# THE
# SHADOW
# GIRLS

ALSO BY ALICE BLANCHARD

*The Witching Tree*
*The Wicked Hour*
*Trace of Evil*

# THE
# SHADOW
# GIRLS

• A Natalie Lockhart Novel •

## Alice Blanchard

MINOTAUR BOOKS
NEW YORK

First published in the United States by Minotaur Books, an imprint of St. Martin's Publishing Group

www.minotaurbooks.com

Library of Congress Cataloging-in-Publication Data

Names: Blanchard, Alice, author.
Title: The shadow girls / Alice Blanchard.
Description: First edition. | New York : Minotaur Books, 2023. | Series: A Natalie
  Lockhart novel ; 4 |
Identifiers: LCCN 2023009264 | ISBN 9781250783080 (hardcover) |
  ISBN 9781250783097 (ebook)
Subjects: LCSH: Women detectives—Fiction. | Murder—Investigation—Fiction. |
  LCGFT: Detective and mystery fiction. Novels.
Classification: LCC PS3552.L36512 S53 2023 | DDC 813/.54—dc23/eng/20230227
LC record available at https://lccn.loc.gov/2023009264

Our books may be purchased in bulk for promotional, educational, or business use. Please contact your local bookseller or the Macmillan Corporate and Premium Sales Department at 1-800-221-7945, extension 5442, or by email at MacmillanSpecialMarkets@macmillan.com.

First Edition: 2023

10  9  8  7  6  5  4  3  2  1

I dedicate this book to Doug, with all my love.

*She was disappearing a little more each day,*
*so thin, so frail, a wisp of smoke.*
*One day she would surely vanish altogether,*
*and there was no way to stop her.*

—ALICE HOFFMAN

*The brightest flame casts the darkest shadow.*

—GEORGE R. R. MARTIN

# THE
# SHADOW
# GIRLS

# PROLOGUE

⟵

BURNING LAKE, NEW YORK
MARCH 12

Thirty-seven-year-old Stevie Greenway drove across town to Murray's Halloween Costumes and parked in the sprawling lot behind the sooty brick building. She hated working alone in that big chilly warehouse in the winter, because it was full of narrow corridors and dimly lit rooms you could get lost in. It creeped her out.

Stevie unbuckled her seat belt, then checked her face in the rearview mirror. She'd put on too much blush this morning, and now she rubbed some of it off her cheeks. She hated getting older. Her lips used to be plump. Now they were thin.

She was barely thirty-seven, and she wanted her youth back. Her friends kept encouraging her to go out more, but she'd been on plenty of awkward dates with men who wanted either marriage or casual sex, and nothing in between. Better to stay home and drink Yellowtail pinot noir, while watching old episodes of *New Girl*.

She got out of her economical Dodge Charger and sighed. Under her winter coat she wore a carefully selected outfit—pale blue dress, white cardigan, pale blue tights, white ankle boots, gold loop earrings, and raspberry lipstick. *Little Miss Upstate New York.* As a child, Stevie had learned to compete in beauty pageants at a very young age. Her mother was her manager and her biggest fan, and Stevie knew how to grab attention. She knew how to charm the pants off the judges. By the time she was nine, she'd managed to snag a bunch of trophies, tiaras, satin sashes, and monetary prizes, and had mastered the art of war. She'd made plenty of tiny enemies. Competition was fierce.

But then, shortly after she turned ten, she blew up like a pufferfish, and her big break never came. During her teen years, she snorted coke and partied like there was no tomorrow. She lost her whatever-it-was. Her heat. Her specialness. She went to college and majored in theater. She had a boyfriend of three years who dumped her. She went broke waiting on tables and working part-time in bookstores in Manhattan. She couldn't afford to pay off her student loans. She returned home in total defeat and took care of her mother, who had Lyme disease. She got stuck working at Murray's, and the years flew by.

Now she understood—you only had a small window of time, a brief opportunity, and if you didn't grab it and run with it, then you'd become like a million other faceless, nameless losers. The world's honorable mentions.

The day was freezing cold, and her skin was wind-burned and prickly. Even though she'd grown up here, Stevie felt like a freak each winter when all her friends talked about was skiing and snowboarding. God, she hated Burning Lake. She didn't want to be here. She'd always dreamed about living in Los Angeles and having lots of quirky friends, like *New Girl.* Now she stared at the 80,000-square-foot redbrick building with its hand-painted signs in the windows: *Prices Slashed! 50% Off! Winter Sale! Everything Must Go!* Nobody needed a Halloween costume in the middle of March. The store would have very few customers today. It was going to be one of those tedious eight-hour shifts where she'd have to take inventory and reorganize the merchandise—basically pretend to be working.

A frigid blast of air blew her coat open, and she belted it shut. She'd worked at the store for twelve years now, ever since she was twenty-five, and she figured she could always quit her job. But that was part of the problem—Stevie wasn't very good at running away. *Little Miss Has-Been.*

She checked her watch—fifty-five minutes until opening. Time to do this thing. She went inside and disabled the alarm system. After securing the door behind her, she turned on the lights, opened the safe, and removed the cash register tills.

It was chilly in here, so she kept her coat on and put away her bag. She turned on the computer and the overhead music system, walked over to the thermostat and cranked the heat. As she was setting the cash registers up, she couldn't shake the eerie, goose-prickly feeling she was being watched.

The large, high-ceilinged lobby was full of animatronic displays and mannequins dressed as gangsters, vampires, werewolves, and superheroes of every stripe. There were three cashier stations with computer registers, credit card machines, and orange plastic bags with MURRAY'S HALLOWEEN COSTUMES printed on the side. More than a dozen doorways led into different parts of the huge commercial space, dusty corridors steering you into rooms full of Halloween costumes, wigs, hats, masks, fake beards, makeup kits, and jewelry. There was a whole section for rental costumes and colonial attire used for theatrical and high school productions in the spring.

Stevie hated working here alone—it was so vast and echoey—but there weren't enough sales in the wintertime to justify more than one employee per shift. Thankfully the owner, Murray Gallo, would be arriving at noon. She counted out the cash and finished setting up the tills, then looked around. Time to do a visual check of the doors, windows, and aisles, just to make sure nothing had been disturbed overnight.

As she wandered up and down the broad aisles, Stevie wasn't bothered by the motion-activated displays that abruptly burst to life as she walked by— the growling animatronic werewolves, cackling witches, and screaming devil babies.

As she came to the bottom of aisle seven, the killer clown lunged for her and flexed his fingers, laughing with maniacal glee. The undead corpse hanging from a netted bag tried to wriggle loose, its insane shrieks bouncing off the high ceiling. She deftly sidestepped the two-foot-long hairy spider that scampered across the floor toward her on its eight disgusting, twitching legs.

Stevie continued up the next aisle, while ignoring the cacophony of unhappy monsters writhing in her wake. This was the western side of the building, where the perimeter door led directly into the parking lot. When she came to the end of the aisle, she froze with surprise. One of the mannequins had fallen onto the floor. What was it doing there? She didn't recognize this one.

Stevie looked around, but none of the displays were missing a zombie. Weirder still, it looked very realistic in its khaki pants, white Adidas running shoes, and green polo shirt. It lay on the floor in a coagulated pool of blood. Its open eyes had a varicose stare. Its face was blue. Its pulpy nose was bulbous and red. Its mouth was open. She could see its receding gums and long yellow teeth. Its neck was cinched with something tight—a wire or a cord—and its head looked like a helium balloon about to float away.

"Oh fuck." Her shivers were off the charts. Stevie tentatively approached the mannequin and touched its shoulder, when all of a sudden the body shifted.

She didn't scream. She was used to horror by now.

Instead, she felt a surreal weightlessness, as if she might pass out.

She realized—like a fool finally admitting the obvious—that no, this wasn't a mannequin at all. It was a large man sprawled across the linoleum, and he was dead. And this man bore an astonishing resemblance to one of her co-workers, Randolph Holmes.

"Randy?" she said softly. Irrationally. "Are you okay?"

He didn't budge. Sixty-four-year-old Randolph Holmes stared at her with his glassy blank eyes. Blood trickled down his forehead, and the big red nose, she noticed, wasn't real. It was one of those rubber clown noses the store sold by the bushel.

Her exhalations grew heavy. She stood up and made a sprint for the exit, where she vomited on the edge of the parking lot.

# I

LANGSTON HOSPITAL'S CRITICAL CARE UNIT
SATURDAY MORNING, MARCH 12

On the twelfth of March, at 8:45 in the morning, Detective Natalie Lockhart took a deep breath and let it out. The private hospital room was full of humming, beeping equipment. She'd been sitting in the same chair for hours now, watching the early morning sunlight play across Lieutenant Detective Luke Pittman's handsome face. He looked so vulnerable lying there, it made her feel all tender and protective inside. She leaned forward and stared at him intently, willing him to come out of his coma, to emerge from wherever it was he had gone.

Luke's right hand twitched, the fingers moving delicately as if striking piano keys, and she felt a ray of hope. "You'll survive this," she whispered with conviction. "You will wake up, Luke."

Several hours ago, one of the nurses had explained that he'd scored a fifteen on the Glasgow Coma Scale. "That's a good thing," the older woman said. "He's responding to stimuli and behaving in an agitated way, trying to remove his IV line. Usually, patients who've scored fifteen on the Glasgow scale have more than an eighty-five percent chance of a good recovery."

*A good recovery.*

*Eighty-five percent.*

Natalie liked those odds—and yet, what was considered a good recovery? Low-grade amnesia? Partial paralysis? Post-traumatic stress disorder?

Luke had a ruddy, weathered face and an athletic body. He ran and lifted weights. He was physically fit. His heart was strong. He would pull through in good shape—she just knew it. Natalie squeezed his hand, but he didn't respond. Where was he?

She watched him a little while longer, then settled back against her chair. Across from her was the closed door. She could hear activity on the other side. They were on the third floor inside a small private room of the Critical Care Unit. She'd been watching over him all night long. Protecting him. Her coat was unbuttoned and she'd unsnapped the holster of her service weapon. She wanted to be able to access her gun at a moment's notice, just in case. She sensed that unknown forces were gathering against them, but perhaps she was wrong. Maybe it was just the lack of sleep and too much caffeine that made her feel so ill at ease. She couldn't tell anymore. Her paranoia was intense.

Four days ago, a beloved, practicing local Wiccan named Veronica Manes had been murdered in one of the most barbaric ways imaginable. On Tuesday morning, March 8, Veronica had woken from a drugged stupor only to realize she was dressed in a Halloween witch costume and chained to the railroad tracks north of town. She'd tried desperately to escape, while the morning express came barreling down on her. She didn't make it.

Natalie and Luke had been working the case nonstop when Luke suddenly went missing yesterday afternoon. Nine hours later, his unconscious body was found two towns over at the bottom of a ravine by state troopers. He'd been beaten and left for dead. His condition was stable, thank God, but none of the doctors could tell her when he might come out of his coma.

She'd learned to her surprise that the medical establishment couldn't agree on anything when it came to comas. Outcomes varied from patient to patient. Some people recovered completely, without any mental or physical disabilities, whereas others suffered irreversible brain damage or sank into a vegetative state.

Natalie wasn't the praying kind, but she had prayed last night. Luke was her touchstone. Her rock. A solid presence in her life going all the way back to her troubled childhood. He'd saved her sorry ass more than once over the years. She needed him in her life. No, it went deeper than that—Natalie couldn't imagine her life without him.

Outside, it had stopped snowing. Inside it was warm and toasty. The room smelled of medicine and perspiration. She couldn't help loving Luke. Whenever she looked at him, she saw herself stretched across the decades—her childhood self, her teenage self, her young adult self—always with feelings of adoration and overflowing love for Luke Pittman. They'd known each other since she was five and he was thirteen. They were so close, it felt almost forbidden to love him. He was her mentor, her trusted colleague, her best friend, possibly the only man in the world who truly understood her . . . so how could she be confused about this? About anything?

Now the door swung open and thirty-six-year-old Rainie Sandhill stood on the threshold, looking slightly surprised. A slender blonde, Rainie possessed the kind of natural beauty that required very little effort to achieve. "Natalie?" she said breathlessly. Her cheeks were vivid pink. "Do you mind if I come in?"

"Of course not." Natalie stood up and hid her service weapon underneath her coat.

"How's he doing?" Rainie asked hopefully. "Any improvement?"

"He's getting restless, which they tell me is a good sign."

Rainie brightened. "Maybe I'll sit with him for a little bit."

"Sure, take my seat. I'll go grab a cup of coffee. Want anything?"

"No, thanks. I'm good." Rainie sat down and reached for Luke's hand, pressing it between hers. Tears filled her eyes. She was casually dressed in sweats, with her long blond hair pulled into a sloppy ponytail, and she seemed totally unaware of her own loveliness. "Luke?" she whispered. "It's me, Rainie. Can you hear me?"

Natalie left them alone together.

Out in the corridor, residents, doctors, and nurses flashed past, their rubber-soled shoes making squeaky sounds on the polished floor. At the other end of the ICU, a maintenance man was mopping up a pool of vomit or blood.

Through the patterned glass, Natalie could see Rainie talking softly to Luke, and it felt like she'd been stabbed with a knife. She lightly caught her breath. She had no right to feel that way. Natalie was with Hunter now, and they were in a committed relationship.

Thirty-three-year-old Hunter Rose was funny, charming, generous, and wickedly seductive. He cared about her. He claimed to be wildly in love with her. He wanted to marry her. He wasn't shy about it. He was busy plotting their future together.

They'd been living together for four months now, and his overwhelming determination to win her over completely, heart and soul, had pulled her into the murky current of her own primitive, subliminal desire to nest and be loved and have a family. Sometimes she felt as if she were suffocating, especially when she could feel her own arousal in response to his touch, the throbbing of her inner blood workings, the stirring of vessels and nerves and hormones. She wasn't used to this. She had no road map. She only knew that Hunter was the physical place where she'd been losing herself lately.

Natalie's mouth was dry as toast. She spotted the vending machines at the other end of the corridor and headed toward them. As she was rummaging in her bag for loose change, her phone buzzed. "Lockhart," she answered distractedly.

"We got a D.B. call, Detective," Dennis the dispatcher said. "You're up."

# 2

Natalie drove to Murray's Halloween Costumes on Route 151, then got out of her car and took a look around. The sky was clear and blue. The snow drifts were sooty. The property was vast, composed of several outbuildings, storage containers, a huge parking lot, and the sprawling two-story nineteenth-century warehouse. She got her crime kit out of her trunk and headed for the main entrance, where a police cruiser was parked, its blue-and-red lights bouncing off the brick façade of the building. She knew the responding officers by their car number—Marconi and Keegan were good men.

As she approached the store, one of the officers came outside and lit a cigarette, his silhouette casting a long shadow in the morning sunlight. As soon as he saw her, he put out his cigarette and nodded crisply. "Morning, Detective."

"Morning, Andy. What's up?"

Officer Andrew Marconi was six foot three and by-the-book. "Keegan's inside taking down statements. We arrived fifteen minutes ago and found two witnesses milling around the crime scene. We immediately cordoned off the area and isolated them in a back office. Their names are Stevie Greenway and the owner, Murray Gallo. Stevie's an employee. She called her boss before calling 911. He got here shortly before we did."

She nodded. "Who's the victim?"

"Randolph Holmes. A long-term employee, age sixty-four. It's not a pretty sight."

"Thanks for the heads-up." Natalie ducked under the crime scene tape and went inside, where the cold quickly penetrated her skin. There was an organic smell of decay in the air. She tried to prepare herself psychologically, but it was always a kick in the gut.

Murray's front lobby was as large as a high school gymnasium, full of attention-grabbing animatronic displays and mannequins dressed up as witches, ghosts, Spider-Man, Captain Marvel, pirates, characters from *The Purge*, Jason from *Friday the 13th*, and so on. The cavernous lobby branched off into dozens of other rooms connected by a series of mazelike corridors. Each room was stuffed with merchandise. It was fairly easy to get lost at Murray's. Natalie had been coming here since she was a girl, and not much had changed.

Now she followed the yellow crime tape down a dusty aisle, where a few items were scattered across the hardwood floor—Halloween masks with their neon green price tags attached, a dozen bags of balloons, and a few packets of fake vampire teeth. Natalie put on a pair of latex gloves, picked up a zombie mask from the floor and studied it. It was concave, as if it had been stepped on.

She placed the mask carefully back down and headed toward an animatronic display of a graveyard with dozens of rubber bats dangling from the ceiling. As she got closer, the bats fluttered their wings and screeched like banshees. Beyond this display, about twelve feet after the aisle ended, was the western-facing side door.

The dead body was contained within a makeshift corral of orange traffic cones and yellow crime scene tape. Natalie put on her disposable foot covers and stepped over the tape, careful not to walk on the trail of blood. She knelt down beside the corpse and examined the victim. It appeared that death was due to ligature strangulation. The wire had cut deep. The body was room temperature, with fully developed rigor mortis. He'd been dead for at least twelve hours now. The victim's open eyes reflected the morning sunlight coming in through the glass door several yards away.

Looking every bit of his sixty-four years, Randolph Holmes had a silver ponytail like a string of saliva spitting out the back of his head. Natalie parted some of his thinning hair and found a deep laceration on his scalp caused by crushing force, indicating a blow to the back of the head.

It was a gruesome visage, one that would surely burn itself into her dreams. The victim's head was swollen and blue, and there were hemorrhages on his face and eyelids, minute blood clots called petechiae. She carefully peeled back an eyelid, since the presence of petechiae on the inner surface of the eyelids was presumptive evidence of death by strangulation. And there they were.

She could now assume that he'd been clubbed on the head, and then strangled.

She took a moment. The way she approached a dead body was to look at it as the victim's final communication to the living. *This is who I am, this is how I died, this is the end of my story.* She wanted to honor the victim's life by absorbing all the grisly details of their death. It was the reason she didn't flinch or look away.

The strangest thing about the crime scene so far had to be the rubber clown nose. Judging by the way the elastic band fit over the wound on the back of the head, Natalie surmised that the clown nose had been secured postmortem. She interpreted this as a final act of humiliation for the victim. The store sold these novelty items, and therefore the killer didn't have to bring one with him. It was most likely an act of spontaneity, meant to mock the dead.

Randolph Holmes wore a short-sleeved green polo shirt, khaki pants, and white sneakers. His wallet was in his back pocket. She held up his left arm and gently turned it over. She did the same with the right arm, searching for defensive wounds, but there were no obvious signs of a struggle. Conspicuously absent from the torso and limbs were any abrasions, bruises, or scratch marks, which meant he hadn't seen the attack coming.

Natalie stood up and stepped outside the perimeter of orange cones and crime tape so as not to disturb anything. Then she followed the cordon of yellow tape north toward a rack of colorful costumes about twenty feet away. On the floor beneath the rack was a bloody hammer.

She had a working theory now. The killer snuck up behind Mr. Holmes and bashed him on the back of the head with the hammer, rendering him unconscious. Once the victim was incapacitated, the killer strangled Holmes with the ligature until he was dead. Finally, the killer secured a red rubber clown nose to Holmes's face and left the premises without triggering any alarms or leaving any bloody footprints behind.

Officer Keegan came walking toward her just then, triggering hysterical screams and howls from the animatronics. This made Natalie realize that if the displays had been switched on last night, then Holmes would have heard the killer coming. Given the evidence, it appeared that the animatronics had been turned off.

"I'm all done, Detective," Keegan told her. "The witnesses are in Gallo's office. I told them to wait for you."

"Thanks, Bill." She stood up and brushed off her hands. "I'll go talk to them."

# 3

Murray Gallo's office was situated behind the cashier station down a dimly lit hallway. Natalie knocked on the open door. Murray and Stevie Greenway were drinking tea together.

"Come in, Natalie." Murray was in his early seventies, a stout, ginger-haired man with an angular, intelligent face and a phlegmatic voice.

"Sorry to inconvenience you," Natalie told them. "But I'll need a little more of your time. Murray, can I talk to you first?"

Stevie excused herself and left.

"Have a seat," Murray said. "Would you like a cup of tea, Natalie?"

"No thanks. I just have a few questions."

His old-school office was full of club chairs and tarnished brass ashtrays. On the wall behind him was a bulletin board full of memos, sticky notes, inventory spreadsheets, and a marked-up calendar.

"I'm usually better dressed than this," he said with an embarrassed smile. He was wearing a faded *South Park* T-shirt and sweatpants instead of the usual rumpled business suit. "This morning, I stumbled out of bed to terrible news and came racing over here to find Randy *like that* out there." He sounded loudly amazed. "My head is still ringing. I can't believe it."

"It must've been quite a shock." She nodded sympathetically, then asked, "How long has he worked for you?"

"Almost thirty years now."

"That's a long time. When did you last see him?"

"Yesterday afternoon. He had the ten-to-six shift. I was here noon to four."

Natalie took out her notepad and jotted it down. "And he seemed okay to you?"

"Fine. We chatted for a bit, then I put him to work doing inventory. Business is slow this time of year, you know? Very little foot traffic. The store closes at four in the winter, and we've been having a bug problem, so I asked Randy to fumigate the basement after he was done with the inventory. I told him he could stay late, and I'd pay him for his time."

"When did he finally clock out?"

"Hold on a second, I'll pull it up for you. Everything's on the computer nowadays." Murray typed a few commands onto his keyboard and squinted at the screen. "Hmm, that's unusual. He forgot to clock out last night, but the back door alarm was turned on at eight fifteen." Murray seemed genuinely puzzled by this.

"Do you have CCTV?"

Murray shook his head. "I'm afraid we've had budget cuts."

"So you don't have any surveillance tapes then?"

"No. We stopped using the security cameras years ago. We never had any problems, so we became lax."

Natalie frowned and lowered her notepad. "How lax?"

"Well, I mean, who's going to steal a bunch of costumes?" He shook his head in disbelief. "Listen, I tried it once. A contractor installed an alarm system nine years ago. CCTV is expensive to maintain, and I'm under constant pressure to cut corners wherever I can. It didn't seem particularly useful. So four years ago, we had the CCTV replaced with a passive infrared motion detector system. It's much more affordable and just as reliable."

"But I've seen the cameras," she said.

Murray shook his head. "They're disconnected. But a thief wouldn't know that."

"Okay, look," Natalie said, "the biggest question seems to be one of access. I'm trying to figure out how the perpetrator got inside without triggering the alarm, and at the same time, I'm trying to figure out who left the store at eight fifteen, since it obviously wasn't the victim."

Murray nodded solemnly. "I don't know. I'm flummoxed."

"But you said you have motion detectors?"

"Well, yes, but . . ." he hedged. "During the first couple of years, right after we had the infrared system installed, the alarm would go off in the middle of the night for various reasons. It's a big building. Whenever the wind blows, it rattles the blinds. A rattling blind can trigger the motion detectors. Especially on a blustery night. Or it could be rats. One guy told me a spider crawling over the sensor could trigger the alarm—can you believe that? A spider? I was constantly getting calls from the alarm company in the middle of the night, and I had to drive out here every single time to deal with whatever was setting off the detectors. Which usually turned out to be nothing."

"But the problem got fixed?" she asked.

He shrugged. "I hired a technician to make a few adjustments to the system so it wasn't as super sensitive as before."

"What does that mean?"

"It's not as hair-trigger as it used to be."

"Okay. So it's possible someone came into the building without triggering the alarm."

"We've never had a problem with break-ins, so it's never been an issue before."

"Until now."

"True." He nodded solemnly. "It's unsettling, to say the least."

"Tell me about Holmes," Natalie said. "What kind of an employee was he?"

"Randy?" Murray rubbed his tired face. "He was a real hard worker. He got along with everyone, but he was a bit of an odd duck."

"Odd how?"

"He liked to finish all his tasks, whether you paid him to or not. Some of his co-workers thought he had OCD, but I wouldn't know about that. He didn't have a wife and kids, so he was always available. He'd work nights or weekends if I asked him to. He was good with his hands. He could build shelves and cabinets and do repairs. If I asked him to finish a task, even if it was after his shift, he'd work until the thing was done."

"So just to clarify . . . if you gave him a particular task to do, he would sometimes stay late just to finish it?"

"Yeah, he'd make himself a cup of coffee. There's a TV in the staff lounge. It's rather cozy back there during the winter."

"So he'd stay after hours and keep working? Maybe take a few breaks?"

"He was a perfectionist, I guess you could say. He was organized and meticulous. Sometimes he overstepped his bounds."

"For example?"

"He could be critical of the other employees if he thought they did a shoddy job. That got on people's nerves."

"Whose nerves?"

"No one in particular. Just generally speaking."

"Did he have any enemies?"

"Oh, Lord no." Murray scowled. "Once you got past the eccentricities, he could be a pleasant enough fellow. He liked to help out. You could always rely on Randy to go the extra mile. He was, if anything, overly conscientious. Like I said, he'd put in his hours, and then some."

"Doing what?"

"There's always something that needs fixing around here. He's knowledgeable about plumbing, electricity, and carpentry. He's a jack-of-all-trades."

"Any thoughts as to who might've done this?" Natalie asked.

Murray shook his head in disbelief. "Honestly? No."

"Any problems lately?"

"Nothing out of the ordinary."

"Any threats made against you or other members of your staff?" she pressed.

"None that I'm aware of."

"What about the clown nose?" she asked.

Murray looked deeply shaken. "I saw that, too. Talk about disturbing."

"Any idea why somebody might've done that? Does the clown nose have any significance?"

He rolled his eyes, then said, "As you know, every year during the month of October, our employees get to dress up for Halloween. It's good for promotion. Every day of that month, we show up in our costumes. And most like to experiment—a witch one year, a ghost the next. But Randy always dressed up as a clown. Here's this guy, he's got almost zero sense of humor, but he wants to be a clown. Never a zombie or a pirate. Nothing else. That's all I can think of."

Natalie nodded slowly. "So it would be someone who was aware of that? Other employees, customers, sales reps, tourists, family, friends?"

Murray shrugged.

"Anything else you can tell me about him?"

He rubbed the gray stubble on his chin and said, "I forgot to mention, he was always volunteering at the local food bank and Toys for Tots, stuff like that. He tried to do some good in this world. What kind of enemies could he possibly have?"

"You'd be surprised. What's his home address?"

"Let me look it up for you." Murray foraged around inside a file cabinet, then took out a careworn manila folder. "This is Randy's personnel file. Would you like me to make a copy for you?"

"Thanks, Murray." She stood up. "In the meantime, I'll go talk to Stevie."

"This is a genuine shock, Natalie. Look. My hands are still shaking."

"Don't worry, we'll get to the bottom of things. I promise." She turned to leave, but he stopped her.

"Just so you know, Stevie and the other girls didn't like the guy very much. But I guess you'll find out soon enough."

# 4

Natalie found Stevie Greenway in the staff lounge sitting cross-legged on the sofa and cradling a mug of coffee in her lap. "Will this take long?" she asked. "I'd like to go home."

"I have a few more questions, then you can go."

Stevie gazed out the window at the parking lot. She was a sweet-looking woman with short, shiny dark hair and vivid blue eyes. "My mother used to buy me Red Bull and caffeine tablets, like NoDoz and Stay Awake—stuff to keep me alert for the competitions I was in as a kid. Beauty pageants," she explained. "There are pictures of me looking totally strung out as I played the violin or paraded down the catwalk in my two-piece."

Natalie nodded but said nothing. The beauty pageant culture for kids as young as two always shocked her. Actually there was a newborn category. Baby Miss.

"You're Grace's sister," Stevie said, turning her attention on Natalie. "You've been in the news lately." She put down her mug and picked up a tabloid newspaper from the coffee table. "You arrested the Violinist. Didn't he kill two women?"

Natalie felt suddenly exposed. She wasn't expecting this. "Yes," she answered.

"You've been in the news a lot this past year, huh? Sheesh. That's the kind of publicity I would've died for once." Stevie put the tabloid down and sighed. "I was supposed to be an actress. I majored in theater at NYU, but then my life fell apart, and I ended up back here taking care of my mom.

She has Lyme disease, which some doctors think is a psychological disorder, but she really is sick. So you solved that serial killer case, too, right?" She checked the tabloid headline. "The Crow Killer? Didn't they find dozens of bodies buried on his property?"

"Nineteen," Natalie said, trying to remain patient. The two big cases she'd solved—dubbed the Crow Killer and the Violinist by sensation-seeking reporters—had been splashed all over the media for months on end, and as a result she was a local hero to some and the subject of scorn to others.

Within the span of a single year, Natalie had lost her sister to suicide after finding out that Grace was a murderer. As if that wasn't deeply shocking enough, she'd also solved New York State's biggest serial killer case ever— the Crow Killer. Samuel Hawke Winston had abducted and murdered dozens of homeless people, along with a handful of tourists visiting the Adirondack Mountains, and his crimes went back decades. And then, six months later, on the day after Halloween, she'd discovered a dead body in a dumpster, a naked woman with an inscrutable tattoo and a strange callus under her chin, the tragic victim of an ongoing murder spree by a deranged and troubled young man—this one dubbed the Violinist.

"And just last week Veronica Manes was killed," Stevie said, her face going pale. "And now this happens to Randy. What the hell is going on in this town? It used to be so quiet and peaceful. When I was growing up, we left our doors unlocked."

Natalie nodded numbly. "I wish I could tell you."

Stevie picked up her mug and took a few sips. "Did you know that your sister and I were in the same grade together?"

Natalie shook her head. "Sorry, I didn't."

"Well, anyway. Grace was very popular. I was a party girl back then. I had a bad reputation. No wonder she never mentioned me."

Natalie nodded vaguely.

"Because, you see, I gained a lot of weight when I was ten, all that pressure from the pageant circuit. Almost overnight, I went from being this adorable, photogenic Little Miss Upstate New York to having pimples and a big tummy. Before then I'd won plenty of awards. They have goofy names for each category, like Mini Miss Glitz, Baby Miss Splash, or Tiny Miss Sunburst. The pressure to be the most talented and the most adorable was *intense*. When I outgrew my cute phase, Mom insisted I still go on auditions, and I was so freaked out, so lacking in confidence that my voice would crack and I'd burst into tears. Not a good selling point. In junior high, I started doing drugs and lost a bunch of weight, but by then it was too late. I was out of the pageant circuit." She paused for a moment. "Sorry about your sister. That must've been hard."

"It was," Natalie said, shifting uncomfortably. "Very difficult."

Stevie drank her coffee slowly. "So anyway, here I am. The ex-pageant princess who found the dead guy. Maybe I'll finally get in the papers." She smiled ironically.

"Trust me," Natalie said. "You don't want to be in the papers for that."

She shrugged. "I shouldn't be joking around. It'll bring more bad luck."

Natalie took out her notepad and pen. "Tell me what happened this morning?"

Stevie put down her coffee and crossed her arms. "Like I told the officer, I didn't notice anything out of the ordinary. There weren't any customers clamoring at the front door. Believe me, it's no fun getting dressed up in the dead of winter when the whole town is bored with the one thing you sell—Halloween costumes." She shrugged. "Anyway, I did a walk-through, you know . . . a visual check to make sure nothing had been disturbed overnight. That's part of the protocol. And then I found him—" She stopped speaking.

Natalie nodded, encouraging her to go on, but Stevie seemed to be riffing silently on her own shock. So Natalie said, "Murray tells me Randy was alone in the building last night, fumigating the basement."

Stevie blinked. "Yeah, we have a bug problem. Silverfish and cockroaches."

"Tell me about Randy. What was your relationship?"

"Our relationship?" she scoffed. "Nonexistent. We were co-workers, that's all. He was a quiet, kind of weird dude. All into himself. But basically a nice guy. He did all the heavy lifting whenever Belinda, Tori, and I were working. He'd tell us—you girls shouldn't move anything, let me do it. He had one of those lifting belts, you know?" Her eyes grew solemn. "Anyway, my mother says, if you don't have anything nice to say about someone, then don't say anything at all."

"Why? What do you want to tell me?" Natalie asked, leaning forward.

"Nothing specific. But none of us girls wanted to be alone with him."

"Why not?"

"He was prickly. He didn't like being interrupted or given suggestions. If he had a job to do, for instance, he'd start from the beginning and go all the way to the end without stopping. I mean, he was a hard worker, he did his job—no fuss, no muss. He wasn't emotional, he just put his head down and got it done. In that sense he was fine. But he really didn't like it if you interfered with the way he was doing things. Not a team player. He could be difficult to deal with, which explains why he didn't have anybody waiting for him at home." Stevie laughed harshly. "Jesus, who am I to talk? Neither do I. But I like to at least *pretend* I have a life, you know? Anyway, the winter is pretty dead, so Murray usually has us taking inventory, reorganizing the merchandise and packing up returns—and that's when Randy was at his worst. He makes all these lists and becomes super inflexible. And that just makes a boring task less tolerable, you know? I've thought about getting another job, but the pay isn't bad. I have health benefits, lots of sick time and two weeks' vacation. And Murray lets me have a flexible schedule in the summer so that I can do community theater, which I love. Besides, who would hire me now . . . you know, blah-blah years old with limited skills?"

Natalie smiled sadly.

"Sorry, I'm babbling." She blushed.

"I'm still not getting what made you so uncomfortable around Randy?"

"Gee, I don't know," she said sarcastically. "Some childless, single dude in his sixties with no life to speak of who meticulously organizes objects and insists on doing things his way, or else he'll hold a grudge, like, forever . . . lurking around like a resentful troll. What would make me uncomfortable?"

Natalie couldn't help smiling—she'd painted quite a picture of the guy. "Tell me what the procedures are for the last employee on the premises?"

"Okay, so," Stevie said, counting on her fingers, "first, you make sure the tills and settlement reports have gone into the safe. No, wait. Randy doesn't do any of that. Murray, Belinda, and I are in charge of the financial stuff."

"Okay, so what would Randy typically do before he left for the day?"

"Last night, he would've emptied the trash receptacles, wiped down the cashier counters, and swept up. You're supposed to rinse out the coffee pot and get it ready for the next morning. You replace the paper towels and toilet paper in the restrooms. You do a final walk-through of the building, just to make sure that nobody accidentally gets trapped inside."

"Do people ever get trapped inside?"

Stevie shrugged. "It's a huge space with lots of rooms and storage closets and stairwells and hallways leading to dead ends. Sometimes you'll find a customer wandering around at closing time."

"So it's possible for someone to get lost inside the building? Or maybe hide inside the building?"

Stevie blinked at her. "That's never happened before, but yeah, it's possible. There's tons of displays and storage rooms full of junk . . . it's spooky here at night."

"So you don't check the *entire* building, then, do you?"

"No. That would take hours. Just the areas a customer might be."

"Okay," Natalie said. "What happens then? After the walk-through?"

"Then you turn off the computers, shut down the animatronics and kill the lights. You activate the alarm system and exit the building."

"Which door do you exit?"

"Either the main entrance or one of the perimeter doors. Randy usually leaves by the back door because he parks behind the building."

"So he'd type in the security code and lock the door behind him?"

"Exactly," she said. "We each have a set of keys and the alarm code. Last person to leave is supposed to activate the alarm. The code is eight numbers long."

"Show me," Natalie said.

They headed down a corridor toward the back of the building, where the stockroom and shipping-receiving were located. They walked past shelving units crammed with merchandise, a cluttered receiving desk, empty dollies, and towering stacks of boxes. The back door was painted glossy black. There was an alarm panel on the wall to the right of the doorframe. Stevie was about to demonstrate by raising the plastic panel and typing a code onto the keypad when Natalie stopped her.

"We have to check for prints first. Just tell me the number."

Stevie nodded, took a step back and rattled off the alarm code.

Natalie suddenly noticed a piece of paper taped to the wall not far from the panel, with the same eight numbers written on it in pencil. "Isn't that the alarm code?"

"Oh, gee." Stevie nodded. "Yeah, that's for Murray. He forgets."

"So the alarm code is right there for anyone else to see?" Natalie gave her a skeptical look. "On the wall right next to the door?"

Stevie blushed. "I never thought about it that way," she admitted. "Murray doesn't always remember things. But you're right. Anyone could punch in the alarm code and exit the building. But they'd have to have the building keys."

"Does Randy have a set of keys?"

"Always. They're on a ring looped around his belt."

Natalie returned to the lobby, where she searched Randy's belt for the keys, but they weren't there. She went through his pockets, and then checked the area around him, but the set of keys Randy always kept with him were gone.

She thanked Stevie and left.

It was time to find out who Randolph Holmes really was.

# 5

Randolph S. Holmes lived at the end of a dead-end street in northwest Burning Lake. The property was isolated, surrounded by woods. The nearest neighbor was half a mile down the road.

Natalie got out of her car and took a deep breath of cold, fresh air. She could smell pine and wet earth mixed with ozone. The mid-twentieth-century clapboard house was washed in sunlight. In the front yard, the carcass of an old truck lay rotting away on a scraggly patch of winter weeds, its leather seats eaten through by mice and raccoons. A barbed wire fence delineated the property, and nailed to the fence posts were several NO TRESPASSING signs.

She took the muddy flagstone walkway to the front door and felt a chill as she rang the bell. "Hello? This is the police. Anybody home?"

Announcing herself was part of the protocol, even though she already was aware there was nobody home. Then again, you never knew.

In the distance came the lonely cry of a hawk. Natalie tried the door but it was locked. She checked under the welcome mat for a spare house key. On a hunch, she walked down the steps and overturned a heavy ceramic urn on the lawn. Underneath the urn, she found the spare key. She unlocked the door and went inside.

"Hello?" she called out again. "This is the police. Is anybody home?"

No answer.

The kitchen was full of old but dependable appliances, simple pine furniture, floral-patterned wallpaper, and varnished woodwork. It smelled of burnt coffee.

The living room had twelve-foot ceilings and maple plank floors. The furniture was plain but comfortable-looking. The old-fashioned window shades were up, and brilliant rays of sunlight lit the walls. But that wasn't what grabbed her attention.

On all four walls of the living room hung dozens of display cases full of insects—butterflies, dragonflies, beetles, moths, spiders, and so on. She'd seen these type of "shadow boxes" at the natural history museum. Each display case held a grid of insects pinned to a foam board backing. The acrylic panel top cover gave you a clear view of the specimens inside.

Natalie picked up a nausea she couldn't shake, and it burned in the pit of her stomach. Everyone was entitled to their hobbies, and plenty of people collected insects, but something felt "off" about the fact that the entire living room was dedicated to this particular avocation. Every available surface was stacked with boxes of entomology supplies and brand-new shadow boxes sealed in plastic. The big oak desk in the corner was littered with jars of dead insects, bottles of acetone and isopropyl alcohol, cotton balls, a package of plaster of paris, and glass mason jars with screw-top lids. On a nearby worktable were packets of brackets and hooks for hanging pictures, a stack of foam board panels, a plastic tray full of entomology pins, a microscope, and tubes of glue. Scattered around the room were dozens of catalogs from companies selling entomology supplies.

Natalie walked over to one of the display cases and rested her fingers lightly on the cold smooth surface of the clear acrylic glass cover. Inside the shadow box were twenty or so mounted monarch butterflies, meticulously pinned to the foam board, their wings brilliantly patterned in oranges, golds, and reds. Underneath were tiny labels with the scientific names of each specimen spelled out in elegant handwriting.

She rummaged around in her bag, took out Randy's personnel file and perused it quickly. His job title at Murray's was listed as sales clerk, but his job description said he was also responsible for repairs and maintenance. Murray had noted in the margin that Randy knew how to safely install electrical systems and do rudimentary plumbing. The file didn't mention if a background check had been performed. Before he'd gotten the job at Murray's thirty years ago, Randy had been a part-time handyman and worked for a pest-control company. Randy's employee evaluations were across-the-board positive.

She skim-read the employee evaluations. "Randy has maintained good attendance throughout the year . . . he's achieved stability in number of sales this year . . . maintained a positive attitude . . . is highly organized and efficient . . . is very good with his time management skills . . ." On the negative side, he wasn't always an effective communicator with other staff members and his preference was to work alone rather than with the team.

Natalie put the file away, then walked through the first and second floors, looking for more clues. Randy's bedroom on the second floor smelled like a gym locker. There was an old pine bed and matching bureau, a careworn corduroy armchair and a wooden desk in the corner—pencils in a cup, a stack of legal pads, a calendar, and a cheap-looking roller chair. Outside the window, a tree branch stirred in the wind, tapping thinly against the glass.

The bathroom toilet was shiny clean. The faux-slate countertop was neatly stacked with male grooming products—shaving cream, a folded-up tube of toothpaste, stick deodorant. There were bath towels and dirty clothes in the hamper.

The spare bedroom at the other end of the hall appeared to have been converted into a library for Randy's collection of glossy entomology magazines. The built-in bookshelves were crammed with subscription magazines going back to at least 2010. There was a rocking chair by the window, next to a side table and lamp. Behind the table was a Victorian-era wooden trunk with dull brass corner pieces and a stained leather handle.

Natalie opened the storage trunk's lid and peered inside. A musty smell wafted up. The trunk was full of seven large three-ring binders, the kind of office binders that had the capacity to hold almost a thousand pages each. She put on a pair of latex gloves, then carefully picked up the first one. On the front cover was a computer printout that read "SUBJECT 001: August 3, 1988."

With a touch of anxiety, Natalie opened the binder. Inside were perhaps five hundred pages of handwritten notes, done in the same neat script as she'd seen in the shadow boxes downstairs.

*May 12, 1988: No captures today. Must be patient.*

*May 23, 1988: I spent the entire day on Conklin Avenue observing some of the local scum gobbling up all my lovelies — it was heartbreaking to watch.*

*June 2, 1988: The unseasonably warm weather has drawn out my lovelies early this year. They are so quick it's difficult to catch them. They hover and dodge, changing directions on a whim. The second I try to lure one of them into the shadows, they are gone.*

*June 15, 1988: Outstanding summer day. They are so pretty they take my breath away. I watched them for hours, while they made the most amazing choices. They will literally go with anyone who pays the least bit of attention to them.*

On and on it went. It chilled Natalie to the bone.

Finally, she found this: *August 3, 1988: My first capture. A little messy and difficult. But she's mine.*

Heart pounding, Natalie rifled through the remaining pages of the binder, pausing to read random journal entries. Randy Holmes described, in minute detail, the daily habits of Subject 001, including her sleep patterns, her menstrual cycle, when she ate, when she defecated, how long she watched TV or listened to the radio, bouts of crying, bouts of screaming, bouts of pleading. He detailed his and subject one's "sexual interludes"— assaults, Natalie corrected his insane euphemism, rapes—and included various Polaroid pictures of a slender young woman in various poses— never showing her head, just her naked body.

The final entry was extremely distressing: *May 1, 1991: For everything there is a season. A time to die, and a time to weep.*

She turned the page. That was it. No more pages.

She put the binder down and opened the next one. Natalie spent the next hour going through all seven binders. He referred to his victims as Subject 001, Subject 002, Subject 003, et cetera—no names or ages were given, as far as she could tell. There appeared to be one binder dedicated to each victim, and the dates of the kidnappings appeared to be 1988, 1991, 1994, 1997, 2000, 2003, and 2006. In total, this looked like a series of well-planned and well-executed abductions of seven individual women.

Deeply shaken, she placed the binders back inside the trunk exactly the way she had found them and closed the lid. She would have to sort through it more carefully later on—after they'd officially taken the trunk into evidence.

Mike Anderson was in charge of the chain-of-custody process now, and she would have to wait a couple of days to tackle this terrible treasure trove, despite her burning desire to do a deep dive into what it all meant.

With a heightened sense of apprehension, Natalie finished her walk-through of the property. There was nothing of significance in the attic or in the backyard, except for a charred burn barrel. She found a stick and stirred the ashes. Whatever he had wanted to get rid of, it was gone now. There was nothing left.

Finally she checked out the basement. The wooden stairs were narrow and creaky. The fluorescent lights were harsh. It smelled of mold and dead mice down here. The concrete walls were mottled gray, spotted with a white powdery substance her father used to call efflorescence—it happened when moisture passing through porous concrete walls left a residue of mineral salts behind.

At first glance, it appeared to be a typical basement—garden tools, bags of dry cement, a shovel and bucket, a buzz saw bench, a woodworking table, a furnace and hot water heater, a pegboard full of tools, and shelving units for stashing oil cans, wrenches, rags, and packages of d-CON for killing rodents.

As Natalie circled the basement, she wondered why it was so much smaller down here compared with the rest of the house. The upstairs floor plan seemed much larger.

She also noticed that the basement floor was uneven in places. He had thrown a threadbare rug over the most trafficked area—from the stairs to the fuse box. The rest of the concrete floor was laid bare—cracked, pitted, sloping in places, a patchwork of different colored mortars in various stages of disrepair.

Now she paused in front of the north-facing wall, where a large pine cabinet was positioned in front of a blue plastic tarp, and partly visible beneath the tarp was a doorframe.

Using as much muscle as she could, Natalie pushed the heavy pine cabinet away from the wall, then swept the tarp aside. A plume of dust flew up, making her sneeze.

Behind the tarp, there was no door at all—just a concrete wall, chipped and cracked with age. Judging by the dust and spiderwebs, it hadn't been touched in years. Best guess, whatever lay behind this door had been sealed up at least a decade ago.

Natalie's nerves lit up. Randy Holmes was—for all intents and purposes—a trusted employee who fed the homeless and delivered Toys for Tots, and who liked to dress up as a clown for Halloween. He also killed and mounted insects in shadow boxes, documented his sick fantasies or real confessions in seven office binders, and had a sealed-up doorway in his basement.

Who the hell was this guy?

She took out her phone and called Detective Lenny Labruzzo down at the station.

"Natalie?" he answered.

"Lenny, I'm at Randolph Holmes's place," she said, running her finger over a seam in the cement. "We need demolition equipment down here right away. I found a hidden passageway in his basement, among other things, and it's raising all sorts of red flags. Could you arrange it for me?"

"Sure thing. But, Natalie," Lenny said, "haven't you heard?"

"Heard what?"

"Luke's out of his coma. He's been asking for you."

# 6

The post-holiday blues had descended upon the midsized town of Burning Lake, New York, population 50,000. Upstate winters had a tendency to drag on, and this year was no exception. A big snowstorm had blanketed everything in white this past November, and the winter storms kept coming. Now everyone was praying for an early spring.

Located south of the Adirondack Mountains, at the midpoint between Albany and Syracuse, Burning Lake was an important tourist destination for fans of Halloween, rivaling only Salem, Massachusetts, in popularity with its monthlong schedule of festivities, including haunted guided tours, museum exhibits, and witch-themed balls. For the local business owners, fall was their season. Halloween was huge.

It all began in 1712, when three innocent young women were executed for the sin of witchcraft, and for centuries afterward, the town fathers had struggled to keep Burning Lake's shameful history hidden from view. The town's rebirth began in the 1970s, when a book about the witch trials was published to critical acclaim, drawing hundreds of curious tourists. By the 1980s, the town finally realized its potential and went full-bore Salem. A cottage industry blossomed around Abigail, Sarah, and Victoriana's tragic demise, and now the commercial district was full of occult gift shops, historical inns, and New Age boutiques selling everything from spell kits to magic crystals. In October, the leaves blazed spectacular orange, red, and gold colors, and thousands of people came from all over the world to celebrate All Hallows' Eve.

As for the rest of the year, there were plenty of things to do in Burning

Lake during the warmer months, and thousands of vacationers came here to enjoy the natural beauty of upper New York State and all it had to offer— hiking, rock climbing, bike riding, fishing, camping, and cave-exploring.

Downtown was clean and safe for the most part, and the business community worked hard to keep it that way. Main Street, with its Victorian-era buildings and tree-lined sidewalks, featured plenty of jazz clubs, bookshops, cafés, and art galleries. There was a summer music festival and a Performing Arts Center that headlined off-Broadway plays. Not that the town was perfect. Far from it. Gossip was a form of entertainment in these parts. The winters could be bitterly cold, and heating bills were a burden. Finding a bar wasn't difficult in a town where the temperatures could dip to twenty below and the waterfalls could freeze solid.

Natalie found a parking spot for her silver-gray Honda Accord and got out. She'd been born in Langston Memorial Hospital, and so had Luke. Last night, she was worried he might die here, too.

This morning, icicles melted down the hospital's postmodern facade of metal and glass. Hundreds of vehicles gleamed in the strong sunlight, and the edges of the lot were crusted with dirty snow. Her long hair fluttered in a chilly breeze. She was still shaken from her recent finds on Randolph Holmes's property, but she would have to keep a lid on it for now. There was no telling how much information Luke was capable of absorbing, and she didn't want to overwhelm him.

Bursting with nerves and excitement, Natalie pocketed her keys and went inside. The atrium was full of activity; visitors, staff, and residents rushing around. She crossed the crowded glass-walled lobby and headed for the elevators, wondering what sort of state she would find him in. Lenny hadn't given any details over the phone, and Natalie was afraid to ask. She was hoping for the best. She wanted the old Luke back but was too superstitious to wish for it so badly.

Upstairs, she paused in the doorway of Luke's private room. The scene was striking. He was sitting up in bed, chatting with the other detectives from the unit as if nothing had happened. He looked perfectly normal, except for the hospital johnnie and plastic ID bracelet. It felt like a miracle. There was a lot of laughter. A bouquet of Mylar balloons was tied to the end of the bed, and a bunch of "Get Well Soon" cards were propped up on the nightstand. Within all this celebration, Rainie sat quietly in a chair next to the bed, holding Luke's hand.

Just then, Lenny said, "Natalie, come join the party!" and waved her inside.

Everyone stopped talking and turned their heads. All her colleagues from the police department were there—detectives Augie Vickers, Brandon Buckner, Mike Anderson, and Jacob Smith, along with officers Keegan, Goodson, Prutzman, and Marconi.

Rainie stood up and said, "Here, Natalie, take my seat. I'm going for coffee. Want anything, Luke?"

He shook his head and said, "I'm good." His eyes were fixed on Natalie. It felt like just the two of them in the room.

Passing her in the doorway, Rainie said brightly, "Go on, take my seat."

One by one, the guys excused themselves.

"Stay safe out there," Luke told them as they headed for the door.

Before he left, Lenny pulled Natalie aside and said, "I sent a team of officers over to the Holmes's property to demo the wall. I'm heading over there myself now."

"I'll join you shortly," she said. "And have Brandon do a background search on this guy. Something's hinky. You'll see when you get there."

"Sure thing."

After Lenny was gone, Natalie settled into the chair, still warm from Rainie's body. The hospital bed with its starched sheets and steel guardrails looked uncomfortable, but Luke seemed remarkably relaxed. It was amazing how he could keep his composure under the most extreme circumstances.

"How are you feeling?" she asked.

"None the worse for wear," he said with an ironic smile.

"Seriously, though, are you okay?"

"Physically, I feel fine. The doctors say I'm neurologically in good shape, but they need to do more tests. I just want to get back to work. The sooner the better."

All the tension was released from her body. "Jesus, that's a fucking relief."

He grinned at her. "Yeah? You thought I was a goner, huh?"

"Shut up." She couldn't help smiling. "You scared the hell out of me."

"I heard you stayed up all night long watching over me."

She blushed. "What else was I supposed to do?"

"I don't know." He shrugged, watching her expectantly.

She shook her head. "What happened, Luke? The last thing Lenny and

I know, you went off the radar. We figured you went to find Murphy and confront him about the missing evidence."

He nodded. "When I explained we had proof of his malfeasance, he became belligerent and attacked me. I should've been ready for it. I was standing on an incline when he sucker-punched me. I lost my footing and fell. Last thing I remember is hitting my head on a rock."

"Thank God you're okay. We were all worried sick."

"It's hard to believe. I mean . . . *Peter Murphy*? That guy?"

"I know," she said with equal disbelief. "We'll find him. There's a state-wide APB out, and we're tracking his credit cards and cell phone. It's a high-alert situation. We've got everybody working on it."

"Good. I want to be the first to interrogate him," Luke said darkly.

She asked, "Did Lenny tell you about the lockbox?"

"No. What about it?"

"A couple of hours before you went missing, Murphy popped in at the crime lab to ask a few questions. But after he left, the lockbox was gone."

Luke frowned with renewed concern. "Why would he steal the lock-box?"

"I don't know, but it establishes a pattern of wrongdoing. I mean, come on . . . tampering with evidence, stealing evidence, attacking you, and go-ing on the run?"

It should have been obvious all along that forty-five-year-old Detective Pe-ter Murphy was gaslighting them. He was the first to volunteer for the thank-less job of cataloging the evidence—he'd been the crucial link in the chain of custody for all of their most high-profile cases. Evidence was not only missing from the manifest in the Veronica Manes case, but they'd had problems with the Violinist and the Crow Killer cases, as well. The chain of custody always pointed back to Murphy, every damn time.

Murphy was an average-sized middle-aged man with slick dark hair and thick, dark eyebrows. Some of the guys jokingly called him Bert, because of those Muppet-like eyebrows and his world-weary hapless demeanor. He had a dour sense of humor and knew a lot of trivia, and he and Natalie used to get along quite well, but last year his feelings had soured toward her, and now theirs was a contentious relationship. It all started when Murphy accidentally lost a crucial file from the Missing Nine case, and Natalie let him know how much his carelessness pissed her off.

And who was Peter Murphy? He was a blank slate. He had no family to worry about and very few responsibilities. He was an affable guy and a me-diocre detective. What did they really know about him? And why would he do such a thing?

The lockbox was an extremely disturbing item that Natalie had found during her investigation of Veronica Manes's homicide. Having been bur-ied in the ground for decades, it contained evidence of foul play by an unknown assailant, including a torn piece of pink polyester fabric with bloodstains on it; a desiccated leather coin bag full of ashes; a pair of black lace mesh spandex panties; and a Polaroid picture of a girl who appeared to have been kidnapped—with the date of the film stock and identifying numbers cut out. The girl was bound and gagged, with her back to the cam-era, and she peered over her shoulder, one terrified eye looking straight into the lens and staring bleakly into a future beyond her own death.

At least, that was Natalie's chilling interpretation.

Natalie had managed to link the mysterious lockbox to a high school cult from the mid-1970s. She'd discovered a connection between several key members of this cult, including Ned Bertrand, the abusive father of the Violinist, and Dottie Coffman, a former English teacher who'd influenced a group of high school students into experimenting with the occult. One of those students was Natalie's sister, Grace. So far, everything pointed back to this 1975 student cult.

"Why would Murphy steal the lockbox?" Luke asked now. "What pur-pose could it serve?"

"For him? No purpose at all."

Luke squinted at her. "What are you implying?"

"Someone might've hired him to steal it."

"So you think this is all part of a cover-up?"

"Whoever was responsible for that Polaroid and the bloody piece of cloth certainly didn't want the police to have it."

"Fuck," Luke muttered. "I hate that you could be right."

"There's more." She paused. "Lenny found a preliminary match between the dark blue fibers in Murphy's van and the blue fibers on the witch cos-tume Veronica was wearing the night she died. He sent samples off to the state lab for verification, and if they can confirm it's a match, then it would prove that Veronica was in Murphy's van after the kidnapping took place."

"Okay, so why would Murphy kill Veronica? For what twisted reason?"

"That's the million-dollar question. Whatever his motivation, it doesn't explain why he's been manipulating and corrupting the evidence from our other cases, too. And it fails to explain why Veronica's homicide was so . . ." She shuddered. "So deeply personal. Whoever did this wanted to humiliate and punish her."

Everyone in Burning Lake knew who fifty-eight-year-old Veronica Manes was—a beloved local Wiccan priestess, head of one of the oldest covens in town. She used to live in the historic Bell House on 8 Plymouth Street, and many years ago, she'd written several books under a pen name, Corvina Manse—a clever anagram of her own name. She was known to host quarterly moonlight rituals on her property and was the best person to talk to if you wanted to understand modern-day witchcraft. She had shoulder-length gray hair and wore informal, mismatched clothes—turtlenecks, cardigans, stretch pants, New Balance sneakers. She was a perfectly ordinary, kindhearted person who just so happened to be a witch.

Now she was dead. Chained to the railroad tracks north of town and hit by a train.

The most intriguing clue they had to go on was the fact that Veronica had been researching the history of Burning Lake before she was killed, and the murderer had also ransacked her house. Cabinets and drawers were thrown open, possessions were tossed about in a frenzy. It was clear they were looking for something specific, since several of her devices and hard drives were missing, along with stacks of handwritten research notes. No silverware, no cash, no jewelry—nothing of value had been taken, only things relating to her new book. Whatever the case, Natalie believed that Veronica had stumbled across important information that powerful players in this town wanted to keep buried. What did Veronica know? What was the terrible secret she had unearthed?

"I'm still kicking myself," Natalie confessed. "I didn't suspect Murphy of any wrongdoing. Not even after the Crow Killer evidence went missing. I thought it was sloppiness or incompetence. But it should've been a red flag."

"None of us suspected a thing," Luke told her angrily. "We were all duped."

"In the meantime, I've been assigned to a new case," she said. "An employee at Murray's was killed last night in the warehouse. I won't burden you with the details. We can talk about it later, after you get a clean bill of health."

He smiled warmly at her. "I feel fine."

They locked eyes for a moment.

"Almond croissants, your favorite," Rainie announced from the doorway. She was holding a paper bag and two carryout coffees. "I went to Starbucks. Better than lime Jell-O, right?" She walked into the room.

Natalie stood up. "I was just leaving."

Luke shot her a brief look. "We'll talk about your case later on."

"Okay. Take care, Rainie."

"Good-bye, Natalie. Be safe out there."

She walked out of the room feeling as if they'd left so much unsaid.

# 7

Out in the corridor, Natalie glanced back into the room. Rainie was sitting on the edge of the hospital bed, sipping her coffee. Luke was smiling, and the two of them were talking quietly. He took a bite of croissant and got powdered sugar on his lips, and Rainie leaned forward to brush some off. A spike of goose bumps tingled the back of Natalie's neck.

Now she heard a familiar voice echoing down the hallway. "No, that wasn't the deal . . . yeah, exactly. Okay, call me back in ten." She turned and saw her boyfriend over by the nurses' station. Founder and CEO of the biggest tech company on the East Coast, thirty-three-year-old Hunter Rose wore a full-length winter coat, a black scarf, and black leather gloves, his face still rosy from the cold. His hair stuck up in wild tufts, and he smoothed it down as he walked past the glass-enclosed station, where all three nurses inside were watching him.

"Damn, you look beautiful," he told Natalie, pocketing his phone and smiling broadly at her.

"More like sweaty and gross," she said with a smirk.

"Yeah, well, you make sweaty and gross look yummy." He gave her a kiss.

They'd been texting each other periodically all night long, and he knew about Luke's recovery, but she hadn't told him about her new case yet. She wasn't expecting him to show up at the hospital, either. His eyes were bloodshot from lack of sleep, glazed and red-veined. He clasped her face in his hands and said, "How are you doing? Are you okay?"

"I'm fine. What are you doing here?"

He shook his head. "Couldn't sleep. I've been worried sick about you." Then, almost as an afterthought: "How's Luke?"

"Good. He's sitting up and talking. It's as if he was never in a coma."

"Well, that's good news. No lasting damage?"

"They're still doing tests, but it looks like he dodged a bullet. Listen, Hunter, I forgot to tell you, it's been such a crazy morning . . . but I caught a new case. A homicide at Murray's. I'm right in the middle of the investigation, so I can't talk long."

His eyes grew solemn. "Are you serious? It had to be you?"

She drew back a little. "I'm on-call this week."

"They couldn't assign it to anyone else? After all the bullshit you've been through?"

"We're two men down," she said defensively. "Murphy and Luke."

He rolled his eyes. "Come with me."

"Where are we going?"

"You'll see."

"Hunter . . ."

"Trust me." He led her down the hallway, moving with catlike grace past the vending machines. He looked so elegant and confident in his black cashmere coat and leather boots, his physical presence awakened all the conflicting emotions she'd been suppressing over the past twenty-four hours. Natalie could feel Hunter now in the steady pulsing of her blood. He was pulling her—ever so slowly—into the nest he was building for them. A safe, secure future with marriage and children and lots of fucking. And Natalie had to admit that part of her wanted this, desired this very thing, to give into her passion and helplessness in the presence of his predatory physicality.

Now he led her into an empty waiting room with blond-wood furniture and washed-out seascapes on the walls, then slipped his arms around her waist and said, "Listen, once this deal goes through, I'll be opening a branch in Denver next year. We could move there and start over."

She shook her head. "I can't think about that right now."

"I'm just saying there are options." His arms tensed around her waist. "Come on, Natalie. Nobody's going to be the least bit surprised if you quit your job. They all know what kind of hell you've been through. Who's going to blame you for turning your back on this fucking town?"

She lightly touched his face. "Go home and get some rest. You look exhausted."

Very tenderly, he cupped her face in his hands. "Last night, when you said you were cursed . . . you have no idea how much that upset me. You, of all people, aren't responsible for any of this. You do realize that, don't you?" He rested his hands on her shoulders. "I care so much about you, I hate to see you in pain. I love you too much. Run away with me. Let's get the hell out of Dodge."

She shook her head. "You know I can't. Not when Peter Murphy is still out there, and Veronica's death remains unsolved. Besides, I've just been assigned this new case."

He drew back. "There's always going to be a new case, Natalie."

"I know. Look, I'll be home tonight, and we can talk about it then, okay?"

"I want to take care of you. Let me take care of you."

"Hunter, please don't do this now."

His phone rang, and he checked the number. "Shit. I'm sorry, babe. I have to take this. But we'll have a long talk tonight, right? We'll be honest with each other."

"Tonight," she affirmed.

"Be careful, Natalie." He strode off down the hallway. "Hello? Good afternoon, gentlemen, let's find a solution and close this deal . . ."

She stood for a moment feeling a static discharge on the back of her neck. She'd been living with Hunter for four months now inside his rambling stone mansion—a Romanesque Revival constructed in the late-1800s and nestled on twenty acres of rugged wilderness, like a decaying fairy-tale castle. As she watched him leave, she could feel his vulnerability pulsing toward her through the air. His anguish, his overwhelming love, his concern, was like a thorn. It jabbed. It hurt her heart.

She absently reached into her coat pocket and took out the rumpled letter of resignation that she'd written last week. She unfolded it and read, *"Dear Chief Snyder, Please accept my letter of resignation from the position of CIU detective . . ."*

And yet, she hadn't signed it.

She hadn't resigned.

Right before Natalie planned on handing it in, Veronica Manes was killed in the most horrific way imaginable, and the letter never got delivered. It was still folded up in her coat pocket.

There was something very evil woven into the fabric of this town. It was almost too much to bear. In many ways, Hunter was right in pressuring her to leave.

# 8

The sound of a jackhammer greeted Natalie's ears as she opened the front door of Randy Holmes's house. *Rat-tat-tat-tat.* She went downstairs to the basement, where Lenny and his team had just broken through the cement wall, and now clouds of powdery dust hung suspended in the air. The officers had BLPD stenciled on their jackets and wore protective masks, and they took turns using a sledgehammer to knock out the rest of the doorway. Soon all that was left was a rectangular-shaped hole.

Natalie put on latex gloves, slung the department camera on its vinyl strap around her neck, and waited for the dust to clear. Then she turned on her flashlight and entered the gaping hole into a narrow, dark-paneled passageway that smelled of mildew and decades' worth of old garbage. It was like entering a mummy's cursed tomb.

The claustrophobic passageway extended fifteen feet or so toward a chained and padlocked door at the other end. "We need the bolt cutters," she told Lenny, who had paused in the entranceway.

"Coming right up." In his late fifties, Detective Lenny Labruzzo had a pruney face and a fast-receding hairline, and even though he referred to himself as a fossil, he worked twice as hard as guys half his age. Since the BLPD couldn't afford a CSI unit, Lenny was their primary crime technician, in charge of processing trace and prints, and he'd been teaching Natalie everything he knew. No one was indispensable, but Lenny might've been the exception to that rule.

He brought the bolt cutters into the passageway, then clipped the lock. They unraveled the chains, pushed the slightly stuck door open, and found themselves inside a labyrinth of dank, windowless rooms connected by truncated passageways. The floors were covered with old newspapers. The surfaces were tacky, and the smell was stomach-churning.

"Christ, what's that smell?" Lenny hissed.

Natalie's nostrils flared with revulsion at a potent combination of feces, urine, burnt hair, and dirty feet. She'd suspected something was seriously off, but the shock of this discovery made her numb. "He kept someone down here," she whispered, as if the place were sacred.

"So the binders upstairs weren't a figment of his twisted imagination," Lenny said gruffly. "This place has obviously been sealed up for quite some time. This is really sick stuff."

She turned to him in despair. "Seven victims. I was hoping it wasn't true."

They went methodically room by room, careful not to disturb anything. The hairs on the back of Natalie's neck crawled as she took pictures of this secondary crime scene. Flashes lit the rooms. Everything was covered in cobwebs.

"Windowless, doors locked from outside," Natalie said. "It's a dungeon."

One of the rooms functioned as a bedroom. The old pine bed had a pair of handcuffs attached to the headboard, which repulsed her even more. The thin mattress and blankets were moth-eaten. Debris littered the floor—a woman's underclothes, a baseball cap, dozens of dog-eared paperback romance novels, stale packets of peanut-butter crackers, crumpled aluminum cans, a popcorn bag, and the core of an apple.

"So if the binders are real, then he kept seven women down here," Lenny said.

"Not all at once, though," she said, snapping pictures. She lowered her camera and explained, "According to the binders, the abductions seem to have been spaced three years apart, give or take. And did you see the last entry? It said the same thing in every binder. 'For every thing there is a season. A time to die, and a time to weep.'"

"So he killed them and replaced them with a fresh victim." Lenny shot her a disgusted look. "Jesus Christ, will the madness never end?"

She went over to the bureau and opened one of the drawers. She picked up a T-shirt and checked the label. "Women's size six." She rummaged through the rest of the drawers. "Blouses, sweatpants, sweaters, jeans." She picked up a pair of panties from the floor and checked the label. "They're all women's size six."

She shone her light over a sweat-stained pillow, moldy towels, a couple of camping chairs, a small folding table, and a flashlight. She tried to turn it on. "Batteries are corroded." There were no windows down here. There was no natural light. She shook her head, disgusted by the fetid, cloying odor of the room.

On top of the bureau was a hairbrush. She picked it up. There were long dark hairs entwined in the brush bristles. "We need to process for trace. Hairs, prints, bodily fluids. I'm sure we'll get DNA. Some of these hairs have the root bulbs attached."

"I'm already on it," he said with a nod.

The cramped bathroom made her feel physically ill. There was an old-fashioned tub, a rusty pedestal sink, and a plastic shatterproof mirror covered with greasy hand prints.

"I'll dust the mirror soon as we're done here," Lenny told her.

Natalie nodded. "It could be a gold mine."

The counter was cluttered with shampoo bottles, curlers, deodorant sprays, wet wipes, and hygiene products. Natalie picked up products at random. "Hmm. That's interesting. All of these expired around 2009 or earlier."

Inside the medicine cabinet were tubes of spermicidal jelly and a box of condoms. Under the sink was a large box of tampons, extra rolls of toilet paper, and a makeup bag full of outdated lipsticks and eye shadows.

Natalie shone her flashlight into the bathtub and immediately drew back. There were reddish stains around the drain that could've been blood. "Lenny?"

He peered into the tub. "Yeah, I'll test for blood, but it could be iron ochre."

She nodded. She knew what iron ochre was—whenever there were high levels of iron in the soil, it could build up in the drainage system. Iron ochre stains were very stubborn, almost impossible to clean. So was blood, which was rich with iron.

In the living room, they found a plaid sofa, a worn leatherette chair, an old television set, a boom box, and piles of fashion magazines. Most of the magazines dated back to the late-nineties and into the 2000s. The latest date she could find was January 28, 2007. Everything seemed to be stranded in time.

Inside the tiny kitchen, the Tupperware containers were full of moldy,

rotten food. There was a hot plate and a mini-fridge, but no sink. The cupboards held plenty of paper plates, plastic cups and canned goods well
past their expiration dates. Natalie checked a few—the baked beans and
noodle soup had expired in 2009, the bottled water had expired in 2008.
The silverware drawer contained an abundance of those soft, child-safety-
approved, virtually useless plastic utensils, a handheld can opener, and an
old bag of Hershey's Kisses. Everything was coated with dust.

The entire underground complex was abysmal, squalid, filthy. She couldn't
imagine any sane person living there, let alone how Randy Holmes managed
to live with his own conscience.

"Let's talk about that basement floor," she told Lenny. "I think we should
excavate for dead bodies. The floor's uneven, cracked and sloping in places.
It looks as if it might've been torn up in places, and new concrete poured."

Lenny nodded. "I agree. We should at least get a cadaver dog down here
to scope it out. I'll call Gossett and put in the request." He left her alone to
go make a call.

Natalie felt trapped. This was a very lonely space. Isolated. Punishing.

She spotted a stuffed animal on the sofa and picked it up—a smiling
calico kitten, its fur worn bare in places. It was well-loved. She tried to
imagine the horror these girls must've gone through, and who they were,
and where they'd come from. Her heart ached for everything they'd lost.

Now her phone buzzed, and she checked the number. It was Barry Fishbeck, the coroner. "Natalie," he said by way of a greeting, "the autopsy
starts in one hour."

"I'll be there," she said and hung up.

# 9

Sixty-four-year-old Randolph Holmes's naked torso lay under a sheet on the stainless steel autopsy table. His feet were blue. There was dark matted blood in his silver hair. The ligature had been removed from around his neck, leaving a deep cut. The rubber clown nose had been placed into an evidence bag for processing, along with the victim's clothes and other belongings.

Coroner Barry Fishbeck had a fleshy face, heavy jowls, and a mild temperament. He'd always been supportive of Natalie's career, which she appreciated, but he had a tendency to overexplain and talk too much. She didn't mind, because she always learned something—for example, the right lung was bigger than the left lung to make room for the heart, which weighed the same as both kidneys—but today the clock was ticking. Her time was precious.

The lighting inside the autopsy suite was merciless. Barry's long-sleeved gown, shoe covers, apron, hair covering, and latex gloves protected him from the deceased's bodily fluids, as well as preventing cross-contamination. He adjusted his splash shield and said into his digital recorder, "Male Caucasian, five eleven and a half, weighing approximately two hundred pounds. Sixty-four years old. Hair is silver and shoulder-length, pulled into a ponytail at the back. Eye color is brown. There's a deep laceration on the back of the scalp from blunt trauma. Radiographs show the circular depressed fractures of a hammer blow to the skull. Since a bloodstained hammer was found at the scene, and the fracture pattern matches the blunt end, we can say with confidence that

this is the murder weapon. A single blow to the skull rendered him unconscious. Once he was incapacitated, the perpetrator had a relatively easy time of
it. Death was caused by occlusion of the vessels supplying blood and oxygen to
the brain due to the tightening of a ligature around his neck."

"What type of ligature was it?" Natalie asked.

Barry pointed with his scalpel. "Here's where it gets interesting. I've
seen quite a few ligatures in my time—electrical cords, neckties, lengths of
rope, pantyhose, dog leashes, you name it. But never this." He held up an
evidence bag with a length of wire coiled inside. One end of the wire was
threaded with blue and gold silking that ended in a small blue ball.

"Is that a violin string?" she asked, feeling the surprise in her bones.

"Violin or viola. This one's sixteen and a half inches long."

Natalie's first thought was of the Violinist, the deranged psychopath
who'd placed one of his victim's severed arms inside a violin case. But he
was behind bars in a supermax facility, serving a life sentence.

Then she thought about the hundreds of musicians who flocked to
Burning Lake during the fall, spring, and summer months, when all the
local bars, nightclubs, music halls, and other venues hired musicians to
entertain the thousands of tourists who flocked here from all parts of the
country—rock bands, rhythm and blues, honky-tonk, rockabilly, fiddlers,
classical chamber ensembles, and string quartets. A nationally renowned
music conservatory was only a thirty-minute drive away from Burning
Lake in Chaste Falls, New York. Not to mention, the annual Halloween-
themed music contest and the summer music festival that was held every
August in Percival Burton Park. Both of these major events drew thousands of musicians from all over the world.

Then she thought of Stevie Greenway, who'd mentioned that one of
her talents in all of those grueling childhood beauty pageants had been
playing the violin while strung out on NoDoz. Stevie didn't like Randy.

Finally, Natalie briefly thought about her childhood friend, Bella Striver,
a promising young violinist who'd gone missing on the night of their high
school graduation many years ago. Bella's disappearance had changed Natalie's life forever.

Setting aside the evidence bag, Barry said, "One more thing." He lifted
the sheet and showed Natalie the victim's lower torso. "He's had his testicles surgically removed. The scars are well healed. I looked up his medical
records. He was diagnosed with early stage testicular cancer in July of 2009

and underwent surgical removal two months later. Both testicles, as you can see. However, there was no follow-up radiation treatment or chemo, as far as I can tell. According to his medical records, the cancer didn't metastasize and never returned."

"Is that unusual—no follow-up chemo or radiation?"

"Not especially. Testicular cancer has become a model for curable neoplasm," Barry explained, drawing the sheet back over the victim. "Surgery alone could've done the trick, if caught in the early stages. Or the patient may have refused treatment for whatever reasons. It's unknown."

The rubber clown nose, the secret dungeon, a violin string used as a ligature, the shadow boxes full of dead insects, the obsessive journals about "my lovelies."

Who the fuck was Randolph Holmes?

# IO

The commercial district was bustling today. Natalie circled the block several times before finally parking on a deserted side street. It was so nice out, she didn't mind walking to the music shop, tucked in between an insurance company and a gift shop selling incense and crystals.

Kentucky Jardine sold musical instruments, sheet music, and everything else music-related. The brick storefront had a sign in the window that read KENTUCKY'S MUSIC SHOP, FORMERLY KNOWN AS STRIVER'S MUSIC SHOP. It used to belong to Bella's father. He used to teach violin to local kids, but after Bella disappeared, he stopped giving lessons and devoted himself exclusively to his music shop until his death in 2015.

Mr. Striver was gone now, and the shop had been sold to the highest bidder to pay off his debts. But the house where Bella had grown up had been sold to a blind trust. Natalie had looked into it briefly, but the whole point of a blind trust was to keep the owner hidden away from scrutiny. Rumors circulated that nobody had been inside the house since Mr. Striver's death, and the neighborhood kids claimed it was haunted.

Corbin Striver had lived vicariously through his only child, Bella, who was a musical prodigy. Being a typical stage father, he had forced Bella to perform at various venues and pushed her to succeed. All that pressure only made her resent him more—but not the music. Never the music. Bella loved her violin so much she sometimes jokingly covered it with kisses.

A little bell jangled when you opened the door. Classical music was playing in the background. It smelled of lemon-scented wood polish in here. Nice. The shop was small but comfortable, with large aisles you could spend hours browsing through, perusing stacks of sheet music or trying out the wind instruments. The antique musical instruments were stored in glass cabinets, and you could read the little placards placed in front of them explaining where they were from, who made them, and other historical information. Walking into the shop was like stepping back in time.

She spotted forty-something, salt-and-pepper-haired Kentucky Jardine fussing with something behind the register. The seasoned blues musician looked like one of those people you tried to avoid in public—a distracted, spiky-haired adult who lived primarily in his own little world and perhaps didn't change his clothes often enough.

"Mr. Jardine?" she said, showing him her badge. "Detective Lockhart."

He stared at her for a moment, eyes slowly rolling focus. "Oh, hello!"

In front of the register were the last-minute impulse buys—container trays of drum sticks, guitar picks, saxophone mouthpieces, jars of rosin, and other paraphernalia for the local musicians. There was a section for old records, too. Albums. They were all fitted in protective plastic sleeves and cost at least ten dollars apiece.

But the shop's mainstay was classical music equipment—horns, strings, wind instruments. The rarest violins were locked away in display cases, whereas test models of the modern instruments hung on the walls. Bella used to say, "Playing a new violin in public is obscene. It feels like foreplay."

"How can I help you?" Kentucky asked, eyes twinkling. "Are you taking up the guitar, Detective?"

"Ha. No. Not today. I wanted to ask you a few questions."

He smiled and scratched his chin. "Store's empty. Give it your best shot."

"Right." She smiled. She liked his sense of humor. "I'm curious about your viola strings."

"String curious, are you? Sure. What about them?"

"Do you have anything with blue and gold threads on one end?"

"Sheep gut or steel?"

"Steel," she said.

"Small, medium, large, or extra large?"

"Wow. That's a lot of choices. It's sixteen and a half inches long."

"Got it. You're talking about the D'Addario Helicore viola string set, with blue and gold silk threads at the ball end. That's one of our most popular brands. They're right over here." He walked down an aisle and picked up a packet of strings. "This is for a long scale viola, medium tension. Sixteen and a half inches long, stranded steel core. These produce a clear, warm tone. And there's a quick bow response for classical and alternative styles. Not overly bright. So there you go."

Natalie accepted the packet. "May I open this?"

"Well, uh . . ." He hesitated, rubbing his chin. "Once they're open, we can't resell them. Sorry, Detective."

"How much?"

"Seventy-nine thirty-eight."

"Eighty bucks?"

"Being a musician ain't for the faint of heart," he said with a smile.

Natalie took out her credit card. While Kentucky ran her card through the charger, she opened the package and took out a C-string. She held up the string like a ligature, looping each end around her index fingers and pulling the string taut, judging its strength, flexibility, and tension. You could definitely kill an unconscious man with this.

Kentucky handed her the credit card and a receipt. "That stranded steel core contains steel wires braided together to produce the cable core. You've got great strength and flexibility in that one."

Natalie nodded. "Do you have a bag?"

He opened a small plastic bag with a flourish and popped everything inside, including the receipt.

"Did anybody buy these same strings from you recently?" she asked.

"A full set of D'Addario Helicore?" He shook his head. "How recently?"

"I don't know. Let's say in the past three months."

"Oh, sure. We get quite a bit of traffic for replacement strings. Especially for the violinists. Violas are a little less common, but the string community in general is pretty large in these parts. Violin, viola, cello, bass, fiddle, acoustic guitar."

"Could you get me a list of people who've purchased these strings recently?"

"A list?" He frowned. "I'd have to go through my records. A lot of people buy their strings online nowadays, so we have to be competitive. We offer a customer loyalty card, similar to those coffee-stained, hole-punched cards people use to score free lattés with. Only with our cards, you can get a twenty-percent discount off a major purchase. And it's not a physical card, either, it's a digital app you can download."

"So then, you'd have a record of those purchases?"

"Yes. Plus regular credit card purchases. When do you need it?"

"As soon as you can get it to me."

"Probably this afternoon."

"Thanks," Natalie said. "Also, do you have any surveillance tapes?"

"Me?" He laughed. "Nah. I don't believe in that shit. Big brother is watching you. That's not my bag.

She studied him inquisitively. "You've never gotten ripped off?"

He shook his head. "Let me show you something." He took out a key chain, walked out from behind the counter, and unlocked one of the antique cherrywood cabinets. He picked up an antique violin. "There's a song my niece loves to hear me play." He picked up the old bow. "It's called 'Witches' Dance' by Niccolò Paganini."

He closed his eyes and began to play a haunting melody, a musical prose poem about love and loss. A wild grief-stricken work of genius that dissipated toward the end like a puff of smoke.

When he was done, he put the violin and bow carefully back inside the cabinet and locked it again. "My little shop isn't just a place to buy instruments for the high school band, you know. I wanted to make it an immersive experience. You can feel history surrounding you, all those geniuses who composed music that envelops your senses and fills you with emotion. It's magical. There's more than one kind of magic in Burning Lake, you know."

"That was beautiful," she said.

"And I will protect this modest little shop by any means necessary." He stood there, flexing his fingers. "My hands are strong from playing the violin, but I also do a lot of target practice down at the range. Nobody messes with me, Detective. Everything's cool. We never had this conversation."

She handed him her card. "Lucky for you, I'm in the middle of something. Send me that list to this number."

"I'll get it to you this afternoon."

"And we aren't done talking," she warned him. "I've got some better options to recommend. You don't want to shoot anyone."

He grinned. "I've never had to. Just showing them what I got tucked away behind the counter is deterrent enough. It's not loaded. Don't worry."

"Oh come on, Kentucky. Get the damn CCTV."

"I'm telling you, deterrence is better than waiting for the police to identify some guy on a blurry videotape, especially if he's wearing a mask."

"I'll be back. Lock that thing away so I don't have to arrest you, hear me?"

# II

Back inside her car, Natalie felt clammy and sweaty beneath her jacket. Like Joey used to say, *You can't fix everything. Keep your focus on the case.*

She opened her wallet and pried out the snapshot of herself and her father on her police academy graduation day. Joey was beaming from ear to ear and hovered over her like a proud papa bear. She pictured the service revolver in his hand, the barrel pressed against his temple, his finger teasing the trigger—the same hand that had taught her how to play "Chopsticks." Instead of pulling the trigger, though, he let the cancer devour him. Every time she thought about it, her blood thrummed a little deeper.

Officer Joseph "Joey" Lockhart had been blue through-and-through until the day he died, a proud member of the Burning Lake Police Department for thirty-five years. He spent his career directing traffic, rescuing kittens, breaking up bar fights, and arresting drunk drivers. He was a fitness buff with scruffy brown hair and warm hazel eyes, and as the father of three daughters, he'd always wanted a son. But after Deborah put her foot down and said, "No more kids," Joey scooped up his youngest daughter—the one who adored him, the one that he'd named after Natalie Wood—and taught her everything he knew about being a cop.

One of his best pieces of advice to Natalie was about looking instead of talking. He used to say that every crime scene was full of obvious things, if only you took the time to observe them. Natalie decided to go back to Randolph Holmes's house and look for the obvious things.

By the time she got to the property, the other officers were gone. Lenny had finished sweeping through the house with his equipment, lifting loose fibers off the furniture, dusting for prints, and collecting valuable trace evidence. It was just Natalie and the long afternoon shadows.

She liked being the only detective at the scene. She could think without disruption and absorb any hidden clues that others might have overlooked. You usually got one shot at a crime scene. In a department struggling with a budget crisis, time was a limited resource.

Downstairs in the basement, Natalie entered "the dungeon" and saw patches of colorful print powder on the pertinent surface areas. Lenny had done his best to collect whatever trace he could find in a limited time period—fingerprints, fibers, hairs with roots (you could get DNA from those), footprints, bloodstains, blood spatter, documents, weapons, or anything else that pointed to criminal intent or could possibly identify the victims.

Tomorrow they would bag and tag as much evidence as they could, including the women's clothing and shoes, the handcuffs, birth control, anything else of significance, and transport it down to the station for processing. It was too soon to speculate, but Natalie suspected that Holmes had kidnapped at least seven women—re: the seven binders—and held them against their will down here in his basement dungeon, sexually abusing and perhaps even killing them. It was horrific. Hopefully, using DNA and other techniques, they would be able to identify the victims and match them against databases for missing persons or unidentified Jane Does.

During her second walk-through of the dungeon, Natalie couldn't find any evidence of torture besides the handcuffs—no chains, no metal cages, no bondage equipment or restraints. Just a dirty, soundproof bunkerlike complex hidden behind a chained and padlocked basement door.

Randy Holmes was clearly a monster.

Until they found solid evidence, however, legally it was all circumstantial. It infuriated her. She decided she would find more solid evidence if it was the last thing she did. She'd stay down here all week if she had to.

Natalie swept her flashlight beam over the moldy walls of the dank passageways and cramped, smelly rooms. It was unsanitary and windowless. A terrible existence. Floors strewn with debris. Brutal. Horrifying. How had they managed to survive psychologically with the threat of rape or even death over their heads? She could barely wrap her mind around it.

The so-called living room reeked of its former captives, a cloying sweetness permeating the walls and carpet. A sickly sweet smell that turned Natalie's stomach. A smoky acrid stink. Cigarettes, greasy scalp, potato chips, coffee grounds, body odor, stale donuts, rotting strawberries. No matter how many times you scrubbed and vacuumed, you would never be able to get rid of that smell—like expired milk, souring week after week. They would have to burn the place down.

Once again, she assessed the living-room furniture—a plaid sofa, a coffee table, a pole lamp, old movie posters on the walls. *Ghost, Forrest Gump, Indiana Jones.* There was a bookcase full of board games, stacks of dog-eared fashion magazines, and a moth-eaten blanket on the old armchair. None of the magazines were dated after 2009. It was as if time had stopped in February of that year.

Her gaze settled like a leaf on the sofa. She lifted a greasy, flattened throw pillow. There were ugly gashes in the plaid fabric underneath. A chill ran through her. Terrible secrets had been buried here, like mushrooms growing in the dark. Natalie knew she shouldn't be thinking about Bella right now, but she couldn't help herself. It was the binders upstairs that made her think about her old friend.

In the binders, Randy had referred to his victims as Subject 001, Subject 002, Subject 003, et cetera—no names or ages were given. There was one binder per victim, and the dates of abductions appeared to be 1988, 1991, 1994, 1997, 2000, 2003, and 2006. Which turned out to be every three years or so—a deliberate cycle.

Natalie had taken criminal psychology courses in college and knew that most sexual deviants had a predilection for victims of a certain age, sex, and physical appearance. For instance, one deviant might prefer seventeen-year-old blond Caucasian females, whereas another might prefer ten-year-old Asian males. They wouldn't want each other's victims. Any straying outside of these narrow parameters, and they'd get turned off.

However, she hadn't been able to find any descriptions, names, or ages of the girls in Randy's binders. And every three years or so, there was a new binder—a new victim.

It was apparent that he had kept all seven victims down here in the dungeon. There was only enough room for one victim at a time—two at the most. There was only one bed. There were no other sleeping bags or mattresses on the floor. The bathroom held just enough products for a single person—one stick of deodorant, one brand of shampoo, one type of moisturizer for sensitive skin. The clothing in the bedroom belonged to only one woman, size six. Natalie found slippers and sneakers strewn about, all of them size seven.

Randolph Holmes wasn't your typical sex criminal, and why would anyone expect him to follow the classic textbook profile? He'd been described at his job as being obsessive-compulsive, and this was also borne out by the fact that he collected and preserved insects in a fastidious, meticulous way. The abductions had occurred at regularly spaced intervals, approximately three years apart, and they'd ended with the 2006 kidnapping of Subject 007, which meant that the next abduction, if it had ever happened, would've taken place in 2009—the year that Bella disappeared.

But almost immediately, Natalie saw the fatal flaw in her thinking.

The last victim was a size six, whereas Bella was a size four.

Bella's foot size wasn't seven, it was a size six and a half.

There was no eighth binder. No Subject 008.

Therefore, it might be mere coincidence that the abductions ended in 2009.

These crimes weren't disorganized, which ruled out schizophrenia. Instead, the killer was careful, methodical, alert. Perhaps a highly intelligent sociopath, playing out some sort of psychodrama by abducting and controlling his vulnerable victims.

Bella had large almond-shaped eyes, a mischievous smile, and tousled dark hair. She liked to say things that shocked people: *Get straight A's, succeed, and get into a top college so you can have sex and get an abortion. It's not okay to do drugs, but here, take this Ritalin and Adderall. Fuck the world, I give up.*

Nobody else gave Natalie that look—a stubborn fury born of absoluteness. Bella was right, and everybody else was wrong, and there was no use arguing. For such a big personality, she occupied very little space. She claimed she wasn't superstitious, but she had a lucky hat. She made beautiful music. Her fingers smelled of violin resin. She wasn't afraid of the dark. It was very dark down here.

Could Bella have been one of Randy's victims? But she disappeared in June of 2009, whereas down in this dungeon, everything appeared to have frozen in time at around February or March of 2009.

Since Natalie couldn't prove it—there was no eighth binder—she decided to set her concerns aside and stick a pin in it for now. Weird coincidences happened all the time in police work. You had to learn to separate the wheat from the chaff.

*For everything, there is a season . . .*

Natalie walked into the bedroom again—handcuffs on the headboard, mildewed mattress and box spring, rickety nightstand, a lamp, a chest of drawers. Posters of rock bands and pop singers from a bygone era—

Nirvana, Blondie, Alanis Morrisette. A mess of stained pillows, sheets, and blankets spilling from the mattress onto the dirty floor.

As Natalie crossed the room, she almost tripped over a braided rug. She knelt down and turned the rug over. There was something on the cement floor underneath it—repetitive scratches in the cement. She pushed the rug aside. You could see where the chest of drawers had been pulled away from the wall—repeatedly over time. The cement floor was scratched in a curved pattern. The scratches originated from one of the dresser legs.

Natalie shouldered the chest of drawers and pushed it away from the wall, then aimed her flashlight at the white-painted wall. There was nothing but cobwebs and dust.

She pushed the chest a little further away from the wall, and looked at the unvarnished back panel of the chest. The surprise hit her with a whoosh of breath. Someone had scratched words on the wooden backing. Correction—*several* people had scratched words over every inch of space with a nail or a screw. She ran her flashlight slowly down the panel. In places the scratches overlapped.

*"I will not die in this place."*

*"God will save me."*

*"Do what he asks so he lets you live."*

*"I am 21 years old. I want to see my mom again."*

*"I miss my little brother. His name is Kane."*

*"Stay strong. Don't let the bastard wear you down."*

There were hearts, four-leaf clovers, and rainbows. Her heart began to break as she took pictures with her crime scene camera.

*Joy Westport, Sept 14, 1988.*

*Tati Sanriquez, 7–10–91.*

*JoJo Barnes, May 5, '94.*

*Kimi Duchamps, 10–1–97.*

*Danielle Coleman, 2000.*

*Remi Johnson, '03.*

*Harmony Sean Young, 7–21–06.*

Natalie's hands wouldn't stop shaking.

Sometimes you had to remind yourself to breathe.

# 12

Natalie walked out of the claustrophobic dungeon into the cramped basement and could not seem to focus. She took out her notepad and stood blankly clicking her ballpoint pen, the one embossed with BURNING LAKE POLICE DEPARTMENT. She stared at the spongy, lichen-colored rug on the basement floor. A smoky glow spilled from the arc lamps in the passageway, casting long shadows inside the dungeon and backlighting swirling grains of dust.

Who were these women?

Natalie packed everything into her crime kit, locked up the house, and went to sit in her car, where she activated her phone and began perusing the internet. Using the names of the seven girls, thinking it was a long shot, she was surprised to find an article about all seven of them entitled "The Shadow Girls."

In 2007, a reporter from the Binghamton *Press & Sun-Bulletin* named Melba Dunleavy had written the in-depth article about the missing women. According to Dunleavy, between 1988 and 2006, seven young women had gone missing from Binghamton, New York. Since all of the missing girls were sex workers, none of the various law enforcement agencies involved had bothered to connect the cases until Dunleavy started investigating on her own. She dubbed the missing women "The Shadow Girls" because the typical law enforcement attitude toward prostitutes and runaways at the time was that they weren't important enough to prioritize. They were invisible members of society who'd simply slipped off into the shadows.

Another reason the police hadn't connected the missing girls together was because no bodies were ever found, and therefore it was impossible to prove if the Shadow Girls had met with foul play. Theoretically, they could've gotten on a train or a bus and gone elsewhere. In that sense, it was similar to the Missing Nine case, Natalie thought, except for the fact that Binghamton was a large city with a substantial population of people in need, including drug addicts, homeless families, sex workers, and criminal elements, which unfortunately would've made it much easier to abduct vulnerable young women.

Melba Dunleavy's point was that if the police had bothered to talk to the friends and family of the missing girls, they would've understood that these poor victims couldn't simply have disappeared, because they either had children or close family members and friends who cared about them, and they'd all disappeared while working late at night in isolation.

All of the girls were eighteen or nineteen when they were abducted. All were sex workers and shared certain physical similarities—petite, small breasts, long legs, wide eyes, cupid-bow lips. They varied in race, hair color, and eye color, which meant that Randy wasn't fussy in that area. In two instances, the victims were heard screaming, but the witnesses didn't respond and instead brushed it off as kids fooling around. In several instances, a red van was reported to be in the vicinity, a dark red van with a company logo on the side. No one could remember the logo, but the guesses were varied—a maintenance and repair shop, a gardening company, plumbing, electricity. One witness saw a bug stenciled on the van.

Natalie felt prickles travel across her scalp. She put down her phone and took Randy's personnel file out of her bag. She checked his previous employment listing and found the fumigation company name—Gardner Pest Control. They specialized in fumigating office buildings and industrial parks in Binghamton, New York.

Natalie had already done a walk-through of Holmes's backyard, and she had been inside his garage. She'd taken pictures of a red van up on cement blocks. No tires. Now she clutched the department camera and scrolled through the digital images, and there it was.

She got out of her car and went to check out the garage again. The van was over three decades old and streaked with rust. Holmes had taped off portions of the vehicle and had begun spraying the body white, but you could make out patches of red and a company logo underneath—Gardner Pest Control. On one of the door panels was the silhouette of a cockroach.

# 13

Back at Langston Memorial Hospital, Natalie moved swiftly down the brightly lit corridor, then struggled with impatience as she waited for an elevator.

The third-floor corridor was painted in earth tones. Nurses, residents, and orderlies bustled past, attending to other patients in the critical care unit. The sound of squeaky, rubber-soled footsteps represented busy people saving lives.

Natalie approached the door to Luke's private hospital room cautiously. She had important things to discuss and didn't want to have to spend time chatting with Rainie Sandhill. Natalie wasn't good with small talk.

She was relieved to find Luke alone in the room. "Hey. How are you feeling?"

"Bored." He smiled at her. "But I'm good now."

"Can you talk a minute?"

"I've got nothing else to do."

Thirty-nine-year-old Luke Pittman had the kind of handsome, weathered face that suited his chipped, rugged personality. His eyes contained a gorgeous laziness about them that masked an underlying calculating intelligence. You underestimated Luke Pittman at your own peril.

They had known each other since Luke was thirteen and Natalie was five—an eight-year age difference. Luke's backstory was simple—his father had abandoned him, and his mother worked two jobs to keep them afloat. It wasn't long before Joey Lockhart invited the fatherless boy over for dinner, and soon Luke was hanging out with the Lockhart girls in their backyard.

Grace, Willow, Natalie, and Luke.

She'd fallen in love with the tall, skinny boy who had rips or holes in every single one of his T-shirts. His sneakers were threadbare. He couldn't wait to get his driver's license, and as soon as he did, he bought a beat-up Buick Skylark for $500 and got lost on the back roads of Burning Lake while blasting the B-52s' "Dirty Back Road" on his crummy Radio Shack speakers. He was proud. He was vengeful. He kept score. He was a misunderstood superhero. He was Wolverine.

Luke had been there during the most crucial events in Natalie's life. They shared such a rich history that their current situation felt awkward at times, as if they were forever stepping over the line, and then retreating. For years, she'd had a dreamy-eyed crush on Luke, but their timing was always off. By the time Natalie hit puberty, Luke was in college. By the time she'd kissed a boy, Luke was getting married and having a baby. By the time she'd entered college, he was divorced and in the army, being deployed overseas. By the time she'd joined the BLPD, Luke was a rock star detective and Natalie was dating Zack Stadler, her erstwhile boyfriend of three years.

Now Luke was miraculously sitting here before her. He'd come out of his coma looking and sounding perfectly healthy. She pulled up a chair and asked, "Did Lenny tell you anything about my new case?"

"Randy Holmes? Yeah, he filled me in briefly. What have you found, Natalie?"

She told him about the viola string, the clown nose, the insects, the dungeon, the binders, and the Shadow Girls. "Seven young women, still listed as missing, no bodies have ever turned up," Natalie explained. "Look at this." She showed him pictures of the messages the victims had left behind on the chest of drawers, etching their names into the wood with a nail or a screw.

"Fuck," he whispered, truly alarmed as he scrolled through the images.

"Melba Dunleavy's article was published in 2007," she said. "She found out there was a gap of about three years between each disappearance, which matches the binders we found in the house. It implies that he replaced one victim with the next. Maybe he liked them a certain age. Maybe when they got too old, or too rebellious, he killed them and then went hunting for his next victim."

"Why did he stop in 2006?" Luke asked.

"That's a good question. I think he actually stopped in 2009, three years after he abducted his last victim, Harmony Sean Young. Remember, he kept them alive for three years. Each of the binders ends with the same ominous biblical verse: For everything there is a season. A time to die, and a time to weep."

Luke nodded. "So it all ended in 2009?"

"Around that time, he was diagnosed with early stage testicular cancer. In September of 2009 he underwent surgical removal. Both testicles. I think that's why he sealed up the dungeon and began to focus on his insect hobby."

Luke nodded slowly, letting the information sink in. "We'll need definitive proof that at least one of those girls was actually in the dungeon."

"I just forwarded Lenny this new information, so now he has seven names to work with. He's been looking in the state and federal databases for fingerprint matches. He sprayed with luminol and found bloodstains inside the bathroom, along with dozens of hairs with roots. He sent everything off to the state lab for testing. He says it'll take a while to get the DNA results back."

"Tell him to put a rush on it."

"If Randolph Holmes held these young women hostage for three consecutive years inside a concrete bunker he built in his basement, then he probably murdered them, too. He wouldn't want to leave any witnesses. I think we should dig up the property—backyard, front yard, basement floor. There's a checkerboard of concrete areas that look as if they've been repoured and patched."

Luke nodded solemnly. "The ground is still frozen, but I'll ask Lenny to get a cadaver dog over there to start the process, so we can see if there's anything worth pursuing. I'll approve ground-penetrating radar, too."

"Thanks, Luke." She blushed. She sat smiling uneasily, while he watched her closely. She wasn't used to being scrutinized by such intense blue eyes.

"What?" he said, raising a careful eyebrow.

"Nothing. It's just good to have you back."

He smiled broadly at her. "It's good to be back."

Before the moment became awkward, a nurse chased Natalie out of the room.

Back outside the hospital, she stood for a moment in the darkening air, watching her chalky breath clouds dissipate before her and trying to delete the ugly images inside her head—images that were sure to provoke feelings of hopelessness and despair if she didn't shut them off. The handcuffs, the condoms, the squalid lightless existence.

Her phone buzzed in her coat pocket, jarring her.

It was Hunter. "How's it going, babe?" he asked softly.

"The usual. Falling down rabbit holes, one right after another."

"What's your ETA? Are you coming home any time soon?"

She looked at her watch. Her vision was blurry. She was exhausted. She'd been up for the past thirty-six hours. She'd spent most of last night watching over Luke, and now her head was pounding. "Now, I guess," she said.

"Good. I'll have dinner ready."

She hung up and drove back to the station.

There was one last thing she needed to do before heading home.

# 14

As Natalie drove back to the police station, she passed a handful of satellite vans camped out on the village green. Three days ago, the national news outlets had picked up the shocking news of Veronica Manes's death, and the front steps of the station house had been jammed with reporters and camera crews muscling their way forward, squeezing up against one another and shouting questions at Chief Snyder—no wonder they called it "the press." *The Burning Lake Gazette* had run stories about Veronica's local Wiccan coven and the tabloids had gotten hold of some shocking crime scene photographs, the aftermath on the train tracks. It was grisly stuff, but more than that it was disgusting. No wonder the police didn't trust the media.

Natalie swung her Honda Accord into the parking lot behind the station and eased into her spot, determined not to let any information about the Randolph Holmes's case leak to the media. She didn't want any more attention focused on her than was absolutely necessary. It was much better to work in obscurity. Inside, she collected her mail and took an elevator down into the basement, where the evidence storage room was located.

Access to the storage area was restricted. There was an intrusion alarm for the doors and vents, but no infrared motion sensors. An entry code got you into the security hallway leading toward the evidence room with its bulletproof transaction window, where she found Officer Hughie Siskin behind the thick pane of glass.

"Natalie, how's tricks?" Hughie said through the two-way intercom.

"Tricks is good, Hughie. Did you hear about Luke?"

"My wife's been praying for him. Sometimes the good guys win, huh?"

"Absolutely."

Hughie rapped his knuckles on the countertop. "So what can I do for you tonight?"

"I'm looking for an archived file. Bella Striver. 2009."

"Sure thing. You know the drill." He pushed a clipboard across the counter and through a narrow opening in the transaction window, and Natalie picked up the pen and filled out the form.

"Don't forget the case number," Hughie said, pointing with a damp finger. He could be an impossible man to deal with, full of bluster and self-importance, and his incompetence was legendary. However, Officer Siskin had been with the department forever, and you didn't want to get on his bad side. He could slow the process down to a snail's pace. Also, he'd said some really nice things about her father at the funeral. So she was quick to forgive him.

She added the case number, along with the summary information and her detective ID, then handed it back.

Hughie stared at the request form. "Is that a P or a B?"

"P for Missing Persons. Case number MP-060209–01."

"Okeydokey." He disappeared into the back.

The evidence was organized into general categories—firearms, drugs, cash, jewelry, trace. Every piece of evidence was identified, tagged and put in a property box, which was then assigned a number corresponding to a specific location inside one of six property rooms. The boxes might sit for weeks, months, or even years before they were needed for court proceedings or further lab analysis. It should have been an easy task to retrieve any given box, but Hughie Siskin was in charge, and that meant everything was stored in a seemingly haphazard fashion, dust rising up wherever you poked around.

Natalie could hear him shuffling things around in one of the back rooms.

"Got it!" he shouted, returning to the window with a heavy-looking storage box in his arms. He opened the door and set it down on the floor.

"Well, that was relatively painless," Natalie said with a smile.

"I aim to please."

"Have a good evening, Hughie."

"Cheers, kiddo."

She carried the archives upstairs to her third-floor office, where she set the box down on her worktable. The unit was empty this evening. All the guys were either off their shifts or out in the field, searching for Peter Murphy. She wiped the dust off the lid and opened the box.

Thirteen years ago, eighteen-year-old Bella Striver had been a whip-smart beauty with a promising future ahead of her as a gifted violin soloist. Her father—a former wunderkind himself—was a strict disciplinarian who'd encouraged Bella to show off her skills. He was obsessively attentive and harsh in his criticisms. Over the years, he lost sight of who she was—a teenaged girl with typical girl struggles—and his blind ambition for his only child eventually drove her away from him.

After their high school graduation ceremony, Natalie, Bella, and their closest friends, Max, Bobby, and Adam, celebrated that evening by meeting at their favorite hangout, an abandoned theme park in the woods. They called themselves the Brilliant Misfits, and that night they got stoned in Funland's old derailed train and ended up perched on the edge of the crumbling Bridge to the Future, wondering where they'd all be ten years from now.

Later on that night, after Bella went missing, Natalie's father, Officer Joey Lockhart, got involved in the search for the missing girl, and at one point Mr. Striver came under suspicion. But the primary suspect turned out to be Nesbitt Rose, Hunter's younger brother, who'd had cognitive problems since birth and was allegedly the last person to have seen Bella alive.

Three weeks after Bella's disappearance, on a drizzly rainy night—after being hounded by the media, with the whole town in an uproar—Nesbitt sucked on the nozzle of a vacuum cleaner and put an end to his misery. He had loved Bella better than any of them and didn't understand the increasing calls for his arrest.

In a strange turn of events, several months after she disappeared, Corbin Striver received the first of several letters from Bella containing Polaroid pictures that proved she was alive and well. She was fine, she said. She simply needed time to think and space to heal. Natalie also received a couple of letters from Bella explaining why she'd run away. Mostly she blamed it on her egocentric, overbearing father. She didn't want to be a violinist anymore. "Tell everyone to stop looking for me," she wrote. As a result, the police had labeled Bella a runaway, and the missing-person case was closed. And now, here it was in Natalie's hands. All that anguish, all that heartache and pain, reduced to a bunch of paperwork and dusty evidence bags.

But the pain had endured. In the aftermath of Nesbitt's tragic death, his older brother, Hunter Rose, had sued the police department and the local papers, blaming them along with the small-town mentality that had contributed to Nesbitt's suicide. The city settled out of court, but it took Hunter years to get over it. Except that Natalie wasn't sure he was entirely over it. Now he was one of Burning Lake's most prominent citizens, a wealthy entrepreneur with friends in high places. He pulled the strings and other people danced.

Eventually, Bella's letters stopped arriving, and no one ever saw or heard from her again. They all assumed she'd gone off to find herself, perhaps to the point of leaving the country. Natalie still missed her. There was a hole in her life where Bella's mischievous, warm personality belonged.

But life wasn't fair or predictable.

Now Natalie combed through the box and found what she was looking for—the Polaroid pictures that Bella had sent along with her letters to prove she was okay. Each of these pictures was allegedly taken in a different location over a six-month time period—postmarked Los Angeles, Seattle, San Francisco, Denver, Chicago, and New York City. She didn't appear to be intimidated, scared, or suicidal. In her letters, Bella insisted that she'd left town of her own free will and was traveling around the country, staying at various youth hostels and making new friends.

However, there was something about them that had irked Natalie to this day.

In every picture, Bella was seated on the floor, leaning against a white wall and smiling at the camera. She seemed happy and relaxed, but far too pale for the California sun. This was back in 2009, before cell phones and selfies. In her letters, Bella never mentioned who had taken the pictures or where she'd gotten the money to travel or who her new friends were. The Polaroids were all close-ups of her, from her collarbone to a foot or so above her head. You couldn't see the rest of her surroundings, just the white wall behind her. Always a white wall.

Four months ago, Natalie had shown her old friend Max Callahan—now a building contractor—these Polaroids. After carefully studying the images, Max told her something was definitely "off," because the white walls looked the same in every picture, despite the fact that they were supposedly taken in different locations. As a matter of fact, he came to the conclusion that it was the *same wall* in every photograph.

Max, an expert in building construction, pointed out that each wall had the exact same flaws in it. He explained about the effects of gravity on old buildings. The weight of the floors above, plus the movement of people, could produce a "turning effect," also called a "moment." If the moment was large enough, then, under catastrophic conditions, the walls might collapse. But if the moment was small, which most of them were, then a wall could form discernible cracks over time due to tension and compression forces. Each new crack was unique, like a fingerprint.

But the cracks in all of Bella's Polaroids appeared to be identical. So the question was—how could she have possibly posed in front of the same wall every single time, while claiming to be in different locations? Had she left Burning Lake voluntarily? Or was she kidnapped? And what eventually had happened to her?

These were the questions that ate a hole in Natalie's heart.

# 15

One time, many years ago, Natalie accidentally saw pictures of a dead girl in her father's study. The girl had been stabbed multiple times, and it took her several agonizing seconds to realize that she was looking at color photos of her older sister's corpse. Willow Lockhart's bloodstained body.

It had traumatized her. It kept her awake at night. She couldn't tell her father what she had seen, couldn't bring herself to talk about it. She kept the image of Willow's ashen face, pale blue lips, and glazed-over eyes buried in a dime-sized corner of her brain where it slowly rotted and turned black. Who knew that there could be such evil in the world?

Now she pulled up in front of Randolph Holmes's house and parked. The property looked eerie in the moonlight. She got out and automatically checked her weapon, her eyes drawn to the moon shadows.

Inside, the house was dead silent. The basement was dark. Natalie switched on the arc lamps set up inside the narrow, dusty passageway. Her heart beat erratically as she entered the tunnel and went through the second doorway, where the arc lights couldn't reach.

Natalie switched on her heavy-duty flashlight and stood in the middle of the living room. The beam of her flashlight scanned the sagging plaid sofa and leatherette chair, the old analog TV, and stacks of pawed-through magazines and careworn romance novels.

The living-room walls were painted white. On a hunch, she activated her phone and scrolled through the stored digital images, until she came to the series of Polaroids Bella had sent her and Mr. Striver so long ago. Bella always posed in front of a white wall, just like these white walls.

Now Natalie held up her phone screen and tried to find a match between Bella's Polaroids and the dungeon walls. She methodically went around the living room, studying cracks and divots in the plaster and paint. She paused. To the right of the television set was an empty space large enough for a human being to sit on the floor and lean against the wall.

Feeling little prickles of fear mixed with excitement, Natalie crouched down and studied the cracks and flaws in the paint. It looked like the same wall to her—but she was no expert.

She grabbed her camera and snapped a bunch of pictures from different angles. She couldn't keep her mind from racing. Was it possible Bella had been kidnapped on the night of their high school graduation in 2009 and brought here? Had she been held captive inside this dank and putrid place? But then, where was the binder for Subject 008? Why were the clothing sizes all wrong? What happened in 2009?

Natalie couldn't stop imagining her best friend—so sharp and funny and ambitious—trapped inside this prison. Crying for mercy. Sobbing for help. Picking at her own skin, scratching her face, pulling on her hair. Beating the walls with her fists, blisters of paint granulating under her fingernails, while her mind slowly disintegrated and fragmented away.

Where was Bella now?

Was she dead?

And what about the Shadow Girls? What had happened to them?

Were they all dead? Would Holmes have left any witnesses?

And who had murdered him last night? Why?

Natalie studied the heaps of clothes and garbage bags full of trash, the smelly, tangled nest of blankets on the thin mattress, the single overhead bulb, the empty soda cans and crumpled packages of food, and her eyes filled with tears. She stayed until she couldn't stand it anymore. She went outside and stood in the snow, staring angrily back at the house. The last rays of pink sunlight lit up the sky. The day was done.

She called Max Callahan. "I need your help, Max. I'm no expert."

"What's up, Natalie?"

She explained the situation to him, while leaving out all the confidential information. "Can you come over and take a look at this? Make a comparison?"

"I'm at a work site. How about tomorrow?"

"Sure. When?"

"Tomorrow at one?"

"Sounds good, Max. See you then." She hung up.

Max would meet her here tomorrow, and together they would find out if this wall was the same wall that Bella had posed in front of many years ago. This idea calmed her. Max would help her figure it out. The thought was like a soft, comforting paw on her shoulder. Now she could finally call it a day.

# 16

Natalie powered down her window and let the chilly night air hit her face. It had started snowing again—gentle flakes twirling in the moonlight. She'd left downtown Burning Lake behind and was heading north into the woods. She took the bridge across Swift Run Creek, then drove past turn-of-the-century homes nestled in old pine groves. The northern part of town consisted of conservancy lands and wealthy neighborhoods where the estates had been passed down from generation to generation. Hunter lived here. Now she lived here, amazingly enough.

A pair of headlights flashed in her rearview mirror, and she noticed a red Nissan sedan following her. She took the next right, and the car followed her onto a quiet residential road.

Natalie kept an eye on the driver behind her. He had curly dark hair and wire-rim glasses, and she vaguely recognized the ex-journalist-turned-Substack-blogger from Rochester who kept calling her to ask about the Crow Killer and Violinist cases.

She took another turn down a country road, winter-bare trees gliding past in the gathering darkness. The Nissan followed her down two more side streets, until they were quite isolated, with nothing but woods all around.

Natalie hit the brakes.

The Nissan stopped abruptly behind her, his tires skidding over an icy patch on the road. She got out of her car and unbuttoned her coat to display her weapon. She might've been mistaken about his identity, and she hated stalker-ish behavior. She put her arms down by her sides and stood in the glare of his high beams.

The reporter gave her a smug smile. She'd forgotten his name. Kip something. He got out of his vehicle and strode confidently toward her. "Detective Lockhart, remember me? I'm Kip Edwards, I used to work for the *Daily Record,* but now I've got a blog with over eight hundred subscribers and thousands more readers. I must've left a dozen voicemails on your work number . . ."

"Why are you following me? What do you want?"

He stopped smiling. "Can you tell me anything about Detective Murphy?"

"No comment," she said, heading back to her car.

He jogged toward her. "Wait! What happened? Did Detective Murphy assault Lieutenant Pittman? Was he involved in Veronica Manes's murder? I heard he's been stealing evidence from the police station, is that true?"

"Who told you that?" she demanded to know.

"I can't reveal my sources."

She held his eye. "You're no journalist. You're a blogger."

"I'm an independent journalist."

"Get out of my way," she said firmly.

He raised his hands and said, "Sorry, sorry." He stepped aside. "Come on, Detective, use me. I'm a resource. I can post anything on my blog, and maybe you'll get a response."

She got into her vehicle and locked the door. Then she rolled down her window and said, "Kip."

He leaned in. "Yes?"

"Off the record."

"Yes?" he said anxiously.

"Leave me the fuck alone, okay?" She rolled up her window and drove away.

# 17

It had stopped spitting snow, and the dying sun cast scarlet streaks across the windblown surfaces of the clouds as Natalie pulled into the long gravel driveway and parked next to Hunter's BMW. The eerie-looking stone mansion was called Romanesque Revival. It had conical towers, bay windows and sculpted copper claddings. Constructed in the late 1800s, it was four stories high, with twenty-eight rooms and six stairwells. There were thirteen steps per staircase. How deliciously creepy.

There were unconfirmed rumors that the Boston steel magnate who'd originally lived there had lost three children to accidents on the property, and so at the turn of the century, the bereaved man had sold it, and it was subsequently turned into a luxury resort. In the 1920s, it became a sanitarium for tuberculosis patients. In 1935, it was abandoned and left to rot until the mid-1980s, when Hunter's father bought it and restored it to its former glory. On the eastern side of the mansion, a well-tended lawn gave way to a tennis court and small orchard. On the western side was a greenhouse and a detached garage for Hunter's vintage motorcycle collection.

Natalie and Hunter had dated briefly one long-ago summer, when she was in college and he was an aimless grad student. They'd fucked on his parents' king-sized bed while the Roses were traveling in Italy, and afterward Hunter showed her where he used to ride his skateboard up and down the austere second-floor hallway.

But life had intervened, and Natalie became a cop, Hunter became an entrepreneur, and they went their separate ways. They hadn't seen each other in years until just a few months ago, when the Violinist's second victim showed up dead in a dumpster and Hunter inadvertently became embroiled in the case as a witness. For some reason, they clicked. Perhaps it was their shared grief—her sister Grace had recently died, and Hunter still hadn't gotten over Nesbitt's tragic demise. Or maybe it was his charm and persistence. He was ready for love, and so was she.

One year ago, Natalie had broken up with her ex-boyfriend, Zack Stadler, and it was during this interim between Zack and Hunter that she had hoped—oh God, she'd been so embarrassingly hopeful—that she and Luke might finally connect, that they'd grab hold of each other and never let go. After all, she used to believe it was their destiny.

Now she understood something about herself, something that she couldn't share with anyone else. She had always been in love with Luke Pittman, ever since she was ten years old and had carved her and Luke's initials into the bark of her favorite Witch Tree on the edge of McKinley Forest in Black-thorn Park. As legend would have it, if you carved your deepest desires into a Witch Tree, then over time, as the tree grew taller, the bark would swallow up the carving until it became indecipherable, and only a witch could read it.

Only the witches of Burning Lake knew how much Natalie loved Luke.

But then, totally unexpectedly and with much accompanying drama, Hunter Rose came into her life at that exact moment, and he'd flipped the board over, scattering all the pieces. He was charming and relentless. He was ready for love, and he chose her. He had the most physical presence of any person she'd ever met—a natural grace, a tanned, ropey physique, and he loved to use his body in an exploratory way. Their chemistry was unde-niable. His body played her body like an instrument. He had a natural grace and a brooding moodiness that reminded her of a character from an Em-ily Brontë novel. He touched her like an elegant, lovestruck vampire who was afraid he might lose his last thread of self-control and drain her of all her blood, and thereby risk losing her. He was afraid to show her how very much he loved her, and so he held back, sitting on his feelings until they became unbearable, and all this love finally came pouring forth, threaten-ing to bury her.

And so, when Natalie had found herself mourning her dead sister, when it hurt more than anything else in the world, when she was broken and saturated with grief and loss, he had grabbed her in his muscular, protective embrace and refused to let go. He had kissed her so passionately, she'd almost died. He had sworn his love almost immediately, too soon. He had rubbed his stubbly cheeks over her face, peppering her with little kisses and making her feel sore and tickly all over. He had fucked her until she couldn't fuck anymore, and so they would lie around in bed, eating takeout and watching old movies until the soreness left them, and then they'd fuck again. During the day, he would watch her the way a cat watches its prey, before it attacks, waiting oh-so-patiently. When he pounced, his love bit deep, like a terrible secret. And for the first time in a very long time, Natalie felt vividly alive— stirringly, kinetically alive—and she wanted to feel this way all the time. She was paralyzed by it.

# 18

There was nothing so lovely as a winter evening under a cold pale moon and crystal bright stars. Bone-tired at the end of an eventful day, Natalie stood for a moment in Hunter's front yard, enjoying the brisk wind in her face—hoping it would blow reality away, just for a little while. Then she went inside.

It was refreshing to hear classical music drifting from the living room. The house was full of savory smells. Hunter was cooking dinner. She could hear him rooting around in the cupboards, rattling pots and pans, and pinching his fingers in the silverware drawer. "Ouch. Shit."

"Hunter, it's me," she called out.

"Natalie. Just a second, I'm juggling recipes . . ."

She hung up her coat, gloves, and scarf. She kicked off her boots, then carried her shoulder bag into the living room, where she set it down on an antique side table. The interior of the house was composed of dark varnished paneling, tall echo-y ceilings and sinuous mahogany staircases. To a middle-class kid like Natalie, the house spoke of great wealth and generations of secrets behind its elaborately carved wooden doors.

Through the arched doorway, she could see the long mahogany dining table set for two—tapered white candles, a pitcher of ice water, the Rose family silverware, and antique Limoges floral dinnerware. Hunter believed in using valuable things instead of packing them away like assets for future appraisal. If a dish broke, so what? That's what dishes were for, to be used and enjoyed.

"Dinner's almost ready," he said. "Come sit." He smiled and gallantly held her chair out for her. "I made you something special. I hope you brought your appetite." He was being ironic—he never said things like that without being utterly ironic. She smiled and let herself relax. He held her attention for one brief, anticipatory moment before slipping back into the kitchen.

Natalie draped the linen napkin across her lap. She wasn't very hungry, just numb. The flickering candles cast delicate, animated shadows. She thought about the rubber clown nose and wondered what the killer had been referencing there.

"Are you ready?" Hunter carried two sterling silver serving dishes through the arched doorway and set them down on the table with a flourish. "Risotto with porcini mushrooms, perfumed with truffle oil."

He poured them both a glass of white wine. "My wine guy recommended this today. A 2019 Louis Jadot Pouilly-Fuissé from Burgundy, France."

She smiled, amused by his performance, but also not quite knowing what to say or how to react. Whenever Hunter was feeling especially nervous or uncomfortable about something, he became super animated and busy. He liked to cook. He was good at it. He was good at a lot of things. He probably wanted to eat a good meal, drink a splendid wine, and fuck her to death. But Natalie wasn't in the mood for fucking.

Now he took a seat and draped his linen napkin across one knee. "Do you like it?" He drank some wine. "Mmm. Not bad. What do you think?"

"It's very good."

"My wine guy knows of what he speaks," he said, gently mocking himself.

"Your wine guy has never steered you wrong," she said with a smirk. His wine guy, his trainer, his interior designer, his maintenance staff, his security team. Hunter was embarrassed about his wealth, his possessions, his entourage, which was why he constantly poked fun at himself. Natalie chimed in because it was true—it was ridiculous to have "your people."

"I should adopt him. I'm glad you like it." He had exquisite manners—especially when he was bothered by something. And something was bothering him now. She could tell, even though he hid his feelings well behind a flawless coat of varnish. He carefully set down his wineglass and asked, "How's your risotto?"

She wrinkled her nose delicately. She rested her fork on the edge of her plate.

"Come on, sweetie. Have something. You must be famished."

"The truth is I can't taste anything."

"Okay." He put his fork down and gazed at her. "What happened today, Natalie? Talk to me. I want to know what you're going through. I want to be involved."

"Sometimes there's too much to process. I need to digest it all before I can share my feelings with you. So much has happened in the past few days, it's overwhelming."

"I get that." He nodded. "I do."

"And it's not that I don't want to involve you, it's just that I can't."

"So this guy, this new case . . . I heard about it on the news."

She nodded. "Randolph Holmes. He worked at Murray's Halloween Costumes."

"Out on Route 151. They said he was murdered. Strangled."

"Right."

"Okay." Hunter took a sip of wine and put it down with exquisite care. "And Peter Murphy, they're still looking for him? He had something to do with Veronica's death, right? It's all over the news. It's not a secret."

"Right."

"Is there anything else?" he asked. "I mean, are you handling everything okay?"

She nodded. "I just want to figure out what's going on, that's all. I get impatient with the process. Justice works slowly, and that sucks."

He frowned thoughtfully. "More Pouilly-Fuissé?" He refilled their glasses, and Natalie drank half of hers down. "There you go. Drink up."

She took a few more sips, then said, "I may have to reopen Bella Striver's case."

"Really?" His entire mood shifted. "Why?"

"I can't say too much. It's all speculative at this point. But we may have found evidence indicating she didn't run away."

"Really?"

"Sorry, I can't tell you any more than that."

His mood darkened. "I never quote you, Natalie."

"I know. I'm just saying . . ."

"I don't talk to people about your job, Natalie." He seemed angry.

"I know. It's just that my head is throbbing."

"So you're going to dig up an old case file that's painful for both of us. I thought your therapist has been encouraging you to move forward. How can you move forward when you're literally moving backwards?"

"That's the very definition of a cold case," she said defensively. "Moving backwards."

"Give me a break," he muttered.

"Jesus, are we fighting now?" She dropped her napkin on the table.

"No," he said heatedly. "We're disagreeing. We aren't fighting."

"Then why do you sound angry? I'm only doing my job."

"Bella Striver? You had to reopen that particular case? Why?"

She felt the tug and pull of her own exhaustion. "I can't talk about it."

"You said you found evidence. Evidence of what?"

"Hunter . . . stop it."

His angry expression didn't change. He finished off the rest of his wine.

She curled her hands in her lap and kept her mouth shut.

"Okay," he said. "Bottom line? I love you. I'd do anything for you, Natalie. Absolutely anything. But look at you. Something really awful has happened, a whole series of awful things have happened in a row, and you were on the verge of quitting last week because of it. And then, Veronica Manes is murdered, and now some guy who works at a costume outlet is strangled, and you immediately go back to work and get involved up to your eyeballs. What is it about this job? Do you honestly think it's worth it?"

He didn't say the words out loud, but Luke's name hung in the air between them. She sensed that Hunter suspected part of the lure for her going back to work was Luke, but that was so insulting. As if her job didn't mean everything to her. As if she needed a man to motivate her to do some good in this world. He reached for her hand, but she drew it away before he could softly catch it. She was furious. Her heart was pounding. Her temples throbbed with blood.

The silence between them this evening felt heavy.

"Look," he said, leaning forward, "I want you to be happy. Not tormented by the past. You've paid a heavy price for this career of yours."

"I'm very aware of the sacrifices."

"Okay. Well, there's one other thing I'd like you to do." He sat back in his chair and looked her straight in her eye. He stared at her. "I want you to make up your mind about us."

There it was.

"Are you committed to this relationship?" he asked. "Are you with me?"

"Am I with you?" she repeated, incredulous. "Of course, I'm with you, Hunter. I'm here, aren't I?" she said defensively. What she couldn't say, what she couldn't bring herself to tell him was that Hunter didn't understand how obvious he was. His desire was written all over his face and embedded in his body language. He liked to sit and watch her get drunk. He delighted in her stories and her laughter. He caught her whenever she was about to tip over, like a dizzy child. He watched and waited, sitting on his appetite for her. She could see all this, and it scared her. His great need for her to be in his life frightened her. Hunter Rose could have had anyone in the world. Why choose her?

"I don't want you to just 'be there' for me," he said, clearly exasperated.

"Then what do you want?"

"Everything. Marriage, kids, the works. Your body, your mind, your soul. Our dream home. Far away from here."

"My soul?" She laughed.

"Fuck it. Why not?"

"Why not?" She honestly didn't understand him right now.

"I'm sorry, is it too much of a reach for you to consider that I also might want you to own me, body, mind, and soul?"

"No, okay, I see what you're saying." She tried to back down off this emotional cliff. "It's just a little melodramatic."

He stared at her. "I hate what this town is doing to you, and it infuriates me that you don't see it."

"I appreciate your concern, but it's my life."

"My *concern*?" He laughed angrily. For a moment, he looked at her as if she were a stranger. Then something ticked through his brain—she could see him thinking—and the derision and irritation melted off his face, and a great warmth suffused his body. He wiped his mouth on a napkin, leaned forward, and said in a gentle voice, "Listen to me for a minute. There's something you should know. We've had a few incidents on the property recently."

"Incidents?" she repeated blankly.

"I'm considering installing a safe room."

She looked at him steadily. "What kind of incidents?"

"Like I've mentioned before, it's not unusual to get people wandering onto the property, the occasional trespasser or some other misguided soul. I'm a prominent person, and you've been quite notorious lately. We're both in the news a lot. Local celebrities, you might say . . ."

"Celebrities? No, we aren't."

"Natalie, come on. You know what I mean. Anyway, most of these folks seem pretty harmless. But there's an individual lately who's been very effective at breaching the perimeter and not getting caught—this one keeps leaving his calling card on the edge of the property. I'm worried about this particular creep. We've caught him on video, but only glimpses and partials. He drives a vehicle, a dark sedan, but the plates are obscured. He wears a ski mask and knows how to hide from the cameras, which means he's staked out the place. All of this makes him potentially dangerous."

"What kind of calling card?" she asked.

"Wiccan objects."

"What kind of Wiccan objects?"

"A couple of witch-bottles so far."

It sent a chill through her. Witch-bottles were dark magic. "What was inside?"

"Pins and nails suspended in some kind of liquid."

"Urine? Did you have it tested?"

"Yes, of course."

"What did they find?"

"Turns out it was animal urine. From a cat. You trust Bill Finley, don't you? Bill's a former PI in Buffalo, he knows exactly what to do. He has a connection to a crime lab in Albany. He's right on top of things."

"Can I see the surveillance tapes?"

"Natalie, let my guys handle it." He shook his head. "Do you want this? This kind of life? Because I'm considering relocating to Denver, and I'd very much like you to come with me."

"Just run away? Easy as that?"

"I didn't say it would be easy. You don't have to give me an answer right away. Just promise me you'll think about it."

She nodded slowly. It was exhausting to argue with him.

"And remember, we can live anywhere in the world."

"The world is pretty big," she said softly.

"Just tell me what you want, Natalie—name anything, and I'll get it for you."

Of all the things she could've asked for—a new life, travel, adventure, a family—the one thing she wanted more than anything else was to solve this bizarre string of homicides, to find out what had happened to Randy Holmes, to Bella, to Veronica, and to her own family—no matter how scary or dangerous it might be.

Her phone chirped, interrupting their meal. "Sorry, I have to take this."

"Yeah, of course." He shrugged, trying to mask his anxiety.

She got up and walked into the living room. "Hello?"

"Detective Lockhart, it's Kentucky Jardine. I've got a list of all the customers who purchased viola strings in the past three months."

"Thanks, Kentucky. Can you send it to me?"

"Sure, hold on. Okay, bingo. Just sent you the attachment. Looks like twenty-three pairs were sold in the last three months, and the POS system shows that twenty of those transactions were either by credit card or using a customer loyalty card, so that means there are three sets of strings that were purchased with cash only." He paused. "Is that helpful?"

"Very. Do you remember any of those cash-paying customers?"

"Nope. Could one of them possibly be the killer?"

She frowned. "How do you know about that?"

"Well, I saw it on the news that Randy Holmes was strangled. Hell's bells, as my mama used to say. And since you're the lead detective on the case, and I watched you open a packet of strings in my shop and use it as a ligature, wrapping the ends around your two fingers . . . I put two and two together."

"Okay." She sighed. "Listen to me, Kentucky, don't share this information with anyone, understand? We want to keep it out of the public eye, and it could be crucial to the identification of the perpetrator. Do you understand?"

"Yes, ma'am. I won't say a word."

"Thanks again." She hung up.

Back in the dining room, Hunter was gone. She walked around the first floor, looking for him. He was holed up in his den. She could hear his muffled voice.

Natalie knocked softly on the door.

After a moment, he poked his head out, still on the phone. "What's that?" he said into the receiver, glancing over at Natalie. "Okay. Call me back. Thanks." He hung up. "The deal appears to be going sideways. I have to make a few phone calls. I'm sorry, babe. Do you mind?"

"No," she said. "I think I'll go lie down."

# 19

Natalie went to bed exhausted. She could hear Hunter's low, melodic voice traveling through the house. She knew he would get what he wanted. Hunter always got what he wanted. Soon she fell fast asleep.

Natalie woke up abruptly at two in the morning. She couldn't remember her dreams—only a lethargic blankness. Hunter was snoring softly beside her, his head buried in his pillow. She carefully peeled back the covers so as not to wake him, put on sweatpants and one of Hunter's flannel shirts over her washed-out BLPD T-shirt, then went downstairs.

The house was quiet. The hardwood floors were chilly. She put on her winter coat in the foyer, pulled on a pair of boots, and went outside to retrieve Bella's case file from the trunk of her car.

Back inside, she set the box on the dining-room table, then opened her laptop to Melba Dunleavy's article. The long mahogany dining table had been built for a family of twelve. She liked to come down here early in the morning, drink her coffee, and contemplate her caseload, but it was eerie in the middle of the night. The French doors didn't have any drapes, and tonight the full moon provided a good view of the manicured backyard and wild woods of Upstate New York. She could feel goose bumps rising on her arms. She wondered if the mysterious intruder was out there. It gave her the creeps, but she also knew that Hunter's security team would be watching over them.

Natalie turned her back on the French doors and read Melba Dunleavy's article all the way through. The seven women were all from Binghamton, where Randy used to work for a pest control company thirty-five years ago. Luring these women into his van wouldn't seem to require much effort if all he had to do was wave some cash around, but being able to slip in and out of the community and harbor these women for years would require extreme mental clarity and discipline.

The FBI had concluded that many serial killers were caught in a progressively intensifying loop of fantasy. Although childhood fantasies were perfectly normal, they could transmogrify into a compulsive form of escapism for children who were abused or traumatized. And many serial killers were severely abused as children, it turned out.

Perhaps the only thing that stopped Holmes from living out his violent fantasies was the operation for testicular cancer in 2009. Perhaps then his quest to experience the ultimate fantasy morphed from abducting, raping, and controlling women into killing and mounting insects? It all seemed to stem from the same obsessive, compulsive, and cyclical nature of serial criminality.

Now Natalie's phone rang, disrupting the silence. She answered softly, "Hello?"

"Hey, it's Luke. Did I wake you?"

"No, I'm up."

"It's two fifteen in the morning. Why aren't you asleep?"

She smiled. "Why aren't you asleep?"

"Because it sucks here."

"At the hospital?"

"Yeah, they keep waking me up to make sure I'm getting enough sleep. Sorry to call so late. Can you talk?"

"Sure." She leaned back in her chair. "What's up?"

He took a deep breath and said, "I'm looking at Veronica's case file right now, and the bulk of the evidence seems to point to Murphy, but we can't ignore the second set of footprints at the scene of the abduction. If it's true that he pulled this off, horrific as it seems, then he must've had an accomplice. As you said last week, it would've been impossible for him to carry an unconscious woman plus those shackles all by himself during a snowstorm, but we need conclusive proof. So far, it's all circumstantial."

It was shocking enough to have learned that Detective Peter Murphy had been lying to his colleagues for years, stealing evidence and covering up other criminal activity, but the fact that he was now the primary suspect in Veronica's homicide was utterly baffling. They didn't have a motive. No one could figure it out. Nobody had seen it coming.

"So the question is—who helped Murphy kill Veronica?" Luke went on. "And if more than one person is responsible for her death, then who was in charge? Murphy or his accomplice?"

"What do you think?" she asked.

"I doubt Murphy could've managed something of this magnitude on his own."

"Me, too."

"And yet, there's no reason in the world for him to have killed her. We can't find any links between them. Plus, look at all the other evidence that went missing on his watch—the Crow Killer and Violinist cases, to name a few. Why would he do that? He clearly wasn't stealing the evidence for his own purposes. What could he possibly do with it? And if Murphy was working for a third party, then we have no idea what kind of people we're dealing with here."

Natalie told him, "Lenny suspects that he may have planted evidence, too."

"Seriously? How did he come to that conclusion?"

"Last week, he did a thorough sweep of the Dodge pickup and found nothing of significance. But then, during a second sweep, he found trace evidence linking the truck bed to Justin Fowler—evidence he'd oddly missed the first time around. And Peter Murphy was the only person to visit the impound lot between those two sweeps."

"So he planted the evidence to implicate Justin Fowler?"

She nodded. "I'm beginning to think that something deeply corrupt is going on in this town, Luke." Moonlight poured in through the French doors and fell gently across the paperwork on the table. "I can't put my finger on it, but what if Murphy's just the tip of the iceberg?"

Luke sighed. "Well, if Murphy is a pawn in a bigger game, then we need to be careful going forward. He had us hoodwinked for years. We don't know who else we can trust."

"Who do you trust?" she asked.

"The guys in our unit. Lenny, Augie, Brandon, Mike, and Jacob. I can't vouch for a lot of the officers, though, with the exception of Keegan, Goodson, Marconi, and Prutzman. They're good men. But for the time being, let's keep it inside the CIU," Luke told her.

"What about Assistant Chief Gossett?"

"I don't know. He seems on the up-and-up, but he's also an ass-kisser, and the guys don't like him. He's got issues. Once we know more about Murphy's motives or anything definitive about his associates, we can pull Gossett in. In the meantime, let's keep a low profile. Direct communications only. Whatever's going on, we have no idea who else could be involved. I hope we're wrong, but we can't mess around."

She shivered. "I hope we're wrong, too."

"Listen, you and I need to sit down with Lenny and go over the details of your new case together, once the lab results are in. Just to see where we are. The doctors have given me a clean bill of health, and I've been cleared for duty. I'll be discharged from the hospital tomorrow and back to work on Thursday. We can meet then." He paused. "How are you handling all of this, Natalie?"

"Okay."

"Just okay?"

"I keep thinking about my old cases. We're supposed to be able to move on, but it doesn't seem possible, does it?"

"Well, just know that I'm here for you."

"Thanks. It's good to know."

"I'm always here for you."

A shimmering silence stretched between them—like the quivery tension of a drop of water clinging to a blade of grass before the inevitable fall.

"Listen, I know we've had this conversation before," Luke said gently. "I know we've made a decision, and we have to stick by it, but I need you by my side, Natalie. I need you strong, ready, close. You're my best detective, and I depend on you to tell me when I'm veering off message or when I'm full of shit. I find your intelligence stimulating. More than that, you get me. Very few people get me. It's rare, this friendship of ours, and I don't want to botch it."

Natalie was speechless. She wanted him to keep on talking, to hear his voice in her ear for the rest of the night, until the first rays of sunlight filled the room. She didn't understand why she felt suspended in time between these two men. These two choices. She couldn't explain it. But she was with Hunter now. Clean lines.

"Anyway," he said with a sigh. "The chief wants me to take a few days off, but I'll be working from home. As of tomorrow, call me anytime. Then on Thursday, we'll meet up with Lenny and do a deep dive into your new case."

"Sounds good," she said.

"Good night, Natalie," he said calmly.

"Good night, Luke." She hung up, feeling a tidal wave of emotion—a sorry combination of remorse, regret, and nostalgia for what might've been.

# 20

SUNDAY, MARCH 13

The following morning, Natalie drove across town to Murray's Halloween Costumes and parked in the empty lot. A cold breeze whipped her hair around as she stepped out of her vehicle and glanced at the sooty brick warehouse. Yellow police tape stretched across the entrance indicating that this was a crime scene, closed to customers.

She knocked on the glass door, and Murray came bustling out of his office to let her in. His face was sweaty and deeply lined, and he looked as if he hadn't slept a wink. "Natalie, they left everything in disarray. There's crime tape on the door, and fingerprint powder everywhere. When can I clean up and reopen for business?"

"I'll ask my team," she said with an understanding smile. "It shouldn't be much longer. I'll get back to you this afternoon."

"They took the body away, thankfully, but there's still blood on the floor! Are you going to clean it up, or should I?"

"I'm afraid you're responsible for cleaning up the crime scene, Murray. I'm sorry. But I'd recommend you hire a professional service. Here's their card."

"Thanks." Murray squinted at the business card. "Upstate Forensic Cleaners?"

"We always recommend it, especially when there's a possibility of bloodborne pathogens. These people are very thorough and compassionate. Quick, too. It'll be done within twenty-four hours."

"Well, that's a relief." He offered Natalie a stick of gum. "Would you like a piece? No?" He popped the stick of gum into his mouth and said, "So how can I help you? What's up, Natalie?"

"I have a few more questions. For instance, did you know that Randy had a hidden bunker in his basement?"

Murray looked confused. "A what? A bunker?"

"In the basement. Take a look at this." She scrolled through the digital pictures on her phone and showed him the demolished wall, the dank interior passageway leading to the padlocked door, and the windowless living room. "The doorway was covered up with cement, and we had to knock it down. Inside, there's a windowless bunker. A cramped living space, with a bedroom, a bathroom, a living area, and a tiny kitchen. Did you know about this?"

"Why, no." Murray gazed at the picture, then up at Natalie. "I had no idea."

"Did you ever visit him?"

"At his house?" He shook his head numbly. "Sometimes we'd go grab a few beers after work. My wife felt sorry for him, so we invited him over for dinner once in a while. But a bunker? No. I have no idea who this guy is you're describing to me."

"And you've never been over to his house?"

"Once or twice. I remember the bugs in the picture frames. I didn't stay long."

Natalie put away her phone. "Did Randy have any romantic relationships or anybody else he may have been close to?"

"Randy?" He seemed surprised. "Not that I know of."

"Who are the Shadow Girls?" she asked, watching carefully for his response.

Murray shook his head, clueless. "I have no idea. Are they singers?"

"Was Randy secretive? Strange? Any odd behavior?"

"Well, like I said, he collected bugs. I guess that's pretty strange."

"Anything else?"

"He didn't talk much."

"So when you went out for a few drinks, what did you two talk about?"

Murray shrugged. "Sports. Work-related subjects. He once told me a story . . . I don't know."

"Yes? Can I hear it?"

"It was about his father. I forget how the conversation started, but he told me about a time when . . . right after his mother's funeral, during the reception, Randy's father got wasted and kept harassing him, and they got into a shouting match, and . . . Randy said his father had a broken leg at the time. At one point, he threw Randy down on the floor and sat on him with his leg in a cast, and Randy couldn't breathe. Then his father leaned over him and punched him in the face. It took three guys to pry him off."

"So his father was abusive?"

"I got that impression."

"Did he tell you any other stories like that?"

"I honestly don't remember." Murray's eyes lit up. "Oh, wait. He once related a story about being locked in a toolshed or something, and he got so hungry he ate a worm. I don't know if he was exaggerating or not. Also, he had bad acne as a kid and called himself an outcast. And when his father died, his aunt took him in, and she was very religious."

Natalie nodded. "Anything else?"

"Not that I recall. I felt sorry for him."

She nodded her encouragement. "What about the rubber clown nose? Any ideas?"

"Only what I told you yesterday. That he liked to dress up as a clown for Halloween. Here, I'll show you," Murray said.

They headed down the hallway toward the staff lounge, where Murray pointed at a bulletin board full of snapshots of his employees dressed in a variety costumes. "Every year, we show off our inventory for Halloween, so we each choose a costume, and Randy always picks the clown with the fright wig."

In all the pictures taken throughout the years, Randy wore the same clown suit.

Murray took one of the snapshots down and handed it to her. "He never gained a pound from year to year, unlike some of us, so the costume always fit."

"Can I keep this?"

"If it'll help."

She pocketed the photograph. "And he has no other family in the area? Brothers, sisters, parents?"

"He has a nephew. He's listed on the insurance form as Randy's beneficiary. It's in the personnel file."

"I forgot my copy. Can you get me the contact information, Murray?"

"Sure, it's in my office. Come on." He led her back down the hallway toward his office. "My God, the world is going crazy, Natalie. I'll never understand any of this."

# 21

Natalie took the exit off the highway and pulled into Woodbine's Pre-Owned Vehicles, a commercial used-car lot full of shiny banners, patriotic balloons, and piped-in music.

She found a parking space near the main entrance, where a couple of salesmen lurked beneath the PARTS AND SERVICE sign, waiting to pounce on customers. One of these men approached her with a jaunty step, saying, "Are you here for the sale? I can offer you a great deal. You don't want to pass up an opportunity like this!"

"Detective Lockhart, here to see Peyton Wolanski," she said, displaying her badge.

"Oh," he responded, immediately losing interest. "He's in his office."

Inside the building, a glass-walled showroom highlighted three freshly waxed vehicles on rotating platforms. There was a customer lounge with a flat-screen TV, and about three other well-dressed salesmen stalked her like prey. She had to keep flashing her badge at them.

It took Natalie a moment to recall who thirty-two-year-old Peyton Wolanski was. It turned out that Randy Holmes had a sister named Jessica who was married to an auto mechanic named Manny Wolanski. They had two kids, Peyton and Darla. Peyton had been one year ahead of Natalie and Bella at school.

She remembered him as a peripheral kid, a skinny stoner who liked to hide out on the fringes of the schoolyard and crack dirty jokes. He was plain-looking, with a shy, elusive demeanor. He'd talk to you out of the corner of his mouth, then glance nervously away when you answered. His shyness could've been interpreted as cool by some, but Natalie saw through it, because she was shy, too. Only she hid her shyness behind a wall of out-spoken rebelliousness and an insolent moodiness.

Natalie could recall only a single incident involving Peyton and Bella, and it happened a long time ago when she and Bella were in the fourth grade. They used to take the bus to school, and one afternoon, after the final bell rang, all the kids ran out of the building toward the idling buses. Peyton got on his bus, which was parked parallel to theirs. The two girls were chatting happily together when they noticed Peyton staring at them through the dirty windows—he was directly opposite them in the other bus. He stared so hard that Bella flipped him the bird, saying, "What is *wrong* with you?" Just then, Peyton smiled and started blowing them kisses. Bella laughed, and in response she blew kisses back. Then he laughed and kissed the dirty bus window. Bella squealed with delight, and she leaned forward and kissed the bus window. Then both buses pulled away.

It never happened again, as far as Natalie knew, and she and Bella never talked about it afterward. A kid like Peyton Wolanski wasn't really on their radar. He was one of those truly invisible kids, a shadow boy running around in baggy jeans and a gray hoodie, skulking around corners, hiding from his teachers, making no bones about how much he hated school, smoking weed during recess. Natalie and her nerdy friends wanted to be rebels, but Peyton and his ilk were the real rebels. They were the genuine misfits.

But that was ancient history.

Now Peyton Wolanski was a high-earning salesman in a used-car lot. He lived three towns over and was married with kids. He stepped out of his corner office, smartly dressed in a crisp business suit, and waved a cursory hello. He was on the phone. Trim and fit, pleasant-looking and impeccably groomed, he winked at her as if they were chummy old friends. He hung up and cut across the polished floor, saying, "Should I call you Natalie?"

"Detective Lockhart's fine."

"Cool. I remember when you were yay high. Step right this way." He lightly touched her elbow and steered her into his office, then closed the door. "Your timing couldn't be better. We just finished our morning pump meeting. Basically, lots of yelling and clapping and trying to get everybody jazzed. Please, have a seat."

She sat in one of two black leather recliner chairs. "I have a few questions about your uncle," she began, then backtracked. "I'm sorry for your loss."

He leveled his gaze at her. "Yeah. That's okay."

"Were you two close?"

He grimaced. "Not really."

"Why not?"

"Sometimes that happens with families."

"So what happened?"

"We just drifted apart, I guess."

"I see." Natalie jotted it down. "But you've been to his house, correct?"

"When I was growing up. But not in the past seven years."

"Why not? What happened seven years ago?"

He shrugged. "After my mom passed away, there wasn't any reason to keep up the pretense."

"When you visited your uncle, though, did you ever go down to the basement?"

"What? No. We'd usually watch the game in the living room. Stuff like that."

"And he never mentioned building a bunker in the basement?"

"A bunker? Like a bomb shelter?"

"Something like that."

"No. I never went down there. My mom and sister and I used to visit Uncle Randy about once a month or so. Darla and I would play in the backyard or watch TV in the living room. But then, after Mom passed away . . ." He glanced out the plateglass window at the car lot. "Leukemia. Yeah. It was rough."

"I'm sorry."

"Thanks. After our mother passed, I didn't feel like seeing him anymore."

"So you stopped visiting your uncle seven years ago. What triggered that?"

He sighed and looked at her. "He was a bit of an oddball. When Mom was alive, she'd drag us over there. But I stopped communicating with him after my mother's funeral. That was it for me."

"Why?" Natalie pressed.

"Because he was a dick."

"Okay. That's one way of putting it. So you had a general feeling of dislike for your uncle? Was there anything in particular about his behavior that put you off?"

He shrugged. "I just never liked him very much."

Natalie decided to take a new tack. "Do you remember Bella Striver?"

He stiffened and studied her for a moment. "Where are my manners. Can I get you anything? Cup of coffee? Coke? Sparkling water?"

"No thanks, I'm good."

Peyton clasped his hands together on his desk. "Yeah, she was a nice kid."

"She bought some pot from you once, I think," Natalie said, suddenly remembering. During their senior year in high school, Bella told Natalie, "Hey, I know this pothead—you remember Peyton, right? The bus-window kisser?" According to Bella, he sold great weed. She bought a few joints from him, and the Misfits would get high in the old theme park. It was the only time Natalie had heard Bella mention Peyton since the bus-kissing incident in fourth grade.

"Why?" he asked. "Are you going to bust me?"

"Just trying to get a bead on things."

"During senior year, yeah," he admitted. "And not just once."

"How many times?"

He gazed out his office window. "I don't know. Dozens." He shrugged.

"Dozens?" she repeated, surprised. "So you guys hung out together?"

He unclasped his hands and leaned forward. "What we had was a transactional relationship. I sold weed, she bought weed. We ran in different circles."

"So it was a business transaction? Or rather, dozens of transactions?"

"She bought pot, we'd smoke a little. She made me laugh. She was a good kid. But obviously, I don't do that kind of thing anymore. I have a wife and kids now. I'm a responsible citizen."

"Right. And the night she disappeared after our high school graduation?" Natalie asked. "Did she buy pot from you then?"

He frowned. "No. That was heartbreaking."

"Where were you at the time?"

"Where was I? Okay." He dropped his hands in his lap. "Probably getting stoned in Haymarket Field with my buddies. All of us losers used to hang out there. But exactly where was I that night? I don't remember."

"So just to clarify, you didn't see her that night?"

"Hello, no. Why?" he said anxiously. "I thought she ran away?"

"That's the official story."

His shoulders sagged. "So she didn't run away?"

"We're exploring the possibility. Did your uncle know Bella?"

"My uncle? Why are you asking me these questions?"

"It's just routine. You don't have to answer."

"I've got nothing to hide," he said defensively.

Natalie nodded. "You mentioned you disliked your uncle. Why's that?"

He sighed and shook his head. "My uncle was a lonely man who didn't know how to be around people, and my mother sort of treated him like this wounded creature she needed to protect. He was always building things. He built the shed and the garage out back, and the renovations to the house, and the back deck. When I was a kid, he'd let me help him. He taught me how to hold a hammer and whack a nail properly. But as I grew older, I became more aware that he was off in his own little world. And after my mom died, there was no reason to go over there anymore."

Natalie glanced around Peyton's office and noticed the family pictures in their wooden frames. She picked one up—Peyton posing with his mother and sister. Peyton was in his late teens at the time. They were all dressed up, and his younger sister Darla was holding a violin. "Your sister plays the violin?"

"She used to be really good. It's more of a hobby now than anything else."

"And Darla is how old now?"

"Twenty-eight."

That meant that Darla was three years behind Natalie and Bella at school.

"I mean, look," Peyton said, glancing impatiently his watch, "my uncle wasn't a bad guy. Just eccentric, like I said. When I was a kid, he took me fishing and helped me build a tree house in the backyard. So I don't know what to tell you."

"But then . . . you cut him out of your life?"

"By that point, after my mom died, he'd turned into a lonely weirdo. At some point he started killing insects and mounting them in boxes to hang on the walls. He showed me his killing jars once—you know, all these glass jars full of dead insects, along with the cotton balls soaked in chloroform." He shrugged. "It freaked me out."

"What else freaked you out about him?"

"He used to line up all the kitchen appliances in a row, so they were identically spaced from each other. I think he had OCD or something. He used to tap his fingers on the table in a peculiar way. He was always very difficult to relate to. I don't know. I have a wife and kids now, I don't have time to pretend that I care. Some people are beyond rescuing."

"I understand," Natalie said. "Did Bella ever meet your uncle when she was buying weed from you?"

He winced. "Not that I recall. Can't help you, Detective. Sorry. I wish you the best of luck. Bella was a sweet kid, and I feel bad for her family. But she had her own orbit, and I had mine. Now if you'll excuse me, I'm expecting an important call . . ." He tapped his watch face.

"If you think of anything else, here's my number." Natalie handed him her card.

"Look, this is highly disturbing, okay? It bothers me—you coming here to talk about Bella. Why's that? We all liked Bella. I was one of the volunteers who searched for her. Just the thought of it sends shivers up my spine. There's no way she would've had anything to do with Uncle Randy."

"I understand. Thanks for your time. Just take the card."

His shoulders sagged. He took her card and glanced at his watch again.

"And please, call me if you can think of anything else."

"Okay." He escorted her out of his office. "Hit the phones, people!" he shouted into the showroom.

# 22

By the time Natalie got back to Randy Holmes's house on the northwestern side of town, Max Callahan was waiting for her in his father's van. Callahan & Son was a construction company that specialized in residential buildings, as well as offering consultations and repair and maintenance services.

Max got out and waved. "Sorry, I'm early."

Natalie checked her watch. "I'm late."

"You're just being polite. I've always been habitually early."

She smirked. "You never got that fixed?"

"No, I still dread being left out of things." Max had aged since their high school days—a paunch over his belt, hair going gray at the temples, crow's-feet around the eyes—but he was the same old Max she'd known since they were kids. Jovial, inquisitive, and comfortable in his own skin.

They crossed the front yard together, then Natalie unlocked the door, and Max followed her inside. The house was silent, a desolate early afternoon light filtering in through the curtains. The floorboards creaked at the lightest step. The tension was palpable.

"Everything I'm about to show you is strictly confidential."

"Absolutely," Max said. "My lips are sealed."

"It's this way." She led him downstairs into the basement, where water seeping from the ceiling hit a stagnant puddle on the floor, the drops echoing. The water heater and furnace hummed and clicked. You couldn't ignore the huge, wrecking-ball hole in the wall or the narrow, dusty passageway inside.

Max looked at her with strained incredulity. "What is that?"

"A hidden bunkerlike space. I'm talking unsanitary conditions. We think he might've been holding at least one captive down here for quite some time."

"A captive?" he exclaimed.

"That's all I can tell you. It's pure speculation at this point, but we believe it was sealed up by around 2009, since most of the canned goods and beauty products expired on that year. You're here to look at one of the walls."

Max swallowed hard. "Okay," he said. "Let's do it."

"We need to mask up." She handed him a filtered mask. "And gloves."

They put on their protective gear, then stepped through the jagged entranceway into a mildew-smelling passage that led to the second doorway, which was covered with plastic sheeting. "This is to protect against asbestos, toxic mold, or any other contaminants." Natalie swept the sheeting aside, and they entered the dungeon.

Max let out a low whistle.

"Remember the old Polaroids I showed you last week? The ones that Bella sent her father and me shortly after she disappeared?" Natalie said as they headed down a dank passageway toward the living room. "In each photograph, she posed in front of a white wall. Do you remember when you told me they looked like the same wall?"

"I do indeed," he said solemnly.

"Well, I need to know if *this* is the same wall as the ones in the Polaroids."

Two arc lamps had been set up in front of the living-room wall. The old rug was worn down in high-traffic places. The plaster ceiling was fissured with cracks.

Her heart beat erratically as she approached the wall space next to the television set. They both stood in front of it. "Do you still have those images on your phone?"

"Yep, hold on." It took a moment for Max to pull up the attachments on his phone. "Okay, got it." He made a few adjustments to the images. "Well, I can tell you a few things. But first, let me check something out." He put down his phone, took out a tape dispenser from his back pocket, and began to measure the wall. "Over time, you'll see the effects of gravity due to a house settling. The weight of the floors above it, plus the effects of the weather and people moving around can create cracks and puckers."

She nodded. "I remember. You called them 'moments.'"

"Right. Or 'turnings.' Every stress point is unique, like a fingerprint. Now here . . ." He tapped the wall with a gloved finger. "You can see this large crack that's very similar to the ones in the Polaroids, only it's slightly longer. Now, this crack here and the other cracks aren't identical, but that could explained away by the gap in time, which is over a decade now. The Polaroids were taken in 2009, correct?"

Natalie nodded. "Shortly after Bella went missing, yeah."

"The more time that passes, the bigger a flaw can become." He put his measuring tape down and picked up his phone again. "So we could presume that, if another decade or so of pressure was applied to this wall, it might explain why the crack is longer and more prominent than the ones in the Polaroids. However, this wall . . ." He patted the dungeon wall. "Look to the right of the crack. See that? It's smooth."

Natalie nodded.

"But in the Polaroids, you can see a dimple about eight-point-five inches diagonal to the right of the crack—see there?"

She leaned over the phone and studied the enhanced images on his screen.

"That's a nail pop," Max explained.

"A what?"

"Nail popping is a common sign of an underlying structural problem. You'll see it with drywall cracks sometimes. It can occur whenever a nail or a screw pulls away from the stud underneath the drywall. Hold on." Max zoomed in on each image, then compared them with the living-room wall. "Do you see what I mean? There's a slight shadowy defect on each of these digital images, and they occur at the same distance from the crack. But there are no nail pops on this wall." He smoothed his gloved hand over the dungeon wall.

Natalie nodded. "So what's your conclusion?"

He shook his head. "Well, for it to be official, you'd need to hire an expert in digital enhancement and evaluation of building structures. I can only share my opinion."

"What's your opinion then?"

"No, it's not the same wall. Sorry, Natalie."

"Because of the nail pop?"

"Yes. In my assessment, these five enhanced images of Bella's Polaroids are more precisely similar to each other than they collectively are to this bunker wall."

"Okay, thanks."

"I could give you the name of an expert, if you'd like."

Natalie shook her head. "No, that's the end of the road for this lead."

He turned to her. "I hope it was helpful."

"Very. You saved me a lot of time and effort. Thanks, Max."

"Any time." He smiled. "Is that it?"

She could tell he had all sorts of questions. "Yeah, I'll show you out."

After he was gone, Natalie stood in the living room and looked around at the collection of mounted insects. The sun was beginning to set, long golden rays of light illuminating the specimens inside their shadow boxes. She could see details—iridescent wings, compound eyes, jointed legs, eyelashlike antennae.

Natalie finally let go of the idea that Bella had been one of Randy's captives. She realized now that she'd created a connection out of thin air because, deep down, she wanted to find out what had happened to her best friend. All she had was a hunch and a violin string—or a viola string. She had the thinnest of reasons to pursue this course of inquiry. She decided to set her theory about Bella aside, to exercise patience and wait for the state lab to conduct DNA testing on the trace evidence Lenny had pulled from the dungeon. To pursue this train of inquiry any further would be a waste of time.

Crime scenes were all about patterns. The human mind had a tendency to find patterns where none existed. Your alarm clock yanks you from a deep sleep. You plunge yourself into your shift and investigate cases. There are countless witnesses to be interviewed, many with conflicting statements. You spend your days verifying alibis, setting up interviews with suspects, looking for holes in their stories, hunting down new leads, and waiting for lab results. You hope for a breakthrough from DNA analysts and fingerprint examiners, but it might take months to get those reports back from the lab.

Her father, Joey, had once told her, "If it's really bad, Natalie, just pretend it never happened. Shut off your emotions and protect yourself, because you don't want to take it home with you."

Natalie didn't know how she could possibly not take this home with her.

# 23

Natalie hurried back to town, almost late for her appointment with Dr. Mazza. The doctor's office was located in a five-story, granite building about a block away from the police station. The office was impersonally comfortable.

Dr. Marybeth Mazza was one of those crisp professionals who had their act together and didn't necessarily appreciate sarcasm. She was smart, intuitive, and inquisitive—all the things you wanted in a therapist. But for some reason, these weekly sessions made Natalie feel like an unruly teenager again, reminding her of the arguments she used to have with her mother. Dr. Mazza would've said she was projecting, but Natalie couldn't stand the doctor's practiced neutrality. She wanted to take a peek behind the curtain and find out what Marybeth really thought of her. Woman to woman.

"Two weeks ago," the doctor was saying, "you told me that Abigail Stuart had cursed the town of Burning Lake and everyone in it. You spoke of the witch trials in 1712 and thought we were still paying for those executions?"

"I don't have to believe in the supernatural to think we might be cursed."

"Do you think your own life is cursed?"

Natalie winced. "No," she admitted. "Not really. But whatever is going on, it's certainly bizarre, don't you think? This spate of horrific murders. And I can't control any of it."

"Regrets and PTSD are part of being a cop," the doctor explained. "You've encountered some extremely unusual circumstances over the past year or so. You've had to be stronger than you ever imagined possible. Yesterday, you thought about Bella because of the viola string, but today you feel that's a remote possibility. And you made that deduction based on evidence. That's your job. That's what you're supposed to do. But it's also perfectly natural to wonder what may have happened to your best friend. You continue to be haunted by the past, but perhaps this is part of being a cop as well—finding patterns in the complexity of reality."

Natalie nodded, then glanced out the window at the fluffy clouds.

"Where are you and Hunter?" Dr. Mazza asked in an even tone, her handsome face set to neutral. She tapped one finger on the arm of her chair, the meter ticking.

Natalie sighed. "He has intense feelings for me, and sometimes it feels a little desperate. I know he loves me and wants to take care of me, and that feels good. But he's also hyperfocused on me."

"How does it make you feel when he's hyperfocused on you?"

"A little smothering. But I understand where it's coming from."

Dr. Mazza tilted her head. "You do?"

"Yes. We both lost a sibling. We both know what it's like to experience such a tremendous blow. Issues of love and trust become burdened with fear. The fear of losing that person."

"Right. You lost Grace, and he lost his brother, Nesbitt. And it's interesting to note that it has become an obsession of his to keep you safe. Perhaps because he couldn't keep his brother safe. He was supposed to take care of Nesbitt. He still beats himself up for not being there when his brother needed him the most."

"He was really upset when I told him I was reopening Bella's case file."

Dr. Mazza nodded. "Perhaps he doesn't want to remember Bella, because it brings up all those bad feelings again? And if your father was part of the investigation that led to Nesbitt's death, then perhaps in a way, Hunter still blames the police, and maybe some of those feelings leak onto you somehow. And by opening up the past, by reinvestigating this tragedy, it might seem to him you're going down a path that is abhorrent to him. Such an intense, all-in guy like Hunter . . ."

Natalie shuddered. She hated how accurate Dr. Mazza could be, like an arrow to the heart. She hated that a professional stranger could know more about her than she knew about herself. It was upsetting to have your psychological landscape spread out before you in such a matter-of-fact way. Like a road map.

"You're right about that," Natalie said. "His desire to leave Burning Lake has intensified since I mentioned Bella. And he seems to want to run away from his past almost as much as he'd like me to run away from mine."

"But what are you supposed to be running away from?"

"The pain, I guess."

"Do you want to leave?"

"I can't. Not now."

"So the pain hasn't gotten bad enough for you to want to leave it behind?"

Natalie rubbed her forehead. "It's pretty damn painful. But I have a job to do."

"And Luke? Where does he fit into all this?"

Natalie paused. She hated it when Dr. Mazza asked about Luke. It made her blush. "He's got something going on with Rainie Sandhill," she said dismissively.

"Do you think Luke is in love with Rainie?"

She paused for a moment, then decided to tell the truth. "No, I don't. I can't imagine it. Rainie is . . . she's all feel-good, sunshiny, rosy-cheeked optimism. I can't picture him talking to her about his caseload or police work in general. It would depress her. She isn't the right person for him."

"Who is, then? In your opinion?"

Natalie checked her watch. "I think our time is up."

Dr. Mazza glanced at the digital clock on her desk. "You're right. But we have a minute or two left. Is there anything else you'd like to add?"

"No, I'm good."

The doctor smiled indulgently. "Okay. Just a second, I'll write that prescription for you. We'll start tapering you off in a month or two. I sense that now's not a good time to cut back." She handed Natalie the prescription slip. "Do you agree?"

"Yes." Natalie stood up. "Thanks, Doc."

"And Natalie, it's okay not to have all the answers. Life is a process."

"Right. See you next week," she said and left.

# 24

When she got home from work that night, Natalie parked her car in the white gravel driveway and got out. A chill wind stirred the trees around. She drew her coat collar closer, while ugly images pulsed like the tide on her mind's eye, washing in and out. It was exhausting. She was in pain. She needed rescuing.

It began to snow. Large ornate flakes swirled through the air, reminding her of the randomness of the universe, but also of its great power and beauty. She held up her hand to catch a few flakes, each one unique, and they melted on her palm. She shivered and checked her watch. Hunter would be making dinner by now.

She was about to go inside when she saw an incandescent beam of light playing in the woods to the east of the house. Not just one—there were two flashlights.

Surrendering to her unquenchable curiosity, Natalie headed across the snow toward the woods. In some places the crusty drifts were over a foot deep, but that didn't stop her.

The woods were dense and pitchy. She was jumpy. She told herself to calm down. There was a sweep of movement to her left, and a figure came loping toward her out of the ground fog. He wore a black cashmere coat and sturdy-looking boots. "You're home early," Hunter said, his breath pluming through the chilly air.

"Who's in the woods?" She could hear a soft flutter of male voices about ten yards away. "What's going on, Hunter?"

He slipped a hand into his coat pocket, then took out a pack of cigarettes and a pewter lighter. Hunter never smoked—or rather, he used to, but he quit five years ago. She'd never seen him smoke before, not once since they'd been together. "Someone left a dead animal on the property. The guys are handling it."

"A dead animal? Can I see?"

He lit his cigarette, inhaled, and let out a ribbon of smoke. "All right. Come on."

They headed toward the activity in the woods, where the flashlight beams spun behind the trees, casting witchy shadows. As they approached the clearing, Natalie saw two men standing over a dark shadow on the snow. About fifteen yards away was the tall cedar fence that delineated the property.

"We think it's a raccoon," Hunter explained. "Hard to tell."

On a slope of snow rested the rotting carcass of a dead animal about the size of a large raccoon. The flies had reached the larval stage, and the creature was infested with maggots, but the maggots on the surface had frozen in mid-squirm.

"How did it get here?" Natalie asked.

"Somebody flung it over the fence and triggered the motion sensor alarm. Bill found it on his rounds about twenty minutes ago," Hunter explained.

She turned to Bill Finley and asked, "Did you see who did this?"

He shook his head. "There's security video of a vehicle on the road, but you can't see the plates. A figure in a ski mask and hoodie gets out of the sedan and tosses something over the fence, then speeds off."

Hunter's security team worked in rotating shifts, and her favorite of these guards, Bill Finley, had the Hulk's physique. He talked about his wife and three kids with sentimental affection, and yet Hunter had assured her that Bill wouldn't hesitate to kill anyone who threatened either one of them.

Several years ago, someone had broken onto the property, smashed out a window and stolen some of Hunter's art—family heirlooms. Ever since then, he'd gotten serious about home security, hiring a security detail and installing a perimeter alarm system to protect the residence, along with upgrades such as double-paned glass on the first-floor windows and steel-reinforced doors. He'd also hired an IT company to prevent any cyberattacks on his business.

Now Bill was holding a shovel and aiming his flashlight down at the carcass.

"Those maggots must've hatched inside a dumpster or someplace relatively warm and protected from the elements," Bill explained. "Otherwise the larvae would've remained deep inside the body cavity to avoid freezing to death. The larvae on the surface died after it landed here in the snow. Whoever threw this thing over the fence also attached that to its leg," he said, pointing at an item lying in the snow next to the raccoon. "It's a poppet, tied to the leg with a piece of string."

Natalie's heart rate accelerated. Traditional Wiccan curses known as poppet dolls were used for magic, supposedly for healing and love, but they could also be used for darker purposes. Revenge curses, bad luck, ill health, even death spells.

She knelt down to look a little closer, and the air smelled pungent. Her eyes brimmed with stinging tears. "I'll go get my evidence kit," she told them. "We need to take photographs . . ."

"Natalie, it's okay. The guys are handling this," Hunter told her, his eyes reflecting flashes of blue from the flashlight beams.

"But we need to file a report . . ."

"And say what?"

"Trespassing," she explained. "Vandalism. Criminal mischief."

"No," he said firmly. "There's no need to get the police involved. This is on private property. We can handle it."

"But we need to find out who did this," she said forcefully, standing up. "Can I at least take a look at the surveillance tapes?"

Hunter gave her a tormented look. "My team will handle it, Natalie. That's what I hired them for. We don't need to make it public. Trust me, you don't want the media crawling all over this. Like I said, Bill's got it covered. Pictures, evidence, labs . . . he's handling it all."

She turned to Bill and asked, "You'll let me know if you find any evidence, won't you? Any fingerprints or trace?"

"Absolutely," he said. "I've got contacts at an excellent forensic lab, and an IT specialist is checking the surveillance feed as we speak."

"And you said the video didn't show any plates?"

Bill shook his head. "They must've obscured the plates with mud or paint. The vehicle stopped by the side of the road in one of our blind spots. We're going to conduct a thorough review of our procedures and protocols tomorrow and make all the necessary adjustments."

Hunter drew deeply on his cigarette and said, "Keep us apprised, Bill."

"Will do, boss."

Hunter turned to her and said, "Let's go."

As they headed back to the house, the frigid air stung Natalie's lungs. She wanted to respect Hunter's decision—it was his house, his property, and Bill Finley worked for him. And Hunter was right—they didn't want the police involved. For one thing, it could end up in the papers, which was the last thing Natalie needed. Still, she was itching to become involved. The good news was that Bill seemed open about sharing his findings, so all she had to do was give him space and let him do his job. She needed to be patient. Now she understood how the crime victims felt, waiting for the police to call with an update.

The overcast sky felt incredibly close, like the domed ceiling of the Sistine Chapel. The yard lights cast pale triangles over the snow. The gutters were laced with icicles. Hunter crushed his cigarette underfoot, and they went inside.

# 25

Natalie put on her sweats and went downstairs to Hunter's private gym, where she trained hard for an hour. Squat rack, bench press, cables and pulleys, dumbbells, pull-up bar, elliptical. Then she got on the treadmill and ran for what felt like miles.

A primitive sense of vengeance took over and infused her veins. Instead of finding peace and calm within herself, she wanted to rip the world apart with her bare teeth, to locate the root of evil and tear it to pieces. She wanted to burn it all down and start over. She wanted to declare war on the unknowable, amorphous evil that had taken over her town, to face it, confront it, and destroy it. In the deep recesses of her body, Natalie wanted to reclaim her honor and win. She wanted to taste victory inside her mouth. Only then would she be able to find any so-called peace.

She took a long, hot shower, then got dressed and went looking for Hunter. The kitchen was empty. There was nothing simmering on the stove. The dining-room table wasn't set. Two delivery bags from Gabriela's had been left on the mahogany sideboard.

Hunter was gone.

The house was dark. She switched on the hallway lights and made her way through the first floor, drifting past an ecology of shadows. She needed human contact, and not just any contact—him.

The door to his study was closed. She could hear him talking on the phone, wheeling and dealing. Spinning endless demands. She placed her hand on the antique glass knob, and the door opened smoothly on its well-oiled hinges.

All the lights were off, except for his classic desk lamp. The brocade curtains were drawn. She could barely make out the peaks and valleys of this nocturnal landscape, and it smelled of old-school masculinity—cracked leather, wood oil, cigars, and port.

Hunter was seated at his desk with his back to her, talking on the phone. "We need to know who's doing this. Never mind the expense. What's that?" He rubbed his sore shoulder. "Yeah, I approve. Overtime. Whatever you guys need. Just get it done. Thanks, Bill." He hung up and sighed.

She felt incredibly moved by him. In the few seconds before he sensed her presence, she almost pitied him. "Hunter?"

He turned with a look of surprise. "Natalie. I didn't hear you come in."

She went over to him. In the soft pink light, she could sense that he was trapped inside a well of sorrow. It was the kind of sorrow you tried to cover up with lots of activity and plans and schemes and dreams. He had lost his mother when he was quite young and had become his brother's keeper. Under his watch, Hunter had lost Nesbitt. Grief was like a membrane that spread over everything, a filter across the old lens you used to see the world through.

She wiped a bead of sweat off his cheek, then combed her fingers through his hair and grabbed two fistfuls, her fingers twisting like roots into those thick luscious locks of amber. She gave him a steely, unrelenting look. "I want you."

He was too stunned to respond. She could feel his heart begin to pound through his clothes. There was a translucence to his skin in the dim light that reminded her of his faded ancestors—the ghosts who haunted this house.

His mouth was wet and open, and his face was flushed and hot. She clutched the silky loops of hair until he winced, then bent to kiss him. She could tell there was something odd about him—great depths of shame and guilt, buried rage and heaps of disappointment. She didn't really know this man, not yet. But she thought that at least she could read him. Perhaps she was wrong.

# 26

At around ten o'clock, Natalie's niece called.

"Aunt Natalie, I've been trying to reach you for days," sixteen-year-old Ellie Guzman said breathlessly. "Are you okay?"

"I'm so sorry, Ellie, I should've called. But it's been chaotic here."

"Did they arrest him yet? Detective Murphy?"

"Not yet, we're still looking. But I'm sure we'll find him."

"I hope so. Is Luke okay?"

"He's much better," Natalie said, lightly touching her forehead. The grisly deaths of Veronica Manes and Randolph Holmes had been all over the news lately, so she shouldn't have been surprised that Ellie knew so much about it.

"So Luke's out of his coma?"

"Yes, and he's fine. Just like the old Luke."

"Thank God. Were you scared?"

"Yeah, I was really scared," Natalie admitted. She could hear activity on the other end of the line.

It was hard to believe that the trauma Ellie had endured only happened about a year ago, shortly after Ellie and her best friends had formed a coven together. There were jealousies over boys and more specifically an English teacher. They dabbled in dark magic, then got in way over their heads, and eventually fell into something monstrous. One night, two of Ellie's best friends dragged her down to Abby's Hex with them, where they attempted to set her on fire. Fortunately, Natalie had found them in time.

Ellie spent the next few months undergoing multiple operations to treat her injuries at the Albany burn unit, but her long-term prognosis was excellent. Last July, she went to live with her father in Manhattan, and all was well. Ellie was safe and in therapy. Fortunately, the burns to her body had healed, but the emotional scars remained. And yet, she seldom spoke of it and never complained. Natalie wanted to protect this wonderful person, like a hand curled around a flame.

"So are we still on for Mom's deathiversary?" Ellie wanted to know.

"Of course. That's a month away, isn't it?"

"Yes, and I can't wait to see you. I really miss Burning Lake. I've missed you so much, Aunt Natalie!"

"I've missed you, too, sweetie. So much."

The end of April marked the anniversary of the passing away of Ellie's mother and Natalie's sister, Grace Lockhart. It also happened to be the deathiversary of Natalie's other sister, Willow—the tall, lovely, ethereal aunt whom Ellie had never met.

Traditionally, at the end of April, Natalie, Grace, and Ellie used to honor Willow's passing by bringing flowers to her grave and sharing fond memories. Now that Grace was gone, Ellie and Natalie would be visiting the cemetery all by themselves. It was going to be a sad day, but Natalie hoped it could also be healing.

"How's your father?" Natalie asked now.

"Good. He's trying out a keto diet. He'll only eat meat and protein shakes. How's Hunter Rose?" Ellie asked.

"Fine," Natalie said, trying not to sound ambushed by the question.

"I saw him on TMZ. God, he's hot."

Natalie smiled. "Yeah, he's a good-looking guy."

"No, he's really *hot*. And rich. And brilliant. I feel bad for Luke."

"Why?"

"Because he likes you so much, and he's such a good guy."

Flustered, Natalie swallowed hard. "Luke and I will always be friends."

"Friends? That sounds like a runner-up to me."

"I'm just relieved he's okay. It's been a rough week."

"Are you and Hunter getting married?" Ellie asked.

Natalie tried to laugh it off. "Not in the immediate future."

"No plans?"

"You'll be the first to know."

"Do you want kids?"

"Fuck, Ellie," she said, exasperated. "I don't know."

Ellie laughed. "Sorry! It's just that it would be so cool to have a bonus sister."

Natalie smiled. "Yeah, well . . . no bonus sisters on the horizon for you."

"You said fuck."

"I know."

"Sorry, not sorry?" She giggled. "But seriously, people's plans can change in two seconds, can't they? You think your life is going to go one way, but then it flips around in the opposite direction. You never know."

"This is true," Natalie said patiently. "So how is your beautiful life going?"

"My life is mezzo-mezzo, thanks for asking. I like school, and I like my new friends. Dad's a pain in the ass, but he can't help himself. He was born with a jerk gene."

Natalie smirked. "Fortunately, you didn't inherit that trait."

She could just picture Ellie in her Billie Eilish T-shirt and fleece joggers, with her jet-black hair and rail-straight bangs, her curious blue eyes, and multiple-pierced ears. Ellie was a stunner, an avid book-reader, both skeptical and innocent, edgy and naïve. Last year, she'd dyed her naturally blond hair raven-black in order to distance herself from her mother, but otherwise she was the spitting image of Grace.

"Dad puts up an obnoxious front, but he's actually a marshmallow underneath," Ellie said. "He got really upset when I told him I was thinking about becoming a detective like you."

Natalie let out a low sigh. This was totally out of left field.

"Dad says it's crazy, but he also thinks I should wait to have sex until I'm thirty."

"Your father's a smart man," Natalie said, feeling a low-level panic.

"Anyway, just throwing it out there. I don't see the point in going to college and majoring in English, just to land a teaching gig. That sounds so boring."

"It's a lot to consider, Ellie. Things are different now than when I first joined the force. Why don't we talk about it at the remembrance ceremony?"

Ellie sighed. "Why don't you want me to be a cop? Where'd my Cool Aunt go?"

"Oh, please don't quote Cool Aunt Natalie to me," she said, only half-jokingly, wondering what Grace would have advised. "You'd be better off listening to your father."

Ellie laughed. "Anyway, I've missed you so much. I can't imagine what you've been through, Aunt Natalie. But I know how strong you are."

"You don't know your own strength, kiddo," she said with a warm smile.

"Yeah, I'm a superstar just waiting to happen," she joked. "Dad says hi."

"Hello back."

"I have to go. See you in a few weeks."

"Can't wait."

"Bye!" She hung up.

Natalie put away her phone and decided that she would have to become as strong as Ellie wanted her to be.

# 27

On Thursday morning, Natalie was glad to see so many people out and about, strolling around the commercial district on Sarah Hutchins Drive. The sky was the palest of blues. She swung her Honda into the parking lot behind the police station, eased into her spot, and got out. It was Luke's first day back on the job.

She tucked a few strands of hair behind her ears, then went inside the building, said hello to Dennis the dispatcher, collected her mail, and took an elevator to the third floor. She could hear people talking as she headed down the hallway toward her office.

The Criminal Investigations Unit consisted of six male detectives (five now, minus Peter Murphy) and the BLPD's first female detective—Natalie. She'd come up in the ranks with the rest of the recruits—working foot patrol, directing traffic, volunteering for overtime, and taking any shit detail she could. Out of a desire to prove herself beyond reproach, Natalie had to work twice as hard as the rest of the guys.

The BLPD was a high-testosterone zone. The language could get pretty coarse. Fortunately for her, she had quite a mouth on her from all those years of hanging out with her father, Joey, and his cop buddies. *Fuck* was just another word in a colorful vocabulary that painted a picture of the glories, the absurdities, and frustrations of the job.

Thirty or more people were crowded into the CIU this morning—an open office space with desks, worktables, filing cabinets, and accompanying clutter. There was a large sheet cake on Lenny's desk that said "Welcome back, Luke!" and now everyone began to sing "For He's a Jolly Good Fellow."

Natalie scanned the room—there was Luke, looking embarrassed, standing next to the two Fossils, Lenny Labruzzo and Augie Vickers, in their rumpled suits and ties; there was Brandon in his standard casual uniform of jeans and a polo shirt, grinning from ear to ear; Aimee Dreyer, the department secretary, stood over the cake like a Roman centurion, knife in hand. Detectives Jacob Smith and Mike Anderson, Officers Bill Keegan, Troy Goodson, and Boomer Prutzman, Dennis from downstairs, and a dozen other familiar faces were digging heartily into the lyrics. "Oh, for he's a jolly good *fellow-owww*!" Only Assistant Chief Gossett looked uncomfortable and out of place in his formal dress uniform—dark blue shirt, pressed blue pants, blue issue tie with a silver tie bar, spit-polished shoes, and shiny badge.

Luke pocketed his phone and smiled at Natalie.

"Lieutenant, get over here!" Lenny said, waving Luke over to his desk. "Blow out these candles so we can stuff our faces with cake."

Everybody laughed.

Luke obliged, and then Aimee plunged the knife into the yellow sheet cake with chocolate icing and started handing out square slices on flimsy paper plates.

Then Luke turned to Natalie and said, "We need to talk."

Assistant Chief Gossett interrupted, calling out, "Okay, everyone, let's gather around." He cleared his throat. "Let's give Luke a hearty welcome home. It's great to have you back where you belong, Lieutenant. Hopefully, you're relaxed, recuperated, and recharged, because there's plenty of catching up to do."

"Hear, hear!" Lenny said.

"I personally look forward to handing over the reins to you," Gossett continued, "and placing these fine people back into your capable hands."

Luke took the imaginary reins from Gossett and said, "Thanks. It's good to be back."

Everyone cheered.

Luke turned to Natalie again and said, "My office."

# 28

Have a seat," he told her, pulling up a chair.

"Thanks."

Once she was settled in, he said, "I'm facing headwinds on the Veronica Manes case. Gossett and the chief want to pin it all on Murphy, but he's still out there somewhere, and there's also the inconvenient fact of a second set of footprints at the scene of the abduction. So we're at an impasse."

"Why the rush to close the case?" she asked.

"The usual suspects," he said. He wore a suit and tie today on his first day back. His hair was the color of dark-stained wood, and his blue eyes were clear and strong. He seemed fine to her, if a bit stiff. "The media's running wild with speculation, and it puts Burning Lake front and center again. Nobody wants that. You've got the mayor, the chief, business interests . . . everybody is anxious to get Burning Lake out of the limelight. But no matter what kind of circumstantial evidence I present them with, at this point, unless it's a slam dunk, they aren't going to listen. Because it's a big fat turd in the punch bowl, and they want closure. They want to put it to bed and get rid of the media attention. I've only been back in the office for fifteen minutes, and already I'm being pressured from the top."

"What about Murphy's phone?" she asked. "His associates? His bank account?"

"Lenny and Augie have been tracking all of those, including his social media and online transactions, and it's like he died or something. Everything appears to have come to an abrupt halt last week. We have no leads on his vehicle so far, no credit card information, no phone information. There's nothing going on. However, they did find out that he bought a crypto wallet two years ago and had a safe deposit box at his bank, but he cleaned that out four months ago. He's been slowly emptying his bank account over the past few years. Regarding the fire at Murphy's residence, the fire chief has officially declared it an act of arson, so either Murphy burned his own house down, or someone else did it as a warning. No dead bodies were found in the ruins. It's as if he's been planning on never coming back and wanted to destroy all the evidence."

"How thorough is our dragnet?" she asked.

"It's all-encompassing. We've got the state police and all local agencies involved." Luke shrugged. "Everybody's out there looking for the guy. We're putting a hundred percent effort into finding him."

"Then we'll find him," she said firmly.

For the first time, he looked a little tired. A little defeated. "I hope you're right. So anyway, where are you on the Holmes case?"

Natalie spent the next fifteen minutes updating Luke on the case. Then she said, "Something changed around the time of Randy's operation in 2009. That's when most of the fashion magazines and the canned goods expired down in the dungeon, around 2008, 2009. Lenny believes the room was sealed up around that time. Randy also began to collect entomology magazines in late 2009."

"So he got cancer and stopped kidnapping women? Turned to collecting bugs?"

"It sort of looks that way."

"And the names on the back of the dresser match the Shadow Girls?"

Natalie nodded. "Every single one. Harmony Young was his final victim, before he sealed up the place, which implies that he held her captive from 2006 until approximately 2009, which fits the MO. Every three years."

Luke nodded thoughtfully. "I've approved the requisition request to excavate the property," he told her. "I imagine it'll be a month or more before that can happen, since frozen-ground excavations are too expensive. So we'll wait until the snow thaws. We're looking at mid-April or later."

She nodded. "It's good to have you back," she said.

He smiled warmly at her. "It's good to be back."

"And you're doing okay?"

"I feel fine now."

There was a long pause.

"Hmm," she said and smiled. "Awkward silence."

"You look good, Natalie," he said softly. He cleared his throat.

She wanted to respond to this somehow. To share some of her thoughts with him. But the mixed feelings of attraction and concern and warmth threatened to suffocate her. So they just looked at each other and let the pain register.

He cleared his throat. "So what's your next move?"

"Well, we've found different blood types and hair samples down in the dungeon, and we're in the process of comparing them to the missing women from Binghamton . . . the Shadow Girls. Fingerprints, too. There was also some fetal tissue found. Lenny and Augie are sorting through the clothing at the impound lot, and they said they have a match for the outfit Harmony was reported as last seen wearing, including a set of sapphire earrings. So we're pretty confident about that one. We're still waiting for DNA results from the lab, but preliminarily . . . Lenny has a match for two of the girls' prints from the bathroom mirror—Harmony and Kimi. Also, he's been able to match multiple hair samples—color, length, thickness—to the descriptions of the missing girls. He'll keep going, but I think we can start building a solid case. I'm convinced these are the Shadow Girls. We've got their names on the bureau, we've got the van spotted by witnesses at the scene of several abductions, and we've got an abundance of trace evidence."

"Sounds good," Luke said. "Anything else?"

She shook her head. "I think we're all caught up."

"Okay." He checked his watch. "I've got a meeting with the chief in five. Keep me posted, Natalie."

"Will do." There was a bit of awkwardness as she left.

Out in the hallway, her phone buzzed, and she picked up. "Lockhart."

"Hey, it's me," Hunter said. "Just checking in. How's it going?"

"Grim," she admitted, heading for the elevators. "But we're making progress."

"Well, this feels entirely inappropriate, but I wanted to invite a few people over for drinks this evening, sort of a celebration. We closed the deal. Oliver Chabert and his wife, Serena—you remember them? They're major investors. Plus Martin and his wife. Is that okay?"

"Of course. That's great news, Hunter. We should celebrate."

"I wanted to ask you first. They won't stay long. Just drinks and small talk," Hunter said. "We're all just so fucking relieved and psyched to be doing business together. This was a long and arduous process. Anyway, it's set for seven."

She glanced at her watch. "Okay, I'll be there."

"Great. And if you change your mind, Natalie, just let me know."

"I'll see you later," she said firmly.

"Later, babe."

She hung up. "Shit," she muttered. She hated parties.

# 29

Outside, it was beginning to snow again. Natalie took out her keys and approached her vehicle, then sensed a presence behind her, hovering on the fringes of her awareness.

"Natalie?" It was Detective Brandon Buckner.

"Jesus! Don't creep up on me like that, Brandon."

"I didn't realize you were so skittish. Let's go talk in my Jeep, okay?"

"Sure." She dropped her keys in her shoulder bag and they walked over to his black Jeep Cherokee, which was parked in his reserved space. Brandon stomped the snow off his boots, while Natalie got in the passenger seat, closed the door, and shivered. "Okay, so? What did you find out?" she asked.

"So regarding the background check on Randy Holmes. He's got a clean record, not even a traffic ticket. Jacob and I contacted some of our sources, and we dug a little deeper, and it turns out he was accused of molesting somebody's teenage daughter on Halloween, and he was dressed as a . . ."

"Clown, right?" she interjected.

"Fuck, yeah. Echoes of John Wayne Gacy."

"What happened?"

"This was fifteen years ago," he explained. "There was an incident where the police were called to Randy's house, and a young woman named Posey Revelli claimed she called 911 by accident. The police were careful to separate the partygoers and get all their statements, but no one was willing to press charges, and the victim walked it all back. So the police made sure her parents were informed before they left. Now, at the time, they thought it might be Randy's nephew, Peyton Wolanski, who was bothering the girl, since the two of them had briefly dated, but Posey insisted nothing happened, that it was a mistake, and that she was just fooling around and never meant to call 911."

Natalie nodded, listening intently. "Then what happened?"

"Well, the girl's parents got upset, of course, and they threatened to press charges, but they never did. This was back in 2007. Rumor has it, lawyers got involved, and the parents were paid off in return for their silence."

"How much?"

"Unknown, but they never pressed charges."

"So tell me about the girl."

"She's a professional musician. Born Posey Barone. She's thirty-three years old and lives in Albany with her husband. She's in a string quartet. And get this—she plays the viola."

"Seriously? Did you talk to her?"

"Briefly, over the phone. She wasn't comfortable talking to a male detective, so I told her you'd like to speak to her, and she said you could call. Here's her contact info." He handed Natalie a slender file folder with handwritten notes inside.

"Thanks, Brandon. This is great."

"Let's nail that sick bastard. Even if he is dead already."

Natalie smiled, relieved that they were friends again. They used to be buddies, until the tragic events of last April had torn their relationship apart. For the longest time, Brandon couldn't even look at Natalie without thinking about his dead wife. For months, he refused to talk to her outside of their official duties. But since then, he'd processed his grief, and Natalie was grateful they were friends again. Now all she had to do was forgive herself.

"So what's next on the agenda?" Brandon asked.

"In light of this information, let's look into Randy's co-workers next," she said. "Stevie Greenway mentioned two other women, Belinda and Tori. She said these women were uncomfortable around Holmes, so we need to find out why. Maybe there were other incidents involving him?"

"Okay. I'll get right on it." He chewed on a thumbnail. "So what do you think? About Luke and Rainie? They seem pretty tight."

She stiffened a little. "Come on, Brandon."

"What? You don't have an opinion?"

"It's none of my business."

He stopped chewing on his thumbnail and just looked at her. "Why the hell not?"

"I'm just relieved he's going to be okay."

"Come on, Natalie." His gaze was slightly mocking. "You and Luke forever."

"Shut up." It pissed her off. Brandon was always getting way too personal for his own good—the one side of his personality she hadn't missed. "Have some boundaries, for crying out loud."

Now he studied her with excruciating honesty. "Are you happy? Just tell me you're happy, Natalie, and I'll shut the hell up."

"I'm happy, of course I'm happy. I'm in a committed relationship."

"A committed relationship doesn't mean you're happy."

She glanced at him, feeling nauseated. "I can't be having this conversation."

"So you're just going to let it happen?"

"Let what happen?"

"Rainie's got her claws in him. Sometimes people take the path of least resistance, it's only human nature. It's a rebound thing. And it's kind of cunning of her, actually. I mean, Luke is at his weakest point, he just came out of a coma. He's probably feeling his age, you know? That sense of mortality that weighs you down when you approach the big whatever-O. You know? In Luke's case, he's almost forty. And she's going to make herself indispensable to him, mark my words. He'll wake up one day and they'll be engaged."

"Listen, Brandon. I wasn't going to say anything, because it's none of your fucking business, but Luke and I had a long talk about this a week ago. We discussed it. It's never going to happen. We're friends. Really, really good friends. He's extremely important to me, but we had the conversation, and that's the end of it."

He rested his broad hands on the steering wheel, perspiration glistening on his forehead. "He's probably still in love with you. He probably thinks there's still a chance. So if you have any doubts about how you feel, Natalie, you'd better figure it out soon. I'm telling you. I can see how things are unfolding between him and Rainie. Don't end up regretting this for the rest of your life."

She gazed at the gently falling snow. She couldn't help feeling guilt sick, as if Brandon had caught her in the act of lying, or acting like a hypocrite, or even worse—of not knowing herself as well as he did. "Well, thanks a lot, fuckhead."

"I love you like a sister, Natalie," he said as she got out of the Jeep and slammed the door in his face.

# 30

That afternoon, Natalie drove down to Albany, where Posey Revelli had agreed to meet her at Esmeralda's Coffee Shop. Natalie got there early and found a corner booth. Frost dappled the plateglass windows. A light snow was falling. She glanced at her watch. Posey was late.

At one thirty-five, the door swung open, and thirty-three-year-old Posey Revelli swept into the coffee shop all bundled up in her winter parka, her cheekbones carrying a high flush. She had sly gray eyes, a great smile, and shiny medium-length brown hair. "Hello," she said breathlessly, taking off her coat and sliding into the booth. She picked up the menu. "Sorry I'm late." She studied the menu. "What are you getting?"

"Just coffee." Natalie noticed that Posey's hand was in a medical support brace. "Is your wrist okay?"

"What, this?" She frowned and held up her injured hand. "No, I have carpal tunnel from playing the viola. I put this brace on sometimes so it won't get any worse. That would be nothing short of disaster for a musician. I'm just hoping it'll heal in time for the summer season. That's when we get most of our gigs, and there's also the music festival. Fingers crossed."

The waitress came over and asked, "Ready to order?"

Posey said, "I'll have a sparkling water with lime. And a blueberry muffin, please. Toasted with butter."

"Just coffee, thanks," Natalie said.

After the waitress had walked away, Posey leaned forward and said, "I'm glad he's dead, to be honest. That guy was a psychopathic liar and a horrible creep. I was eighteen when he molested me, while everyone else was partying in the backyard. He said he had a surprise for me. Well, I hope he was surprised the other night. I hope he suffered."

Natalie was startled by the bluntness of her statement. She paused for a moment, then said, "Well, I'm sorry that happened to you."

"I've hated clowns ever since. It was a Halloween party where this happened."

Natalie nodded. "The police report said it was an accident."

"I lied," she confessed angrily. "Now that he's dead, I can talk about it, right?"

"If you don't mind me asking, what exactly did he do to you?"

She let out a shudder. "I was so naïve back then. Just a kid, really. And I liked Peyton a lot. He was two years younger than me, but he was funny and cool. He invited me to a Halloween party at his uncle's house. They had a huge backyard, and there must've been a hundred people there. There was plenty of beer and pot. Everybody was having fun. I came to the party as Princess Di. And this guy comes over to me, he's dressed as a clown. And Peyton introduced us—it was his uncle Randy. And I was really stoned at that point, I'd had a few beers, and he started telling me about butterflies . . ." She made a face. "For instance, did you know butterflies taste with their feet? They land on a plant and drum their feet until the plant releases its juices. And they live on an all-liquid diet. They drink nectar, but they also drink from mud puddles. And they're nearsighted, but they can see colors. And they can't fly when it's too cold out. Interesting things like that."

"Then what happened?"

"He told me he wanted to show me his butterfly collection. So we went inside. I trusted him. There were so many people there, right? So he leads me into his living room and shows me a box of butterflies. I was so stoned, I thought it was beautiful. I got lost in the colors. I could imagine them flying around. And all of a sudden, I feel a wet cottony thing clamp over my mouth, and it felt like I was suffocating. At the same time, I'm being half dragged into a back room. And Randy's got his hands all over me, and there's this terrible chemical smell in my nose. And I'm about to pass out, so I start fighting back. I scratch his face and run for the door, but he drags me back, and nobody can hear me scream, because of the noise and music in the backyard, and he's got his hands all over me, and he's like . . . pulling his pants down . . . these polka-dot clown pants . . . and I'm fighting for my life . . . and I'm starting to feel drowsy . . . so I try to gouge his eyes out, and then somehow, I get away. Now I'm in the backyard. So I call 911 and tell the police to come get me."

"But then you told the police you were joking around? Why?"

"Peyton begged me not to say anything. He was terribly upset. And his uncle denied the whole thing. He claimed that I'd fainted, and he was trying to help me. That was bullshit, obviously."

"And then what?"

"Peyton convinced me to not say anything to the police, and I just wanted to go home, so I lied and said I never meant to call 911. It was supposed to be a joke. But then, when my parents found out, they wanted to press charges, but they were contacted by an attorney, and so they changed their minds. They got paid a settlement not to file charges."

"How much?"

"I don't know. Enough not to press charges." Posey shook her head. "They didn't want me to have to testify in court, either. I was traumatized enough. My father hired a lawyer, and they got together with Randy's lawyer and came to an agreement. He bought us off, I guess you could say. We moved to Chaste Falls shortly afterward. It paid for my music education. It was enough money that I never had to take out a college loan. My dad wanted to kill the guy. All I remember is that it was enough to make my parents back off."

"And Randolph Holmes paid for all this?"

"I don't know. I guess so." She shrugged. "My parents handled it."

"Can I talk to them?"

She shook her head sadly. "They're both gone."

"Mine, too. Sorry."

"Yeah, it sucks. I miss my mom especially."

"And now you're a musician?" Natalie asked.

"I play the viola in a string quartet. Maybe you've heard of us? The Wild Rose String Ensemble. Wild roses are the state flower."

"How different is the viola from a violin?" Natalie asked.

"Oh, very. Violas are bigger. They're heavier. They require more upper body strength and hand dexterity. I have the smallest size viola, and I love the sound it makes. That's what attracted me in the first place—those deep, warm, mellow tones."

"You didn't want to play the violin?"

She shook her head. "Violins are for extroverts. Violas are for introverts. I can play in an orchestra and not have to worry about any solo parts. There are no viola soloists—only violin soloists. Violins play the melody, whereas violas play harmony. You need a faster bow movement to get that rich, sonorous sound."

"So you're an introvert?"

She shrugged. "I guess it suits me."

"What kind of strings do you use?" Natalie asked, watching her carefully.

"D'Addario Helicore medium scale, medium tension. They produce a warm, focused, not overly bright tone." She shifted uncomfortably in her seat. "Why?"

"Where were you on Friday night?"

"Friday?" She frowned and shook her head. "Here in Albany. Why?"

"Doing what?"

Posey stared at her. "Having dinner at home. Why do you ask?"

"It's a standard question. Were you alone?"

"No. With my husband." She drew back. "Why?"

"It's a routine question. I just need to confirm your alibi."

"My alibi?" she almost spat. "Wait a second. Do you think that . . . just because some guy molested me sixteen years ago, that all of a sudden I'm going to risk everything and drive up there and kill him? Throw my whole life away? After everything I've accomplished?"

"Like I said, I have to ask."

She frowned angrily, then sighed. She gave a reluctant nod.

"Is your husband also a musician?"

"He's the cellist in our string quartet."

"Does he know about Randy?"

"Yes. I told everyone close to me what happened, and I trust them to keep it confidential. That was an extremely difficult time in my life, and it still has resonance. You know what I mean?"

Natalie nodded. Yes, she did know. "How did your husband react when you told him about Randy Holmes?"

"He was furious. He wanted to kill the guy." She caught herself. She looked frightened. "But that was *years* ago."

"Has anything happened recently that might've triggered those memories for you?"

"I like to think I've moved on. Until last weekend, when I heard the news."

"Right." Natalie nodded. "Do you have any proof you were at home last Friday night? Make any phone calls, order takeout? Anything like that?"

"I can't think of anything. I made chicken and rice. We don't eat out anymore. Too expensive. Besides, it's healthier to make your own meals at home."

"And you and your husband were together all night long?"

She blushed and looked away. The waitress brought their drinks and muffin over to the table, then asked if there was anything else and left. Natalie sipped her coffee. It tasted slightly burnt. Posey just stared down at her toasted muffin.

"Was your husband with you the whole evening?" Natalie repeated.

"No." She glanced away, bristling.

"Where was he?"

"He wouldn't do anything like that," she whispered harshly.

"Do what?"

"Kill somebody."

"I believe you," Natalie said, surprised by Posey's emotional response. "I'm just checking off the boxes here."

Posey fidgeted with her napkin, and Natalie took a moment to study the support brace, which was attached to Posey's left hand with Velcro straps. She wondered if it could possibly be covering up another type of injury besides carpal tunnel.

Posey took a sip of mineral water, calmed down and said, "Tony was furious at my parents for letting the guy get away with it. Tony, that's my husband, he said they should've pressed charges, no matter what. He said we should've put the guy away so he couldn't hurt anybody else. But the way I see it, I never could've afforded music school if not for that. And I never would've met my husband. So, I figure it's fate."

Natalie nodded thoughtfully. "But you initially said Tony was with you that night. Then you said he wasn't at home the whole time?"

"No," she finally admitted. "He got home late. His car got stuck. He's a teaching associate. It's a twenty-minute commute."

"Why did you lie about that?"

She blushed. "I don't know."

"Where do you buy your strings for your viola?"

"Online. It's much cheaper."

Natalie nodded. "And when did your husband get home?"

"Around ten."

"But you initially said you two had dinner that night."

"We did. At ten o'clock." Posey opened her backpack and took out her wallet. She attempted to pay for her sparkling water and muffin in cash, counting out the dollar bills and change. "Look, this is absurd. I've tried to answer all your questions, I really have. Now I'm leaving."

"I'll cover this."

"Don't bother." She didn't have enough spare change to cover the bill.

"I'll pay for the rest."

"I just didn't bring enough cash with me," she said defensively. She took out a credit card, looked at it, and frowned.

"It's okay. I got this," Natalie insisted, picking up the bill.

Posey put her card away and refused to make eye contact as she scooped her money back into her backpack. Then she wrapped the muffin up in a bunch of paper napkins.

"How can I reach your husband?" Natalie asked. "I'd like to talk to him."

"Please just leave us alone. I don't want to have anything to do with Randy Holmes anymore, okay? I've suffered enough." She drank some of her sparkling water. She stood up. She took her muffin with her. "Good-bye."

# 31

Back in her car, Natalie called Brandon and said, "We need to find out who represented Randy Holmes on that molestation incident. How could he afford to pay the family so much money on his salary?"

"How much was it?"

"Enough for Posey Revelli's music education. Enough to keep her parents from pressing charges."

"Huh," Brandon said. "Okay, I'll check it out."

"Also, let's try to find out if Randy molested any other teenage girls or young women. Anything else on his record? And one last thing . . ."

"Shoot."

"Posey seems to be hiding something. I need to talk to her husband. His name's Tony Revelli, and he apparently got furious when she told him about the assault. He doesn't have an alibi for Friday night. She said his car broke down. Then she got nervous and cut the interview short."

"Hold on, I'll check online," Brandon muttered.

"Shit, I could've done that," she said with a smile.

"Eh, no bother. I'm just sitting here at my desk, cleaning out my ears with a pencil. Okay, it says here he's a music teacher at Albany-SUNY. You want me to send you his contact information?"

"Thanks, Brandon. You're a lifesaver." She hung up.

Two minutes later, she had Tony on the phone.

"I'm a TA in the music department here at SUNY," he explained. "I teach the cello and something called Classical Music Appreciation."

"I was just talking to your wife . . ."

"I know. She just called. We have to make this quick. I have another class."

"She said your car broke down on Friday night? That you came home at ten?"

There was a long pause. "What's this got to do with anything?"

"I'm trying to eliminate suspects in Randolph Holmes's homicide. It's a standard question."

"Suspects? Just because he molested my wife over a decade ago, you think I'd suddenly get the urge to kill him?" Tony asked angrily.

"I don't think anything. I simply need verification that your car broke down."

"Well, there's nothing to verify. I got a flat tire, I was on an isolated road, and it took a while to replace the tire, that's all."

"You didn't call Triple A?"

"It was easy enough to get out the spare."

"So you replaced the flat tire with a spare tire?"

"Look, this is insulting. What do you want from me?"

"We have specific facts of the case that we can't disclose to the public," she explained. "One of those facts points to your wife. She claims she was at home alone that night, and that you didn't return until ten o'clock. I'm simply trying to validate your alibis."

"Excuse me," he hissed into the receiver, "but this is ridiculous. We were both here in Albany. How could we possibly be in two places at once?"

"I understand. I don't mean to imply anything. I simply would like to find out if you and your wife have anything to back up your statements, regarding your whereabouts on Friday night."

"I don't know. How do I prove where I was?"

"Did you stop for gas? Make a phone call? Did anyone see you on the street replacing your tire? Or maybe there was a traffic camera nearby? Where were you when this happened?"

"Okay, look. I'll try to find some sort of verification, but class is starting. I have to go. What was your name again?"

"Detective Lockhart of the Burning Lake police."

"Okay. I'm making a note of that. I consider this harassment. I'm hanging up now," he said, and the line went dead.

# 32

The trees swayed eerily in the March wind, their bare branches reaching for the night sky under a waxing moon, just a sliver of gold hanging there suspended in the cosmos.

Natalie drove past the police station, where the American flag billowed like a full sail. The sidewalk in front of the BLPD was jammed with reporters tonight. There were media vans parked side by side, and competing television crews had staked out different parts of the block.

She avoided the scene and took a left onto Meadowlark, where the road curved away from downtown. Natalie's radio was tuned to the news. The media attention was relentless. The news outlets were awash with speculation, providing wall-to-wall coverage of the series of recent homicides that had hobbled Burning Lake.

"Police are still investigating the death of Veronica Manes . . . the gruesome murder of a beloved local Wiccan who wrote several books about this unique upstate town renowned for its history of witch trials and its celebration of Halloween . . . in a bizarre twist, at the center of the case, there appears to be the same intrepid detective who solved two infamous homicide cases fairly recently—the Crow Killer and the Violinist . . . Detective Natalie Lockhart is said to have been in pursuit of Detective Murphy when he disappeared . . . what do you have for us, Bill?"

"Mary, I'm here in front of the Burning Lake police department, and it's getting dark as we speak. Still no word yet on whether the police have a suspect, despite a lot of speculation over this past week. There's been a virtual news blackout, Mary."

"And now, astonishingly, police have come across yet another homicide victim in this small upstate town, isn't that correct, Bill?"

"Yes, Mary. According to officials at the scene, a sixty-four-year-old man named Randolph Holmes who worked at a costume store in town was murdered almost a week ago. I've been interviewing his neighbors and colleagues, and it appears that he was generally well-liked within the community. He's been called 'nice' and 'quiet,' a 'hard worker' and 'generous with his time.' He was a volunteer for Toys for Tots and the local food bank. The police are not answering questions, but we'll be here, standing on this very spot, and I'll be giving you updates throughout the night, Mary."

"Thanks, Bill, stay safe out there."

Natalie turned off the news and left the downtown area behind. She headed north into dense woods with nothing but winter-bare trees on either side of the road. When she took a right onto Danbury Lane, a pair of headlights flashed in her rearview mirror, and she noticed the familiar red Nissan sedan following her. She frowned at the driver, the ex-journalist-turned-Substack-blogger from Rochester who kept pestering her for an exclusive.

He followed her another half mile or so, until they were quite isolated, a repeat of the other night. She slowed down long enough for him to pull up behind her. She caught a glimpse of his caffeinated gaze in her rearview mirror. She honked her horn for him to fuck off, but he stubbornly dogged her down another couple of back roads.

"Get lost!" she said with a vigorous wave.

He waved back and kept following her.

Around the next turn, a fox darted out of the woods—a rust-colored blur—and Natalie swerved to avoid it, her headlights illuminating the narrow, curving road ahead. She practically stood on the brake pedal, while her tires skidded over a patch of ice and the car veered toward the tangled underbrush that grew by the side of the road.

Her tires locked as she hit the brakes, and the Honda swerved into a snowbank, hitting it with a loud thump, the impact flinging her forward. Only her seat belt prevented her from smacking her front teeth against the wheel.

She sat for a stunned moment, while ice crystals danced in the glare of her high beams. It was a relatively soft landing into a cushion of snow—the impact wasn't enough to inflate the airbags.

Regaining her equilibrium, Natalie put the car into reverse and backed out of the snowdrift, while ice and slush spit against her wheel wells. Fortunately, she'd replaced her all-weather tires in January, and they held up fairly well. She backed out onto the road, then checked her rearview.

The Nissan stood idling in the road behind her. She cut her engine, unsnapped her seat belt, unlocked the door, and shoved it open. She got out, bristling with irritated energy. "You!" she shouted, approaching his vehicle.

The reporter or blogger or whatever the hell he was—Kip somebody—raised his hands and said, "Sorry."

"Get out of the vehicle. Now."

He unbuckled and got out. He looked like a soggy poodle with his curly hair and wire-rim glasses, and was probably one of the most unpleasant people she'd ever met.

"What's your name again?" she asked.

"Kip Edwards." He wore a guilty scowl and a threadbare parka. Looking into his eyes, Natalie saw weariness and agitation.

"What do you want?"

"I told you, I'd love to tell your side of the story."

"Okay, listen. We both know what it is you really want," Natalie said. "You don't care about the news. It's all about clickbait. How many followers. Substack is a subscription service, right?"

"That's not true. I've wanted to be a reporter ever since I was a snotty little kid. I can't help it if I'm out of work in the days of massive media layoffs. I'm just chasing the most interesting story out there. And that's you."

She believed him. He was a jerk and a pest, but she believed him. "I asked you politely to stop following me, didn't I?" she said.

"I'm sorry. I'll go quietly."

"How do you expect me to react when I'm being harassed like this?"

"Harassed? You won't answer your phone at the police station. I must've left a million messages. What else am I supposed to do?"

"What was your plan, Mr. Edwards? What were you going to do? Follow me home? And then what?"

He was rosy-cheeked from the chilly night air. His wide eyes blinked pitifully as he stared at her. "Come on, Detective, use me. I'm a resource. I can post anything you'd like, and who knows? Maybe you'll get a response."

She got in her vehicle and locked the door. Then she rolled down her window and said, "Kip."

He jogged over to her car and leaned in. "Yes?"

"Off the record."

"Yes?" he said anxiously.

"As you know, we're looking for Detective Peter Murphy. We want to talk to him. Can you post something for me?"

"Absolutely." He took out a notepad and pen.

"Quote an anonymous source as saying that Lieutenant Detective Pittman may be suffering from short-term memory loss."

"Really?" he said, scribbling away. "Is that true?"

"Quote this source as saying he doesn't remember what happened to him. Then quote another anonymous source saying that Detective Lockhart believes Murphy to be a reliable, respected law officer who—as far as she's concerned—had nothing to do with Veronica Manes's death. But the police urgently need to talk to him."

"Okay. Anonymous sources. I got it."

"Don't quote me. I know where you live." She was kidding, but she wasn't.

"Thanks, Detective, this is terrific!"

She revved her engine and drove off.

# 33

Natalie hated parties. She never knew what to say. As a cop, you were trained to sit with your back against a wall in a crowded place, like a restaurant, always on the defensive. Tonight, she sat on the sofa, wearing a royal blue velvet dress with matching Christian Louboutin heels that Hunter had bought for her, and she didn't feel like herself. Not at all.

There was an easygoing rapport among the small group of guests tonight that made her feel slightly alienated. They exchanged clever jabs and observations. Their sense of humor would've bordered on cruelty if they didn't also enjoy poking fun at themselves. They spoke brightly and lightly, as if they were batting around a balloon.

Hunter had two different sets of friends—a large group of local friends, and a scattered group of college friends who lived in New York, Los Angeles, and Sedona.

Here in Burning Lake, he belonged to a solid group of wealthy business associates. Some of them had been his father's friends. She'd seen lots of silver rinses and Botoxed brows at these dinner parties, which were subdued and rather dull, where the men drank port and smoked cigars after dinner, and the wives polished off their desserts with a glass of wine and plenty of gossip.

"Now, I'm no connoisseur," Hunter said from behind the bar, "but I've been told that this 2013 vintage cabernet from Napa Valley has a robust bouquet of roasted coffee, chocolate, and violets. See if you agree," he said, popping the cork and pouring wine into eight long-stemmed glasses. When he was done, he opened another bottle. Natalie happened to know that the 2013 Silver Oak Cabernet Sauvignon was worth hundreds of dollars a bottle.

He passed around their drinks, then raised his glass in a toast. "My father used to say there were three steps to closing a deal. Number one is to find the missing piece. Number two, give them a choice. And number three, shut it down. He didn't say anything about timing, compromise, and luck—but anyway, we did it. Martin, you're a rock star. Thanks for putting up with me. Oliver and Serena, I'm delighted to have you as my partners on this venture. Becky and Stephen, what a brilliant move bringing up that last-second nibble. Thanks to everyone for helping me take Rose Security to the next level. Cheers."

"Cheers!" They all clinked glasses.

Natalie was relieved to discover that Hunter hadn't invited a ton of people over. It was just as he'd said—the Chaberts were there, along with Hunter's second-in-command, Martin Asher, and his wife. There was a third couple she'd never met before.

The house was full of good smells. The fire in the marble fireplace cast a heady warmth into the room. Through the arched doorway, antique glassware and Wedgewood china was on display in the great mahogany hutch behind the dining table, which was set with a centerpiece of fresh flowers.

The wine loosened everyone's tongue. They talked shop for the most part. Twenty minutes later, the women were grouped together around the coffee table, while the men talked business over by the fire. Natalie didn't know how this happened, but it seemed to be the arrangement every time. She didn't resent it, because she didn't care enough. She just wanted the party to be over with.

"You can't protect a child from outside influences anymore," said Serena Chabert, an elegant, attractive older woman who exuded poise and empathy. She was married to Oliver Chabert, a wealthy businessman in his mid-sixties—a slender, fit, energetic fellow who didn't look as if he were about to retire anytime soon. "By the time they're old enough to hold a phone, it's too late. They have the knowledge of the entire world at their fingertips."

"Too late?" Becky Gibson repeated skeptically. Her face was quite puckered and sour-looking for a woman in her forties. "So then, we should give up?"

"You can't shield them anymore," Serena insisted. "They're very sophis-ticated."

Natalie felt edged out of the conversation. She wasn't really there. A million other thoughts occupied her mind. She was faking it. Faking the interest, faking the warmth. In the glow of the Tiffany lamp, she could see the lines of stress on these women's faces and wondered if they were faking it, too.

"What about homeschooling?" Becky suggested. "Or private school?"

"Oh God, Becky, please," Jessica Asher said in a dry, caustic voice. A career woman in her fifties with platinum hair and a sharp, lean face, she came across as the dominant partner in her marriage. Apparently, she and Martin had a thirty-year-old daughter nobody had ever met. "It only takes a year or two of private school to create a little monster."

"Homeschooling, then," Becky suggested.

"Raising alligators would be easier," Jessica said with a scowl.

"What about you?" Becky turned to Natalie with the critical gaze of an older sister. "How would you keep a child's innocence intact in this crazy world?"

"You can't," Natalie said. The tension she'd been feeling all day ratcheted up a notch as the women all stared at her.

"What do you mean?" Becky asked with a blink.

"Even before the internet," Natalie told them, "there have been risks, especially for girls. Boys, too, but mostly girls. It's a dangerous world."

"Well, I suppose you would know about that. Danger." Jessica turned her steely gaze on Natalie. "Can anyone tell me what's going on in this town? What are the police doing about this spate of murders? Is there a plan?"

"Leave her alone," Serena said, smiling at Natalie. She was the quietest and kindest of Hunter's business friends.

"Right," Jessica muttered. "Off-limits. While the whole town falls apart."

Becky nodded sympathetically. "I'm sure the police are doing every-thing they can, their very best. They all live here, Jessica, they all have families. They want Burning Lake to be safe, too. Isn't that right, Natalie?"

"A thousand percent," she said.

Hunter smiled at Natalie from across the room, and she smiled back. His expression said, "Don't be afraid. These are nice people." Only she didn't believe him. *Nice* was subjective.

The other women were looking at her. Natalie felt compelled to say something, so she asked, "Your husband's in real estate, isn't he, Serena?"

"My dear, he *is* real estate," she said with a self-mocking smile.

"Then I have a question for you. Who's buying up the properties in Burning Lake behind a blind trust?"

Serena's smile faltered. "Blind trust? I don't know. Why?"

"It's very odd. I can't figure it out. Do you remember Bella Striver? The girl who disappeared in 2009? Well, after her father died, the house was sold to an unknown buyer. It's in a blind trust now. And whoever bought the property has never fixed it up. It's exactly the same way it was before he died, or so I've heard."

"That's true," Becky interjected. "Nobody knows what the owner plans on doing with the property. But there's no evidence they want to flip it. It just sits there. The same with Brandon Buckner's old house, where his wife died tragically last year in the kitchen . . ." She looked at Natalie. "Oh gosh, I'm sorry. I forgot about your sister."

"That's okay," Natalie said, feeling her cheeks burn.

"And there could be others we don't know about, right? Other properties where tragedies have occurred," Becky said with worried eyes.

"It's probably just a coincidence," Serena told them. "Upstate New York, especially around the Adirondacks, has become a booming market for real estate. Everybody's buying up properties right and left. Maybe even foreign investors, which would explain why they were left as is."

"Well, this seems exactly like the type of thing the police should be investigating," Jessica said bluntly. "Maybe a group of occultists is performing satanic rituals in these places at midnight?"

"Jessica, please," Serena chided her friend.

Everyone laughed, and the conversation moved on.

Half an hour later, the guests got up to leave. It was nine o'clock.

Snuggled inside her faux fur coat, Serena told Natalie, "I want to apologize for Jessica. There's no filter. But the truth is, we're all quite disturbed by the latest news."

"I know. It's a difficult time," Natalie said, an understatement.

"You'll have to forgive us," Serena said gently, peering up at Natalie and smiling kindly at her. "But we're all very curious about you."

"Nobody wants to hear about my cop stories."

"My dear," Serena said softly, "that's *all* they want to hear about." She clutched Natalie's arm as they walked toward the front door together. "Hunter adores you, you know. He talks about you all the time. I'd love to have the two of you over for dinner sometime. Would you like that?"

"Absolutely."

"All right. Let's talk soon and pick a date. Good-bye, my dear." She kissed Natalie's cheek with her paper-dry lips.

# 34

As soon as the guests were gone, Hunter let out a sigh and said, "Thank God that's over with. More wine?" He picked up her glass and went over to the bar.

The fire spat and crackled. Ravel's *Pavane for a Dead Princess* was playing in the background. Natalie eased off her shoes and curled her legs up underneath her on the sofa, while the weight of the day settled against her shoulders.

"That wasn't so bad, was it?" Hunter asked, uncorking the bottle.

"Not too bad. And I like Serena. They want us over for dinner."

"She and Oliver are pretty cool. They have great taste in art."

Hunter returned with her wine. He put the glass down on the coffee table and sat down beside her. She could sense his sadness and exhaustion beneath the polished veneer. "So what do you think? About the cabernet sauvignon?"

She took a small sip. "It's delicious."

"You're delicious." He kissed her. His kisses were ethereal and creamy.

Natalie felt suddenly estranged from him—from everything. The truth was she didn't much care for his business partners. She couldn't relate to them. And she didn't like how Hunter acted around them. He put on airs. He sounded like a highbrow commercial for Sonoma Valley.

"I'm exhausted." She put down her wine. "Been a long day. I think I'll take a shower and go to bed. Congratulations again." It came out sounding stiff and awkward, although that was not her intent.

"Thank you," he said, just as stiffly. He watched her leave the room.

Upstairs, Natalie hung her blue dress up in the cavernous walk-in closet, pausing for a moment to critically assess her own paltry selection of stand-bys from Ann Taylor and Kohl's, with the few designer outfits Hunter had bought her.

The rest of the closet was taken up by his vast collection of cotton shirts by Ike Behar, double-breasted wool-gabardine suits, Bill Blass ties, black silk Prada T-shirts, lace-ups from Brooks Brothers, loafers by A. Testoni, and jackets by Hugo Boss.

She paused to run her hands over Hunter's expensive designer jeans and didn't understand this person. He wore everything with casual in-difference, mixing and matching as if they were interchangeable sweats from the Gap. He would throw on a Ralph Lauren T-shirt, wool trousers by Prada, and sockless Italian leather wing tips, and look incredibly elegant and relaxed. You wouldn't know how expensive his clothes were if you saw him standing there—you'd assume he was one of those rare people who'd been born smart, sophisticated, naturally athletic, and tremendously fit. You wouldn't see the blood, sweat, and tears, the daily grind, the wear and tear most people were burdened with, or the physically draining effort that came from pushing through every day just to survive.

Hunter seemed to lead a charmed life. People orbited around him. Life orbited around him. He always knew what to say and do. Natalie used to make fun of people like him as a defensive mechanism. Now she was par-tially enthralled by him. Who the hell made homemade cannolis for their girlfriend with freshly scraped Madagascar vanilla beans? Who ordered takeout every other night? Who could love someone as messed up and lost as she was? He had ensnared her, somehow, then hustled her into his crumbling castle on the edge of these haunted woods. He was bigger than life, and yet in some ways he wasn't real life at all. He belonged in some YA fairy tale. Not real. Not genuine. A delicious dream. A confection.

Her thoughts scattered. Her body was shaking. She was tired and edgy with raw nerves. She peeled out of her clothes and took a long hot shower, soaping every part of her body as if she might be able to cleanse herself of the tragic, disturbing events of the past few weeks—no, of this past year. Her stomach was in knots.

A shadow drifted over her mind. She thought about her latest case as she shampooed her hair. She wondered what drove a psychopath like

Randy Holmes. Most people wouldn't have noticed him on the street or in a crowd. They wouldn't have given him a second glance. He lived in the shadows and corners of society, quietly going about his business. Randy had lived his whole life ignored, on the fringes of society, forgotten about the instant he walked away.

What was his motive? What drove him? Power, ego, revenge, a desire to be feared? The primal scream. Me, me, me. The insane logic of an organized psychopath. He had found a way to possess helpless young women so thoroughly and completely, that for decades, no one had caught on. Those poor girls had been trapped in a hellish place, smelling of wetness and mold and death. And now their complicated, emotional lives were reduced to little bits of trace evidence—a long blond hair, a short black hair, a specific blood type, individual fingerprints, encoded DNA.

Lingering under the rainfall showerhead, Natalie turned the heat up until it nearly scalded her skin. She let the hot water pummel her. They had names, these girls. Natalie had learned all about them from the missing persons files. Joy's favorite band was the Bangles and she would run around "walking like an Egyptian" until her friends made her stop. Tati loved treating her little sisters to pancakes every Friday night. JoJo's secret obsession was stepping on bubble wrap and listening to it pop. Kimi had a *12 Monkeys* T-shirt she wore until it was so faded you couldn't read it anymore. Danielle kept a pet duck she named Cocoa the Duckess. Remi loved listening to rain on the roof and eating leftover cookie dough. Harmony's favorite TV shows were *The Office* and *Battlestar Galactica*. They were ordinary young women with ordinary hopes and dreams. They were loved. They were valuable souls, and their disappearances were a huge loss to the planet.

Natalie closed her eyes and breathed in steam. Minutes passed. She wasn't aware of the fact that Hunter had stepped into the shower to join her until she felt his fingers lightly touch her arm.

She turned and said, "You scared me."

"I'm sorry." He was naked. He had a thin face, a long lean body, and hungry gray eyes threaded with rust. "Do you want me to leave?"

She didn't answer. Her heart had crawled into her throat.

"I'll do whatever you want," he promised.

"Stop saying that," Natalie said angrily.

"Stop saying what?"

"You'll do whatever I want. That I can leave whenever I want. That I can have anything in the world. That I can go wherever I want to. I can't. I can't have anything I want."

"Why not?" he asked. "Why the hell not?"

For a fleeting moment, she felt like one of the Shadow Girls, held captive by this man's obsessive desire for her—except that his "dungeon" was a seductively gorgeous estate and contained everything in the world that Natalie could ever want or need. She wondered if Hunter's love could heal her and make her whole again. How could she resist being reflected so favorably in his eyes? Or was Natalie a coward, running away from the very thing she wanted the most? Yes, she was a coward. One of life's losers. She should have taken advantage of the opportunity when she had it, when it was staring her in the face.

"You can have whatever you want, Natalie. All you have to do is ask."

She didn't believe him. But she wanted to.

Pulsing with an animal beat, heat rising from her chest to her neck and face, she gave into the physical pleasure of standing next to him and wrapped her arms around him. She felt high when he covered her face with the softest of kisses—dizzy, vague, light-headed, stoned. She could feel the chemical rush flooding her body.

He exhaled deeply, as if he'd been holding his breath. As if he'd been hoping that she would want him. Hoping and praying she would love him back. "You have the most perfect skin." His words fell like snow, soft as fleece, melting as they descended. "I love you." His eyelids sagged, and she watched him fall into a trance of lust. Against her better judgment, she let herself be dragged into his insatiable neediness one more time.

# 35

Natalie woke up abruptly the following morning, fear spinning her around. She felt grimy and confused. Maybe she was done with everything—too much grief, too much horror. Maybe Hunter was right. Maybe it was time to make a clean break.

It was five A.M. She had an eight thirty meeting with Luke. She had emailed him her report last night, detailing her conversations with the Revellis, and Luke wanted to discuss it first thing.

Hunter was sound asleep. She tried to be quiet as she stumbled around in the dark, fumbling through the closet, looking for a suitable outfit to wear—white blouse, tailored pants, matching jacket.

At eight o'clock, Natalie drove to the station where she got herself a cup of coffee. The coffee machine was so old it was coated with lime deposits, but nobody felt it was their job to clean it, and so the machine occasionally malfunctioned. You had to pull the plug, wait a minute, and plug it back in to get it to start again.

Natalie made a fresh pot of coffee, poured herself a cup, and took it upstairs to her office, where she gathered her thoughts. Over the past few days, she'd been spending most of her time supervising the collection of evidence from Randy Holmes's house and going over the findings with Lenny down in the BLPD crime lab. Now Luke wanted an update.

At eight twenty-five, she walked down the hallway to his office. His door was open. He was leaning against the wall, thumbing through a file.

"Hey," she said. "Can I come in?"

The lines of exhaustion and worry carved into his face relaxed and melted away. He smiled and said, "Door's open."

"Right," she said. "When the door is open, it's okay to barge in."

He put down the file. "What's this about the Revellis?"

"Nothing definitive, but I have a lot of questions," she said, taking a seat. "First of all, the ligature was a viola string, a D'Addario Helicore with blue and gold silk threads at the ball end. It's a steel core string as opposed to sheep gut, which makes it a perfect ligature. Posey uses the same strings on her viola, although it is one of the most popular brands."

"And he assaulted her when she was eighteen?"

"That's right. It fits with the pattern. He likes them at that age."

"What else makes you suspect this couple?"

"They gave me conflicting statements and got very defensive when I asked for verification of their alibis. Also, Lenny found tire tracks in the parking lot behind the building that match a Chevy Equinox, which is very common in these parts. Tony Revelli drives a Chevy Equinox."

"Okay, that's interesting." Luke nodded. "What about traffic cams?"

"Brandon's going to be out there today collecting traffic videos and surveillance tapes from all the nearby gas stations and convenience stores around the time of the homicide. Maybe we'll be able to ID the plates, which would expose them as lying."

"Okay, good. What else?"

"The clown nose is significant, since Randy was dressed as a clown at the Halloween party where the assault took place. It seems like a personal statement."

"It does." Luke nodded. "So what's your takeaway?"

"Well, obviously they didn't like the guy. But there's another angle. I think the Revellis are struggling financially. Posey had to stop working recently due to a wrist injury, and Tony is a TA, which means they don't make much. I asked Brandon to look into their finances, and so far it appears they're having trouble making ends meet. I think it's possible they figured that if Randy was willing to settle with her family to shut them up once, then maybe he'd do it again?"

"So it was a shakedown?"

"A shakedown that went terribly wrong."

He frowned. "That's a stretch."

"People do crazy things when they're desperate."

Luke narrowed his eyes. "So walk me through it. How would this unfold?"

She checked her notes and said, "The doors to the warehouse were locked and alarmed when Stevie Greenway arrived on Saturday morning. There were no signs of forced entry. No breaking and entering. So we have to assume that the killer either entered the building on Friday and hid out inside the warehouse until Randy was alone, or else Randy let him in on Friday night. In the Revellis case, perhaps it was a prearranged meeting to discuss the settlement?"

"So at a predetermined time on Friday night, he let them into the warehouse?"

"Yes."

"But there were no phone calls to or from the Revellis on his T-Mobile account."

"Right, however one of his co-workers mentioned he had two phones, so I'm thinking maybe Randy was using a burner phone. Which means we need access to the Revellis' phone accounts."

"Makes sense."

"They were probably wearing gloves. We didn't find any prints besides Randy's on the back door. No prints or trace on the clown nose. No prints on the hammer. No prints on the alarm keypad. Either they came prepared with latex gloves, or else they kept their winter gloves on."

"What else?"

"After Randy let the killers into the warehouse, we can assume they discussed the situation. Now, either he gave them the money, or he didn't. My guess is he didn't, and that provoked an argument. Whatever the case, as soon as Randy's back was turned, Tony or Posey struck him with the hammer."

"You think he refused to pay them?"

"There were no withdrawals from his bank account recently, no credit card transactions. He could've had some cash stashed away, or paid them using some other source we don't know about yet."

"Bitcoin? PayPal?" Luke asked.

"We don't have any evidence of that, but we're still looking."

"Where did they get the hammer?"

"It was Randy's," she said. "Some of his co-workers said he'd bring his tools around with him while doing repairs. So he probably set the hammer down somewhere nearby to let them in."

"What if he had no intention of paying them off? Maybe he used the hammer on one of them first?"

"It's a possibility." Natalie nodded. "Posey's left hand is injured—carpal tunnel, she said. But there was no other trace on the hammer besides Randy's blood, prints, and DNA. And it looks as if he was attacked from behind, taken by surprise."

"So maybe he did pay them off, but then for some reason they attacked him."

"Either one of them could've lost it at the last second." She nodded. "The clown nose could've been an act of spontaneity."

"So this could've been an impulsive revenge killing," Luke said, finishing off his coffee and tossing his take-out cup in the trash. "But do you honestly think that's a possibility? That they stumbled their way into a meeting with a serial killer, and then fumbled their way through a murder?"

"Anything's possible," she said. "But you're right, there are things that don't align with that scenario. They would've had to know that the alarm code was posted by the back door, and Posey would've had to bring the viola string with her."

"Maybe she had one in her bag? It could've been a weapon of opportunity."

"But it feels more deliberate than that, don't you think?" Natalie suggested. "The clown nose, the viola string. It's like they wanted to send a deliberate message."

"Okay, if not the Revellis, then what are the alternatives?"

"I don't know," she admitted. "But there are other possible scenarios."

"Such as?"

"The perp could've entered the building on Friday, along with the other customers, then hidden out in the warehouse until Holmes was alone in the store. Around eight o'clock that night, the killer emerged from his hiding place, grabbed a hammer from the warehouse, approached the victim from behind, and knocked him out. Then he strangled Randy with the viola string, took the keys off the belt loop . . ."

"And the burner phone?"

"In this scenario, there wouldn't have to be a burner phone. In this scenario, the killer knew enough to take Randy's keys and leave by the back way, where the alarm was posted. Then he tossed the keys in the snow, where one of the officers found them approximately fifteen yards from the back entrance during a grid search."

"So in this scenario, the killer would have inside knowledge?"

"A limited amount of knowledge. Where to hide during the day, that Randy would have been alone at the end of his shift, that you'd need the keys and alarm code to let yourself out."

"Which makes it sound like an inside job." Luke frowned.

"But all of his co-workers have solid alibis for that night. Brandon looked into it."

"We need to find out if the Revellis have ever been to Murray's before."

She nodded. "And we need to check those traffic cams. I'm going to drive down to Albany and talk to Tony Revelli today, try to dig up enough evidence to subpoena their phone records."

"Good work, Natalie," Luke said, checking his watch. "Keep me posted. One other thing."

She'd just gotten up to leave. Now she paused. "Yes?"

"There's a rumor going around that I've lost my short-term memory. Would you know anything about that?"

She paused for a moment, considering whether or not to tell him the truth.

"Also," Luke continued, "an anonymous source is quoted as saying you don't think Murphy had anything to do with Veronica Manes's death. Do you know anything about that?"

"Yeah," she said with a shrug. "It's the usual bullshit."

"Someone's setting up a play without my knowledge," he said, watching her closely. Nothing got by Luke.

"But if you knew about it, then that might force your hand," she explained.

"It might."

"And that wouldn't be helpful. Not if you were trying to lure someone out of the woodwork."

"True."

"So at this point, I think it's safe to say that it's just so much media bullshit, and leave it at that. Fog of war."

Luke's eyes clouded over, as if he were assessing his options. Then he tapped his finger on the desk blotter. "Okay, fog of war."

She smiled. A few moments slipped by.

"Anything else?"

"No, I think that's it."

"Okay, Natalie. Good job. But listen, be careful. This job can get to you. Don't let it."

"Oh, it's way too late for that," she joked.

He didn't even crack a smile. "I'll be here if you need me. Anything else?" His voice hardened, but his eyes remained soft as he studied her.

"No, thanks. I'll keep you apprised," she said and left his office.

# 36

The college campus was lovely to look at and covered in snow. The music department was located inside a modern limestone building. Natalie walked past a string quartet playing an ethereal Mozart piece in the lobby. The soundproof rehearsal rooms were located at the back of the building, past the music library and recording facilities.

She found Tony Revelli inside an empty room, sunlight streaming through the narrow windows. There were two rows of metal chairs, each with its own music stand. There was a large, old-fashioned clock on the wall.

"Hello, can I help you?" Tony asked, shaking hands. He was an average-sized thirtysomething with thinning hair, a broad almost childish face, and tremendous strength in his grip. A cellist's grip, she thought.

"Detective Lockhart," she introduced herself. "We spoke over the phone."

"Oh. Right. Like I said, Detective, we have to make this quick. I have a practice session for seniors coming up. We're preparing for the concert next week."

"You're a teacher here?" she asked.

"I'm a TA. I teach the cello and music appreciation."

"And your car broke down on Friday night? You said you got home around ten?"

He nodded. "You can speak to my lawyer about this."

"You hired a lawyer?"

"Yes."

A young woman walked into the practice room carrying a cello case almost as tall as she was. She had short blond hair and wore an ash-gray hooded sweatshirt from the campus store, moccasin boots, and a pleated miniskirt with a ruffle of lace around the hem. She shrugged at them apologetically as she found a seat in the first row.

"Let's talk over here," Tony said, leading Natalie into a quiet corner.

"Did you call Triple A that night? Did you call your wife? How long did it take you to replace the tire? Where did this happen exactly?"

"Look, this is insulting," he said, lowering his voice as more students trickled into the room, each one carrying a heavy-looking cello case. They propped their sheet music on their stands and took out their instruments, pretending not to eavesdrop. "What do you want from me?" he whispered testily.

"I'm looking for verification that your car broke down. Anything. Your wife claims she was at home. I'm simply trying to validate both of your alibis."

"Our alibis?" he hissed. "Are we the bad guys here?"

"You said you'd give me something to prove that you were where you said you were that night. Phone records, gas station receipts, witnesses. We can clear this up right now, and I can cross you off the list."

"What list?"

There was no list. "Can we go somewhere for just a minute?" Natalie asked. "I need you to walk me through last Friday night. Tell me what happened . . . for instance, when did you leave the campus?"

He nodded toward the door, and they crossed the room and stood outside in the large hallway. Natalie could see some of the students craning their necks through the open doorway.

"Just tell me where you were on Friday between six and ten P.M.," she said.

He rolled his eyes. "You can call my attorney if you wish." He fumbled in his jacket pocket. "Here's his card."

She took it. "So you can't answer a straightforward question?"

"Look, it sickens me that Randy Holmes was allowed to walk around, free as a bird, when all that time he could've been molesting other young women. My wife's parents never should have settled with him. He should've been in prison. Am I sorry he's dead? No. But that doesn't mean I killed him. The very thought of it is absurd."

"Then what makes you so upset when I ask about your alibi?"

"I'm not upset." He bristled. "You're interfering with my job. Excuse me." He turned his back on her and went back into the rehearsal room, where he addressed the students. "Hey, guys. Sorry for the delay. First we'll do Dvorak's piece, then Shostakovich's Cello Concerto number two."

Natalie stood in the doorway and watched him gather up sheet music from his briefcase and set it on the music stand at the head of the class.

The blonde in the hooded sweatshirt smiled sweetly at Natalie. As the students began running through the movements, trying various phrasing techniques and creating a calamitous sound, the girl carefully propped her cello in its stand, put down her bow, and left the classroom, saying rather loudly, "Restroom break. Be right back."

# 37

Out in the hallway, the blond student said, "Hi, my name is Amy Rhodes. Are you a detective?"

"Detective Lockhart," Natalie said. "What's on your mind?"

"Tony was with me that night," she explained in a soft, unformed voice.

"Last Friday night?"

"We're seeing each other," she whispered, gesturing for Natalie to follow her farther down the corridor where nobody could overhear them. "His wife doesn't know about us yet. I mean," she whispered, "he's going to leave her, but now's not a good time."

"And why is that?" Natalie asked, feeling sorry for this mixed-up young person. Hadn't anyone warned her there were predators and liars out there in the big bad world?

"Because she's unstable."

"Posey Revelli is unstable," Natalie repeated.

Amy nervously twirled a large silver ring around her index finger. "She's emotionally wounded from being molested when she was a kid. I feel sorry for her, I really do, but Tony says they fell out of love a long time ago. He's been wanting to get a divorce for years."

"He told you that?"

She nodded. "I mean, we didn't plan on falling in love. It just happened. I shouldn't be telling you this. He doesn't want other people to know about us yet."

Natalie wasn't sure what to think, except that Tony Revelli was a scumbag. "He told you about his wife being molested?"

"Oh, yeah. She's neurotic because of it. Tony says she's bipolar. For instance, it was her birthday a couple of weeks ago, and he took her out to a restaurant where the waitstaff brought out a cake with candles and sang 'Happy Birthday.' She got upset, because one of the waiters wore a clown nose, and she's so sensitive about it, she freaked out and wouldn't eat the cake, and they had to leave. It makes things so difficult for us, because now's not a good time to tell her he's in love with someone else."

"I see." Natalie frowned. Maybe it was never the right time to tell someone you'd fallen in love with somebody else. "So Tony was with you last Friday night?"

"After class, we went to my apartment."

"What time?"

"Around five. I kicked out my roommate. She saw me with Tony. She can tell you." Amy began to fidget with her necklace, and Natalie could see the silver pendant with its Wiccan symbol on a long silver chain.

"What is that?" she asked.

The girl blushed, clutching the pendant. "A good luck charm."

"It's the Eye of Horus."

Amy tucked the necklace underneath the collar of her blouse. "My mother's a devout Christian, but I'm not a believer. She thinks I'm following the devil or something. I tried to tell her it's nothing like that."

"Sure, lots of people have embraced Wicca."

"But I'm not a Wiccan, either. I just like it. The eye. It's not the evil eye. It represents an Egyptian god who protects you. It's a symbol of protection and healing."

"I see."

Her eyes sparkled, and she became animated. "Tony thinks I should lose my dependency on my mother. He's teaching me how to be more discerning."

Natalie tried not to show any reaction. She wanted to say, "Yeah, I'll bet." But all she felt was pity—but perhaps that was wrong. Perhaps this fairy tale would have a happy ending? Not for Posey, though.

"And you and Tony were in your apartment that evening," Natalie repeated, "the whole time, between six and ten?"

"Oh." She shook her head. "No, he left around seven. He had to go home. You won't tell anyone else about us, will you? Because he could lose his job if the university found out."

Natalie sighed. "Only if the information proves helpful to the case."

That seemed to offer her a bit of relief. She smiled brightly and said, "Thanks!"

"Only if it becomes necessary . . ."

"I understand. But it won't. He was with me, and my roommate can confirm it. So our conversation doesn't have to leave this hallway, does it?"

Natalie smiled at her naïveté and said, "I have no motivation to use information that isn't significant to the case." It was such a broad statement, it literally meant nothing.

But most people heard what they wanted to hear. Of course the information would be used if Tony turned out to be the murderer. But if it amounted to nothing, then Amy would be in the clear, unfortunately for Posey.

"I'd better get back," the girl said. "Thanks so much, Detective. I'm glad we had this talk. Bye!"

"Bye." Natalie watched her hurry back to class.

# 38

Natalie was checking her text messages back in her car when her phone rang.

"Hello?" she answered.

"It's me," Brandon said. "I've got some information for you."

"Great. Share away."

"So, I tracked down the surgeon who performed the operation on Randy's cancerous balls. Turns out he's retired now, but he agreed to talk to me about it, so I'll be heading over to Little Falls tomorrow."

"Great," she said.

"And I found out who was responsible for negotiating the settlement between Holmes and Posey's parents. His name is Kerrick Maddox, Esquire. He's a partner in an Albany law firm called Fleming, Abercromby and Maddox."

"I'm in Albany now. What's the address?"

He rattled it off.

"Thanks, Brandon."

"Watch your back." He hung up.

The skyline glimmered golden in the late morning light. Downtown Albany consisted of a mixture of old and new—turn-of-the-century brownstones, 1980s office buildings, classical government buildings, Georgian-style museums, and mediocre five-star restaurants nestled along the banks of the Hudson River.

The attorney's office on the tenth floor had recessed lighting and original works of art on the walls. Kerrick Maddox was seated behind his desk, wearing a studious look. His thin, stark face was washed in sunlight. He peered at Natalie through a pair of wire-rim spectacles.

"Thanks for agreeing to see me on such short notice."

"Not at all. Have a seat. Coffee?"

"No, thank you." She sank into a tobacco-colored, leather armchair. "I just found out you once represented Randolph S. Holmes in a settlement between himself and the parents of Posey Revelli, maiden name Barone."

"Right, I saw that on the news the other night. Such a tragedy."

"We're following up various leads, and this is one of them. An important one."

"Okay." He smiled and folded his hands together. "It happened quite a long time ago, but yes, I negotiated on behalf of Mr. Holmes, that is correct."

"He molested Posey Barone when she was eighteen," Natalie said.

"Allegedly. That was the accusation."

"Oh, come on. It's just you and me, Mr. Maddox. Your client is dead."

A small smile was nestled in his lined, aged face. "I'm an attorney. I don't think that way." He nodded politely. "And if you or someone you loved ever got into serious trouble, Detective, you'd be relieved that I don't think that way."

"I doubt I'll ever need your services, but thanks," she said, trying not to sound adversarial but unable to help herself. Natalie had a fuck-you reflex that was baked into her DNA.

Maddox shrugged. "You never know. Take one of my cards."

"Approximately sixteen years ago, at a Halloween party on Holmes's property, Posey called the police after she was assaulted by your client. But before the police arrived, she got talked out of pressing charges. Instead, she lied and said it was a joke."

His brow furrowed as he leaned back in his seat. "I don't recall all the details of the case, but that sounds fairly accurate. In the ballpark."

"And as you know, Mr. Holmes is deceased, so attorney-client privilege is no longer applicable here. I'm working a murder case, Mr. Maddox, and I hope we can have your full cooperation, sir."

"Look," he said with a sigh, "I'm well aware that the rules regarding disclosure of a client's confidences no longer apply. I'd be happy to cooperate with the police."

"Well, thank you," she said. "I'm not here to argue about the incident. Posey told me there was a large settlement, enough to pay for her musical education, which included private school and college. I'm assuming you also charge a hefty fee for your services. I'd like to know how much the settlement was for, and how Holmes managed to pay for it on his salary as a sales clerk in a costume shop."

Maddox cleared his throat. "I'd have to pull those files out of archives to be sure. I'm a stickler for detail. But I do remember the case well, and I can give you an estimate. I believe it was in the seventy-five-thousand-dollar range, and no, he didn't pay for it."

"Who did then?" she asked.

"A woman named Violet Hawke."

Natalie felt the surprise in her stomach. Her heart began to pound a little harder. Violet Hawke was the Crow Killer's grandmother. Samuel Hawke Winston.

"She was quite a character," Maddox went on. "Dressed all in black and dripping with jewelry with occult symbols on them. You know—what are they called? A star inside a circle?"

"Pentagrams."

He nodded without a hint of perturbation. "She was very memorable. Polite, erudite, in a hurry to resolve the entire business. However, like I said, I really should review the files before I give you a definitive answer. It'll take a few days to retrieve them from the archives. We have a procedure . . ."

Natalie leaned forward and asked, "Did she say *why* she was doing this?"

He shook his head. "Just that Randy was a friend of the family. I got the feeling they were close."

Natalie took out her notepad and pen and wrote it all down. "Were there any other similar settlements paid for by Violet Hawke?"

He tapped his finger on his desk blotter. He seemed to be debating whether or not to tell her. "One other incident in 2008."

"Really?" She jotted it down. "What happened?"

"It was a similar situation."

"You mean, he molested another young woman, then settled with the family?"

"Allegedly molested. Yes."

"And Violet Hawke?"

"She paid for everything." He checked his watch. "However, I don't feel comfortable discussing this any further without being able to consult my files."

"I understand. Just tell me the second victim's name."

"Part of the settlement agreement was anonymity for the victim."

"Are you kidding me? I already know about Posey Barone."

"But you found that connection all by yourself, Detective. This would be me betraying my client's NDA. There were two parties involved."

"Just tell me where the incident occurred?"

"In Burning Lake. Spring of 2008."

"And you said Violet Hawke was involved in both settlements?"

"Yes, that's right." He checked his watch again. "Sorry, my next appointment will be here any minute now. If you don't mind—"

"Thank you, Mr. Maddox. I'll be in touch."

"It was nice to meet you, Detective Lockhart. I've read a lot about you."

"Yeah, well . . . I don't like being in the spotlight. I never asked for this. I just want to go home at night, knowing I've done my best. Here's my card," she said, standing up. "Any further details you can provide us with would be greatly appreciated."

"Okay. And why don't you take one of mine," he said, nudging the silver card tray closer. "Just in case."

She smirked. She hesitated, but then she took one.

# 39

Natalie drove into the foothills of the Adirondack Mountains, taking the 87 north, and passed the exit to Thaddeus Falls—Samuel Hawke Winston's hometown, where he'd once lived with his wife and children before Natalie had killed him.

The sun burned off the morning fog, and despite the brilliance of the sky, the day felt solemn and dark. She felt stiff, on edge. During her first year as the designated newbie of the Criminal Investigative Unit, Natalie's assignment was to reinvestigate a stack of unsolved cases called "the Missing Nine"—nine beat-to-hell plastic binders, battered around the edges, their dog-eared pages full of old leads and dried-up lines of inquiry. All the other detectives had taken a shot at the Missing Nine and failed. It was considered tradition to pass along the burden to the newbie, since what was needed was a fresh pair of eyes.

In the past three decades, nine transients had gone missing from Burning Lake—drifters, drug addicts, indigents, alcoholics, the invisible edges of society. The FBI field office had gotten involved back in the mid-2000s, but since the victims were all drifters by nature, it was assumed that they'd drifted through Burning Lake on their way to other destinations.

Last April, after following a new lead in the disappearance of a local homeless woman named Bunny Jackson, Natalie solved Upstate New York's biggest serial killer case ever—dubbed the Crow Killer by the media. A forest ranger named Samuel Hawke Winston had abducted and murdered dozens of homeless people, along with a handful of tourists visiting the

Adirondack Mountains, and his crimes went back decades. The first seven victims were found buried on Samuel's property, and twelve more were recovered from his grandmother's property, which was where Natalie had tracked the Crow Killer down and ultimately killed him in self-defense. His grandmother was Violet Hawke.

After the Crow Killer case was solved, Natalie spent the next few months piecing together the evidence, tracking down all of Samuel's victims and connecting their disappearances to the bodies the police had unearthed. Samuel had left plenty of clues behind, stacks of dog-eared journals full of rambling messages written in indecipherable, minuscule handwriting, like the kind she'd found inside his grandmother's house. You needed a powerful magnifying glass in order to read them—if they could be deciphered at all, since most of the tiny, cramped scribblings remained a mystery.

When all was said and done, Natalie still didn't get it—all those years the Crow Killer had spent hiding behind a veil of normalcy, passing as a loving father, a considerate husband, and a kind and caring colleague, when in reality, he was a savage psychopath, abducting and killing people in the most horrific ways imaginable. She struggled to understand, because she hoped to prevent the next horror from happening, but the answers eluded her. All she knew was that crows liked to stare at their victims for long stretches of time before pecking them to death, just like murderous sociopaths.

Before Samuel's grandmother had passed away, she was living in a town called Hemlock Gate. Her name was Violet Hawke. The town was full of farms, woods, and dead ends. If it was true that Violet had paid off Randy Holmes's settlements, then what was the connection between them? How was this possible?

Now Natalie took an isolated street for forty yards, until she came to a driveway with KEEP OUT signs posted on the gateposts. The rusty old mailbox said HAWKE.

Perspiration trickled down her chest between her breasts as she drove up the steep driveway. It was colder here than in Burning Lake. A chilly wind blew through trees.

At the top of the hilly driveway stood a ramshackle Victorian house with a whimsical roofline full of gables and chimneys like something out of a demented fairy tale. The house had fallen into disrepair, and half the roof shingles needed replacing.

She parked in the driveway and stepped out of her car, fright bubbling up her spine. The last time she was here, a woman was screaming for help inside the house, which had led to her final showdown with the Crow Killer.

Now wind chimes dangled on the front porch, creating a twinkly, carnival-like sound. Ferns grew deep on either side of the road, and all around the property were the towering, impenetrable woods. There was a sign nailed to a tree—NO HUNTING. The only creatures who were ever hunted here were the human beings who'd been preyed on by a madman.

The property looked the same as she remembered, except for a huge collection of junk in front of the house. Natalie walked over to the towering piles of broken furniture, corroded kitchen appliances and old toys, alongside boxes and trash bags full of stuff, and realized that someone was cleaning out the place.

"Hello?" a female voice called out. "Can I help you?"

Natalie turned around.

Samuel's widow, Tracie Winston, stood in the doorway holding a wire whisk. Her cheeks were the same rosy pink as her vinyl jacket. She wore pale blue sweats and a pair of muddy work boots. There was a dark red wool scarf wrapped around her neck, and for a second it looked as if her throat had been slashed.

"Tag sale?" Natalie asked, pointing at the heap of trash.

"No, just throwing it out. But the house is for sale."

Videos of Tracie Winston hiding behind her hands on the courthouse steps had gone viral last year. The media never got tired of showing Tracie's deep shame to the public, juxtaposed against the corny, department-store portrait of Samuel Hawke Winston, New York DWW Forest Ranger, posing with his attractive wife and two adorable children. It was almost as shocking a contrast as the family snapshots of the victims compared with their skeletal remains that had been dug up from Samuel's backyard.

"Spring cleaning," Tracie explained. "Thought I'd make the house presentable to buyers, if at all possible." She wore a confused look. "Wait. Don't I know you?"

Natalie nodded, although she was hesitant to identify herself. "I should've introduced myself. I'm Detective Lockhart."

"Oh." Tracie reacted with a solemn, almost angry nod. "What are you doing here? Should I call my lawyer?"

"No, that won't be necessary."

"I thought the case was closed? They told me it was basically over. They said it was okay to sell the house."

Instead of explaining herself, Natalie asked Tracie, "Are you moving out of state?"

Samuel's wife nodded. "I'm tired of the notoriety. My kids . . ." She had nervous eyelids. "We're going to start over. We're moving thousands of miles away from here."

Natalie nodded. "I understand. And I'm sorry."

"Is that what you came here for? To apologize? Because I've been apologizing for almost an entire year now, to the victim's families, to the press. I had no idea what Sam was up to. I had no clue what he was capable of. The insanity. And now my kids have to live with it. They get ostracized at school. It's so horribly painful, what he did to us, I can't even talk about it."

Natalie nodded. "So you're selling both houses, then?"

"Yes. We're moving across the country. I've got family in Oregon. The kids and I will use my maiden name." She sighed and glanced around. "Anyway, I'm glad to get rid of it. I've hated this house since the moment I first set eyes on it. So big and creepy."

Natalie nodded in agreement. Violet Hawke's house was monstrous.

"He blew up my life," Tracie said with bitterness. "And no, I never suspected a thing. Does that make me ridiculous? Am I heinously stupid?"

"No," Natalie said, her gut clenching. "It just makes you a victim."

"We're both victims, aren't we?"

Natalie nodded. She sympathized with this woman. Tracie hadn't known that her husband was a sick, twisted killer, and Natalie hadn't guessed that Grace was a murderer and a liar. And yet, the feelings of guilt and responsibility ate you up anyway. In the eyes of the public, you were damned. How could you not know that the people closest to you were capable of such evil? How was it possible?

Tracie watched Natalie with keen interest. "I don't blame you, Detective, for shooting my husband. At first I did, but only because I couldn't believe what kind of a depraved monster he was, you know? I was in denial. But now I understand. You had to save that poor woman."

Natalie nodded sympathetically.

Tracie dropped the wire whisk into a box and tied back her hair. "Anyway, how can I help you? I've already told the police everything six times over."

Natalie pointed at the junk pile. "Mind if I take a look?"

She shrugged. "The police raided the house last year, but they left a bunch of stuff behind. Sam's grandmother was a hoarder. Help yourself."

Natalie poked through the trash. Once a person threw something away, it became public property, but since Tracie had also given her permission, Natalie was legally allowed to confiscate it. There were loaf pans, mixing bowls, old videos like *Butch Cassidy and the Sundance Kid*, a sticky game of checkers, a broken metal towel rack, stacks of cheap plates and dishware. There were paperback books so pawed-over, the bindings were wiggly and the pages were stained a dark yellow and loose as an old dog's teeth. There were sad-looking children's toys, empty perfume bottles, and tangled extension cords. There was a bucket of greasy tools—old wrenches, a rusty screwdriver, a broken pair of scissors. There was a folded up carpet, a musty old sofa, a collection of used cleaning products, and the dome of an old ceiling lamp full of dead insects.

"I've hired some guys to transport everything to the dump," Tracie told her.

Natalie found an old journal tucked among a bag of clothes. She took it out and opened it, the yellow pages crackling with age. She leafed through it. The handwriting was just as illegible as it had been in the other journals they'd collected. On every page were inscrutable words, along with drawings of birds, handmade maps, and hieroglyphics. The police must've missed this one.

"What's this?" Natalie asked, holding it up.

"I don't know. Found it in the attic."

"Can I have it?" Natalie asked.

"Please. Take everything. I never want to see it again."

Natalie gathered up the most promising-looking items—an old leather suitcase embossed with Violet Hawke's initials, a few books, two grocery bags full of paperwork and correspondence—then she found an item that shook her to the core. It was an old shadow box containing several dozen preserved and pinned spiders.

"That's so creepy, right?" Tracie said. "I never felt comfortable around her."

"Listen, I know you want to sell the house," Natalie told her, "but I'm working on another case, and there might be a connection to Samuel's case, so we'll need to do another grid-search of the property and look through the rest of this stuff, with your permission. I have to go, but please don't remove anything from the property. I promise we'll make it as quick as we can. Is that okay?"

Tracie frowned, looking extremely disappointed. "Are you serious?"

"Look at it this way. If you ever wanted to make up for what your husband did, now's your chance. This is your opportunity."

"Oh Jesus, that's not a loaded request or anything," she said angrily.

"I know. I'm sorry." Natalie felt desperate and clumsy. She took a deep breath and attempted to explain the significance of what she was asking. "I understand exactly how you feel. I know you've been through so much already, and it feels unexpected and unfair of me to ask you this so late in the game. But it's vital. And I promise you, we'll finish up here as soon as we can. In and out." Natalie handed Tracie her card. "But it's imperative that we search the property one last time. Do I have your permission?"

The woman appeared to deflate like a popped balloon. She studied the business card in her hand. "Can I call you directly? I don't want to get the operator or be put on hold. I need a direct line of communication."

"Yes, absolutely," Natalie said, taking back the card and writing down her personal number. "Call me anytime, day or night. I won't let you down. Listen, I could get a search warrant, but that could take some time, which would only delay your plans. If you consent to a search right now, we can get this over with more quickly."

She nodded, pocketing the card. "Okay, you have my consent."

"Thanks. What's your number? I'll send you a consent agreement."

Tracie gave her the number, while Natalie pulled up the form on her phone. A "consent to search" form was documented proof that the person had waived their rights against an arbitrary search-and-seizure of the property. Natalie made sure to include on the form that the "scope of search" was the house and the entire property. Otherwise, any physical evidence they obtained during the search could be contested as inadmissible in court.

Appearing resigned and a little miffed, Tracie filled out the consent form on her mobile device and sent it back to Natalie. Then she said, "Some people are just plain evil. But how can you tell? They hide it so well. I never knew who I was dealing with all those years. How could I have been so blind? And how do you salvage your life after something like that?"

"I have the same questions," Natalie said, putting away her phone and slipping in behind the wheel of her car.

Tracie lingered with her hand on the door. "I guess you do your best," she said. "I guess you try to focus on what's good in this world. The positive things. Huh?"

"Yes. And I hope you find happiness in the near future."

"You too, Detective."

"I'll be back with some officers later this afternoon." Natalie felt an inexplicable weight fall on her shoulders as she drove away.

# 40

Back at the police station, Natalie headed directly for Luke's office. She knocked on the door, barely waiting for his reply before she swung it open and burst inside. "You'll never guess what just happened," she said excitedly, then stopped short.

Rainie was standing in front of Luke's desk, smiling at him.

"Oh, I'm sorry."

"No problem," Rainie said lightly. "I was just leaving. But I might as well share the good news." She extended her hand and fluttered her fingers. "Luke and I are engaged!"

Natalie stared at the tasteful, antique diamond ring on Rainie's finger. "That's great," she said, trying very hard not to show her disappointment. "Congratulations."

Rainie examined her engagement ring. "It was his mother's. Isn't it lovely?"

"Yes." She swallowed hard. "When's the wedding?"

Rainie laughed. "I'm not sure. But at least he popped the question. Small blessings."

"I'm right here," Luke told them drily.

"I'm happy for you, Rainie," Natalie said with a pained smile. She wanted out of this conversation in a bad way. She glanced at the door, wondering if she should attempt an escape.

But Rainie wasn't finished. "And listen, I'm sorry this is so last minute." She reached for Natalie's hand and squeezed. "But Luke and I are having a party two weekends from now, and we'd love for you and Hunter to be there. Say you'll come?"

Natalie stared at her for a breathless beat. "Sure. I'll see if he's free."

"Please come. It'll be fun. We're celebrating Luke's recovery and our engagement. There's so much to be grateful for."

"I can see that," Natalie said awkwardly. "Sorry to barge in like this. I'll leave you two alone."

"Natalie, what is it?" Luke asked firmly.

"Nothing that can't wait," she said.

"Don't be silly," Rainie said, picking up her bag. "I'll let you two get back to business. See you at the party, Natalie." Rainie flashed her diamond ring again and left, closing the door gently behind her.

Natalie felt flushed and stupid. The news was shocking. It scared her, even though she had no right to feel that way. Somehow, she'd always assumed there would be plenty of time to figure out how she felt about Luke—this thing that continued to live and grow between them. But clearly time had run out.

Natalie forced a smile, pretending to be happy for them. "Congratulations," she told Luke.

"Have a seat," he said evenly.

She sat. "It's a nice ring," she said, her heart racing.

His face was guarded. "When my door is closed, that means . . ."

"I know," she interjected. "I'm sorry. I shouldn't have barged in like that. I feel like such a jerk."

He leaned forward and asked, "What do you want, Natalie? What's that under your arm?"

"A yearbook. We need to talk."

"Sounds serious."

The wall behind him was covered with crime-scene photographs— Veronica's mangled body in the snow, a purple-faced Randolph Holmes with rubber bats dangling over his head, Detective Peter Murphy's house burned to the ground.

A map of their jurisdiction was pinned to the wall with thumbtacks. There was a red dot over Murray's Halloween Costume, a red dot over Randy's house, and another red dot on the railroad tracks north of town. Too many red dots.

Natalie held the yearbook in her lap. "Fifteen years ago, Randy Holmes molested eighteen-year-old Posey Revelli, and then settled the incident with her parents for seventy-five thousand dollars. Guess who paid the settlement?"

Luke shook his head.

"Violet Hawke."

Disbelief flared in his eyes. "The Crow Killer's grandmother?"

"The very same."

"How is that possible?"

"I don't know. It's totally bizarre. So I looked up her information from the old case file. She was born Violet Scranton in 1938. She grew up in Hemlock Gate, then married a real estate agent named Victor Hawke in 1958, and they moved to Burning Lake. They had a daughter named Frances who went to JFK High School in the 1970s. So I retrieved the yearbook from Veronica Manes's evidence box. Remember those pages Veronica had earmarked, where we couldn't identify some of the students in the pictures?"

Luke nodded. "I remember."

"Well, here's what I found." She opened the old John F. Kennedy High School yearbook from 1975 with its dog-eared pages. The seventies fashions were distracting—miniskirts, paisley shirts, earlobe-length hair for the boys, and cat's eye glasses for the girls. There were pictures of "Class Favorites," along with sections for clubs, sports, activities, and awards. Some of the pages had their corners folded over in place of a bookmark.

"So remember we found Ned Bertrand's class photo?" she said, turning to page fifty-two, where the pudgy senior sat scowling at the camera. His yearbook quote was: "They told me to write something. Something." Natalie held it up for Luke to see.

"And we also found Reverend Grimsby's class picture?" On page seventy-one, she located the skinny, pimple-faced eighteen-year-old Thomas Grimsby, smiling awkwardly into the camera. His yearbook quote said: "We are all God's handiwork."

"And then, there's this." On dog-eared page one hundred and twenty-six was the Young Christians Club, consisting of eight kids. A young Reverend Thomas Grimsby stood in the center, surrounded by seven others. There was Ned Bertrand again, and a sophomore named Dottie Coffman, who beamed out from the grainy photo looking fresh-scrubbed, innocent, and wide-eyed, not yet into her occult phase. "We connected Ned Bertrand with Dottie Coffman and Thomas Grimsby. But there was one female student we couldn't identify."

One of the last earmarked sections was called "Student Life," and it consisted of candid shots of various students hanging out together. The last folded-over corner on page one hundred and sixty-nine was a snapshot of four girls posing in front of the Witching Tree. The photograph was of poor quality, and it was difficult to make out their shaded faces, but she recognized Dottie Coffman among them. The caption read: "Witches in training."

"Right," Luke said. "We also know from the photograph we found in the lockbox that Dottie Coffman and Ned Bertrand were in the same coven together."

"Which is significant," Natalie said, picking up the thread, "because Peter Murphy stole the lockbox from the crime lab, and inside was a black-and-white snapshot of four teenagers—Dottie Coffman, Ned Bertrand, an unknown girl, and a boy who's halfway out of the shot. They're holding a cow's skull. We figured it must be Ned and Dottie's coven."

Luke nodded. "Right. So who are the other two kids in that picture?"

"Exactly. Who is she? Well, in the picture, you can see a distinctive mole on her cheek." She took out her phone and scrolled through the digital images, until she came to a picture they'd managed to capture before the lockbox was stolen weeks ago. "Now, on this page . . ." She rifled through the yearbook until she came to a large freshman-class group photo. "Here's a picture of Frances Hawke. She was a freshman back then. Fifteen years old. See the mole on her cheek?"

Natalie carried the yearbook over to Luke's desk, and they leaned over it together, comparing the image in the yearbook to the image on Natalie's phone. "If we can verify that this is Frances Hawke, then Dottie Coffman, Ned Bertrand, and Violet Hawke's daughter went to the same school together. They were in the same coven together." Natalie's heart wouldn't stop pounding. She was standing too close to him, and she wondered if Luke could hear it. "Which means we can tentatively connect the lockbox, the Violinist, the Crow Killer, and now, Randy Holmes and Violet Hawke together."

"Shit," Luke muttered.

"And if you think that's crazy . . . you're not going to believe this." Natalie leafed through the pages of the yearbook again until she came to the H's under the series of senior class pictures. "It turns out Randy Holmes was a senior in 1975. He was in *Ned Bertrand's class*. And Frances Hawke was a freshman at the time. There's your fucking connection."

Luke let out a low, incredulous whistle.

"Veronica must've found out about all this, because she had the year-book in her possession, and she folded over these specific pages, and she was writing a book about it. She didn't have Holmes, though. But all the others . . ."

"So they killed her because of it?" Luke asked.

"Obviously, she knew a lot more than that. I mean, think about it. Ned Bertrand's son grew up to become the Violinist. Frances Hawke's son grew up to become the Crow Killer. And now we're discovering that Randy Holmes was bailed out by Frances's mother." Natalie put the yearbook down and scrolled through her phone again. "I found Violet Hawke's obituary. She went to Erie County Community College, then became a real estate agent for Davidson Realty, where she met her husband, Victor. Her daughter Frances and son-in-law died in a car accident in 1999, and she lost her husband to cancer shortly afterwards. Samuel was thirteen at the time his parents died, and he went to live with his grandmother in Hemlock Gate. There's nothing in the obituary about witchcraft or covens. She died in 2015."

"So what are you saying?"

"I don't know. These are just facts. We need to dig around some more. But it's very strange that they all went to the same school together, they all knew each other, and a lot of really bad things came out of it. We need to reassemble the facts in chronological order and figure out what happened, but it's clear that Veronica was onto something here."

"There has to be some bigger connection between them, something that bound them together in secrecy, that bled into their whole lives."

"Exactly. Like the items we found in the lockbox before it was stolen," Natalie said excitedly. "The Polaroid picture of the girl who was bound and gagged. The bloody panties. Maybe they did something awful to her, and then hid it away from the world. Maybe they killed her in a ritualistic sacrifice? And ever since, they've been bound to one another in secrecy."

"Okay," Luke said, "slow down a second. If Violet Hawke paid for Randy's settlement, then the question is—why? Why would she do that?"

"Maybe Randy threatened to reveal their dark secret?" Natalie suggested.

"Blackmail? But wouldn't he be implicating himself as well?"

"Violet worked as a real estate agent. There's nothing to suggest she could afford to pay anyone that much money. As far as I know, she wasn't well off. And it happened twice."

"It did?"

Natalie told Luke what Maddox had told her.

"A second settlement? Who with?"

"He wouldn't give me a name."

"So then," Luke said, "who actually paid the settlement money?"

"Not Ned Bertrand," Natalie said. "Not Dottie Coffman. Somebody with money. Maybe the unidentified boy in the photograph we found in the lockbox?"

"Let's not get ahead of ourselves," Luke told her. "We're going to have to reopen these cases and reconsider everything. We can't jump to any conclusions."

"But we can agree that they're all connected by the occult. They were in a coven together in high school—it all started there. We need to go through Violet's house again, one last time, to see if there's anything we might've missed. I've asked Sam's widow for permission to search, and she signed a consent waiver."

"Okay, then." Luke stood up. "Let's go."

# 41

The sky had gone from blue to overcast in a matter of minutes, it seemed, and Natalie hoped it wasn't going to snow again—they needed to search the property unimpeded. She parked behind Luke's Ford Ranger in front of the ramshackle Victorian, then several police cruisers pulled up behind her.

A trickle of sweat zigzagged down her neck as she got out of her car. The driveway was slippery with patches of ice. All around the house were the towering, impenetrable woods. Natalie and Luke took the rough-hewn steps up to the front porch, where wind chimes dangled from a beam, creating an eerie music box sound.

Tracie Winston greeted them at the door. "Hello again. Come on in."

Natalie wiped the mud off her shoes on the old horsehair mat. "A couple of officers will be walking around outside and confiscating any pertinent items, including from the junk pile, if necessary. Lieutenant Pittman and I are going to do a walk-through of the house, and we may seize more evidence, if it seems important to the case."

"Do whatever you need to do," Tracie told them. "I'll be in the kitchen, sorting through more boxes."

They walked down the front hallway toward Violet Hawke's living room, where pale blocks of faded wallpaper indicated where family pictures used to hang. It was chilly in here. The electricity had been shut off. The carpet's padding was rotten beneath the old weave. Two ancient armchairs faced a blank wall where the television console used to be. There was an empty china cabinet, a credenza, and a musty old sofa, its sagging arms covered with elderberry-stained doilies.

A lone winter fly buzzed around Natalie's head, and she brushed it away. She recalled the house as it had once been, when she'd first set foot inside over a year ago. There had been a strange fussiness to the décor, a fastidiousness combined with psychosis, which became obvious as soon as you walked into the parlor.

Natalie recalled the fear she felt as she turned the corner—back then, the parlor was full of gruesome occult items, satanic figurines, animal bones, Wiccan texts, and graffiti on the walls—satanic horns, 666, pentagrams. And the birds. Dead crows amateurishly preserved. Whoever the taxidermist was, he'd arranged the beady-eyed creatures in bizarre poses—crucifixions, mummifications, birds stuck with pins, wrapped in barbed wire, soaking in huge vats of liquid.

Now Natalie shuddered, expecting to see this nightmare again, but instead there were empty shelves and a few pieces of furniture.

The police had confiscated the rest. Several law enforcement jurisdictions had been working in the aftermath of the Crow Killer case, coordinating their efforts to locate, unbury, and identify the remains of the dead. Now Natalie searched her phone for the inventory list of evidence that had been gathered from Violet Hawke's house shortly after Samuel's death. Any search for physical evidence was documented thoroughly and systematically. Once a piece of evidence was determined to be recoverable, then a full accounting of the chain of custody was necessary. She pulled up the extensive list on her phone and found out that the taxidermy birds had been collected by local police here in Hemlock Gate and were being held in archives.

As they checked out the bathroom just off the front hall, Natalie recalled the horrid coppery smell of blood and the stench of acid attacking flesh. She'd experienced a living nightmare inside this house and didn't want to relive it in vivid detail. She tried to stay focused on the present.

"There's nothing down here," she told Luke. "Let's go upstairs."

On the second floor, there were four closed doors to choose from. Natalie moved cautiously into the first room, where she had found a poor woman collared to the wall, her head wrapped in duct tape, except for a slit for her eyes and a slit for her mouth so that she could breath.

They went through each of the rooms methodically, checking the top closet shelves for leftover items, the air vents, and built-in cabinets.

Samuel's room was down at the end of the hall. The metal knob had a ding in it. She swung the door open and stepped inside. The lights were off. The striated blinds were closed. She let her eyes adjust to the dimness. There were faded tulips on the wallpaper, and everything was thick with dust.

They investigated the built-in bookcase. They pushed, pulled, and prodded. Natalie pressed her hands against one side of the bookcase, while Luke examined the other side, searching for cracks or hidden latches or buttons. There was nothing.

"Let's check out the attic," she said.

They took the creaky, narrow stairs up to the attic, which was empty now. It used to be full of junk, but now there was nothing but cobwebs, sawdust, and a musty smell.

Luke shone his flashlight into the shadowy eaves. They poked into every corner and tested the floorboards and wall panels. They pushed and pulled on loose boards, and came up empty-handed. She grew frustrated. She shone her light into the deepest eave.

"Maybe there's nothing more to be found," Luke suggested—barely a whisper, as if the house were getting to him, too.

"Wait a minute. I think there's something back there."

"Where?" Luke asked, squinting.

"It looks like a door." She took off her jacket and rolled up her sleeves. Luke held the flashlight while Natalie crawled underneath the dirty eaves until she came to the end, where she found a small hidden door at floor level. It was locked with a brass latch and had been painted shut. She pried it open, then aimed her flashlight into a spidery crawl space full of document boxes.

# 42

Natalie and Luke carried the five dusty legal-size boxes full of paperwork out to his Ranger, where Natalie rifled through one of them. She took out an invoice dated 2004 and said, "It's financial information. Invoices for consulting work, old bank statements, and pay stubs . . . why keep it hidden away?"

"We'll find out later. Let's go thank Ms. Winston for her time and wrap this up."

Back inside, a strong afternoon sunlight slanted through the kitchen windows—the ebbing of the day through a tangle of branches.

Tracie Winston didn't look well. Her skin was pale and her expression was soaked in pain. She was seated at the breakfast table, which was cluttered with dirty dishes and empty wine bottles. The room smelled of wet insulation and moldy leftovers. There were half a dozen trash bags on the floor and a stack of flattened packing boxes.

"Did you know there was a hidden compartment in the attic?" Natalie asked her.

"No." She looked miserable.

"Under one of the eaves. A little access door at the back, with a crawl space big enough for half a dozen boxes. You've been selling things and moving things—you didn't see it?"

She shook her head. "No, I pulled everything out from under the eaves after the police told me it was okay to do so. I sold a few antiques, but the rest is just junk."

"And you didn't know about the compartment?"

"No, and it makes me sick to my stomach. I just want to sell this place and get out of here. Take my kids and go."

"I understand." Natalie nodded sympathetically. "Detective Lenny Labruzzo will be here tomorrow. Once he finishes processing that area of the attic, then you can go ahead and sell the house."

"It eats away at me," Tracie admitted. "I don't understand what's going on."

"If it's any consolation," Luke told her, "we're trying to figure that out, too."

"I just want to be far away when you do."

"Thanks again for your cooperation," Natalie told her. She looked at Luke and said, "Let's go."

But before they left, Tracie turned to them and said, "You know, I've seen that cop before. The one on TV."

They both stopped short. "Cop?" Natalie repeated.

"Detective Murphy." She nodded. "The one who's all over the news. The guy they're looking for? He was here," she explained. "He came to the house with another officer, and they were looking for something. They took away a lot of old documents."

Natalie felt a swell of excitement mixed with confusion. "When was this?"

"About six months ago. I signed a form."

"Six months?" Luke turned to Natalie. "We didn't authorize that."

"Let me check." Natalie activated her phone and scrolled through the evidence compilation list for Violet Hawke's residence. She studied the dates.

"Anything?" Luke asked in a low voice.

"No," she breathed. "Nothing was collected six months ago. The last time was eight and a half months ago." Natalie turned to Tracie. "Are you sure it was six months ago?"

"Yes, it was last September. Mid-September. Around my son's birthday."

"And you're also sure it was Detective Murphy?"

"Yes, I recognize him from the TV. He has those heavy eyebrows."

"And what did the other officer look like?"

She shook her head. "An older guy. I don't remember."

"How tall? How much did he weigh?"

"He was slightly taller than Detective Murphy."

"Five ten? Five eleven?"

"I think so. A big guy."

"Two hundred pounds?"

"That sounds right."

"And he was in a police uniform?"

"Yes, with the sunglasses and the hat and badge and everything. I distinctly remember Detective Murphy, though, because of those eyebrows."

"Right. And they had you sign a form, like the one I showed you today?"

"They handed me a clipboard," she said, "and I signed the form."

"What were they looking for?" Natalie asked.

"They asked about some old documents. I forget now. I showed them down to the basement, where the boxes were stored at the time. None of the state police or detectives had taken them previously. I guess they didn't consider them important."

"Documents, such as what?" Natalie asked.

"Anything like tax receipts, bills, bank statements, utility bills, mortgage payments, canceled checks. Stuff like that. But those two were in the basement for a long time, rummaging around. They took away several dozen boxes. I don't remember exactly. The rest of it got tossed out."

Natalie and Luke exchanged a look.

"I thought it was official police business. Are you saying it wasn't?"

"Don't worry," Natalie told her, "you did the right thing."

"Thanks. We've taken up enough of your time," Luke said, and they left.

# 43

Outside, Natalie turned up her coat collar. There was a steely chill in the air. Soon, the sun would set—a late winter sunset like liquid copper.

The backyard of Violet Hawke's house was dotted with old spring traps made of netting. Natalie had seen these traps before. They were meant for a large species of bird. *What the hawk eats.* Samuel Hawke. Serial killer.

"Murphy must've been looking for the documents we found in the attic," Luke said, and Natalie nodded. "But who was his accomplice?"

"An older guy, five eleven, maybe two hundred pounds. That fits the description of Randy Holmes. Murphy could've stolen a BLPD uniform, for all we know."

He frowned. "Murphy and Randy working together?"

"I know, it's a stretch. It just keeps getting weirder."

"We need to take a look at these documents," Luke said. "Let's get them back to the station for processing. It's going to be a long week."

They walked around to the front of the house and stood in the muddy driveway. They could see the road from here, between the stone gate posts.

Natalie sighed. "I don't get it. Violet Hawke died years ago. Ned Bertrand had a stroke and is incapacitated. The Violinist is locked away in prison. The Crow Killer is dead. Dottie Coffman has Alzheimer's and is confined to a nursing home. And now Randy Holmes is dead."

Luke rubbed his tired face. "What's the connection?"

"That's the question."

Behind them, wind chimes dangled on the front porch as the wind picked up. The yard was an obstacle course of Havahart traps. She glanced back down the driveway, where winter weeds grew thick on either side of the road.

"Why did Randy stop abducting the Shadow Girls?" Natalie asked. "I mean, we can assume that getting cancer in 2009 must've taken away his sex drive—that makes sense, right?"

Luke shrugged. "What else can we assume?"

"Yeah, but do you honestly think a guy who'd been abducting and killing sex workers since 1988 just stopped cold? It was more than sex for him. It was about control and manipulation."

"Getting your balls cut off just might do the job."

"So then, he turned his obsession into collecting insects?"

"It's all conjecture at this point," Luke said. "We know relatively little."

"But we can presume—"

"We can't presume anything, Natalie. It's premature. We need more evidence, more information. At the very least, we need to talk to the surgeon who performed the operation."

"Brandon's meeting with him tomorrow."

"Good. In the meantime, let's take a careful look at these documents. The answer could be in one of these boxes."

It was getting late in the day. The initial rush of adrenaline had worn off. Fatigue was setting in. "It feels awful coming back to this place," she admitted.

"I can imagine," he said, the lines of his face fading. His eyes grew warm toward her.

A dog howled deep in the woods, and she shivered. "I'll never forget when I walked into that room and found Bunny Jackson with duct tape wrapped around her head. The collar around her neck left blisters on her skin. There was dried blood on her track suit. She couldn't sit up because of muscle weakness. She lay curled on the floor, looking up at me through the eye-slits, and said, 'Shh, the Devil can hear you.'"

"I'm so sorry you had to go through that," Luke said solemnly.

She stood nervously jiggling her car keys in her hand and had the distinct impression someone was standing across the street, watching them. She turned to look down the driveway at the road through the stone gateposts. Nobody was there.

"We're going to solve this thing, aren't we, Luke?" she asked, biting back the tears, feeling immensely vulnerable. "We're going to figure it out."

"Yes," he told her with absolute confidence.

Natalie wasn't so sure. "Those young women, they were eighteen. My niece is almost eighteen. They're still children at that age, in a way. I can't imagine the horror of finding themselves in that position, with a man like that. They had dreams and goals, they had feelings, they had a life. And it just ended."

"You saved a life that day," Luke reminded her. "You saved Bunny Jackson's life, and that's a good thing. Hang on to that. Don't forget."

She nodded and took a deep breath. The air smelled of pine cones. A tear slid down her cheek, and she brushed it away.

"It's okay," he said with crystal clear eyes. "You're safe now. You made it out of that house alive, Natalie. And I promise you, we're going to figure this thing out. Whatever the hell is going on in this town, we'll solve it together. Okay?" He teased a few strands of hair out of her eyes. "Don't let it get to you."

Now was the time, if ever Natalie was going to bring up her feelings for him, now was the time to do it. She glanced at his hand, looking for an engagement ring, but there wasn't one. Luke hated rings. He didn't like formalities. She wondered if Rainie was planning a big wedding. Would she have bridesmaids? A videographer? A registry for wedding gifts? Where would they go on their honeymoon? Natalie tried not to picture the two of them fucking on some pristine beach in the Caribbean.

"Anything else?" he asked, eyes brimming with warmth and patience.

The air turned crystalline. It was quieter than it should be. A sense of fatigue came over her. She shook her head. "I don't think so."

"Are you sure?" he pressed gently. "Nothing else on your mind?"

It was just the opening she needed. But before Natalie could respond, she caught a movement out of the corner of her eyes.

A silver pickup truck drove past the gateposts on this little-traveled road. Her heart gave a flutter as she recognized Bill Finley's vehicle as it hurried past. Bill was one of Hunter's most trusted security guards, and there was no reason for him to be out this way.

# 44

Natalie stood in the front hallway, unwrapping the wool scarf from around her neck and shrugging off her coat. She was exhausted to the bone. She found Hunter sitting inside the dimly lit kitchen.

"Can I have a cigarette?"

He turned toward her. "What makes you think I have a cigarette?"

"Oh, come on."

He shrugged, too apathetic to lie anymore. "Okay. I confess. I've been pretty stressed out lately, so I bummed a few cigarettes from Bill. Can we skip the lecture please?" He frowned at her. "Where the hell have you been?"

"Seriously?" Natalie sat down next to him. "You're going to be that asshole tonight?"

He cracked a smile. "You disappeared today. No phone calls, no messages."

She sighed heavily and said, "I saw Bill Finley this afternoon, while I was working the case."

"Now I feel like a cigarette," he confessed.

She studied him. "Did you have Bill follow me up to Hemlock Gate?"

"What? No," he said defensively. "He wasn't following you. He was following one of your stalkers, some reporter guy. I guess that must've led him to you."

She drew back, irritated. "I can defend myself against persistent reporters."

"Persistent? The guy's on Reddit after midnight, weaving conspiracy theories, and they all seem to revolve around you. The guy's a psycho."

"Okay," she said, rubbing her face as if she were trying to rub out a mistake. "You can stop white knighting for me, Hunter. I don't need you and Bill riding to my rescue all the time."

"In this climate? Come on. The guy's a steaming pile of garbage. You should read his Twitter threads, he's quite deranged."

"Was it Kip Edwards?"

"No, his name is Leopold something. Leopold Wolfgang. Sounds made up. One of those anon accounts. We're digging into it, trying to find out who he really is."

Natalie had never been contacted by anyone by that name before, but a lot of reporters had attempted to communicate with her over the past year or so, and she'd stopped reading their Twitter feeds. It was too upsetting. Most of them invented their own spin and ran with it.

"What's wrong, babe?" Hunter asked with deep concern.

She looked at him and frowned. "Today sucked on top of already sucking."

"So it double sucked? Why? What happened?"

She peeled off her jacket. She wasn't sure how much she should share with him. She could see the worry in his eyes. "I fell down another rabbit hole. Things are getting complicated. I don't know." She leaned forward and rested her chin on her hands. "I'm starting to feel lost."

"You aren't lost. You're with me."

She smiled faintly. "You and my ghosts."

"Are your ghosts annoying you now?" He looked at her, full of love. "Grief takes time, Natalie. That's the key ingredient."

"Time," she repeated softly. "The missing ingredient."

"It's actually quite simple. Just wait long enough, and the pain will fade away."

She smiled sadly. How long would she have to wait for today's pain to fade away.

"Anyway, I got you something," he said, picking up a small plastic bag from the Apple Store and handing it to her.

She reached into the bag and took out a blue plastic tile. "What is this?"

"A tracker tag. Pending your approval, of course."

She held it up to the light. "You got me a tracking device?"

"To keep with you always. That way I'll know where to find you."

She looked at him angrily. "Have you been spying on me?"

"Spying all over the place." He cracked a smile, then realized she was serious. "Come on, Natalie, we just had that conversation. No. What are you talking about?"

She looked him in the eye. "Swear to me that Bill wasn't following me today."

"I swear to God. Jesus, how many times do I have to say it?"

"Because I can handle myself. You realize that, don't you?"

"I know you can, Natalie. But there's been another incident . . ."

"Another one?"

"Someone drove by the property last night and threw an object over the fence. The footage is dark and grainy, so it's hard to pin it down, and once again, they obscured their plates. I think we should take every precaution until this thing is resolved."

"Why didn't you tell me?"

"You weren't answering your phone, remember?" Hunter sighed. Then he studied her for a moment. "Let me help you, Natalie. Temporarily. Until this thing blows over."

She had to admit he was partly right. You never knew about people. And she didn't want to be put into the position of having to use her weapon again. That was to be avoided, if at all possible.

She could tell he wasn't going to drop it, either. It would probably eat away at him until she caved. "All right, I'll keep the tracking device on my key chain. But only until things quiet down."

"Thank you," he said with vast relief.

"What kind of item was it?" she asked.

"What's that?" He frowned.

"What did the guy throw over the fence this time?"

"Oh. An old, cracked porcelain doll's head from the 1800s. Not the body, just the head. And stuffed inside was a dried lizard tied up with what looks like human hair."

She drew back. "That's Wiccan dark magic."

"I know."

Hunter's personal security team was highly skilled at performing background checks on persistent reporters and serial-killer fanboys, screening visitors, and examining the mail. They used closed-circuit TV to monitor the house and grounds. There were alarms and panic buttons. The only thing missing, Hunter joked, was a designated safe room. And he was thinking about that.

Natalie was grateful for the protection. Living with the founder of Rose

Security Software had given her a chance to hide out from the press. She hadn't asked for the notoriety. She hadn't set out to solve two of the biggest serial murder cases in Upstate New York. It just happened. The only thing she knew was that she couldn't keep living this way.

She gave a reluctant nod. "Okay. For the time being."

"Good." He took the little bag and set it down on the table as if she were a special guest, an ambassador from a faraway land, and not his girlfriend. "Now," he said, "what do you feel like? There's leftovers in the fridge. Thin-crust pizza, pad thai, chicken masala."

She shook her head. "I'll grab something. I've got a lot of work to do."

He checked his watch. "Me, too, unfortunately. I've got to prep for back-to-back meetings in the morning. Big decisions coming up. Contracts to review. I'll be working in my study. Help yourself to whatever." He kissed her on the lips. "Don't stay up too late, sweetie," he told her and left.

# 45

Upstairs, Natalie stripped out of her clothes, put on clean sweats, then locked herself in the bathroom. She felt a surge of bad feelings wash over her and opened the medicine cabinet, then took down her prescription bottle of antianxiety meds.

It was empty. There were no pills left. Dr. Mazza had written her a refill, but Natalie didn't have time during her hectic week to pick it up from the pharmacy. She checked her watch. The pharmacy was closed.

She stared at her face in the mirror. She looked so pale and unhappy. Her heart was racing. She wasn't feeling well on several levels—physically, emotionally, psychologically. She tried to slow her breathing. It felt as if she were suffocating.

Natalie took a couple of ibuprofen with tap water. As she was brushing her hair, she couldn't stop thinking about the Shadow Girls. Tati Sanriquez was a beautiful and talented child, destined for greatness, a cheerleader, a popular A student, joining every club and team she possibly could. Some people called her a go-getter. But after losing both her parents in a tragic car accident, she ended up on the streets.

JoJo Barnes had always struggled with her future—"I'm going to open a ceramic store! I'm going to become a mathematician!"—but everything fell flat. JoJo's mother encouraged her to try different things—music, a business degree, teaching, something, anything—but all JoJo wanted to talk about was boys and marriage. Her head was filled with average things—and there was nothing wrong with average. When she got pregnant, her boyfriend paid for the abortion, but JoJo was never the same again. All the doctors told her the pain she felt was imaginary. She got into opioids and ended up on the streets.

From an early age, Harmony Sean Young was a great negotiator, a cool, calm, and collected middle kid. More practical and less adventurous than her big sister, she could've gone to college. She could've been anything she wanted to be. But something stopped her. She ended up selling her body on the streets to pay for her meth addiction.

It hurt Natalie to know these things.

She wanted to solve this abysmal puzzle, once and for all.

She looked in the mirror again and tried to brush a few strands of hair out of her eyes, and that was the moment when everything broke inside of her. Natalie crawled deep into herself and curled up in a ball on the bathroom floor and stopped speaking. She didn't scream or burst into tears. She didn't move a muscle. She was barely breathing.

Inside this dissociative stillness, Natalie's sister Grace stepped out of the shadows and took a seat on the side of the tub, her body drenched in river water and laced with seaweed. Her hair was wet. Her clothes were soaked. The fabric clung to her skin.

"Grace?" Natalie whispered. She knew she was looking at a specter— glassy eyes, wet mop of golden hair, lifeless skin, shock-white mouth. Grace's nails were painted raspberry pink, and the seaweed made paisley swirls over her bloodless cheeks. Natalie could count the delicate veins on her eyelids.

The shock of it—the cold, sharp shock—jabbed at Natalie. She reached out for Grace's blue hand, her mind spinning in circles, but the illusion abruptly washed away, and she could see that it was just a bath towel draped over the side of the tub.

*Willow, Grace, Bella, the Shadow Girls.*

She struggled to catch her breath, a sickening feeling. She just wanted to fall sleep and never wake up. She wanted to be Sleeping Beauty. *Wake me up when the nightmare's over.* And yet, exactly who would be her Prince Charming? Whose kisses could reanimate her frozen body? Was Prince Charming AWOL? Was he kissing some other beauty awake?

Hunter knocked on the bathroom door. "Natalie?" he said with gentle urgency from the other side. "Are you okay?"

The ball didn't budge.

"Natalie, it's been over an hour. Are you all right in there?"

She took a deep breath, then struggled to sit up. She leaned against the bathroom door and said, "Don't come in."

"I won't. I just need to know that everything's okay."

She sat there, feeling both grateful and resentful. She wanted to be rescued, and yet she didn't need saving. "You asked me how I'm feeling. Physically, I feel fine. But emotionally and psychologically, I'm seriously fucked up. I'm so fed up with everything, my anger exhausts me."

"I'm here. Do you understand? You're safe with me. Do you understand? You're safe in this house. What else can I do? How can I help?"

After a pause, she said, "She hated shellfish."

"Who?" Hunter asked.

"Bella."

There was another long pause. Then he said, "She did, huh?"

"She was afraid of public restrooms—she'd rather pee in her pants than use a public toilet. And she had a lucky bucket hat she never washed, because she was afraid it would get ruined in the dryer, and then she'd be unlucky forever. I don't know why I keep thinking about her all the time." Her eyes fogged with tears. "I'm so tired, Hunter. I'm so fucking tired I can barely breathe."

"Hey," he said. "Everything's going to be better in the morning."

She shook her head slowly. "It doesn't feel that way."

She could hear him shifting positions as he leaned against the door on the other side. She pictured them seated back-to-back, with something solid in between them.

"You know how cruel kids can be?" he said, settling against the door. "How siblings can hurt one another without ever meaning to? Well, my brother used to be terrified of the dumbwaiter, because it made such a racket. There were no shock absorbers back then, so when it struck the top of the shaft, there was a loud bang. And the ropes were loose, so they'd slap against the walls, making a poltergeist sound. The rusty pulleys squealed like shrieking mice whenever the cart traveled up and down, and the old electric motor made a low rumble like distant thunder. So Nesbitt figured there must be monsters inside. I tried to explain to him how it worked, but he wasn't convinced . . ."

She shivered and hugged her knees to her chest, drawing into herself.

"Anyway, when I was twelve and Nesbitt was eight, I had this brilliant idea," he went on. "I decided to prove to him once and for all that there were no monsters in the dumbwaiter, so one day I shoved Nesbitt inside and closed the door. He was traumatized, of course. He immediately started screaming and banging for help. Only the maid was home during this time, and she was downstairs doing the laundry. When she heard the racket, she ran over to the dumbwaiter and pressed the button, and the dumbwaiter traveled down into the basement with Nesbitt still trapped inside. He thought he was going to hell. He was a complete wreck by the time she pulled him out, and she tried to comfort him, but he wouldn't stop freaking out. She knew it was all my fault, but I denied having anything to do with it. I lied, because I didn't want to be the bad guy. Because in my mind, I was only trying to help."

"Poor Nesbitt," Natalie said.

"I know. I felt terrible about it," Hunter confessed, "especially when he became more convinced than ever that there were monsters inside the dumbwaiter. Great. So the next time we were home unsupervised, I crawled in there myself and shut the door, hoping to prove to him once and for all that there was nothing to it. But then I got locked inside, and it was frankly terrifying. As it turns out, the more darkness there is, the more your primal brain rips a hole in your heart. It's evolution, it's genetics—this fear of the dark. And I'm only sharing this with you because of the riddle."

Natalie's heart skipped a beat. She knew exactly what he was talking about. Right before he took his own life, Justin Fowler had tried to warn her about a bigger evil engulfing Burning Lake.

*"You realize this isn't the end of it, don't you?"*

*"What are you talking about?"* she asked.

*"You're not seeing the bigger picture, Detective."* His pain was palpable.

*"What bigger picture?"*

*"You have no idea what you're dealing with here."*

*"Stop talking in riddles! Tell me what the fuck you mean!"*

*"You want a riddle? Here's one. The more of it there is of this, the less you can see."*

*"I don't know. What?"*

*"Darkness."*

That was when Justin pulled a pistol out of his pocket, stuck the barrel in his mouth, and blew his brains out all over the virgin snow.

"I've been thinking about that riddle you told me," Hunter said softly from the other side of the door, and Natalie was afraid to ask where this was going.

"It's such a bleak message," he said in his most comforting voice. "Like a terrible curse. And you took it to mean that whatever is lying in wait for you out there is full of malevolence. But I think darkness can also be a force for good."

Natalie frowned. "How?"

"Because, and I honestly believe this . . . the more darkness there is, the *more* you can see. When I was trapped in the dumbwaiter, it was pitch-dark, and I couldn't see a thing, except for my own ignorance, my own selfishness, the crassness in my heart. And after I calmed down, I figured a way out. There's this little lever, a latch on the inside of the door. You can let yourself out. Anyway, I apologized to Nesbitt, but he was more terrified than ever of the dumbwaiter, because in his eyes, the monster had gobbled me up. So . . . how did I cure my brother of his irrational fear?"

There was a long beat of silence.

"I don't know," she said, impossibly sad.

"I asked our chef, Teddy, to make Nesbitt's favorite dessert in the whole world—chocolate bread pudding with real whipped cream—and had him deliver it to my brother on the third floor, via the dumbwaiter. Nesbitt had to confront his worst fear if he wanted his bread pudding. And he did. Every night for the rest of the year. That's how he got cured."

Natalie took a shaky breath, tears trickling down her cheeks.

"Bread pudding cures everything."

"You think so?"

"I know so."

She wiped her face, got up from the floor, and opened the door.

# 46

L et's get you to bed," Hunter said. "You're exhausted."

She stood for a moment, feeling a static discharge on the back of her neck as his arm tensed around her waist.

"Come on. One step at a time. I've got you."

Hunter used all of his persuasive techniques to get her to shed her clothes like breadcrumbs. He helped her put on her favorite oversized BLPD T-shirt and a pink pair of boxers, and then guided her into bed.

They didn't make love. "I'll watch over you," he promised. They fell asleep in each other's arms, and Natalie woke up after midnight, feeling like a dreamer waking up inside another person's reality. The rest of the world seemed sterilized and dead to her.

Hunter's side of the bed was empty. She thought she heard the *ding* of an oven timer beyond the closed door of their master bedroom. She got up and walked into the dimly lit, second-floor hallway. "Hunter?"

The house smelled like a French bakery. A warm, melty chocolate smell.

Something hummed and clicked. It was the dumbwaiter down the other end of the corridor. Her arms prickled with goose bumps as she padded toward the dumbwaiter in her bare feet.

The dumbwaiter stopped with a loud thump. Sometimes, when they had guests over, Hunter liked to demonstrate how it worked as part of the house's historic charm. The turn-of-the-century lift was hidden behind a carved mahogany door, and inside was a wonky wooden cart fitted with gears and pulleys that hauled food or linens to the upper rooms through a narrow shaft. The contraption used to be controlled manually with ropes and chains, Hunter explained to their guests, but then, in the 1930s, an electric motor was installed, and now it was operated by pushing a big red button.

Now Natalie opened the dumbwaiter's carved mahogany door. Inside was a tray with a silver serving bowl of chocolate bread pudding, a small dish of whipped cream, a china plate, a dessert spoon, and a folded linen napkin.

She didn't react. She didn't know what to think.

Actually, she thought it was pretty creepy.

The bread pudding was steaming in its serving bowl, and a delicious smell wafted toward her—semisweet chocolate, brown sugar, butter, brandy, vanilla beans, and a hint of espresso.

"What do you think?" Hunter asked from the second-story landing.

She turned. She hadn't heard him come up. "You made this just now?" she asked, her stomach clenching. She breathed a little faster.

"Try it. Go on," he said, leaning against the wall and watching her.

Natalie reached for the tray, put it down on the carpeted floor, then sat with her legs crossed. She dished out a heap of pudding, added a dollop of whipped cream, and took a bite.

"Well?"

"It's delicious." Suddenly, she was famished.

She wolfed down the rest of her dessert. The spoon made greedy clinking sounds against the china plate, *clink-clink*. She could feel the aromatic heat emanating from the bread pudding while Hunter watched her eat. She froze, staring numbly at his face. She became hypnotized, pulled along, dragged under. She wanted to explain that she would never stop being a detective, and that she wanted to solve this case more than anything in the world, to find out what was inside the riddle. She wanted to run away from Hunter and his stories, as far away as she could, but felt herself being sucked into the undulating heart of his oversized, personal narrative.

"You've got chocolate on your lips," he said, approaching her with his hand held out, as if she were a wild animal.

"Don't come any closer," she hissed.

He crossed his arms. Surprised. "I won't," he said.

"I need some space," she explained, ignoring his wounded look.

"Okay, I'll go sleep in the guest room." He was trying to show her that he could be sensitive to her needs—and that he wasn't confused by this sudden alienation.

"Thanks." Her breathing came out quick and irregular as she licked the spoon.

Now his phone chirped loudly, interrupting this strange interlude between them.

Hunter answered crisply, "Yes? What is it?" He glanced back at her. "Yeah, okay." He closed his phone. "I have to make a few calls. I'll see you in the morning, okay?"

She nodded.

He paused. "I'm sorry. Was it too much? The bread pudding?"

"A little."

"I thought it would be comforting . . . I'm sorry. But I don't want you to be afraid of anything, Natalie. I'm here. I'll take care of you. I'd do anything for you. You get that, right?"

"Yeah," she said irritably. She got it. She more than got it.

"All right." He stopped talking, sensing he was only digging himself a deeper hole.

Natalie dropped the spoon on the tray, left it there on the carpet, and shuffled down the hallway toward the master bedroom. She closed the door and locked it behind her. She didn't want to talk to him anymore. She didn't want to look at him.

She pressed her ear to the door. She could sense him standing there in the dark. She imagined him rolling his eyes or shaking his head. Natalie heard him pick up the tray, dishes rattling as he headed back to the stairs. She heard him pause—ever so briefly—in front of her door. Then he moved quietly down the hallway, and the stair treads creaked under his weight as he took the tray down to the kitchen.

# 47

Early mornings were cold and dark in March. Natalie felt chilled to the bone. She stood inside the dining room, sipping her coffee and gazing out the French doors at the woods. She was jumpy. She told herself to calm down.

Last night there had been another snowfall, but now it was dissipating. The ground was lacy blue in the predawn moonlight. She caught a movement out of the corner of her eye and stared into the dense, pitchy forest that surrounded the house, wondering if someone was out there looking in at her. But it was just the wind shaking patches of snow off the trees.

Natalie relished the quiet of early mornings before Hunter got up, and today was no exception. She put down her mug and opened the box she'd taken out of the trunk of her car—one of the boxes she and Luke had salvaged from the crawl space of Violet Hawke's attic.

It was five in the morning, and Natalie had been sorting through documents for over an hour now. What she'd found so far was remarkable. It seemed that Violet had once worked for Davidson Realty, where she met her husband, Victor. Davidson Realty shut down in 2001, two years after Victor died of thyroid cancer. Shortly after his death, Violet got a job with another real estate company called Caden Walsh Realty. When that company closed in 2010, Violet started working as a paid consultant for a third firm, this one called Northwood Properties. Violet passed away in 2015.

When Natalie typed all three names into the search engine, she discovered they were linked to an investment firm called Bluebird Real Estate Investments, or BREI. The name sounded vaguely familiar. Ten minutes later, she had identified the principals of BREI as Oliver and Serena Chabert.

Shock was not the word for it.

Natalie felt electrified by the news. Stunned with a cattle prod. She'd met the older couple several times before at Hunter's parties, and she liked them better than any of his other business associates. They were warm and wise and seemed genuinely interested in her. It felt like a hammer blow to the heart.

And yet, she had to check her trepidation, because it could be a coincidence. After all, they would've had to invest in a multitude of upstate real estate companies to become as powerful as they were. And if you dug deeply enough, surely you would find connections between plenty of surprising people you wouldn't think were related in any way whatsoever.

The next thing Natalie did was to collate Violet's bank account statements into separate piles—she and Victor once had twelve separate accounts between them, in six different banks—and now Natalie was assembling the pieces.

Soon she noticed a pattern of transactions—what appeared to be a money-laundering operation, where Violet Hawke was paid consultant fees through a vassal company, which she then deposited into separate LLC bank accounts. From these business accounts, she made payments to independent contractors, and among the independent contractors were two names Natalie recognized—Randolph S. Holmes and Peter Murphy. Ever since the early 1990s for Holmes, and as recently as 2013 for Murphy.

Okay, this she couldn't chalk up to coincidence.

Natalie brushed the hair out of her eyes and stood there, stunned. Inside this box were answers she'd been seeking for over a year now. Her heart raced as she surrendered herself to this dark knowledge.

But there was more to learn. After tracing the Hawkes' various bank statements, Natalie found out that Violet had paid both of Randy's settlements via the law firm of Fleming, Abercromby & Maddox, totaling seventy-five thousand and sixty thousand each. There were also payments made to Samuel Winston—the Crow Killer. Violet's grandson. These payments seemed to sync up with the dates that a handful of tourists had gone missing in the Adirondacks, according to Natalie's extensive knowledge of the case.

Samuel Hawke Winston had abducted and murdered dozens of homeless people, along with a handful of tourists visiting the Adirondack Mountains, and his crimes went back several decades. Natalie had never been able to figure out why he'd gone after the tourists, since his predilection was for homeless people. Now she wondered if he'd been paid to do so.

At the bottom of the box, she found an unmarked folder that held dozens of newspaper articles inside, all concerning the disappearances of those tourists—a handful of upstate businessmen who were potential rivals of Bluebird Real Estate Investments. In the same file, she found newspaper clippings about the various acquisitions of BREI in the months and years after the businessmen had disappeared in the Adirondacks.

Natalie sat back, stunned by this gold mine of information.

No wonder Murphy had tried so desperately to confiscate it from Violet's house.

It appeared obvious to her now—although it wasn't what you'd call conclusive proof—that BREI had hired people to operate outside the law. Their crimes quite possibly included such things as money laundering, criminal profiteering, bribery, fraud, manipulation, even murder. If what she surmised was true—that BREI was hiring criminals to do their dirty work and eliminate the competition—then this was the kind of case that a D.A. could try under RICO laws. It appeared to be a terrible conspiracy that reached across generations.

No wonder they had killed Veronica Manes. She'd been nibbling around the corners of this network of evil and corruption, threatening to expose it. This was such mind-blowing information, Natalie couldn't sit on it for another minute. She had to tell Luke.

Footsteps overhead.

Natalie froze, the hairs on her arms bristling.

Hunter was up. He couldn't see any of this. Serena and Oliver were his friends and business partners. They couldn't know that the police were in possession of such explosive information. She jammed everything back inside the dusty box and closed the lid just as Hunter came shuffling down the stairs, talking on his phone.

"Yeah, okay, Martin, let's deal with this later." He pocketed his phone and stood in the doorway, smiling sheepishly at her. "How'd you sleep?"

"Pretty good. You?"

"Not great."

She took the box off the table and set it down on the floor. She smiled. His voice was low and husky. His eyes were bloodshot from lack of sleep.

"Natalie, are we going to be okay?" he asked with a baleful look.

"Yeah, we're fine," she lied.

His expression darkened. "Please don't blow me off like that."

"I'm not," she said dismissively. "Everything's fine. I have to go." She picked up her box and went to leave, but Hunter blocked her path. It felt as if he were about to sweep her up in his arms—and yet he didn't touch her.

"I'm sorry about last night," he said. "I know it was over the top."

"It's okay," she said lightly. She didn't like lying to him. She should've ended it last night.

He took a step forward. He shook his head. "Can't we please talk about this?"

"Yes," she agreed. "Later."

"When?"

"Tonight."

He nodded slowly. "Okay." He stepped aside. "We'll talk about it tonight," he said, his eyes full of hope.

# 48

Natalie took the quickest route across town to Luke's house. Her hands wouldn't stop shaking. She could barely breathe. She didn't like this feeling of emotional vulnerability. She wanted to be stronger.

A light snow was falling. She hoped another big storm wasn't headed their way. She desperately wanted to dig up Randy Holmes's backyard soon and make sure that each of the Shadow Girls got a proper burial.

She parked in Luke's driveway and got out of her car. She impatiently rang the bell and knocked on the door. She barely waited for him to swing the door open before she burst inside and said, "You're not going to believe what I just found . . ."

Luke watched her with veiled warmth. It was always strange to see him out of his work clothes, which consisted of a suit and tie. This morning he wore a pale blue flannel shirt, well-worn jeans, and black running shoes. The shirt matched the pale blue of his eyes.

"Natalie?" a female voice said behind her.

She spun around.

Rainie was standing in the kitchen doorway, looking radiant in a white blouse with a Peter Pan collar, a tweed blazer, and dark tailored pants. She gave off a fresh-scrubbed, country-club vibe.

"Oh, I'm sorry!" Natalie said, blushing fiercely. "Am I interrupting . . . ?"

"Don't be silly," Rainie said. "Would you like some coffee?"

"No, thanks. I'm here to talk about the case," she apologized. "Something urgent has come up, and I had to inform Luke, so . . . here I am."

"I'll go upstairs," Rainie said, "and let you two talk shop."

Luke nodded, and Rainie smiled and hurried up the carpeted staircase.

Once they were alone, Luke looked at Natalie and said, "Have a seat."

She sat down. "For fuck's sake, I'm sorry. I didn't realize," she blurted. "I didn't mean to barge in on you like that."

He took the seat opposite her. His face was guarded. A flush crawled up his neck. He leaned back in his chair and asked, "What did you want to tell me, Natalie?"

A cold wind rattled the old-fashioned windows, but the blazing fire in the hearth warmed the modest house.

"I was looking through one of the boxes we found in Violet's attic," she said, then proceeded to tell him about the Chaberts and their connection to the other real estate companies, and the proof she'd found that Violet Hawke had paid both settlements. She told him about the businessmen who'd been killed in the Adirondacks, and the business transactions that had followed to benefit the BREI.

Luke let the information sink in. They both knew how earth-shattering this could be if proved true. When she was done, he shifted slightly in his seat and said, "Okay, we need to officially go through every scrap of evidence in those boxes and build a solid case. I'll approve whatever overtime you need. This is promising stuff, Natalie, but we'll need to definitively link it all together before we can act on it."

Natalie nodded solemnly. There were faint violet shadows beneath his intelligent blue eyes, which indicated he hadn't been sleeping well. The stresses of the job appeared to be piling up on him, and she didn't want to add to that burden.

"As for the boxes," he told her, "let's get them down to the station now. Mike Anderson's in charge of cataloging the evidence in conference room C. Pick a team to work with and start sorting through the material. We need to carefully document and track every single transaction between these folks. This is a huge dislocating piece of information, if true, and it points to a bigger conspiracy. We need to develop a working theory ASAP."

"Okay, I'll get right on it." Her phone rang, startling them both. "Lockhart," she answered.

"Hey, it's me," Brandon said. "I've got some interesting information for you. Turns out the surgeon who performed the operation on Randy's balls tells me it was a *voluntary castration*."

"What?"

"Voluntary. Castration."

"Why would a legitimate doctor do such a thing?"

"Well, for one thing, he never told a soul about it until yesterday."

"But how could he get away with something like that?" Natalie asked.

"Dr. Fulmer didn't graduate at the top of his class, to put it mildly, and he didn't work for a prestigious hospital or anything like that. He worked at a third-rate clinic for thirty years, and now that he's getting up in age— dying of heart disease, he tells me—he wanted to confess. Get it off his chest."

"And he got paid under the table to do this?"

"Back in 2009, he received a boatload of money to perform the ball-sectomy. But the cover-up is always worse than the crime, right? He said it was fairly easy to lie about the tests, because he was paid in cash, and so there were no insurance forms to fill out or anything like that. He says he used another man's cancer diagnosis and X-rays, and never got caught, although he kept expecting somebody to come after him. But they never did. So he forgot about it and lived his fullest life as a medical quack and total scumbag."

"What was the reason Randy gave for wanting the operation?" she asked.

"He complained about his destructive sex drive. And the doc says there was a woman with Randy—he described Violet Hawke to a tee. Anyway, this woman appeared to be in charge. She did most of the talking and was the source of the cash. The doc says Randy did whatever he was told, and the operation went off beautifully."

"Wow. Is that it?"

"That's all she wrote."

"Good work, Brandon." She hung up and told Luke about it, and they both wondered at the bizarreness of it all. Then she said, "I'll bring those boxes over to the station house and set up a team. Then I'd like to talk to Peyton Wolanski again. We need to find out if he recognizes any of these people—Violet Hawke, the Chaberts, Peter Murphy. If we can show that they visited Randy at his residence, that would be another significant connection between them."

"Sounds good." Luke checked his watch. "I've got a conference call with the chief in ten minutes. We all done here?"

"Yeah." She stood up, then hesitated. "Luke . . ."

"I'll see you out," he said in a formal, distanced way. Sounding so un-Luke-like.

He showed her to the door, but then they both paused, a tender silence lingering between them.

"Listen, be careful, Natalie. If even half of what you found out today is true, then things are about to ramp up to eleven. We don't know who else might be involved. I'd like you to get a burner phone. I'll get one, too. That way, we can have a direct, unencumbered line of communication where we can raise our suspicions without having anything on record."

"Okay." She tilted her face toward him. "Luke—"

"Don't say it," he interrupted.

"Don't say what?"

"Whatever it was you were about to say." He stared at her solemnly. "We don't need to talk about that. Ever."

"Yeah, I get it." She nodded.

Luke said nothing. His eyes were blank. She wanted to slap him.

"Fuck," she muttered.

"What?" he said loudly. Concerned. Startled.

"Nothing. I'll catch you later." She left as quickly as she could, but then she thought she heard him mutter, "Fuck," behind her.

# 49

During the winter months in Upstate New York, snow slowly accumulated layer upon layer, until the drifts reclined against the sides of buildings and buried the cars and trash cans under a dirty white blanket. By mid-February, the mail carrier would have to dig out the mailboxes with his gloved hands. In March, everyone prayed that another big nor'easter wouldn't sweep through at the last minute and bury half of April.

So far, so good, Natalie thought. It was a sunny afternoon, with clear blue skies. Last night's snow was already melting. She escorted Peyton Wolanski into the interview room at the police station. "Thanks for coming in," she said. "I know you're busy. Coke, Pepsi, coffee . . . ?"

"I'd like a glass of water," he said, looking less put-together than he had the other day. His face held onto a sheen of sweat and his tailored suit was slightly rumpled.

"Have a seat." She turned on the video recorder. "I'll be right back."

She went to fetch a bottled water, leaving Peyton alone inside the oppressive room. It was windowless and sparsely furnished, with a table, two chairs, and a camera on a tripod. It was more than a little intimidating. There were techniques you could use to relax a witness or suspect and catch them off guard, but Natalie preferred to go in the opposite direction and just be honest with him.

She came back into the room, handed him a bottled water, and said, "Let me tell you why you're here. I'd like you to identify any of these people, if you can." She spread out several photographs—of Oliver and Serena Chabert, Detective Murphy, Violet Hawke, and Samuel Winston.

Peyton unscrewed the bottle and drank. Then he leaned over the photographs and said, "I know this one—it's the Crow Killer, right? I've seen him a lot on the news."

"Did he ever visit your uncle?"

"No." Peyton tapped Detective Murphy's picture. "Also, this guy. He's been in the news, as well. Detective Murphy. They're still looking for him."

"Right. Did you ever see him at your uncle's house?"

"No."

"What about the last two pictures?"

Peyton squinted. "I've never seen them," he said of the Chaberts. "But this woman looks familiar."

"Okay," she said, taking a seat. "Tell me about her."

He shrugged. He took a few more gulps of water. "I saw her a couple of times at my uncle's place. Once she was leaving just as my mom and sister and I arrived. Another time, she and Uncle Randy were talking in the front yard, then she drove off."

"Did you overhear their conversation?"

"No."

"Did he say who she was?"

"Sorry, no." He shook his head. "Look, and this is the God's honest truth, Detective. I knew absolutely nothing about the dungeon in my uncle's basement, okay? Zero. We never went down there. He wouldn't let us."

"So he forbid you to go down into the basement?"

"It's more like . . . you can hang out in the living room or the kitchen, and you can play in the backyard, but the rest of the house is off-limits." For the first time, he became evasive, drumming his fingers on the tabletop and looking around. There was no place to rest your eyes, except on the detective seated opposite you.

"And you said he could be a nice guy?"

"Yeah, he helped my mom out a lot after Dad died. Uncle Randy would have backyard barbeques in the summer, and around the holidays we'd sing carols and open our Secret Santa gifts together. I thought he was pretty cool when I was a kid, because he built this ant colony once. I got to feed the ants grains of sugar and watch them scamper around."

She sensed he was holding back information. "What about Posey Revelli?" she asked, and his eyes widened. "Did you know about the settlement?"

"Yeah. So what?" he said defensively.

"She was assaulted by your uncle at a party, and you were there. This was back in 2007. You were—what? Sixteen, seventeen?"

He shook his head, but then his shoulders slumped as if he'd been holding his breath. "Yeah, I remember what happened. She said my uncle molested her."

"And?"

"And I believed her."

"You did? Why?"

"I told you, he was a bit of an oddball. But I didn't take it seriously at the time."

"Why not?"

He shrugged. "Everybody knew he acted inappropriately sometimes, especially when he was drunk. You just sort of steered clear of him."

"Did you know there was another settlement the following year?"

He looked at her and said, "You mean with Bella?"

Natalie felt the shock in her bones, but she somehow managed to keep her voice steady. "Yes, that one."

"My uncle apologized and said he was drunk."

"When was this?"

"At a Christmas party at his house."

"Who else was there?"

"A bunch of my friends, my sister and her friends. My mom. Uncle Randy. He let us play loud music and everything. It was pretty cool, until . . ."

"What happened?"

"Bella said he grabbed her. She went to get a Coke from the kitchen, and he cornered her and grabbed her, then tried to pull her down into the basement with him, but she got away and screamed bloody murder. Uncle Randy immediately apologized and said he was drunk. But Bella insisted that he tried to take her down into the basement."

"Did she call the police?"

"No, my mother smoothed things over."

"So your mother convinced Bella not to do anything?"

"Yeah, like I said, she was protective of Randy. He was her younger brother."

"Then what happened?"

Peyton shrugged. "Lawyers got involved. Bella's father was offered a settlement, and as far as I know, he took it. Then the whole thing disappeared."

"What do you mean, disappeared?"

"Just that . . . she never mentioned it again."

"Was this around the same time you saw Violet Hawke at your uncle's place? The woman in the picture?"

"Could be. I don't remember."

"But you knew about the settlement?"

"Bella told me a little while later that her father got a lot of money, and she was supposed to keep her mouth shut. She said she was going to take the money and travel around Europe, but her father wanted to use it for her education instead. She was pretty pissed off. I guess she got into that music school . . ."

"The Harrington Brock Conservatory?"

"Yeah, I think so." He shrugged. "But listen, I honestly can't believe my uncle would be capable of doing something like that. I mean, he had a pretty rough upbringing, so maybe that's what was wrong with him. When I was a kid, he helped my family out quite a bit. He'd come around and repair things that needed fixing inside the house. He'd mow the lawn or build a shed out back, clear the brush or shovel out the driveway, stuff like that. He could be a nice guy. It's almost as if he had two sides to him."

"What was the other side like?"

"He had this weird way of greeting you, like when Darla and I were kids, his way of saying 'hello' was to sort of slap my face a few times, then ruffle my hair. I hated it. He'd pinch Darla's cheek until she shrieked. He'd fake-punch me in the gut, and then laugh when I jumped away. He thought it was hilarious. You know, one of those jovial, over-the-top bozos. I think he had a rough upbringing. That's what Mom always said."

"Rough how?" Natalie asked.

"His father—my grandfather, who I never got to meet—was apparently very strict, according to my mom. There was this story about Randy being locked in the cellar for days at a time. I think they didn't feed him, so he'd end up eating worms or bugs down there. And he had bad acne as a kid, which made him an outcast. After my grandfather died, Uncle Randy and my mom were left in the care of a religious aunt, who was also very strict. But my mother grew up to be a good person, whereas Randy could be such an asshole sometimes. He'd show Darla and me horror movies, then laugh when we got scared. Those slasher movies gave us nightmares."

Natalie waited a beat, then asked, "Do you think your uncle had something to do with Bella's disappearance in 2009?"

He took another swig of bottled water and wiped his mouth with his hand. "Jesus, I hope not," he said.

"And your sister? Did she have any unpleasant encounters with Randy?"

He nodded reluctantly. "Just once."

"What happened?"

"He was fumigating our house one summer. We had termites. Uncle Randy was preparing the house for the fumigation, and Darla was helping my mom clean up the place, and she was about to head out to go to a movie with her friends when he touched her inappropriately. He'd been drinking."

"What happened?"

"Nothing. She left for college shortly after and stayed away. She never felt comfortable around him again."

"How old was she?"

"Eighteen."

"I'd like to talk to her," Natalie said.

"She got married and moved to California. Her name's Darla Hagel now."

Natalie waited a beat, then asked, "There's nothing about any of this in Bella's missing-person file. Why didn't you tell the police about your uncle after Bella went missing?"

He took another swig of water, then put the bottle down and said, "Mom told us not to breathe a word of it to anyone. And the police never asked, so I figured it was better to let sleeping dogs lie."

"So the police never asked about your uncle?"

He shook his head. "I thought maybe Nesbitt Rose had something to do with it at the time. I thought something bad must've happened to her. I volunteered for the search and put posters up all over town. We combed the woods for weeks . . ."

Natalie nodded. She remembered.

"But then, around the middle of August, when the first letter arrived, the police called everything off. They called off the search, and everyone in the volunteer group was pretty upset. We couldn't figure out why Bella would let the whole town suffer like that . . ."

"Let me ask you again," Natalie said, leaning forward slightly. "Do you think your uncle could've had anything to do with Bella's disappearance?"

"But she didn't disappear."

"Theoretically."

"Honestly?" he said, looking down at his hands. "No."

"Even after you knew about those three incidents? Posey, Bella, and Darla, your sister?"

His face flushed. "I know it sounds lame, but I never suspected him of anything like that. I mean, I couldn't imagine it. He apologized profusely every time it happened and promised to quit drinking. It was a pervy thing to do, for sure. My friends used to call him Handsy Randy. But Mom insisted he was harmless."

"She did?"

"Yeah, she told Darla to forgive him. And then he got cancer. Mom believed in forgive and forget." He checked his watch. "Listen, I have to get back to work."

"Just a few more questions," she said.

He put the cap back on the water bottle. "I hope this was helpful."

"It was, but I have to ask . . . were you able to verify where you were the night that Bella Striver disappeared in 2009?"

"Why?" He squinted at her as if she'd just spoken in tongues. "Like I told you, I was probably getting high with my buddies in Haymarket Field."

"Could you write down the names of your friends for me?"

"Their names?" he repeated irritably. "What for?"

"I'd like to talk to them and see if they remember anything."

"For something that happened over a dozen years ago? You think they're going to remember where they were that night?"

"It was high school graduation. That's a big deal in a small town. Everyone's in a celebratory mood. Lots of parties. Can't you remember?"

"Look, this is ridiculous," he said. "Bella wrote and said she was fine, right? That's what it said in the newspaper. She ran away, right?"

"Peyton," she said, "did you or your uncle have anything to do with Bella's disappearance?"

"What?" he exclaimed. "What the hell is this?" He suddenly realized where the interview was headed. His eyes widened. "I guess this is the point where I ask to talk to my lawyer."

"Just answer the question. Did you or your uncle have anything to do with her disappearance?" she repeated stubbornly.

He took out his phone. "Yeah, okay. I'm calling my lawyer and you can talk to him." He stood up. "Jesus, I was trying to be helpful, and you're twisting my words all around. I'm free to go, right? Am I free to go?"

"Yes," she said.

He walked out the door.

# 50

Natalie drove across town to Murray's Halloween Costumes and parked in the sprawling lot behind the old warehouse. It was early in the afternoon, and the sunlight shone in her eyes as she gazed at the 80,000-square-foot redbrick building with its huge hand-painted signs in the windows: *50% Off! Winter Sale!* The store had very few customers at this hour.

Today's revelations had knocked her sideways, and now she struggled to form an overarching theory. All she knew for sure was that the seeds of evil had been planted a long time ago, probably in 1975 at John F. Kennedy High School.

The news about the Chaberts was deeply disturbing, and she sincerely hoped it wasn't true, for Hunter's sake. Her mind was a maze of connections and links, and the more she thought about it, the more disturbing and unbelievable it became. Hard to imagine.

Natalie reached into the Target shopping bag on the passenger seat beside her and took out the burner phone she'd just purchased. She didn't know who to trust at this point, and so, on her way over to Murray's, she'd stopped at a Target outside of town and bought a prepaid mobile phone with cash. She'd asked the clerk to activate the phone using the SIM card number. That way, she didn't have to give up any personal information. No credit cards, no debit card, no ID.

Now she plugged the Nokia into the car's USB port and set it aside on the passenger seat. Most burner phones were lightweight and had excellent battery life, so this one should last for days on a single charge. She wasn't expecting to use it all that much. It was a just-in-case purchase in order to keep certain calls private, since there was a chance that, if Murphy had been so easily compromised, then perhaps some other officer in the department might also have been corrupted. If Natalie decided to speculate and share her suspicions with Luke, she didn't want to leave any record behind.

Now she took out her iPhone and called Luke at the station.

"Natalie, what's up?" he answered.

"I got a burner phone."

"Great. I'll pick up one on my way home tonight."

"Who do you trust besides the guys in the CIU?" she asked Luke. "Do you trust Gossett?"

"I don't know him well enough."

"Me neither. For the time being, let's keep the circle small—just the seven of us," she said. "Once we know more about Murphy's motives or something definitive about those documents, we can pull in more people, including Assistant Chief Gossett."

"Agreed."

She gazed out her windshield at the old converted warehouse. "Peyton Wolanski says he never suspected his uncle of anything nefarious, but he just admitted that he knew about the two settlements. And guess who Randy assaulted in 2008?"

"No idea."

"Bella Striver."

"Seriously?" Luke said, his voice rising with incredulity.

"Randy assaulted at least three eighteen-year-old girls that we know of—Posey in 2007, Bella in 2008, and Darla Wolanski, Peyton's sister, in 2009."

There was a pause. Then Luke asked, "Do you think Peyton has told you everything he knows?"

"I thought he was being pretty honest with me. But then he lawyered up."

"Shit."

"It's my fault. I kept pushing him about Bella. In the meantime, Brandon found out that the Revellis are deep in debt. Credit cards and a mortgage. Posey can't play her viola due to her hand injury, so they're going through a rough patch."

"Okay, but would that make them desperate enough to try to squeeze more hush money out of Randy?"

"It's possible, right? If you think about it, Posey has a very good reason to hate him. And she uses the same brand of strings Randy was strangled with. Her husband drives a Chevy Equinox. Neither one of them has an alibi for the crucial window of time that night. Where were they? It's possible Tony convinced his wife to blackmail Randy, and they went to see him at the warehouse, but then things went sideways. The guys are still gathering traffic cam info, but it'll take a while to collect and process."

"Did Bella ever mention Randy Holmes to you?"

"No. Nothing," Natalie said. "Probably because those were the terms of the settlement. It bought her silence. However, I know she wasn't happy about the prospect of going to the music conservatory. She was rebelling against her father, and what she really wanted to do was travel that summer. She wanted to see the world. She asked me to go with her at one point, but I didn't take it seriously. I thought she really wanted to be a musician, despite her father's suffocating ambition for her. Anyway, I fully intended to go to college in the fall, and I always figured Bella would, too.

"But it's incredibly suspicious that she had an encounter with Randy in 2008, and then one year later she disappeared. Peyton kept reminding me that she didn't disappear, but now I'm not so sure. Remember those Polaroids with the same, identical white wall behind her? It's entirely possible that her kidnapper might've forced her to write those letters. He could've taken those Polaroids of her as 'proof' she was still alive. If there's any chance that Randy abducted her, then we need to examine all the walls down in the dungeon and look for a match."

"I thought you looked at the walls?"

"I only asked Max to examine one spot in the living room. Besides, I think we need to hire an expert to take a look at all of those walls."

"We may not need to hire an outside contractor," Luke told her. "Lenny's working out the logistics for tearing up the basement floor, and he's still processing all the trace you found in the dungeon and the van—prints, hairs, fibers, semen, blood. He's including Bella Striver's prints, dentals, and DNA along with the Shadow Girls, so we should know something definitive about the victims within a month. Once we've excavated the grounds, then hopefully we'll have our answers."

"In the meantime," Natalie said, "I've asked Lenny to reprocess the envelopes and letters Bella sent to her father and me for prints or potential DNA—anything we can trace back to Randy. If he managed to kidnap Bella in 2009, and then forced her to write those letters to get the police off his trail, then he might've licked the stamps and handled the envelopes. That could tell us more."

"Good thinking."

"In the meantime, I'll call the Revellis' lawyer and try to set up a formal interview with them. I've also asked Brandon to look into the background of Peyton's sister, Darla—any anger management issues, mental health issues, DUIs, traffic tickets, pending bankruptcies."

"Sounds good, Natalie."

"Right now, though," she said, checking her watch, "I have to pick up my prescription from the pharmacy. Then I'll head over to the station and help Mike process the documents."

"Okay," he said. "And don't worry. We've got a lot of evidence to sort through, but that's a good problem to have. I have a feeling we'll solve this thing sooner rather than later."

"Let's hope so," she said.

There was a long awkward pause.

Then Luke said crisply, "I think that covers everything. Good job, Natalie. Call me if you need me."

Before she could say anything, he hung up.

# 51

By the time Natalie got to the pharmacy, the clouds had blown away and the sun was shining brilliantly in the sky. It felt as if Burning Lake had finally woken up from its winter hibernation. People were out shopping and walking their dogs. Spring was coming. Hope existed.

She found a parking space in front of the corner pharmacy, a small rectangular family-owned business with narrow aisles and neatly stacked shelves. She handed the pharmacist her prescription, then picked up a shopping basket and filled it with random items—moisturizer, deodorant, a new lipstick that looked pretty.

"Detective Lockhart?" the pharmacist said.

She listened patiently while he went over the instructions, swiped her card, put everything in a paper bag, and handed her the receipt.

She snagged the little bag and went outside.

Maples and oaks swayed in the breeze. She was reaching into her shoulder bag to fish out her keys when her iPhone rang. She answered, "Detective Lockhart."

"Hello, Natalie, this is Peter."

She froze. Her sense of reality flipped over. "Murphy?"

"We need to talk. Can I trust you?"

"Yes," she said quickly. "Where are you?"

"I need to know you aren't being followed, so I'm going to give you some instructions. Stick to them closely, or this isn't going to happen. Agreed?"

"Okay," she said, fear seizing her. She stood in the middle of the sidewalk, paralyzed, unable to move forward.

"Drive to one-eleven Coyote Lane. Come alone and unarmed. Don't call the police. Do not contact any friends or colleagues at the station. You have fifteen minutes." He hung up.

Fear clotted her mind. She couldn't think straight. Her heart was racing. She checked her watch. Fifteen minutes. Getting to Coyote Lane from here on a good day took at least twelve minutes. There was no time to waste.

# 52

Natalie's Honda Accord roared through the countryside, needle grazing seventy. She was heading into the northwestern corner of town where the state park took over. She had to slow down as she navigated the back roads, bumping over potholes left by February's turbulent storms. She retrieved her cell phone from her jacket pocket and called Luke.

"Hello?"

"Luke, it's me. Murphy just called. He wants to talk."

"Murphy?" he repeated with dull shock.

"I'm supposed to meet him in fifteen minutes. He wants me to come alone and unarmed. I'm on my way to one-eleven Coyote Lane, but I'm sure he'll ghost me at any sign of police presence, so we need a plan."

"Okay, I'm leaving now. I'll stay out of sight."

She nodded. "Don't tell anyone else about this."

"I won't," he promised. "Stay on the line."

"No, I can't. I'll call you back when I'm almost there." She hung up.

Time slowed way down. The sky was an intense blue. Sweat broke out on her skin. Ten minutes and counting. She was terrified that she might somehow screw this up.

Sunlight poured down, and she fished around in the glove compartment for her sunglasses. Her heart was beating like a drum. She headed north through the woods, the noontime shadows dancing across the country roads. She knew this desolate part of town. At night, during a full moon, the tree branches looked as tangled as witches' hair.

With two minutes to go, Natalie called Luke back. "I'm almost there."

"I'm about ten minutes behind you. Try to stall him."

She bit her lower lip, worried they would lose Murphy if they weren't careful. "I'll do my best. Just stay out of sight." She hung up.

The vacant two-story house at the end of 111 Coyote Lane was as tall and slab-like as a gravestone, ugly and unadorned. The property was isolated with nothing but snowy woods for miles around.

Natalie parked by the side of the road and waited. The large, lumbering, bare-branched trees in the front yard were centuries old—western hemlocks, oaks, big-leaf maples. The owner wasn't interested in selling, and the house had been vacant for years.

The jarring ring of Natalie's cell phone startled her. "Hello?" she answered.

"Get out of your car and walk over to the mailbox."

She got out of her car. At the end of the driveway was a rusty-looking mailbox with a faded surname on one side. JAMESON.

"Open it."

She opened the mailbox. There was a Kyocera burner phone inside.

"Take the phone. Put *your* phone inside. Close the lid and step back."

She did as she was told, reluctantly placing her iPhone inside the mailbox.

Now the Kyocera burner phone in her hand rang, and she answered, "Yes?"

"Show me your weapon," Murphy instructed.

She glanced up at the house. The windows were dark and empty, but he could have been hiding inside. However, there were no vehicles parked nearby.

"Open your jacket and turn around slowly."

Her heart began to pound with fear. Was he watching her from inside the house or from somewhere in the woods?

She unbuttoned her jacket and turned around, displaying her holstered weapon.

"I asked you to come unarmed."

"Sorry. Force of habit." Natalie steadied her breathing. She was going to do this thing. Murphy held the key to nearly every one of her questions.

"Put your weapon in the mailbox," he instructed.

Natalie removed her jacket, then hesitated. She squinted into the woods.

"Put it in the mailbox and step back," he said gruffly.

She did as she was told. "Okay, Murphy, I did what you asked. I came alone. I didn't tell anyone. You have my word. Now let's talk."

"There's a foreclosed farm on Meadow Lane," he said. "At the dead end of the road. Go there and wait for my call. Do not diverge from these instructions. Do not call for help. I can track your location and usage on the Kyocera. If you're not at this location in twenty minutes, you'll never hear from me again. Do you understand?"

"Yes . . . but wait!"

The dial tone sounded in her ear.

# 53

Natalie headed back to her car, tossed Murphy's burner phone on the front seat next to her Nokia, and peeled away from the curb. She knew where she was going. The Grayson family hadn't been able to keep up with their loan payments for the expensive farm equipment they'd purchased, and Stewart Grayson had taken his own life when the bank foreclosed.

The sun shone mercilessly down—blazing, golden, glorious. Natalie glanced at the Nokia on the passenger seat—shit, that was prescient. She unplugged it and dialed Luke's number. It took him five rings to pick up.

"Hello?" he said.

"Luke, it's me."

"I didn't recognize the number. Where are you?"

"Murphy made me lose the iPhone. He's instructed me to head over to Stewart Grayson's place, you know the old farm on Meadow Lane? I'm on my way there now. He gave me a burner phone that he can track. It's a Kyocera. So I'm using the Nokia for you, and the Kyocera for him."

"Jesus, that's fucking lucky. Thank God you picked it up. Be careful, Natalie. I'll follow you to Meadow Lane and stay out of sight. Call me the instant anything goes sideways."

"I will." She hung up and tucked the phone underneath her seat. She took a hard left onto Pemberton Avenue, then drove past the old railroad depot. After the next intersection, she turned right onto Jolene Avenue.

The west side of town was a depressing confirmation of the economic downturn. Most folks here had it hard. The main drag consisted of fast-food restaurants, big-box stores, motels, and auto-body shops. Then came the sprawling farms and dying orchards. After several more miles, she took a dead-end, little-used road called Meadow Lane.

The run-down farmstead consisted of an old Dutch barn encircled by boarded-up sheds. The weathered farmhouse sat crouched self-consciously at the end of a snow-covered driveway. The abandoned farm was a popular hangout for underage partying in the summertime. The barbed-wire fence was choked with winter nettles.

Just as Natalie pulled up in front of the property, the Kyocera rang. "Murphy?" she answered.

"Step out of the car," he said calmly.

She got out of her vehicle, then stood squinting at the various outbuildings—an old pigpen, a chicken coop, a broken corral for sheep. Perhaps he'd rigged the abandoned property with a CCTV camera and was monitoring her now. "You're watching me?"

"Open all the doors of your vehicle," he instructed her. "And the trunk."

She opened the car doors, then popped the trunk, and stepped back. "There's no one inside the vehicle," she told him. "I haven't called anyone."

"Where's your off-duty weapon?"

Natalie shook her head. "Not wearing one."

"Raise your pant legs so I can see. Lift your jacket way up."

She raised her pant legs, one at a time, turning her leg this way and that to show him that she didn't have her off-duty weapon with her. She emptied her jacket pockets, then removed her jacket completely and turned around slowly. "I went to the pharmacy this morning, Murph," she told him. "I didn't bring any other weapons with me. Okay?"

He didn't answer.

"Stop playing games, and let me help you," she said angrily.

He sighed. "Listen carefully. From here, you're going to take Route 9 north until you get to exit four. Then you'll be getting on the I-87 North. Drive for approximately forty-five minutes, then stay in the right-hand lane. I'll call you in forty-five minutes with further details."

Dial tone.

# 54

Forty-five minutes later, Murphy called Natalie with instructions for getting off the I-87, and as soon as they hung up, she called Luke. Following Murphy's directions, she ended up in the foothills of the Adirondacks in a town called Portia Falls, fifty miles north of Burning Lake.

Natalie took a little-traveled country road onto Cobb Lane, marked by a slightly bent street sign, and pulled over to the side of the road in front of a crumbling colonial-era stone wall—exactly where Peter had instructed her to park.

She'd called Luke five minutes ago while en route with the rest of the directions, then had turned off her Nokia burner phone and slid it way under the passenger seat just in case Murphy decided to search her vehicle in person. Luke was ten to fifteen minutes behind her. Now she was stranded in a place she didn't recognize without any weapons or phones. Maybe this wasn't such a great idea.

Natalie got out of her vehicle, stood in the middle of the road and turned full circle. She was deep in the woods about an hour north of Burning Lake. Winter birds were singing. She checked her watch again. It was almost one o'clock.

The Kyocera in her jacket pocket rang in the clear bright air, startling her. "Hello?" she answered, trying not to sound as anxious as she felt.

"Walk up the road about twenty yards, you'll see a cabin. Knock three times on the front door and wait there."

"Okay," she said, suspecting that he was in full-blown paranoia mode.

Twenty or so yards up the road, a cabin came into view. It was a modest structure with a brick chimney and an A-frame roof. There was an Audi Quattro parked in the driveway—a four-door sedan, navy blue, with a rental sticker on the back.

Natalie paused for a moment, hoping she wasn't walking into a trap. Then she crossed the yard and knocked on the cabin door three times.

The green-painted door swung open. Detective Peter Murphy wore a dark winter coat with a gray hoodie underneath, a pair of jeans, and winter work boots with a bit of snow on them. He looked as if he'd just come from outdoors. His face was flushed and his breathing was labored, but she would've recognized those thick, Muppet-like eyebrows anywhere. "Come in," he said gruffly.

Natalie put on her game face and went inside. She was about to tell a pack of lies in order to get him to open up. She would do anything at this point to find out what was going on. "I'm glad you called me, Peter. I want to hear your side of the story and find out how we can resolve this thing."

He held her eye for a suspicious beat. "First I'll need to pat you down."

"Really?" She frowned. "Come on, it's me."

"You can leave if you want."

"Okay. Fine."

He did a quick pat down, nothing too intrusive, then took away his Kyocera burner phone. He was more disheveled-looking than usual, more exhausted for sure, and he smelled as if he hadn't showered in a week. "Have a seat, Natalie. Coffee?"

"Thanks." She figured it would be good for him to keep busy. She blinked a trail of sweat out of her eyes and entered the living room. The furniture had been chosen for comfort over style. There were upholstered chairs with permanent sweat stains and ugly toss pillows, liquor bottles and a toaster on the cheaply constructed kitchen island. A living room, a kitchenette, a front hallway. In back was the bedroom and bathroom, she presumed. "A statewide APB has been issued for you," Natalie told him. "Everybody's out there looking for you."

"I know." He handed her a cup of coffee, then said again, "Have a seat."

She took a seat on the sofa and set her cup down on the coffee table.

Murphy opened the front door and stood for a moment watching the road. There was no traffic. Finally, he closed the door, dragged a chair over to the woodstove, opened the cast-iron door, and fed a few logs on top of the dying embers. He added a rolled-up newspaper, then found a book of matches and lit a fire.

In his midforties, Murphy had a receding hairline and a pair of permanent worry lines between those thick eyebrows of his. Today he looked bone tired. His fingers trembled. "I want immunity," he told her. "Full immunity."

Natalie nodded. "What for?" she asked gently.

"I don't know where to start."

"Start anywhere." She girded herself. She wanted him to reveal all, and she was both mortified and excited by the prospect.

"Okay." He dragged his chair across the floor and parked it in front of the coffee table so that they were face-to-face. "I have a gambling problem," he confessed.

Natalie nodded, afraid to respond in any way, because this hounded, paranoid man might take it the wrong way and stop talking. And it was vital that he tell her everything.

"Eight years ago, I had gambling debts all over the place." He gritted his teeth and winced—it was obviously very painful for him to admit this. "I kept it hidden from everyone, but during my spare time, I was always at the casinos or gaming online, doing sports betting. I had accounts in various upstate casinos. I'd applied for credit lines and made thousand-dollar bets. I lost a lot of money. I tried to quit. But gambling's an addiction, you know." He released a sigh, then wiped his sweaty forehead with his hand.

"You couldn't pay off your debts?" she repeated.

"Not on my salary. And not only that . . ." He stared down at his interlaced fingers. "I got involved with a mob-controlled gambling ring five years back. That's when things turned deadly serious for me. Illegal sports betting. It goes like this. You place your bet online, and then a runner will come over to square up, either collecting the money owed, or else paying out your winnings. I lost more than I won. And this is organized crime we're talking about."

"That's pretty serious."

He nodded slowly. "I have a mortgage. I have responsibilities. A sick brother."

She drew back. "I didn't know you had a brother, Murphy."

He smoothed his hands together. "I don't talk about him much. He lives in Tennessee. He's got MS. He's got unpaid medical bills. Like I said, I have responsibilities, and here I was, owing money to the mob. And so . . ." He leaned forward and looked at her. "What would you do if somebody came along and offered to pay all your debts for you? Every last one? Plus provide you with some extra cash. And all you had to do was perform one simple favor?"

Natalie frowned. "I'd be tempted. Depends on what they asked for."

"Believe me," he said with a pained look. "I thought about it long and hard."

"Was this the mob?"

"No. A third party. Totally unrelated."

"So I'm guessing you did this person a favor, and they paid off all your debts?"

"Every last cent." Murphy threw up his hands, as if he still couldn't believe it. "They saved my life."

"They?"

He shook his head. "I can't say more until I get total immunity. Guaranteed."

Total immunity would provide Murphy with a shield against any future charges based on other matters related to his testimony. New York State offered total immunity, also known as transactional immunity.

"So just to clarify," Natalie said, "the overwhelming burden of your debts, plus the dangerous situation you found yourself in, was big enough to convince you to cross the line? To tamper with evidence? To steal the lockbox? Even worse things?"

"You've got it all wrong," he said, leaping up from his chair. He glared down at her. "At first, it was little things. Practically insignificant. But then it became a slippery slope, and once you cross the line, yeah, sure . . . you're blackmail material. You're done. You're toast. It's over."

"So it started small and gradually escalated?"

"Yes, that's what I'm saying." He walked over to a window, where he stood gazing outside at the road. "I think they're after me. I need witness protection, Natalie. I need full immunity from prosecution. Then I'll talk. I'll give grand jury testimony. You haven't heard anything yet."

She nodded carefully, taking in the full scope and breadth of what he was saying. New York State provided grand jury witnesses with automatic transactional immunity, which meant that he could never be tried for Veronica's murder or any other crimes he may have committed, and about which he'd testified, even if his testimony turned out to be completely false. It was a blanket pardon.

"I understand," she said. "And I'm going to help you get immunity, because I believe you, Murphy. I know you didn't do this all by yourself. If you'll cooperate, we can bring the real perpetrators to justice."

He spun around and studied her carefully. "What do you already know?"

She hesitated a beat before telling him the truth. "We know you weren't working alone the night Veronica was abducted. You had an accomplice. We also know that you and another person—we don't know who yet—illegally removed evidence from Violet Hawke's house, a number of boxes of documents that weren't listed on the manifest."

He nodded, then watched her curiously. "Is that it?"

"We know Veronica was doing research for her new book, and that she was very interested in a high school yearbook from 1975."

Murphy nodded. "JFK High."

"We suspect that a group of students started a coven back then, and that they may have abducted or killed a fellow student. A young girl—we don't know her identity yet. We had the evidence in the lockbox, but then you stole it from the crime lab."

"I was instructed to retrieve it," he said with a grim nod. "You seem to have figured out quite a bit on your own."

"Not the bigger picture," she admitted. "We have a few names—Randy Holmes, Frances Hawke, Dottie Coffman, and Ned Bertrand. But there were a few others we can't identify. And we haven't been able to fit all the pieces together yet. We need your help."

She was lying to him, holding back information. She didn't want Murphy to know everything they knew—she needed to make sure he wasn't lying, either.

"I'm not going to tell you anything else until I get immunity," he said. "I need written guarantees, and I want you to handle it, Natalie. I've got a lawyer on retainer, and I'm not saying another word until you get me a deal."

"That sounds reasonable, Murph. Sit down, you're making me nervous."

"I'm fine," he said angrily. His hands were balled shut. He was clearly afraid of something. His eyes were a bit wild.

"I just need to confirm that you were involved in Veronica's homicide, is that correct?"

"What did I just say?" he shouted. His face grew red. "I'm afraid for my life, don't you get it? These people are dangerous . . ."

"What people?"

"They're going to kill me. I know too much. Okay, look." He began pacing nervously back and forth in front of her. "Somebody very powerful— through a proxy—paid off all my debts. Once my debts were paid off, I had enough extra to afford better care for my brother. They were very generous. I started treating it like a job. It was easy at first. It didn't bother my conscience too much. But then they asked me to do some things . . . awful things . . . and I realized this wasn't what I wanted to be doing with my life. It was like waking up inside a nightmare, you know? After this last job, the lockbox, I was going to leave the country and disappear, but now there's an APB out for my ass. Worse than that . . . much worse, there's a bounty on my head. I'm not so much afraid of the police as I am of them. I know they're after me. They're very good at this."

"And if we can work out an immunity deal, you'll tell us who these people are?"

"Plus witness protection."

"Right. Of course," she said. "But if we can come to terms, you'll tell us who killed Veronica Manes, how it worked, all the entities involved . . . in other words, you'll give us the names of all your accomplices, as well as the people who are blackmailing you, your handlers? You'll tell us everything?"

"Yes," he said, wiping the sweat off his brow. "Everything. I'll turn state's evidence, just as long as I'm protected."

"All right," she said.

"And listen, Natalie. I have a kill switch. Anything happens to me, God forbid . . ." He crossed himself, which was unusual, because she'd never known Peter to be religious. "If anything happens to me, I've got a kill switch. These are damning documents, okay? And a videotaped confession. Everything I know. So after we depart today, should anything happen to me, then you listen to this . . ."

"I don't understand."

"Shh." He put his finger to his lips, then came over and knelt down in front of her. "You're smart, Natalie," he whispered. "You'll figure it out. It goes like this . . . when I was a kid, I threw a rock at Billy Durkins. He wouldn't let me pitch a single game. He wouldn't stop picking on me, so one day after school, I followed him home. He always took this shortcut through the woods, and I followed him that day. I found a good-sized rock and nailed him right between the eyes. He dropped like a sack of hammers. I thought I'd killed him. So I ran home and hid in the basement.

"Ten minutes later, Mrs. Durkins called my mother, and Mom looked all over the house and property for me, but I was hiding. When she couldn't find me, she called my dad at work. He knew right where to look. He knew about my secret hiding place. He found me, and we had a long talk. He didn't lay a finger on me. He made me ashamed of myself. First time I ever understood what a guilty conscience was." He stopped talking and stood up.

Natalie blinked. "Is that it?"

"If anything happens to me, you'll figure this out." He grimaced. "But I need guarantees. Total immunity and witness protection. Write it up." Murphy stared out the window again. She watched him tense all over. She could hear the low rumble of a car engine outside. "What the fuck," Murphy barked through gritted teeth. "Is that the lieutenant?"

"What?"

He swung around. "Did you tell him about me?"

"No, wait," she said desperately. "Luke's here to help . . ."

"You lied. You fucking lied to me." He reached under his coat, drew a Glock from his holster and pointed it at her. "Don't you move, Natalie. Stay right where you are."

# 55

Murphy grabbed Natalie around the neck and, pressing the barrel of the Glock into her cheek, dragged her outside with him. It hurt badly, as if her teeth were going to crack. Murphy was sweaty and shaky, and she might have been able to get away, but she was convinced that if she ran he'd shoot her in the back.

They stood painfully entwined in the front yard together—the hostage-taker and his hostage—while Luke's Ford Ranger came to an abrupt halt in the middle of the road with a squeak of tires on ice. He slowly put his hands up. "Don't hurt her, Murphy!" He stared at them from behind the window of his Ford Ranger.

"Get out of the vehicle!" Murphy shouted, digging the barrel of the gun deeper into her cheek.

Very gingerly, Luke got out of the Ranger and stood with his hands raised high over his head.

"Toss your weapon toward me. Toss it!"

Luke cautiously reached for his holstered service weapon, then threw it into the snow. "Easy, Murphy. Nobody's here to arrest you. Don't hurt her . . ."

"Shut up!" Murphy made Natalie walk backward toward his vehicle, which was parked in the driveway, while Luke backed away from the Ranger with his hands held high in the air.

"Don't hurt her, Murphy. She had no idea that I'd followed her here."

"Liar! You two need to get your stories straight." Murphy dug the cold barrel into Natalie's cheek and said, "I can't believe I trusted you." Then he shoved her down into the snow, got into his car, and sped off, rear tires spitting slush all over her.

Natalie had landed hard, hurting her shoulder. As soon as Murphy peeled away, she stumbled to her feet and stood rubbing her shoulder, her head going all swimmy for a second.

Luke retrieved his weapon and ran to her side. "Are you okay?"

"He wants to immunity, Luke. He was going to give us names and everything. We can't let him get away."

"Let's go." They got in his Ford Ranger and took off after Murphy.

# 56

The national park consisted of millions of acres of old-growth forest and was larger than Yellowstone and the Grand Canyon combined. Anyone who underestimated its scope and raw power could easily get lost in this treacherous terrain.

Deep in the woods, they caught up with Murphy, pulling up behind him and catching a glimpse of his adrenalized gaze in the rearview mirror—his eyes two desperate glints. Luke honked his horn, trying to pressure Murphy into surrendering, but he pulled away with a furious squeal of tires and a roar of slush.

"Check the glove compartment," Luke told her. "My off-duty weapon's in there."

She took out the Glock 19, checked that it was loaded, then scooped up the radio and called for backup, while at the same time she issued an APB for the Audi Quattro in case they lost him, reading the number off the license plate.

Now Murphy took a right turn onto a narrow road, and Natalie's stomach lurched as they followed suit. These fire roads were loosely packed with gravel and rocks that made for a rugged ride—choppy, noisy. There were numerous hairpin turns and sections of road without any guardrails. The area was prone to avalanches and mudslides due to the steep terrain, and you couldn't find a place to turn around if your life depended on it. The route was extremely dangerous.

"Hold on," Luke told her, and Natalie cinched her seat belt tighter.

They were heading farther into mountainous terrain, full of gorges and canyons. Soon the valley would be below them, with mountains all around. Luke's speedometer nicked sixty—way too fast for these rutted, icy, washed-out roads. He clutched the wheel, white-knuckled, while all around them trees swayed in the wind and the clouds began to congregate overhead. What had been a gorgeous morning was turning into an ominous afternoon.

They climbed steadily, engine grinding, until they'd reached the crest of a ridge, where the road leveled out. The spine of the mountain range between the next two watersheds was especially dangerous, Natalie recalled, with sharp bends and massive drop-offs on one side. The road got a lot of snow in the winter, and there were no guardrails to allow for plowing. It was a beautiful but precarious drive. You had to take it seriously. The trip took roughly twenty-five minutes on a good day, and the only alternative route took four hours due to the ruggedness of the terrain.

This area attracted a lot of tourists who wanted to photograph the stunning views. But it was common knowledge that you shouldn't be driving here if you were unfamiliar with the roads, especially during the winter. The sight of a three-hundred-foot drop-off without any guardrail could panic people. The narrow, windy roads didn't leave you much time to react, and you had to be extra careful at night, when wildlife randomly darted out in front of your car. There was no place to swerve.

Now they sped along the ridgeline, chasing the Audi Quattro. Murphy was about twenty yards ahead when the road curved and he suddenly disappeared from view.

Luke eased his foot off the gas as the desolate stretch of road began to curve to the right. Natalie felt her center of gravity being pulled like a magnet as the road kept curving toward the right.

Around the bend, they didn't see Murphy's vehicle until it was almost too late. There he was, right in front of them, veering over the side of the cliff.

Luke cut the wheel sharply and pumped the brakes. Natalie was thrown sideways, her seat belt cutting into her flesh. Gravel pinged against the wheel wells as they skidded forward, then came to an abrupt stop just a few feet away from the cliff.

Everything went silent except for the pounding of her heart as she watched the Audi Quattro plummet over the edge of the world.

Then they heard a loud thud.

It took her a moment to catch her breath and contain her shock.

Then they got out of the vehicle and went over to the precipice.

Murphy's rental car had flipped over and landed on the hillside approximately a hundred and fifty feet below, the force of the impact leaving a mangled wreck. The door panels, hubcaps, and other vehicle parts had gone flying. There was no way he could've survived that crash.

They waited for more than an hour for the rescue team to arrive, along with New York State troopers and deputies from the County Sheriff's Office. The rescue was conducted by a mountain team made up of local volunteers, along with a number of New York's DWW Forest Rangers, who were stationed throughout the state.

The road was closed following the accident, while the vehicle-recovery team and specially trained state troopers climbed down the steep cliff to recover the driver from the wreckage. Detective Peter Murphy was pronounced dead at the scene.

# 57

Are you sure you're okay?" Assistant Chief Gossett asked Natalie.
"I'm fine," she said, trying to stay focused. They were back inside
Murphy's cabin, and she was seated in one of the ugly armchairs. Two state
troopers and a sheriff's deputy stood talking quietly by the front door.

Luke was standing next to Gossett, a concerned look on his face.

"Sheriff Huddleston will be here any minute," Gossett told them. "His
men were the first responders to the call. It's their jurisdiction. I got here
as fast as I could. What happened?" he asked. "How did you two end up
here?"

"That's a long story," Luke said, answering for them both.

Gossett studied him carefully. "Well, that's why I'm here."

"Oh God." Natalie leaned forward in her chair and cupped a hand over
her mouth, feeling nauseated. Her forehead was throbbing. Her rib cage
ached dully from where the seat belt had cut across her ribs. "I feel queasy.
I need some air."

"Let's go outside," Luke suggested.

"I'd like to get your statements first," Gossett told them.

"She needs some fresh air," Luke insisted. "Come on, Natalie, let's go."

They went outside and stood in the snowy backyard where they could
talk without disruption. Natalie took a deep breath. The air smelled of pine
sap and Douglas firs. "How much do we tell them?" she asked Luke.

"The bare minimum. Don't go into any details."

"Tell the truth, but keep it short?"

He nodded. "Murphy called you out of the blue. You informed me, and I followed you up to the cabin. Murphy asked for immunity. He wanted you to negotiate for him. As soon as he saw me pulling up in front of the cabin, he panicked, drew his weapon, and held you hostage. He fled the scene, and we gave chase. Just state the facts—that while in pursuit of the suspect, he lost control of his vehicle, veered off the road, and plummeted down the side of the mountain."

She nodded. "So nothing about his gambling problem or the rest of his confession."

Luke shook his head. "Let me talk to the chief first. We can't let anyone else know what Murphy revealed to you today, not yet. It's too risky. We don't know who to trust. For the time being, it's just you and me, Natalie, until I figure out a strategy going forward. I'll call you tonight."

"Okay." She breathed in the bone-dry winter air. Her lungs felt raw. "Murphy was scared, Luke. Genuinely afraid for his life. These are powerful people."

"I know."

"What are you going to tell the chief?"

"Don't worry about that. Let me handle it. The main thing is to keep it close to your vest until we can figure out the best way forward. I'll talk to the chief as soon as we get back to Burning Lake. In the meantime, keep your burner phone handy. I'll pick one up later on. Direct communications only. We need to be extremely careful, Natalie."

They fell silent for a moment. They gazed into each other's eyes.

"Luke . . ."

"It's okay." He cut her short.

"I just wanted to thank you." She gave up resisting the impulse and wrapped her arms around his neck, hugging him hard. She could feel his body tense all over, but then he warmed toward her. He didn't so much hug her back as let her hold him for as long as she wanted to.

When they pulled apart, his gaze lingered. It felt shockingly good to stare at him.

Luke forced himself to look away and said, "Okay. Let's go back inside."

As they turned toward the cabin, Natalie spotted a silver pickup truck driving past on this little-traveled road. Bill Finley was behind the wheel, taking pictures. Her pulse quickened as Finley spotted her and the truck sped away.

# 58

When Natalie got home that evening, she collapsed on the sofa and didn't budge until Hunter came out of his office and found her sitting in the same position she'd crash-landed half an hour before, still in her jacket and boots. She was numb with exhaustion, outrage, and confusion. Her leather bag was on the floor where she'd dropped it.

She felt his hovering presence and opened her eyes.

"Hey, you." He plopped down beside her. "How was your day?"

"Not great."

"I'm sorry, sweetie."

"Hunter. Don't."

He drew back. "What's wrong?"

She sat up straight. "Bill Finley followed me again."

"Natalie . . ."

"Don't lie to me, Hunter."

His face hardened. He stood up and paced back and forth in front of her, then looked at her with a churning restlessness. "Sorry, but I did it for your own protection."

She grew livid. "My protection?"

"Yes," he said sincerely. "I told you, I was worried about you."

She stood up. "So you sent your security team out to spy on me?"

He rubbed his face with frustration. "Look, I didn't want to alarm you, but last night we found another dead animal on the property, and it was obviously part of an occult ritual. These incidents seem to be escalating, and I don't know how I'm supposed to react to them, but my first instinct was to protect you."

"Please don't turn this around," she said heatedly. "It's unforgiveable that you're having me followed without my knowledge."

"But I thought we agreed about the tracking device?"

"For emergencies only."

He took off his jacket and draped it over the back of a chair, his fountain pen clinking against the carved oak. "I apologize. It won't ever happen again."

She had to sit down. Her ribs hurt, making her wince.

"Are you okay?"

"Do you know what happened today? Have you seen the news?"

He picked up the remote and turned on the flat screen. He flicked through the channels, stopping at a random cable broadcast. A blond anchorwoman was talking over video of rescuers in neon emergency gear climbing down the side of the cliff toward the wreckage.

". . . where the body of a veteran law enforcement officer from Burning Lake, New York, was hauled up a hundred-and-fifty-foot drop and pronounced dead at the scene," the anchorwoman said. "The accident occurred at about two thirty this afternoon on what authorities have called a dangerous stretch of road between Portia Falls and Hickory Hollow. That section of the pass was closed for five hours before being reopened. State troopers tell us the driver of the vehicle was traveling at a high rate of speed when it careened off the roadside. His name is being withheld until family members have been notified. The incident remains under investigation."

Hunter turned off the TV. "You were involved in that?"

She nodded numbly. "Luke and I were in pursuit of Peter Murphy when he lost control of his vehicle. We almost went over ourselves."

"But I thought you and Luke were working on separate cases?"

She stared at him. "Did you even hear what I said? Don't you care?"

He swept an arm aggressively through the air. "Of course I care! But I can't think straight, not when . . . fuck." He took out his phone, swiped his thumb over the screen, and showed her images of her and Luke standing in front of Violet Hawke's house yesterday. Luke was lightly touching Natalie's face, and the moment came across as tender and intimate. Then he showed her a series of images of the two of them hugging in front of Murphy's cabin today.

"Are you in love with him?" he asked with a deeply wounded expression.

"No," she lied.

"Because it looks like you're in love with him."

"We were working the case together," she insisted angrily. "It was terrifying. We almost went over the cliff. I wanted to thank him for saving my life. So I hugged him, so what? And yesterday, we were strategizing, and then two seconds later, I left. Those pictures are totally deceptive."

"That's not what it looks like to me. And that breaks my fucking heart."

She didn't know what to say. She felt like crying. Their world was falling apart, and she couldn't do a damn thing to stop it.

"Just tell me the truth, Natalie." He held her eyes with a fierce expression. "Are you in love with him or not?"

"It doesn't matter. Luke and Rainie are getting married."

He studied her for a moment. "But you love him in some way."

She hesitated, because she wanted to tell him the truth. She gave a reluctant nod. "I love him in the sense that I care deeply about him. We practically grew up together. You know the whole story. His father went AWOL, and his mother was always working, and so we sort of adopted him into our family. I've never lied to you about my relationship with Luke."

He glanced away. "I think you love him in a way you don't love me."

She sat breathlessly, waiting for him to go on, and could feel a prickly, unpleasant heat crawling up her neck and spreading across her cheeks. They'd had a couple of late-night conversations about previous lovers, hookups, and physical attractions. Natalie always danced around her feelings for Luke, trying to lessen the impact it might have on Hunter. She didn't want to hurt him, so she'd downplayed their relationship, but now she could see that he'd known all along how deep her feelings went.

"Why are you lying to me?" he asked. "I know it goes deeper than that."

She clenched her fists to keep her hands from trembling.

He reached for her hands and forced her fists open. "Just tell me," he whispered.

She pulled away from him and stared at her unadorned nails. Her shoulders sagged. A deep-seated weariness came over her as she looked at him and said, "I need you to listen to me."

He nodded. "I'm listening."

"No, I mean . . . I'm going to tell you something because I care about you."

He sat on the edge of the sofa and turned on the Tiffany lamp. A reddish greenish light shone on all the hollows and lines of his handsome face.

"You have a beautiful soul. You're a beautiful man," she told him. "You say you love me. You've asked me to marry you. You want to take me away from here. You seem to care very much about me. But you don't know me, Hunter. I'm not like you. I can't just drop everything and go wherever I want or do whatever I feel like doing. I have roots. I have obligations. I love this town. I grew up here. I was shaped by the people who love me. My father. My sisters. My mother. And besides that, I'm a cop to the bone. I want answers. I want to find out what's going on. Why it happened. How it happened. I can't just pick up and leave. I don't want to leave. I belong here."

"What are you saying?"

"I need time to think. I need a little space."

"No, no, no," he whispered.

"I'm sorry, Hunter."

His face fell. "Look, I deserve your scorn. I've been a complete asshole. But we can work it out, right? That's what couples do."

She realized how cold she was, how bone tired.

"Natalie, don't give up on me so easily. I thought you were committed to this relationship? Were you lying the whole time? Am I just a pit stop for you?"

She stared furiously at him. "Listen, you aren't aware of this, but just last week, Luke and I had a very sobering conversation about our relationship—how we've never taken our friendship any further than that. And I decided that, no matter what, I was committed to you. *You*, Hunter. And this happened not just once, but twice. Do you realize what that means? I validated my relationship with you *twice*, and now you're implying that I don't have the best of intentions? Well, fuck you."

She could see by his expression that he knew he'd gone too far, and he wanted desperately to dial it back, but it was too late.

"I didn't mean that, Natalie. Wait."

Her heart hardened. "I'm sorry. But I think this is over."

"No . . . please."

"I'm going upstairs. Don't follow me."

"Don't shut me out, Natalie. Not now. Natalie?"

Upstairs in the master bedroom, she moved back and forth between the closet, the bureau and her suitcase lying open on the bed, as if she were sleepwalking.

She scooped out an armload of T-shirts and underwear from the bureau drawer, carried it over to the bed and dropped everything in her suitcase. She entered the walk-in closet and took her old clothes off the hangers—three pairs of dress pants, a velvet jacket, a dozen blouses, a couple of dresses, and a few black skirts. She left the designer outfits Hunter had bought her. She folded her dresses and blouses and pants carelessly and dropped them into her suitcase. Then she got her hair dryer and beauty supplies from the bathroom.

"Please don't go," Hunter said from the doorway.

She turned to study him. He looked as if he were about to sweep her up into his arms—and yet he didn't touch her. He had once wielded a soft, all-encompassing power over her, but today that connection had snapped.

"Will you be coming back?" he asked.

"I don't know."

All hope drained from his face.

She crossed the room again. There was a little pile of things on the bureau top, and she scooped them up.

"Natalie, just stay the night. We can talk it out in the morning."

She dropped the pile of things into her overnight bag, then opened the nightstand drawer. She scooped up two barrettes, her reading glasses, and her birth control pills.

He reached for her hand, but she refused to let him hold it. "Natalie, listen to me." His voice hardened, but his eyes remained soft as he studied her. "I was only trying to protect you. I told you I'd do anything in my power to keep you safe, and that's exactly what I did."

"By having me followed? By not trusting me?"

They stared at each other.

"Just do me a favor," he said. "Try to forgive me."

She removed the blue tracking device from her key chain and left it on the night table. She closed her suitcase and zipped up her overnight bag. She picked them up and looked around the room to make sure she hadn't forgotten anything. Her shoulder bag, winter coat, and boots were downstairs.

"This doesn't have to happen," he said, blocking her way. "I won't ever do it again. I'm sorry. I had no right to distrust you. That was stupid of me." His eyes grew soft and fragile. "Will you give me another chance? Please?"

It was late. She was exhausted. "No, Hunter, I really need to get some space. I need to spend some time alone. I'm sorry."

# 59

The house on Wildwood Road was quietly reproachful, as if it resented Natalie for abandoning it for so long. Each chilly room echoed with her footsteps and was cluttered with books, half-packed boxes, and little piles of laundry. There was expired food in the fridge, and there were dead plants on the windowsills.

Soon, it began to rain. An icy winter rain. She listened to the pitter-patter on the old shingled roof as she wandered through the frozen landscape of the house, which had once been so full of life, full of her sisters' laughter and mellow jazz from her father's radio. Now there was nothing. She shivered, feeling alienated from everything and everyone.

Natalie carried her bags upstairs to her old room, where she unpacked and put everything away. The muted green chaise in the corner still held her shape, her stamp. The four-poster bed with the walnut posts and spade feet had once held a myriad of well-loved stuffed animals. Late at night, as a kid, Natalie would drape a bedspread down from one of the posts so that it formed a tent, and she would read her favorite books by flashlight—*Matilda, Charlotte's Web, The Outsiders, Willy Wonka and the Chocolate Factory*—while the light made patterns on the Indonesian print.

Now the horrors of the day crashed down around her. People could be monsters. Life was a mystery. She didn't want her niece growing up in a world where women were snatched off the streets and held inside dungeons for years until they were broken and forgotten. Where teenage girls went missing forever. She didn't want Ellie to see it on the news or read about it on the internet. It was too terrible.

The hurt and pain of ending her relationship lingered with a dull ache. Hunter was the only man who'd ever asked her to marry him. He wanted to take her away from this troubled place and travel around the world and experience life. Just live. Just relax and have fun. Start a family. Have kids. Move to Denver. Build their dream home. He wanted her to start painting again. Do her art. Have a normal life, for once—whatever that meant. How could she possibly feel so betrayed when he had offered her so much?

It was raining harder now, the old-fashioned windows rattling in their frames. Natalie dragged the quilt off her bed and carried it downstairs, then made herself a cup of tea. Chilled to the bone, she took a seat on the living-room sofa and pulled the quilt up around her. She sipped her tea and dialed Luke's number.

She braced herself while it rang. She stared at the eggshell white walls, smudged with fingerprints. These walls hadn't stayed white for very long.

"Hello?" he answered.

"I left him," she said. "I wanted you to know before you heard about it from anybody else. I moved out, and I'm back home. I'm okay. You don't have to say anything, Luke. I just wanted you to know."

He said nothing.

She hung up, thoroughly shaken.

She waited for him to call her back.

She drew the quilt closer and gazed out the windows. Rain danced on the panes. Rain made ever-changing streaks of amethyst and green on the glass. Shadows trembled on the walls and plank flooring. Lightning flashed and rumbled—a shimmering intrusion that lit up the entire house. This morning, life had been simple. She missed this morning.

Luke didn't call her back.

Natalie finished her tea, then went to wash her cup in the sink. A pair of headlights splashed across the kitchen ceiling, and a car pulled up in front of the house and parked. She heard the engine cut off, and the thump of a door swinging open and shut.

"Shit," she said, thinking it was Hunter, come to plead his case. She didn't want to argue with him. She didn't want to fight anymore. She only wanted to protect this newfound freedom of hers.

Natalie opened the front door and saw Luke standing in the rain. He stood very still on the front yard, heat steaming off his skin.

"I wanted you to know before you heard about it from anybody else," he told her over the storm's uproar. "I broke up with Rainie. It's over. You don't have to say anything, Natalie. I just wanted you to know."

She was feverish and freezing at the same time.

A wet wind gusted, making the treetops writhe and groan.

Luke lifted his face to the rain, while the wet branches swayed in the wind, shaking off droplets. Everything was muted, faded, indistinguishable. He wore a blue T-shirt and Wrangler jeans under his open parka, his chest muscles rippling with tension.

Natalie opened the door wider. "Come in," she said.

He approached the house slowly, holding her steady gaze. He stood on the threshold. He'd gotten soaked. Rain clung to his skin. She impulsively flung herself at him.

He caught her, smiling. "Hey," he said, delighted with this gift.

She wrapped her arms around him and kissed him. She could feel the throbbing of their blood like the distant boom-boom of drums.

"You're getting wet." He swept her inside and leaned her up against a wall. "Better?"

She nodded.

He cupped her face between his hands and asked, "Are you sure about this?"

Natalie smiled. "Uh-huh."

He shook his head stubbornly. He looked so hungry for her, she wanted to cry out in frustration. He ran his hands down her arms, just the tips of his fingers. "You're shivering. Are you cold?"

She shook her head. "I'm just so happy right now."

He smiled, and she led him into the living room and pushed him down on the gray-speckled sofa. Before she could kiss him again, he said, "Look, if we do this now, it points to the lie we've been living. It means we've deceived two innocent people. It means we've been selfish."

"I don't care," she said flippantly, and she meant it.

In truth, love had never gone away. Love had remained asleep in her breast like a sturdy houseplant that never died. You could neglect it. You could forget to water it. You could let dust settle on its leaves. Spiders could invade its tangled stems. But still it would grow. Still it would thrive.

She liked his straight white teeth and his forgiving smile. He got her. Luke understood who Natalie was to the bone. She studied his brushstroke eyebrows and the faint violet shadows underneath his intelligent blue eyes. He had a defined, weathered face and a long healthy body, and his hair shone like polished mahogany in the lamplight. Whenever she thought about kissing him, she could feel a dull ache in the swelling of her flesh.

He sat there, observing her thoughtfully. He was deciding something. He was working things out—morally, ethically, right from wrong. He was being Luke.

"We can't just break up with people we've committed ourselves to," he reasoned, "and then jump into bed together. We'd be hurting them badly."

"I don't care," she insisted.

"That's not true. You care about everything. Don't kid yourself."

A soft silence descended over them. It was true. She did care.

Guilt singed her cheeks with a special kind of shame. She decided that true love was a form a madness. Ripping apart everything in its path and tossing it into the air. Destructive and all-consuming. Luke would be her universe from now on, while everything else receded into background noise. Wherever he was inside the house, whatever he was doing, she would seek him out and wrap her arms around him, pull him closer, and tug at his clothes. He would smile his luscious Luke smile, and he would take her. She would press her body against his and feel his skin burning next to hers. It was a dream she wanted to disappear into forever.

Luke grew agitated. He got up and went down the hallway. A few seconds later, he came back and tossed her a bath towel. "Here," he said.

She dried her hair with the towel, then handed it back. She sat motionless with her chin raised. She sat very still in a glaze of lust and terror, feeling the pull and tug of the darkness that stretched between them. She wanted Luke. Her body was feverish for him. "What should we do then?" she asked.

He looked completely lost. He couldn't stop staring at her.

"Do you want to leave?" she asked.

His smile vanished. His mood shifted and darkened. "No."

"No?" She could feel an enormous tension building between them.

"Sleep with me." He kicked the coffee table out of the way and pulled her down onto the sofa with him. He kissed her, touched her face, ran his hands over her body, pawed at her clothes, lifted her T-shirt, tugged down her jeans. They were each other's source of gravity. She felt the pull of the sun and the moon. Luke was surprisingly muscular and strong, and he knew what he wanted. He rearranged her body beneath him, and drew her legs toward him. She wanted to be devoured like this, whole, while outside the rain pummeled the earth.

# 60

In Natalie's dream, they were chasing Peter Murphy's car into the mountains, when they skidded to a hair-raising stop just a few feet short of the end of the world.

She woke up in a cold sweat, panting for breath and staring at the familiar wallpaper. Her thoughts were a maze—she knew the answer was in there somewhere. She reached for Luke's side of the bed, but he was gone.

The sun was shining. It was a beautiful morning. She found him downstairs in the kitchen. He was leaning against the counter, wearing the same pair of jeans and the same T-shirt as yesterday, holding a cup of coffee in one hand and his cell phone in the other. He was busy texting with his thumb.

"Good morning," she said.

He looked up and smiled. "Good morning."

"You're up early." She went over and kissed him. "Mmm. Coffee lips."

He put down his coffee and, still holding his phone, wrapped his arm around her, pulled her close, and kissed her long and hard. Then he said, "Help yourself."

"To you?"

"To coffee. I made a fresh pot."

"Don't mind if I do." She opened a cupboard, grabbed a mug, and poured herself a cup of coffee. "You didn't happen to go out and get any breakfast pastries, did you?"

"There's oatmeal," he said, still texting.

"You're pretty good with that thumb," she said, sipping her coffee.

He burst out laughing but kept texting. "There's orange juice in the fridge. Help yourself to anything."

"Anything at all?"

He glanced up. "What's yours is mine."

"Oh goodie," she said, opening cupboards and poking around in the fridge. "Where's the bread? Where are the eggs? I'm out already?"

He smirked at her. He put down his phone and reached for her. "Come here, you." He swung her carelessly toward him.

"What?"

"What?" he repeated. He kissed her again, teasing her with his lips.

She snuggled against him.

Somehow they fit perfectly together. Somehow this worked.

# 61

Natalie and Luke spent the rest of the weekend together. It was beautiful, impossible, fragile. The sight of him got her heart thumping. It never failed to amaze her how handsome he was—now that she could look at him whenever she liked. Luke had a strong jawline and incredibly icy blue eyes that became suffused with warmth whenever he studied her face. His shoulders were broad, his arms were sinuous, and his mahogany hair curled damply at the edges whenever he worked out. He looked really good in his sweats. He was in his sweats now.

She let herself drown in his arms, and he gladly drowned with her. She pictured the two of them entwined, drifting toward the weedy bottom of the lake. They had a lazy, seductive, romantic Sunday, kissing like teenagers. He gazed into her eyes as if there were depths and clouds and misty woods and legends and promises of many good things to come. He could see all the way to her soul.

Luke indulged her by buying her cherry Pop-Tarts from the corner store. He was insatiable and insatiably curious. They fucked late into the night, then stayed up talking until they drifted off to sleep in the wee hours of the morning. They slept late. They ate breakfast in bed. They shared many common interests, not just law enforcement. They talked about books they loved and places they wanted to visit and shared their opinions about art and history. His heart beat steadily against her. The moonlight coming in through the windows glowed softly in his eyes and highlighted the stubble on his face. He rubbed the beard stubble on his cheeks and chin briefly, then looked away. He was modest. He was proud. He was wildly in love. She felt his smile in her heart. She felt a joyous, wordless recognition between them—this one is mine. Mine for good.

# 62

On Monday morning, Luke had a meeting with the chief he couldn't miss, so he reluctantly released his grip on her, took a shower, got dressed, and kissed her good-bye at the front door. They stood in contemplative silence for a moment. He clasped his arms around her and squeezed. He pulled her into him, then rested his forehead against hers. "See you soon," he promised and left.

Luke and Chief Snyder were going to discuss the situation regarding Detective Murphy and figure out how to proceed going forward. A small law enforcement agency such as theirs couldn't afford a squad of officers assigned to internal affairs. The BLPD had its own system for policing the police. Since it would've been a mistake to have one officer dedicated to internal affairs—too much power, too much opportunity for corruption—the way they usually handled it was to assign the task to a superior officer or a detective who reported directly to the chief.

In Luke's case, it was a little more complicated than that, since he'd been involved in yesterday's incident. It was quite possible that the chief would decide to assign the task to somebody who wasn't involved with the CIU where the corruption had taken place. However, given the delicacy of the situation, Luke thought it might be advisable to keep the circle as small as possible.

Regardless of the outcome, Natalie had decided to work from home today. Not only did her ribs still hurt, but she didn't want to have to answer any of her colleagues' questions about the accident—not until the issue was resolved. Murphy's shocking confession had ripped open an extremely serious problem within the department, and she only hoped Luke and the chief could find a solution soon. She needed to know what her boundaries were moving forward.

This morning, before typing up her reports, Natalie decided to clean up the place a little. She hadn't been home in months, and the house was stuffy and dusty. She opened the windows to get a cross breeze going. She did a huge load of laundry. She unpacked her bags and put everything away. Then she made a fresh pot of coffee and opened her laptop at the kitchen table.

Natalie double-clicked on the folder containing Peter Murphy's digital personnel file. She was looking for the kill switch. That was her top priority. Murphy had told her—"You're smart, Natalie. You'll figure it out." She found his emergency contact list in the personnel file. There were two people listed, and one of them was Murphy's brother.

Natalie tried the woman's number first. She turned out to be a former employee at a group home where Murphy's brother currently lived. Apparently, Murphy hadn't updated his emergency contact form. She gave Natalie the number of the group home, and after a handful of phone calls, Natalie finally got to speak to Murphy's brother. She knew he had multiple sclerosis and that it might affect his speech.

"Hello," Malcolm Murphy answered. "Who's this?"

Now Natalie had the unpleasant task of telling him that his brother was dead.

After ten minutes of back and forth, with Malcolm alternately crying and recalling some of the good times they'd had, his voice at times strained and harsh, his speech slow and occasionally slurred, Natalie decided to turn the conversation to the one thing she wanted to know.

"Do you remember Billy Durkins?" she asked Malcolm.

"Yes, I do. He was a kid in our neighborhood."

"Peter told me a story about Billy," she explained. "He got into an argument and threw a rock at him, then ran home and hid in a special hiding place . . ."

"The furnace," Malcolm said without hesitation.

"What?"

"We had a coal furnace . . . in our basement . . . Peter used to hide there . . . whenever he got in trouble. Spring and summer, you could . . . crawl inside the furnace and hide."

"Malcolm," she said, "where is your childhood home?"

"We lived . . . in Portia Falls. But my parents sold it a long time ago, and . . . and . . . the developers put up . . . an industrial park. It's not there . . . anymore."

Natalie thanked him, said she was sorry for his loss, and let him go. She had given his caretaker all the information Malcolm needed to handle what remained of Murphy's estate.

The only reason she could think of for Murphy to have told her such a story was because he'd hidden the "kill switch" inside a coal furnace. But if his childhood home no longer existed, then he must have hidden it in some other coal furnace.

She decided to check out his residence in Burning Lake and see if it had a coal furnace. She drove across town, taking the exit to Bakers Mill Hollow and Meadow Lane. As soon as she pulled into Murphy's neighborhood, she smelled smoke in the air. It had been only two weeks since Murphy burned his house to the ground, along with any evidence of his criminal wrongdoing.

She parked by the side of the road, got out and stood studying the charred remains at the end of Meadow Lane. The windows had blown out. The roof had collapsed. A burnt-fuel smell tainted the air.

She removed her sunglasses. The fire was still being investigated, but she'd received a preliminary copy of the inspector's report, and they'd determined that the incident was due to arson.

Only the front façade of the house remained standing. The back was reduced to charred rubble. She could hear glass crunch underfoot as she crossed the yard. A neon orange sign had been stapled to the door that warned, THIS BUILDING IS CONDEMNED—NO TRESPASSING.

Natalie entered the abandoned building, her senses immediately heightened as she crossed the threshold. She gingerly picked her way across a precarious clutter of charred cross beams, caved-in walls freckled with soot, and glass shards flashing in the morning sun. What was left of the floor wobbled underfoot, and she struggled with the bitter realization that she could go no farther. It was too dangerous.

Outside, Natalie called the inspector's office and got one of his assistants on the line. She explained what she needed to know—did Murphy have a coal furnace at this particular residence? She was put on hold for several minutes.

Finally, the assistant picked up again. "Hello?"

"I'm still here."

"No, he didn't."

"No coal furnace."

"No. It was a gas furnace with radiant heating. And that didn't cause the fire."

"I read the preliminary report. You determined it was arson."

"That's right, Detective. It looks as if the fire was deliberately set. We found evidence of an accelerant and a book of matches. Is there anything else I can do for you?"

"No thanks, you've been extremely helpful." She hung up.

*"You're smart, Natalie. You'll figure it out."*

So, if the kill switch—meaning documents and a taped confession— were hidden inside a coal furnace, then where was this coal furnace? Not in his childhood home. Not the house on Meadow Lane. Not the cabin— there was no basement up there, just a woodstove, and Murphy had lit a fire in it.

She thought about all the places Murphy had visited recently.

Then it dawned on her.

There was only one other place to look.

# 63

Natalie parked in front of Violet Hawke's ramshackle Victorian at the top of the hill, her car squeaking to a jerky stop. She unbuckled her seat belt and got out. The piles of junk were gone. A FOR SALE sign was planted in the snowy front lawn. She shuddered with inner tension as she approached the house and rang the bell.

Tracie didn't answer this time. The house was empty.

Natalie recalled seeing the old coal furnace on her previous visits, but she hadn't put it together until now. Six months ago, Murphy and an accomplice had spent quite a bit of time down in Violet's basement, rummaging through boxes and confiscating old documents that might implicate Violet and her cohorts. He also might have assumed that the house would be vacant for another year or so. Perhaps he had hidden his "kill switch" down in the coal furnace, thinking he could retrieve it at a later date?

Now she took the creaking, narrow wooden treads down into the basement, where she skimmed her flashlight beam over the old stone walls and aging copper pipes, shadows playing tricks on her eyes.

And there it was.

She crossed the room and walked up to the obsolete coal furnace, a bulky metal contraption that looked like a seventies sci-fi movie robot with mechanical arms. You could still see the black anthracite dust on the floor from the nearby coal bin.

Natalie opened the heavy wrought-iron door and pointed her flashlight inside. The grimy interior was laced with cobwebs. She reached her arm into the empty chamber and groped around with the flat of her hand, feeling the contours of the inner furnace and batting away cobwebs. She desperately wanted Murphy's kill switch to be here.

*"If anything happens to me, I've got a kill switch. These are damning documents, okay? And a videotaped confession. You're smart, Natalie. You'll figure it out."*

There were molded iron ledges inside the chamber. She felt around, afraid of what she might find. She tried the right side first, and then the side facing her. She was reaching way up on the left side, when suddenly she touched something plastic, and her hand began to tremble as she strained to reach the object. He had hidden it way up on a dusty ledge, just out of reach.

Now her fingers closed around the corner of a box wrapped in plastic. She gripped it until it tipped off the ledge and fell down onto the filthy iron grate. Natalie sighed deeply, pockets of tension loosening inside her as she picked up a package about the size of a shoe box, wrapped in waterproof sheeting and sealed with duct tape.

Natalie shook the box and could hear something rattling around inside. It was fairly heavy. She put it down on a workbench and looked around for something to cut it open with. She found a serrated knife and sawed through the heavy plastic. She popped the lid of the shoe box and felt a hit of adrenaline as she peered inside.

An hour later, Natalie was back at the police station taking an elevator to the second floor. Full of nerves and raw adrenaline, she headed down the long L-shaped corridor toward Chief Roger Snyder's corner office, then hesitated in the doorway. Luke was already there, seated in one of two guest chairs, and both men turned to acknowledge her.

"Did you bring it?" the chief asked.

"Right here." She held up the USB flash drive. "Lenny has the other copy, along with the original documents and video recorder. He's processing everything for prints and trace, then he'll lock them away in the safe."

"Good job, Detective," the chief told her. "Close the door, please."

She closed the door and handed Chief Snyder the flash drive. His office windows overlooked the commercial district of downtown Burning Lake, and the winter snowscape was like a faded Victorian Christmas card. He inserted the USB into his computer, and Murphy's videotaped confession began to play. His heavy eyebrows were knitted together, and his tired, sweaty face filled the screen.

"Have a seat, Natalie," the chief said, pausing the video until she took a seat. He was a barrel-chested man with a puglike face and a pragmatic smile. His gold badge gleamed on his pressed uniform, and you could tell by his demeanor that he believed in formalities, rules, and regulations. Law and order and the chain of command were more important to him than abstract concepts like good and evil. "Now, without further ado, let's watch the tape."

He pressed play, and the three of them watched Murphy's taped confession.

"My name is Detective Peter R. Murphy. Today's date is March tenth, and what I am about to tell you is the truth, the whole truth, and nothing but." The frame filled with a tight shot of his tense-looking face. You could count every pore. He paused to run his hand across his sweaty forehead, then continued. "I took money from very powerful people, who paid off my gambling debts and also helped me with my brother's care. Per their instructions, I stole evidence from the Crow Killer case. I also stole evidence from the Violinist case file and took the lockbox from the BLPD crime lab."

Luke glanced at Natalie with a look of intensity—*This is it*, his expression said.

"I also stole evidence from Violet Hawke's house. And here comes the big one—I kidnapped and killed Veronica Manes. Randy Holmes was my partner in crime. I did all this under great duress and threats to my life—however, no excuses. I burned down my house and attacked Detective Pittman when he confronted me about my involvement in Veronica's death. I never intended to hurt him. I never intended to end up here. I never wanted any part of this, but I felt trapped. It's my own fault, and I own it. But very powerful people have me by the balls. They've made it impossible for me *not* to break the law . . . let me explain."

# 64

Murphy stared a hostile beat into the camera, then said, "Once I was caught up in it, I was toast. These are very manipulative people, heavily into the occult. Once they had me in their web, I was trapped. So I compartmentalized these events in my mind. Not that my behavior didn't sicken me every second of every day." His face cracked with emotion, and he lowered his head to mask the pain and sighed heavily. Then he looked at the camera again. "Anyway. No excuses. I know full well what I've done." He reached out and turned off the camera.

There was a slight jump in the tape, and the camera flickered on again. This time it was a wider angle. Dying sunlight illuminated a large barren room, an unearthly scarlet painting the far walls. Murphy wore faded jeans and a black T-shirt. "I've got nothing left to hide," he said, sitting down on the sofa in front of a coffee table.

On the battered table in front of him was a half-demolished six-pack, a beveled glass ashtray, and a pack of cigarettes. "Regarding the death of Veronica Manes . . . Randy was the leader. Randolph Holmes. I basically followed orders. We went to her house shortly after midnight. I rang the doorbell. She was in her nightgown and bathrobe. I told her that Justin Fowler was in trouble and needed help. I made up some bullshit story, and since Justin was her friend, and since I'm a cop, she trusted me completely and put on her coat and boots, then grabbed her keys. We walked to the van, and once we were inside, I injected her with ketamine. Randy took over from there."

Murphy rescued his smoldering cigarette from the glass ashtray and took a nervous puff. "Who are these very powerful people? Who's in charge, you might ask?" he said in a calm, reasonable voice. "Oliver and Serena Chabert are their names. They own Bluebird Real Estate Investments. They're heavily into the occult. They believe in all that supernatural shit. When I was first introduced, I thought they were nice people, but it turns out they're dangerous psychopaths. They were part of a coven back in the seventies that included Randy Holmes, Frances and Violet Hawke, Ned Bertrand, and Dottie Coffman. There are others, but I don't know all their names. How I became involved . . . it's a fucking slippery slope. I had a gambling addiction. I was in serious trouble. They sought me out."

He picked up the last sweaty beer can and finished it off, then crumpled it up and set it down gently next to the others. "Anyway, the documents in the shoe box will help expose these people and what they've been doing for decades, including using me, Randy, and Samuel Winston to kill, threaten, torment, and harass people into giving them what they want. What do they want?" he asked rhetorically, then answered his own question. "Money, power, ego trip, their very own real estate empire, mixed with cruelty, sadism, and sociopathic tendencies."

Natalie could feel the hairs rising on her scalp as she listened with disbelief and stunned clarity. Everything he was saying aligned with the evidence they had so far.

"Most of what I did," Murphy went on, "was part of a series of ongoing cover-ups for things that had happened decades ago. Oliver's a businessman, but Serena is the heart and soul of the group. She terrifies me. And it's not as if the authorities were about to stop them. A huge law firm handles their business affairs. I don't know much about the attorneys at Fleming, Abercromby and Maddox, but they seem to turn a blind eye to what's going on, and they've pretty much done Oliver and Serena's bidding, as far as I can tell. Meanwhile, Frances and Ned raised their children in the dark arts, so they became twisted and perverted. Basically, they raised monsters."

Murphy scratched his head, his gaze expressionless. "The girl in the Polaroid that was found in the lockbox? That's basically what started it all. She went to school with Serena. Her name was Amber Caplinger. She was a bit of a flirt, from what I've heard, and Serena became jealous, because Oliver liked Amber. As a result of all this, Serena convinced the group to kidnap, torture, and kill Amber Caplinger. Then they used her image and bloody clothes in their rituals. Everything was about gaining power through the occult."

"Jesus." Luke grimaced.

On-screen, Murphy shook his head, then reached for the camera and zoomed in on his face. "You should look into several influential people who've vanished off the face of the earth—mostly in the Adirondacks—over the past couple of decades. I'll give you a few hints—check out Gerald Bartel, Troy Kraus, and Ashley Wittmeyer. They were all successful real estate people who didn't want to do business with BREI, or else they were in direct competition with them, so the Chaberts had them 'disappeared.' This allowed them to advance their agenda and majorly grow their empire." Murphy paused. "Okay, so. A lot of the activity I was involved in was about covering up for past mistakes. The girl in the yearbook, Amber, was rumored to have run away, and this became the official conclusion at the time. They instructed Dottie to destroy the lockbox, but instead she buried it in her backyard, which became problematic.

"Randy told me what really happened. They killed her in a ritualistic fashion, and then buried her in a remote part of the state forest where no one will ever find her," he went on. "After they killed her, the coven was bonded for life over this terrible act. Oliver and Serena blackmailed, bribed, and terrorized everyone else involved. They were all sworn to secrecy. But then, when Veronica started to snoop around, doing research for her next book, Serena had her killed to shut her up, and as a warning to the others. It was a particularly gruesome death, because . . ."

Murphy stopped talking. He lit another cigarette, drew on it deeply, and exhaled a plume of smoke. "Because a long time ago, Veronica had an affair with Oliver when he was married to Serena. Serena never forgave her for it. And when Veronica started poking her nose in their business after all these years, everybody knew she had to be dealt with. But Serena's jealousy reared its ugly head, and she couldn't help herself. That's why the murder was so vicious and gruesome." Murphy scowled and rubbed his face hard, then stared into the camera with bloodshot eyes. "Listen, just to set the record straight, I wanted out years ago. Long before this thing with Veronica, I wanted out. I couldn't live with myself anymore. I wanted my freedom back, so I've been plotting my escape. I have an offshore bank account and a bitcoin wallet. I've rented a cabin under a false name. I have a connection who's provided me with a fake ID. I plan to use this confession as a kill switch in case they come after me. I've securely stashed away the original, plus several copies in various different locations, because I'm no dummy. I'll be leaving the country for sure to destinations unknown. I'm convinced the Chaberts will go to any lengths to protect themselves. I suspect they've already instructed Randy to kill me. So now we come to my current dilemma."

It was deathly silent inside the room, the three of them riveted to the computer screen. Natalie felt prickles running up and down her spine.

Murphy put out his cigarette and stared intently into the camera. "I'm going to kill Randy Holmes. By the time you see this—whoever the fuck you are—Randy will be dead. I've done my homework, and I've decided to frame a couple from Albany for the murder. Turns out they're the perfect foils. I have a plan, and it's already being put into action. Hey." He scowled. "What else am I supposed to do? The Chaberts are coming after me. I know too much, and now the police suspect me. I'm a witness, and the Chaberts don't leave any witnesses behind." Murphy shrugged. "Hopefully, whoever is watching this, I'll be long gone. You won't find me. Believe me, I've worked very hard to cover my tracks." He stared into the camera. "One last thing I'll leave you with. A heads-up or a warning, depending on who's watching. Natalie Lockhart is in almost as much trouble as I am. They're going to have her eliminated."

Luke glanced at Natalie with stark fear in his eyes.

"She keeps messing up their plans. She killed Samuel, who was doing a good job of getting rid of the competition. Those five wealthy tourists who disappeared in the Adirondacks, that was Samuel's main mission. The Missing Nine were just a distraction. Smoke and mirrors. The rest of his victims were for fun. Samuel was a sadist. But Natalie messed it all up, and on top of that she arrested Ned Bertrand's pride and joy. They'll do to her what they did to Veronica . . . only this time I refuse to have any part of it. I'm out. This is my confession, my official statement. Hand to God, I'm telling the absolute truth."

Murphy stopped talking. His pupils had gone a dull, enamel black. He reached out and switched off the camera, and the screen went blank.

# 65

Over the next two weeks, Natalie, Luke, and the rest of the CIU went to the mattresses, living almost full-time at the station while they put together a solid case against the Chaberts and five co-conspirators.

Oliver and Serena split their time between Upstate New York, the Hamptons, and Colorado. It was a beautiful spring day in early April when Natalie and Luke went to arrest them, along with Assistant Chief Gossett and the Syracuse PD as part of a joint task force.

The Chaberts lived in an exclusive, gated community where the pine woods were veined with crystalline streams. A phalanx of cruisers and unmarked vehicles pulled up in front of the faux-Georgian mansion, where oak branches scattered the sunlight over the manicured lawn.

A slender, silver-haired maid answered the door. "Are they expecting you?"

"We're here on official business," Assistant Chief Gossett said.

"Come in." The maid stepped aside, and Natalie and Luke, along with the arresting detectives and officers from the Syracuse police, entered the light-filled foyer. They were here to serve papers—two arrest warrants and a search warrant.

"Please wait in the living room," the maid told them and walked briskly away.

The sun-filled living room was tastefully decorated with priceless paintings and antiques. The drapes were parted, revealing an expansive view of the stables out back.

Oliver and Serena came downstairs. He was impeccably dressed in a gray business suit, and Serena's high heels clacked against the parquet floor as they entered the living room together with a tight, guarded look around their eyes.

"What is the meaning of this?" Serena demanded to know.

"You're under arrest for the murder of Veronica Manes," Gossett told them. "We have a warrant to search the property." He handed her the paperwork.

Serena looked it over, then expelled a long breath. "You should have called our attorney. Oliver?" They stood together studying the paperwork.

Natalie and Luke stayed in the background, while the arresting officers formed a loose circle around the couple, their hands folded nonthreateningly in front of them. Then Syracuse lead detective Dawkins pulled a "rights card" out of his pocket and rattled off the Miranda warning. He finished by asking, "Do you understand your rights? Do you comprehend what I'm saying?"

Serena wore a furious scowl beneath her carefully made-up face, and Natalie couldn't believe that this was the same person she'd felt so warmly about at Hunter's party several weeks ago.

"Oliver," Serena said angrily, "call our attorney."

Oliver's mottled hands shook as he dialed the number on his phone.

Serena shot Natalie a death stare—now she could see her true nature.

More patrol cars with sirens blaring and lights flashing pulled up in front of the house. A dozen more officers poured out of their vehicles.

"We'll be conducting a search of the entire residence and property," Dawkins told the Chaberts. "We appreciate your cooperation. Will you come with us, please."

Serena asked her husband, "Did you call Maddox?"

"He'll meet us at the station," Oliver said.

"There's obviously been some sort of misunderstanding," she told Dawkins.

"After you, ma'am," he said.

As the couple passed Natalie, Serena's eyes hardened to a furious glare inside her fleshy, florid face.

Natalie could taste her own burning anger mingled with a gut-dissolving fear. This woman had fooled everyone. Only Veronica Manes sensed the evil lurking behind her bland, privileged exterior, and for that she had paid the ultimate price.

# 66

Two days later, they were tearing up the earth in search of body parts on Randy Holmes's property in Burning Lake. Natalie watched as the backhoe dug into a cordoned-off area where ground-penetrating radar had indicated that another body would be found.

She felt a shiver race through her. Dump site. Burial grounds. This was the raw challenge. You solved the riddle and arrested the bad guys. You became a hero in your own mind—at least for a little while. Except in this case, the bad guys were either in jail, incapacitated, or dead, so there would be no crystalized sense of justice.

She chugged her bottled water, then stared at the ugly gash in the earth where the eroded crustal soil had pulled apart like a gaping wound—the last of seven excavation pits. A stoop-shouldered man named Joseph was operating the backhoe. "Detective?" he said. "I think we got something."

She ducked under the yellow crime tape and cautiously approached the perimeter. Natalie needed to see for herself. She needed to touch the dirt. She needed to identify the victim. She needed to say hello.

Luke came up behind her. The backhoe swiveled away, and the loader bucket dumped the last of the rich-colored soil onto a growing pile. Part of a floral shower curtain jutted out of the spongy ground.

The police cadets formed a tight circle around the grave and dug with their trowels. Fifteen minutes later, they pulled out the remains wrapped in plastic, tied with butcher's string. Feeling a tightness in her chest, Natalie whispered, "Rest in peace."

At last they had them all. Seven missing women. The Shadow Girls. There were no more. The medical examiner had identified the victims using dental records. Because of the age of the remains, there would be no definitive cause of death. The hyoid bones weren't broken, and there were no indications of stabbings or strangulation. One could only speculate. Perhaps they'd been chloroformed and smothered in their sleep.

As she knelt on the ground, Natalie recognized Harmony Sean Young by the small silver christening bracelet worn around her left wrist. It was satisfying to have them all accounted for, while at the same time it was still baffling and horrifying. Just like the other victims, Harmony lay inside the shower curtain on a bed of dead roses, all the shriveled petals fallen off, leaving only the thorny stems. Her hands were folded together as if in prayer. Her nails had been painted pearlescent pink, and her pretty dark hair had been carefully brushed back and pinned with butterfly barrettes. She wore a blue dress, a white sweater, pantyhose, and blue flats.

With utter revulsion, Natalie realized that whoever had done this to Harmony had also loved her—in his own obsessive, fastidious fashion, the only way Randy Holmes was capable of loving anyone. There was a mother's touch about the exceptional care taken with all seven bodies, everything neatly polished and pressed and fastened and applied. The final Shadow Girl was somehow perfect in death, her hollow gaze fixed upon the clear blue sky.

Natalie swallowed the bitter taste of bile and stood up. It was early spring in Burning Lake, and new signs of growth were everywhere. Purple wildflowers sprouted through last autumn's leaves, protecting the body like the guardians of lost souls.

Now a large flock of crows erupted from the nearby forest with a cacophonous sound—dozens upon dozens of them, an eerie assemblage. There was a reason they were called "a murder of crows." They were scavengers, and they would eat anything. They preyed on the dead. Their angry-sad cries sent shivers cascading through her body as they circled toward the valley.

She couldn't stop thinking about her family and how much she had lost. Mother, father, both sisters. She gently pushed these thoughts aside. Sometimes while working a case, you had to get out of the way of yourself. There was still a lot to do. After all, not every single question had been answered. Not every thread had been tied up in a neat little bow.

# 67

## TWO WEEKS LATER

On a Monday evening in mid-April, Natalie stopped at her favorite corner store on her way home from work and picked up a bottle of wine, a loaf of French bread, and a bouquet of purple irises, hydrangea, and eucalyptus.

On the surface, at least, everything had been resolved. The Chaberts and their associates were being charged with crimes in several different jurisdictions. An internal investigation of the BLPD was ongoing. Hunter was moving away. He'd found a new investor to partner with in Colorado. He was going to sell the mansion. It relieved her to know that he'd be leaving Burning Lake for good.

Hunter had attempted to reach out to her in the initial days following their breakup, sending her multiple text messages and bouquets of white roses. She'd talked with him for half an hour over the phone, explaining her decision at length and trying to help him find closure. Eventually, he'd given up.

In early April, they'd had a brief interaction at the police station following the Chaberts' arrest, where Hunter had volunteered to give an interview, offering complete transparency in all of his business dealings. Due to the sensitive nature of the situation, Assistant Chief Gossett had questioned Hunter personally.

According to Gossett, Hunter was genuinely shocked and thoroughly distraught. He had solid alibis for all of the key dates and produced plenty of receipts—phone records, bank statements, business transactions, meeting schedules, and videotape from his security team. He gave the police access to anything they wanted and provided a list of witnesses who would vouch for his whereabouts in every questionable instance. He was willing to cooperate for as long as they needed him to. He was an open book. Gossett concluded that Hunter Rose wasn't involved in any criminal activities and wasn't even aware of the dark dealings of his business partners, the Chaberts.

Natalie was relieved. She didn't want him to be involved in any of this.

Maybe now, she thought hopefully, they could put it all behind them.

Maybe now everything would return to normal.

Tonight, Luke would be working late. He was still knee-deep in the internal investigation, searching for any possible links between Murphy and other employees at the BLPD. He was methodically interviewing everyone in the department, working his way from the center outward. It wasn't quick, but it would be thorough. So far, he hadn't found any other complicit parties, and things were looking good.

It was six thirty by the time Natalie got home. She arranged the flowers in a vase, took a shower, put Billie Holiday on the sound system, and prepped the meal. Since it was too early to start cooking, she poured herself a glass of wine and took her laptop into the living room, where she sat typing up her reports.

Ten minutes later, her phone rang. "Hey," she answered.

"Hey, you," Luke said in a low, affectionate voice.

She smiled. "How's it going?"

"We're halfway through the rank and file. So far so good."

"Maybe it all ended with Murphy?" she said hopefully.

"It's looking that way."

"When are you coming home?"

"No later than eight."

"Do you want spaghetti for dinner?"

He laughed. "I didn't know you cooked."

"I'm a terrible cook, but I'm good at three dishes. Pizza, spaghetti, and cheeseburgers."

"Spaghetti sounds fine. Your place or mine?"

"Mine," she said. "I can't wait to see you, Luke."

"Me, too," he said, then hung up.

Around seven, she heard a scraping sound and got up to check it out.

The living-room windows overlooked the front yard. Wisps of fog shivered across the road. The moon had slid behind the congregating clouds. There were very few streetlights on this side of town, and the isolated darkness gave her chills. She caught an erratic movement out of the corner of her eye—but it was only a few bats traveling across the night sky.

In the spring, the bats would come out in droves, fluttering overhead. When you lived out in the boonies, encounters with wildlife were common. She'd seen plenty of wild turkeys and foxes in these woods. You could follow the deer paths through the underbrush. Late at night, raccoons would rattle the garbage cans.

There was an odd rattling sound now. She stared at the misty front yard, but nothing was out there. She crossed the room, took her Glock out of its holster, stepped into her boots, threw on her jacket, and paused in front of the door, listening.

She could hear footsteps on the other side. Somebody was running away.

Natalie flung the door open and found something waiting for her. Sweat clung to her skin. She didn't see anyone fleeing the scene, only shifting wisps of fog.

She picked up an old glass mason jar filled with a suspicious yellow liquid and shook it gently. There were a couple of opals on the bottom, along with a skinny braid of human-looking hair. She unscrewed the lid. It smelled like piss.

Okay, somebody had left her a witch bottle. In Wiccan folk magic, jar spells consisted of specific herbs and potions that were sealed inside "witch bottles," which kept their power concentrated and prevented any hexes from escaping before they had done their job.

She looked around her property. Traffic was sparse this time of night. The moon slipped behind the clouds, and she was bathed in darkness for a moment. She tried to shake off the creep factor, unnerved by the subtle shift in the atmosphere.

The moon reemerged from behind the clouds. Across the street were the cedar and pine woods, thick and sweet-smelling. She didn't see any mysterious figures lurking in the shadows.

She took the mason jar inside and sealed it in a freezer storage bag. She would ask Lenny to dust it for prints in the morning. As she was examining the jar by the kitchen light, a vehicle pulled up to the house. Moments later, the doorbell rang.

"Shit, now what?"

She flung open the door.

Kip Edwards, the ex-journalist-turned-Substack-blogger, stood on her doorstep. He wore jeans, a faded *Star Wars* T-shirt, a baseball cap, and a green vinyl jacket. "Hi, Detective Lockhart. Sorry to bother you, but—"

"Were you just here?" she interrupted.

He seemed taken aback. "No. Why?"

"Somebody was just here. You didn't see anyone passing by on the road?"

"No," he said, pushing his wire-rim glasses back up his nose. "Is everything okay? You look upset."

"No, I'm fine."

"I came to ask you a favor, Detective. I know you don't like to give interviews, but if I could just ask a few questions . . ."

"No comment," Natalie said, about to close the door.

"Wait! You owe me, Detective," he said, scowling at her through his wire-rims. His salt-and-pepper hair was curly damp from the fog. "You used me to get a response from Detective Murphy. Didn't I tell you it would work? Well, I did you a huge favor, so the way I see it, you owe me one."

She hesitated—it was true, she had used him for her own purposes, which involved solving a major felony. "Look, Kip," she said. "I really don't want to be the focus of an interview. I have my reasons. I appreciate your help. All I can promise is that it won't go unnoticed. Okay?"

"What do you mean, it won't go unnoticed?" he pressed. "Does that mean you'll give me a heads-up the next time something exciting happens?"

"I mean it won't go unappreciated."

"Tit for tat?"

She hesitated.

"Because in that case, I have some information you might be interested in."

"What kind of information?"

He smiled. "It's about Bella Striver."

Natalie paused, chewing on her lower lip. "What about her?"

His face lit up. "Follow me in your car. It's better if I show you. More impact."

"Are you serious?"

He was already halfway across the yard, heading for his red Nissan sedan. "Come on!"

# 68

Natalie followed Kip Edwards across town and parked behind his Nissan in front of the overgrown acre of land formerly owned by Corbin Striver. Nothing had changed in this Sleeping Beauty landscape. Weeds grew thick and clotted on the front yard. STRIVER was painted on the old mailbox. A sturdy chain-link fence encircled the property, and wired to the fence were spaced-apart metal signs that read PRIVATE PROPERTY—NO TRESPASSING.

Natalie got out of her car and studied Bella's childhood home in the moonlight—a modest Edwardian covered in crawling vines. The windows were locked. She felt a sick chill. She hadn't been to this place in almost a decade. The nearest neighbor was far enough down the road not to see the two of them standing there. A dense all-encroaching forest grew around the property, hugging it protectively.

She turned to Kip and said, "Okay, I'm here. What's this all about?"

"I was recently contacted by two amateur ghost hunters who stayed overnight in this house. Follow me."

"Where are we going?"

"Trust me." He gave her a petulant look. "Don't you trust me by now?"

"No," she said. "But lead the way."

They tromped through the weeds that grew around the fence for ten or so yards, until Kip pointed out a place where the rusty chain links had been busted through. It was obvious trespassers had broken in multiple times. You could see a visible trail in the weeds leading toward the back of the house.

"Okay, so here's the scoop," Kip explained quietly. "Last month, Miles MacDonald and his girlfriend, Felicia, decided to camp out here overnight and videotape their exploits. Miles said it was pretty creepy but uneventful for the most part. But then, around two in the morning . . ." He took out his phone and showed her a YouTube video. "They captured this. Look." He showed her several minutes' worth of scrambled, confusing video footage of a figure being chased through the woods—flashes of a hooded parka racing away from the scene, accompanied by lots of shouting and yelling from the pursuers. "They swear it was Bella Striver, but they didn't capture her face on video."

"Unfortunately, that's not proof of anything," Natalie told him.

"Yeah, I know, but look. They found these Wiccan symbols drawn on the walls of her room. Wait. I'll replay it for you, hold on." He scrolled through the video, then hit pause. "See there?"

Natalie squinted down at the screen. She recognized the faded violin wallpaper from Bella's old room, and someone had used a Sharpie to write Bella's name in all caps next to a large Awen symbol on the wall. As the camera panned around the rest of the room, there was evidence of recent trespassing—a stash of junk food, crumpled fast-food wrappers, rolls of toilet paper, a sleeping bag, some bottled waters, and other evidence that the room was being occupied.

"Well?" Kip said now, watching her expectantly.

An Awen was an ancient druid symbol signifying creative awakening and divine inspiration. It looked like three rays of light drawn inside a circle.

"There's nothing definitive that says Bella was here." She shook her head. "It could've been anybody. Miles and his friends might've staged it."

"Oh come on," Kip said. "Give me something, Detective. This is good stuff."

Just to get rid of him, she said, "Email me a few questions, and I'll answer them for your blog."

"Really?" He beamed. "That's great. Thank you!"

"You'd better go now, before I change my mind."

"Okay," he said, tucking his phone away. "Listen, I admire you, Detective. You're my hero." She didn't know whether he meant it ironically or not. It was hard to tell with this guy. He walked back to his car and drove away, leaving her alone in the moonlight.

# 69

Natalie fetched her flashlight from the car, then stood for a moment looking around the property. She would have to tread lightly, since there obviously could be trespassers or squatters inside the house. She pushed the broken part of the fence aside and crawled through the gap. She emerged onto the weedy front yard.

Natalie trekked around behind the house, where she took the rough-hewn steps up to the porch and knocked on the weathered door. The paint had peeled off a long time ago. The doorbell was broken. There was no response. Nothing stirred inside—no squatters or wild animals or Bella in her gray hoodie.

Natalie cupped her hands over one of the porch windows and peered inside. She could make out the familiar shadows of the Strivers' old kitchen.

She rattled the doorknob, then rammed the door with her shoulder, attempting to break the lock. When that didn't work, she tested the porch windows, but they were all sealed tight. She picked up an old brick and broke the glass, then reached inside and unlocked the window, slid it open and crawled inside.

Natalie landed on the kitchen floor, instantly recognizing the cramped little table where she and Bella used to sit after school and do their homework together. Bored, Bella would kick the wooden chair legs with her heels, and her father would turn and say, "Bella, don't kick the furniture," and she would reply, "I'm practicing Handel's sonata in my head." That always made him smile.

After a dinner of mac and cheese, the girls would clear the table and run upstairs to Bella's room, where they'd stay up half the night giggling and sharing their opinions about everything, along with all their hopes and dreams.

Now Natalie went into the living room, where the old-fashioned windows splashed a sheen of moonlight across the dusty walls. The varnished moldings were cracked with neglect. The vents and light fixtures were congested with dust. During the summer months, it used to be air-conditioned to the point of chilliness inside the house. Mr. Striver sweated a lot, and his face was like a pitted road. In the background, jazz songs about lost love were constantly playing.

Upstairs, Natalie swept her flashlight beam over the cobwebs in Bella's room. It was disorienting. Nothing had changed. The room was like a shrine to her memory, with movie posters on the wall—*The Matrix, The Sixth Sense, Titanic*—and CDs in the bookcase—Nirvana, Salt-N-Pepa, Pearl Jam. In the closet were Bella's old T-shirts, flannel shirts, worn jeans, Doc Martens, and Converse high-top sneakers.

The floorboards creaked as Natalie tiptoed around, trying not to awaken Bella's ghost. There was a small closet, a cracked vanity mirror, Bella's old music stand and an army of Troll dolls gathered on the bedside table, staring solemnly at Natalie.

She felt stuck in a time warp as she shone her light over the faded bedroom walls and saw the prominent Awen along with other Wiccan symbols scrawled across the fading wallpaper. It was eerie. What was the message here? There were several images of the Waxing Moon. For Wiccans, it was the maiden phase or "naïve" phase of the moon, when the Goddess was at the very beginning of her journey.

Now something crunched underfoot. Natalie took a step back, and there was a loud snap. One of the rotting floorboards gave a little underfoot. It shifted beneath her weight, revealing a narrow opening in the floor.

There used to be a rug here, Natalie vaguely recalled. She knelt down and pried up the splintery board. It took a bit of muscle, but the next board came up more easily. There was a stash of stuff hidden under the floorboards, rolled up inside a plastic bag.

Natalie upended the contents onto the floor—a few joints in a baggie, a roll of rumpled twenty-dollar bills held together with a rubber band, and a paperback copy of *On the Road* by Jack Kerouac. Natalie counted the cash—$140 total. She picked up the book and was flipping through its pages, when all of a sudden a Polaroid snapshot fell out.

She picked up the Polaroid. It had been taken more than a dozen years ago. Bella and Hunter Rose smiled at the camera. He had his arm around her slender waist, and Bella was smoking a joint in a comical fashion, holding it with her pinkie finger extended.

Natalie turned the Polaroid over. Nothing was written on the back. She opened the book and found an inscription inside the front cover. She recognized Hunter's handwriting—those flourishes, the looping *g*'s and unambiguous *B*'s, and finally the bold strong strokes that composed the stand-alone *H*, which was how he signed his first name. *H. Rose.*

The inscription read: "We'll be on the road soon enough, Bella Button, xox, H."

# 70

Bill Finley let Natalie into the mansion on 73 Hollins Drive. Bill was clearly surprised to see her there but hid it well beneath his professional smile. "Mr. Rose is in the living room," he told her, then exited the house, closing the front door behind him.

Natalie walked across the front hallway into the glowing living room. Her stomach tightened and her face burned as she paused in the doorway to take it all in.

A harvest gold archway divided the living room from the dining room. Radiant moonlight sparkled through the western-facing windows. There was the familiar blue velvet sofa, along with the wingback chairs, the nine-foot ceilings, and rococo brass sconces. A fire blazed in the hearth. However, the rest of the furniture was covered in drop cloths, and there was a stack of moving boxes in one corner.

Hunter was seated in silhouette on the plush velvet sofa, his face lit by the glow of the fireplace. He wore a contemplative expression. He turned when he heard her come in. There was a blip of pain in his bleary eyes. "Natalie? What are you doing here?" He stood up. He was holding a bottle of wine.

"We need to talk about this," she said, handing him the old paperback.

Hunter blinked at her. He fumbled for a moment, dropping the book and then picking it up from the floor. "Where'd you find this?"

"In Bella's house."

He looked at her. "I can explain. Have a seat. Are you cold? I'm cold. It's chilly." He put the wine bottle and paperback down on the coffee table, then went over to the fireplace. He knelt in front of the hearth and fed the crackling fire.

They used to fuck in front of that fireplace. One of his favorite activities was feeding the flames on a cold winter night. His other favorite activities included pouring them drinks, reading the newspaper, and watching her surreptitiously from across the room as she performed the most mundane tasks. Then sneaking up behind her and grabbing her around the middle and nuzzling her neck. Fucking her. Natalie was one of his favorite activities.

Now the Black Forest clock chimed on the mantelpiece. Moonlight pressed in around the house, filtering through a tangle of branches and casting jigsaw puzzle pieces on the antique rugs. Hunter brushed off his hands and went to sit on the velvet sofa again. He picked up the bottle and said, "Zenato Amarone 2016 from Veneto, Italy. It's supposed to have hints of violet, dried cherries, and roasted plums. I personally can't taste it. Would you like a glass? I can uncork another bottle . . ."

"No, thanks." She stared at him.

He watched her self-consciously. "You're making me nervous. Please have a seat."

"I'm not sitting down. We aren't having a friendly chat."

"No?" He smiled. "I talked a lot of shit today. Phony shit. So now, whenever I open my mouth, it feels like I'm vomiting disconnected words . . . a word slushy. Like all this nonsense is spilling out of my mouth. You know? Talking shit." He nodded. "I find myself wandering into bullshit land. And I don't want to do that with you, Natalie. So I'm asking you to sit down and talk to me. Person to person. Please."

She sat in one of the wingback chairs. Muted firelight filled the room. "All right." She held out the Polaroid picture. "Tell me about you and Bella."

Hunter nodded. "She wanted to travel that summer, really badly. She persuaded me to go with her. I didn't have anything better to do. My parents were in Europe. I've told you what a total fuckup I was. Anyway, we figured we'd drive out to the West Coast, and then head down to Mexico. I had friends in Santa Barbara. We were going to crash with them, then head south. We had big plans. But obviously, it all fell through."

"What happened?" Natalie asked, her heartbeat ticking nervously in her throat.

"Bella didn't want to tell anyone where she was going, especially not her father. She hated him for having so much control over her life. She was pissed at the world, and in retrospect, I think she wanted to punish him. So—me being a complete jerkoff, I agreed, and we snuck out of town that night."

"The night of her high school graduation?"

He nodded. "She told me where to pick her up, and I did. We took off. She called it liberating. We partied hard for a couple of weeks—weed, coke, hash, you name it. We were totally out of it. Somehow, we ended up in this run-down motel in a cheesy border town, where we partied for twenty-four hours straight. Just enjoying each other's company. We had no idea what kind of chaos we'd left behind. We had no clue what was going on back home. We were oblivious. We slept all day, then got drunk, and explored the nightlife. If we'd known what was going on, Bella would have called you, Natalie. She would've called her father. But that's not what happened."

Natalie nodded slowly. "So what happened?"

"We got hold of some heroin. We crashed, two days passed, I think. When I woke up, I swear to God, I thought she was dead. She was cold and blue. She wasn't breathing. There was vomit in her hair. I tried to revive her, but nothing I did roused her. I thought for sure she was dead, so I panicked. Pure panic. I'd heard about Mexican prisons, and I wasn't about to trust the local cops. So I packed my stuff and got the hell out of there. We'd already paid for the room in cash and given them a phony name, and so I just took off. I never told a soul."

"You just left her there?" she repeated incredulously.

He nodded slowly. "I thought she was dead."

"Why didn't the motel alert the authorities? They would've had to tell someone there was a dead American on the premises, wouldn't they?"

Hunter looked at her. "You'd think so, wouldn't you?"

"What's that supposed to mean?"

"It means it didn't go down that way." He took a swig from the bottle.

"When you got home, why didn't you tell anyone about it?" Natalie asked with total disgust.

"Because by then it was too late," he said numbly. "There was a huge search party full of police and volunteers. Everybody was looking for Bella. At that point, I realized that I'd be blamed for her death. But then, things took an even worse turn."

"They blamed Nesbitt," Natalie said, remembering.

"The police suspected Nesbitt, and instead of intervening, I just let it happen. I didn't know what else to do. I felt paralyzed. I watched it unfold like a fucking nightmare. He was innocent. My brother loved Bella. I should've spoken up, but honestly, I had no idea that he'd end his own *life* over it. I figured things would work out somehow. I'd always been lucky. But his death is on me. It's all on me." He took another swig from the bottle. "And I'll have to live with that for the rest of my life."

"What about Bella's letters?" Natalie asked. "And the Polaroids proving she was alive? Did you do that? Did you write them?"

"No." He looked at her and said, "Do me a favor. Go over to that wall where the credenza used to be."

Natalie frowned. She didn't know what he was implying. She glanced at the white wall, exposed now. She got up and went over to look at it.

She noticed a familiar crack and ran her finger lightly over it. There was a nail pop approximately eight inches diagonal to the right of the crack, just like the flaws in the Polaroids Bella had sent home. This was the same white wall Bella had posed in front of all those years ago.

Natalie could barely catch her breath to speak. She drew her weapon. "Hunter," she said with strained authority. "Raise your hands. Slowly."

He didn't move.

"Keep your hands where I can see them."

"Go ahead. Put me out of my misery." He raised the bottle to his lips.

"Don't you move," she said with gritted teeth. "Not one muscle." A glaze of sweat broke out on her face. "Put that down and slowly raise your hands."

Hunter's eyes grew as heavy as stones. He put down the bottle and showed her the palms of his hands. He sighed as if a burden had been lifted. "Let me tell you about that wall."

The silence in the room grew malevolent. She kept thinking, This is crazy. She was so angry, her heart gave a twitch.

"Natalie, there's more to the story. Lower the gun, please," he said.

She could feel the blood draining from her head. Her hands were buzzing. Her feet were lead weights. She knew that things could turn tragic very quickly if she wasn't careful. "Oh, really? You can explain this one away?" she asked cynically.

"Yeah." His features grew still. "Stop pointing that thing at me."

Her fury spiked. She sighted down her weapon. "Did you kidnap Bella on the night of her high school graduation? Did you kill her, Hunter? An-swer me!"

"Of course I didn't kill her," he shot back angrily. "I've been trying to keep her from killing you!"

# 71

Natalie's heart was beating painfully hard. It took a moment for the shock to recede. "What the hell are you talking about?" she demanded.

"It's true, I took those Polaroid pictures of Bella the previous spring," Hunter explained. "She liked hanging out at my place. We joked around and got high. She was fun and imaginative. She asked me to take a series of Polaroids for this collage she was making for her art class. She wore different outfits and different moods, but she posed against the same wall. It was all her idea."

Natalie shook her head sadly. "She never told me any of this."

"Right, because she was jealous of you," he said bluntly.

"Jealous?"

Hunter nodded. "Very competitive. I think she seduced me to get back at you."

"Oh, she seduced you?" Natalie said angrily.

"You don't have to believe me." He took another swig from the bottle. He was silhouetted against the fire, and she couldn't read his expression.

Natalie was beginning to realize that perhaps she didn't know Bella at all, and that their relationship had been an illusion. Best friends. Maybe, maybe not.

Or perhaps Hunter was lying.

"Wait," she said. "How did the Polaroids end up in those letters Bella sent home? If I'm to believe she went on a road trip with you, that means she must've taken those pictures with her?"

"She took lots of things," he explained. "Her violin, her diaries, those Polaroids, her sketchbook . . . she wanted to document our experiences on the road. Anyway, I don't know what happened after the incident at the motel, but she obviously didn't die."

"But you said you tried to revive her," Natalie countered, full of doubts. If he was trying to gaslight her, that made him highly dangerous.

"I know," Hunter said defensively. "Maybe in my crazed panic state, I assumed she was dead. She certainly looked dead. She was fucking blue. She didn't appear to be breathing."

"Appear? Jesus. So you're saying she didn't die? That she sent those letters home? What for? Why not just come back to Burning Lake?"

"I have no idea. All I know is that she found out about the media interest in her—the news crews, the search parties, the volunteers. Maybe she liked the attention? She used to wonder what it would be like to attend her own funeral. But it was Bella writing those letters, and she included the Polaroids we'd taken the previous spring as 'proof' that she was alive. That's when I realized she'd survived the overdose, and that's when she started to torment me."

"Torment you?" Natalie repeated, lowering her weapon. "How?"

He scowled as if it were obvious. "She could've come home immediately and cleared everything up with the police. At any point Bella could have returned to Burning Lake and ended the questions about her disappearance. She knew very well I couldn't tell anyone that I'd abandoned her in Mexico. She was holding the sword of Damocles over my head."

"All you had to do was tell the truth."

"By that point, my brother was dead, and the town was in an uproar. She could've invented any lie she wanted to about me. She could've said I abducted her, or that I raped her. They would've hung me in the town square. She was very aware of what she was doing. She called me out of the blue that August to ask for money."

"Did she tell you what happened to her?"

He nodded. "She woke up in a pool of her own vomit. I wasn't there. She felt abandoned. Another American we'd met at the motel helped her out. He invited her to go back to Monterey with him. He offered her a place to stay. They did drugs every day for a month, but then he dumped her. That's when she called me, demanding to be compensated for her trouble and threatening to tell the press a pack of lies about me. She promised if I wired her the money, she'd leave me alone. She wouldn't tell anyone what had happened in Mexico, or that I was involved in her disappearance. I wired her five thousand dollars, hoping that would be the end of it."

"But it wasn't," Natalie guessed.

He shook his head. "That's when she started writing letters to you and her father, explaining that she'd run away. She included those Polaroids, which I thought was a nice touch. She was threatening me. She was laughing in my face."

"And then the police closed the case," Natalie said. "But it wasn't over?"

"Of course not. Two or three times a year, I'll get a call from Bella asking for more money. I ended up wiring cash to Italy, England, France, Asia, and all over the United States. It never lets up. It's never the end. I could tell her drug habit was getting worse. Over the years, her health has deteriorated, to say nothing of her mental state. She just wants money from me. I'm supporting her lifestyle. Her requests come with the unspoken threat that at any point in time, she can reveal what kind of a monster I am."

Natalie was surprised by his candor. Usually, you had to pry the truth out of people who'd buried their secrets so long ago, even they didn't recognize the truth anymore. "And what has she been doing all this time, besides traveling?"

He shrugged. "Way back when, Bella told me she wanted to lead a vagabond life. She wanted to watch the sunset from a beach in Thailand and play her violin in the Black Forest. I honestly don't know. I don't ask. She never volunteers. She doesn't ask about her father or talk about Burning Lake. She's never asked about you. It's like half of her isn't there anymore. As if she lost part of herself in Mexico. I don't know."

"So she calls you several times a year to ask for more money?"

"Our conversations are very brief. Very disconnected. Like I said, she's not all there, Natalie. She's not the person you remember. Maybe she never was."

"And when was the last time you were in touch with her?"

Hunter crossed his arms and looked at her. "Three days ago."

"What?" she gasped.

"Everything changed last year when you solved the Crow Killer case. You were in the national news for a while, and that must've jarred something loose in her. So she came back to Burning Lake three months ago, and she's been threatening me with all sorts of things. She's been threatening to hurt you. She's the one who left those dead animals on my property, along with the Wiccan objects. I've been trying to buy her off, but she's elusive, and there's something wrong with her, Natalie. She believes she's a witch on a journey. She said something about you being in her way spiritually. That's why I wanted you to move away with me. I thought you'd be safer someplace else. That's why I gave you the tracking device."

Natalie was blown away. "Why didn't you tell me any of this before?" she shouted. "Why'd you keep this information from me?"

"Because I thought I'd lose you," he admitted sadly. "I lost you anyway."

He put the bottle down with exceeding gentleness. "Just because she didn't die back then, it doesn't make me innocent. Like I said, we were partying a lot, booze and coke and weed and pills and what have you. We were burning through cash, but I could afford it. We'd get baked half the day, and the other half we'd be looking for drugs. She was a free spirit. She was always doing crazy shit, like talking to biker gangs or throwing things at me. I was attracted to her energy, until it became malevolent," he confessed. "The truth is, I realized I'd gotten in over my head. I was almost glad when I thought she was dead. That's an ugly thing to say, I know . . . but I want to be truthful with you."

Natalie felt a strange mix of sympathy and revulsion. Hunter was good at explaining himself. She felt sorry for him, but she knew her empathetic feelings could also be a trap. She hardened her resolve and asked, "How does she contact you?"

"She buys burner phones, probably a lifelong habit from doing drugs. She'll call or text me out of the blue, then tell me where to meet her, and I'll go there and we'll talk about the payout. She keeps demanding more every year. She thinks she can score big this time. I wanted to go to the police, but it would only make me the target of an investigation, and I can't afford that. It would hurt my business, everything I've built for myself. That could all go away. I honestly didn't know what else to do. I didn't tell you, because I thought it would put an end to even the remote possibility we might get back together. Natalie, you're the most valuable person in the world to me. I love you. I care about you more than anyone else on the planet."

The blood left Natalie's face. He had done awful things while insisting that he loved her. He had tracked her whereabouts, lied to her, deceived her. He'd been love-bombing her. He was manipulative and persuasive. And now she couldn't help feeling sorry for him, but this was a mess of his own making.

"Do you have her phone number?" she asked.

He dug a piece of paper out of his pocket and said, "It keeps changing, but here's the last one she gave me."

Natalie holstered her weapon. "I want you to call her and set up a meeting for tonight. As soon as possible."

"Okay, I'll try." He took out his phone and texted a message.

They waited in silence.

Natalie recalled a memory—the time Bella jokingly licked Natalie on the face with her wet tongue. She'd been acting like a dog, prancing around, wagging her tail, and barking, and making the other Misfits laugh.

When Bella disappeared on the night of their high school graduation, both girls were on the cusp of exciting things. Natalie had gotten into Boston University, and Bella had gotten accepted at the Harrington Brock Music Conservatory. All Bella wanted to do was escape. *Let's travel around the world and stay in youth hostels across Europe.* She'd marked up an atlas of all the places she wanted to visit. *I love the idea of India, don't you?*

During their sleepovers, Natalie and Bella would confide their deepest secrets. "I don't want to play concertos," Bella told her once, "I want to *live* them. Let's have big bold lives, Natalie. Those old composers had the most amazing adventures. Bach played his violin in the middle of the Black Forest, Peter Warlock dabbled in black magic, and Franz Liszt had affairs with married women. We could have affairs with Italian men. Italians make the best lovers, you know," she said, as if she knew. *"Avoir une bonne vie.* Have a good life."

Bella hated her father's ambitions for her and called Mr. Striver "my smother-mother daddy." She said he kept her in a box. "Not a literal box," she explained, "but a psychological box where I can't breathe. He's got my whole life planned out for me, and basically I'm going to be a violin soloist, whether I like it or not."

More than once, Natalie had witnessed Mr. Striver's overbearing attitude toward his daughter when she visited Bella at home or at Striver's Music Shop after school. He would say inappropriate things like, "Bella's violin costs more than my car!" He'd make cringeworthy jokes about the f-holes in a violin. Bella would say, "Dad, you're so embarrassing!" He would constantly remind Bella, "Recital face, sweetheart! Remember to smile!" Behind his back, Bella made monster faces and called him her stage mom with a dick.

*The day before I decided to do it, to finally run away from it all,* Bella had written to Natalie in one of her 2009 letters, *Dad was in the kitchen making pancakes and listening to Prokofiev. His eyes were closed, and he was swaying to the music when I walked in. "Listen to this cadenza, Bella," he said. He had a glass of wine in one hand and a spatula in the other. Wine for breakfast again, huh, Dad? "We're going to put a little meat on Bella's bones," he said. He ruffled my hair, and each time he dropped another pancake on my plate, he said, "Here you go, my angel. Eat up. Put a little meat on those bones." All of this would've been too much for me, if I didn't have a secret plan out of Dodge.*

A secret plan.

Bella had never explained in any of her letters how she'd gotten the hell out of Dodge. All she said was that she was happy now, still playing her violin and at peace with herself. There was a hippieish tinge to her newfound freedom—*I'm more "me" than I've ever been before, Nat. I've found peace and I hope you do, too.* Bella was satisfied, content, and fulfilled with her life—or so she claimed—and she wanted the same for Natalie. That was the last letter Natalie had ever received from her old friend, and then the police closed the case. Bella Striver was officially declared a runaway.

Now Natalie felt a dark energy surround her. She grew cold. Hunter's eyes were tracking her with nervous calculation. Suddenly his phone rang, interrupting the silence.

He read the text message aloud. "Meet me at the old theme park. Fifteen minutes. In front of the bandstand."

"Tell her you'll be there," Natalie instructed. "Then sit tight. If she texts you again, tell her you're on your way. Don't say anything about me. Understand?"

He nodded and texted Bella back. Then he said, "Be careful, Natalie. I'm serious. She's not well."

# 72

Outside, eerie moon shadows slithered across the landscape. Natalie unlocked her car and got in, feeling the prickles racing across her scalp. What Hunter had just revealed, peeling back layers of history, was shocking and confusing. She had to fight her own numbness as she backed out of the driveway and pulled out onto the road.

When she reached the end of the street, another vehicle's brights blotted out her vision for a second. Headlights splashed across her face and washed over her head as the vehicle did a three-point turnaround in the middle of the road, then peeled away, tires screaming.

Natalie tentatively identified it as a Chevy Cavalier, dark blue or black. She had seen the driver only for a brief flash, but that was enough—a woman with wild dark hair and angry, spinning eyes, who looked like an older, more savage version of Bella.

"Fuck!" Natalie muttered, hitting the gas and speeding after the receding taillights. She clasped the wheel between her sweaty palms and felt the blood rush from her head. There were spots dancing in front of her eyes, and she blinked them away.

She took one country lane after another, following the vehicle deeper into the woods, driving for another mile or so until she recognized where they were headed—they were speeding along Solomon Road toward the old ruins that lay hidden on the edge of town, exactly where Hunter was supposed to meet Bella.

A few minutes later, the Chevy came to an abrupt stop ahead of Natalie, and a slender figure in a gray hoodie got out and ran into the woods.

Natalie's high beams cast crazy shadows over the nightscape as she squealed to a stop. Her stomach clenched as everything snapped into focus. She scooped her flashlight out of the glove compartment and got out. The wind howled through the woods as she reached into her shoulder holster and took out her semiautomatic Glock. She popped the magazine and saw that a round was chambered.

The Chevy Cavalier was parked haphazardly in the road, its emergency lights blinking and the driver's side door flung open. The car's brightly lit interior showed that it was empty.

Weapon drawn, Natalie slowly approached the abandoned car. The LED lights had been removed from the license plate well, and the rear plate was smeared with mud. A familiar sound was coming from the Cavalier—*ding, ding, ding*. The open-door alarm. It reminded her of a windup toy crashing a pair of cymbals together. *Ding, ding, ding.*

She spun around and pointed her weapon into the woods, then strained to pick up any stray sounds. A few seconds later, she heard footsteps and spotted the hooded figure running in an easterly direction, darting through the trees.

"Freeze!" she shouted.

The figure didn't stop.

Natalie ran after her, plunging through the underbrush, her boots sinking into the muddy ground with a weighted diving-bell feel. She took an unmarked trail into the park, running for many yards until she came to a broken fence knee-deep in undergrowth. She could hear the dance of her own heartbeat as she stepped over the fallen fence with its rusty KEEP OUT sign and entered the old theme park on the outskirts of town.

# 73

Funland Village had been decommissioned half a century ago, pad-locked and left to rot. Now the old theme park was officially part of the vast state forest that spread into the Adirondacks and beyond. Fifty years later, the boarded-up concession stand and abandoned ticket booth were buried in tangled vines. The "sculpture garden" was populated with huge, crumbling cement figurines from Grimm's fairy tales—a headless Evil Queen, Jack and his beanstalk, a mossy-eyed Cinderella and her ugly stepsisters. Everything in this apocalyptic playground was drowning in underbrush, having been devoured by nature long ago.

Natalie and her high school friends used to hang out here after school. They'd get high and laugh at the big goofy demented-looking giants and elves and twisted old crones. Now a shiver ran through her. The trek through the woods was spooky at night.

Beyond Rapunzel's tower was the collapsed stone bridge that she and Bella jokingly called "The Bridge to Nowhere." Beyond the bridge was the old bandstand, an elevated stage with a gazebo roof where musicians used to play. Circling the gazebo was a modest dance floor, and around the pe-riphery of the dance floor were a handful of evenly spaced wrought-iron benches, now covered in forest debris.

Natalie's next move would be critical. "Bella?" she called out, then scanned the woods, trying to locate her old friend, the same person who'd left those dead animals on Hunter's property, the same person who'd carved Natalie's name backwards into a tree in Blackthorn Park, the same person who'd gifted her with a mason jar full of urine on her front porch, the one who'd been trying to frighten and intimidate her for the past three months.

A wave of nausea engulfed her. The treetops danced in the wind. The large fairy-tale figurines appeared to be wading through a river of weeds. It reminded her of a haunted topiary garden—hedges trimmed to resemble monsters. She listened to the rush of wind through the undergrowth—a ghostly, pleading sound. Begging for forgiveness. A reprieve from the past.

Natalie tried to slow her racing pulse, while she aimed her weapon around and got her bearings. Behind her were more woods. To her right was the Tilt-A-Whirl, and in front of her was the haunted mansion, or what was left of it. Half of the brick building had fallen down and been swallowed up by forest growth.

Now she heard footsteps running through the underbrush and caught a movement in the broad dark shadow of the haunted mansion. Fear caked her heart. A lone figure was jogging through the theme park—jeans and a hooded sweatshirt.

A swift rigidity fell over her. "Bella?"

This person, this stranger, stopped in her tracks. Natalie could see her eyes through a curtain of hair, and there was the suggestion of fear in her crimped mouth.

"We need to talk, Bella. It's me, Natalie!"

She darted into the haunted mansion and disappeared.

# 74

A shudder crawled up Natalie's spine as she entered the ruins and aimed her weapon at every shadow. The haunted mansion used to be full of spooky, amateurish displays—a marionette leaping out of a closet, a demented-looking baby doll in a carriage, a dusty skeleton stretched out on the rack, a basket of decapitated mannequin heads under a guillotine spattered with fake blood—but the place had deteriorated like the rest of the theme park, and now half the interior walls had caved in, and the half that remained standing were unstable. Just past the CONDEMNED sign was a treacherous pile of bricks, broken boards, and shattered glass.

It was dark inside, with scattered holes in the roof letting in shards of moonlight. Natalie heard footsteps and followed the sound over to a dank stairwell. She aimed her flashlight and her service weapon into the tunneling darkness, then descended the creaky wooden steps.

At the bottom of the stairs, she paused to listen, then heard the sounds of footsteps receding down the corridor ahead. Her flashlight beam danced over the cobweb-covered walls and ceiling, just enough to light the way.

Natalie kept one shoulder pressed against the tight walls of the passageway as she chased Bella through the basement of this tumbledown building. The narrow passage ended abruptly at an open doorway, and Natalie entered a square room, then froze for a terrified moment when she felt the cold barrel of a gun pressing into her temple.

"Don't. Move." A harsh whisper.

Natalie became paralyzed with fear. Bella's voice was older, more authoritative, but still somehow softly lyrical. Familiar, yet completely unfamiliar at the same time.

"Drop it."

Natalie released her grip, and her Glock clattered to the ground.

"Flashlight, too."

She dropped her flashlight, and it rolled into a corner of the room, where it illuminated a cluster of crawling vines and spiderwebs.

Bella kicked the Glock away, then pressed her own gun to the back of Natalie's head and commanded, "Go on. Straight ahead. Keep going."

She force-walked Natalie into another passageway that led to an exit at the back of the ruins, blown out and desolate. The gaping hole was caught in a net of climbing hydrangea. Natalie welcomed the moonlight. At least she could see now.

"I forgot how cheesy it is down here," Bella said, no longer whispering.

Natalie stood inside the numb, unfeeling space where her heart was supposed to be, dancing between stark fear and utter disbelief.

"Turn around. Slowly."

Natalie turned. Her heart rate spiked. The grown woman holding the gun in her face was slender and lean, almost malnourished, beneath an extra-large gray hoodie. She was about five six, and her tangled dark hair trailed across her shoulders. Her hoodie was unzipped and her T-shirt said I HATE MONDAYS. She stared at Natalie with a deep-seated fury bordering on madness.

Time crawled to a stop. The air became electrified.

"Please, put the gun down," Natalie said softly, trying not to alarm her.

Bella lowered the gun, and Natalie could feel it pressing into her rib cage now. She ran through her options, wondering if she could make it into the woods before getting shot in the back.

# 75

Bella Striver was all grown up, with a matted mane of long dark hair, pale, almost pearlescent skin, and haunted-looking eyes. Although they were the same age, thirty-one, Bella resembled a much older woman who'd been terribly beaten down by life. Gutted and flattened. Her life experience was carved into her gaunt face and the edgy set of her shoulders.

"Please, Bella," Natalie said. "Drop the gun and let's talk."

She smiled with cruel eyes, cruel beyond her years. She looked as if she hadn't slept in a decade. Her hands trembled as if she were ill. "I used to think you knew everything. Isn't that funny?" she said with a sarcastic smile. "You were the confident one. The cool one. I looked up to you, Natalie. I really admired you. I thought you were my best friend. Best friends for life—isn't that what we said? And yet, after I disappeared—what did you do? Nothing."

Natalie swallowed hard. Her heart wouldn't stop racing. "I thought you were dead, Bella. And that broke my heart. And then you wrote and explained you'd just decided to run away. What else was I supposed to do? I spent a lot of time missing you. Grieving the loss of you. I wondered about you for years."

"Ah. You *wondered*." Bella gripped the gun in both hands. It looked like a short-barreled Ruger revolver, with a capacity for five bullets in the chamber. "Jesus, you're so good and pure, aren't you? Such a local hero." Bella's finger trembled on the trigger. "You should've come away with me when I asked you to. Why didn't you come away with me, Natalie?"

Natalie tried to maintain her composure, but it took all her energy just keeping her legs steady. Any second that gun could go off, and she would be dead.

"I didn't think you were serious," Natalie said softly. "Now put the gun down."

"Are you kidding me? You didn't think I was serious?" Bella's eyes were two furious glimmers in the dark. "We used to talk about it all the time!"

Natalie shook her head. "You mentioned it a few times, and it sounded like fun. But we were both headed for college in the fall. It wasn't feasible."

"Not feasible?" she repeated angrily. "Do you remember the things I told you about my father? That he touched me? That he molested me?"

"No," Natalie said with genuine surprise. "You never told me about that."

"I didn't?" she practically screamed, her finger nervously flexing on the trigger.

"Just stop . . . let me help you now," Natalie said, raising her hands a little higher.

"We used to talk about all the awful things he did to me, right? Calling me lazy. Calling me spoiled and ungrateful. Wishing I'd died instead of my mom. Controlling my entire life. Yelling at me when I didn't feel like practicing. And then perving on me," she insisted shakily. "Barging into my room without knocking and hoping to catch a glimpse of me naked. Accidentally touching my breast while we were making dinner together. Accidentally touching my ass."

"Your father?" Natalie said, astounded by this revelation. She recalled that Mr. Striver could be strict, that he was demanding, that he wanted his daughter to succeed where he had failed. He'd raised Bella to be a violin soloist, above and beyond anything else, and that wasn't fair. He didn't let her have a normal childhood, which was what she craved. Natalie had always sensed Bella's father had boundary issues, but not this.

"You never came out and said he abused you," Natalie protested. "Did he? Is that true? Because I don't remember you saying anything about that . . ."

She laughed. "Right. No clue. Blame the victim."

"I swear to God, you never told me this." Natalie shook her head, certain now. "Because if that's true, then I'm sure I would've done something. My father would have tried to help. He cared about you, Bella. So did I, enormously. But we had no idea this was happening."

"Anyway, it's too late. Water under the fucking bridge."

"You're not listening to me!" Natalie shouted. "We were all heartbroken when you went missing. The guys and I were devastated when you disappeared, Bella. You have to believe that. And your father was interviewed by the police at least a dozen times. They searched his house. They considered him a potential suspect, until they were able to verify his alibi for that night, and then—"

"And then, you all went on with your lives. How convenient for you." Her wild, matted hair blew gently in the wind, and a swollen vein popped out on her forehead. "Fuck you very much."

"We didn't give up on you, until those letters began to arrive." Natalie's arms were getting tired, and she lowered them an inch or two. "You said we should leave you alone, that you were alive and doing well. You sent pictures of yourself to prove you were okay. The police did the only thing they could've done at the time and closed the case."

Bella grew furious. She stood staring Natalie down, a sour smell rising from her clothes. Her hoodie looked starchy under the armpits. "Move."

"Where are we going?"

"Turn around."

Natalie turned around and could feel the barrel of the gun pushing her forward a few more steps. Now they stood facing the moonlit clearing where the sweetbriar grew in the spring. Natalie felt a massive discharge of adrenaline and tensed all over, poised for flight or fight.

"I begged you to go away with me that summer," Bella said, "but you wanted to follow in your father's footsteps. You wanted to go to college and become a cop. If you'd come with me instead, then maybe none of this would've happened."

"You can't blame me for that."

"You didn't do enough to find me. Neither did the police. The fact that Hunter was gone for a while should've clued them in, don't you think? You abandoned me. You went away to school and forgot about me. You've had a pretty good life, Natalie, and on top of all the shit I went through with Hunter, you somehow ended up with him. He loves you, he told me so. He's terrified that I might kill you. So maybe I should kill you just to get that motherfucker back? What do you think?"

# 76

Natalie slowly turned around to face Bella. "I thought you were dead," she said again bitterly. "I was sick about it. I didn't start putting the pieces together until very recently. You have to believe me. Hunter only revealed the truth this evening."

"Did he tell you everything?" she demanded, her face contorted with rage. "Did he tell you he left me for dead? That he abandoned me, without a ride or cash?" Her nostrils flared delicately. "Did he tell you he got me hooked on heroin?"

The revelation slammed into Natalie's consciousness with terrifying clarity. She shook her head.

"When I woke up, I was in a very dark place," Bella whispered with glazed eyes. "I wanted to die. After he left me there to rot in that sleazy motel, I had to claw my way back to America. I was desperate. I was in a bad state for years. After a while, I didn't want to be found. I wanted to be lost."

"I'm so sorry," Natalie said with deep regret. Bella looked feverish. She'd bitten her nails to the quick. Natalie felt sorry for this person—hovering somewhere between civilization and savagery. "But please, I'd like to help you now, Bella."

"Oh Jesus," she spat out fiercely. "You don't care. Nobody cares. Girls go missing all the time. Girls get raped and killed. They disappear, and everyone forgets until their remains turn up years later. It hits the news cycle for a few days, and then people forget all over again. Nobody cares about girls who go missing!"

"I do," Natalie said just as fiercely. "I fucking care."

"Really?"

"You don't believe me?"

"You? With your bottles of wine, and loaves of French bread, and your bouquets of flowers inside your nice warm house? Who were you expecting for dinner, Natalie? The table was set for two."

It chilled her to the bone that Bella had been lurking outside the house tonight, watching her. "What do you want from me?" Natalie asked defiantly.

"Don't you know?"

"No. Tell me."

Bella didn't look well—her eyes were glassy, her face was flushed. "We were supposed to be there for each other, Natalie. Always and forever. Best friends for life."

"I tried, Bella," she whispered.

"I needed my *best friend* to help me. I was drowning. Nobody understood that more than you. Or so I thought. Stupid me."

Natalie swallowed hard. "You're trembling," she told her gently. "Let's go someplace warm where we can talk. If I failed you before, then let me take care of you now. Please, Bella."

She shook her head and pressed the barrel of the gun into Natalie's stomach. "I met a witch in London who taught me self-respect. She showed me how to cast spells. I'm only at the beginning of my journey, Natalie. It's only fair, otherwise there'd be no meaning in the universe. You have to create order and justice out of chaos, and that's what I'm doing. And I'm good at it, so don't fuck with me."

Natalie glanced down at the Ruger and wondered if she could grab it without getting shot. "Look, I'm really sorry I can't fix the past. But I can try to make up for it now."

"Are you kidding me? Sorry doesn't cut it." Bella's mood darkened, her face chaotic in the glow of the moon. She gave off an aura of isolation and loneliness. "Katrina was the only person in the world who gave a damn about me. She lost her daughter. She missed her daughter. I filled a hole in her life. She shared all her knowledge with me." Her eyes grew fragile. "The dark arts. The magic circle."

"So she rescued you," Natalie repeated, chilled to the bone. *Just keep her talking.* "And her name was Katrina?"

"I loved her like a mother," Bella insisted feverishly. "She protected me. She was so kind to me, it made me weep for joy. She taught me how to get power from this world, Natalie. She showed me how life can't defeat you if you learn all its secrets. She taught me how to fight back with everything I had. How to create magic, how to dig the heart out of a bullfrog and eat it raw, how to cast spells on everyone who'd ever wronged me. She taught me about the dark arts, the terrible arts, and after she died, I ran away and lived in my car like an animal . . . but as soon as I found out that you and Hunter were living together . . . I came back home. And I know what I'm going to do."

Natalie held her old friend's eye, trying to persuade her. "I can help you, Bella. None of this is your fault. You didn't do anything wrong. Hunter hurt you badly, he used you, and he abandoned you. But you don't want to hurt anyone else. Let me help you. Please."

Bella stared at her with outraged eyes. "It's way too late for that."

Natalie could see the madness worming through her brain. She could no longer be reasoned with. She couldn't be bargained with. The old Bella was gone.

"Things could've gone so differently, Natalie. Remember when I asked you to come with me that summer? How I pleaded with you? Let's travel around the world and stay in youth hostels across Europe? I marked up an atlas of all the places we wanted to visit. I said we should have big bold lives, remember, Natalie? *Avoir une bonne vie.*" Bella's expression hardened. "Get down on your knees."

"Wait. Bella." Natalie swallowed the dry lump in her throat and said, "Let's talk about this. Let's go somewhere and figure it out together . . ."

"Be quiet." Bella brought the gun up hard onto Natalie's forehead, and the blow knocked her sideways. Everything went dark.

Seconds later, a sparkly landscape blossomed in front of her eyes. For a few seconds, she swam in a fizzy, electronic sea of pain. Then the stars blinked out, and all she could feel was a sharp ache at the center of her forehead.

"Hunter, it's me," Bella said above her. She was talking on her phone. "I've got Natalie with me. Well, fuck you, what do you *think* I mean by that?" she shouted. Then she calmed down and said, "I want double. Okay? Yes, double. I've got her right here. Do you understand? Remember what I said I'd do to her? Good. Okay, send it to the same overseas account. Call

# 77

Five minutes later, Bella was pacing back and forth, constantly checking her phone. "Come on, come on," she muttered.

Natalie was on her knees with her hands raised, feeling a primal dread. She could hear her own rattled breathing inside this exhausted space, which was about as abandoned as abandoned ever got. Broken bricks and boards with rusty nails jutting out, everything layered with dirt, leaves, and bird droppings.

Bella's phone rang, and she picked up. "Hello? You did? Okay, I'm going to check it out now. Call you back." She hung up and bent over her phone, frantically keying in a sequence of numbers.

Natalie looked around, wondering if she could make it out through the opening in time, which was a good ten yards away across a precarious pile of rubble. Bella was as distracted as she was going to get, but something made Natalie hesitate—a change in the shadows outside.

"Come on, come on. Where is it?" Bella muttered, glaring at her phone screen, her face eerily illuminated from below. "I don't fucking see it . . ." She pressed more buttons and swiped her finger repeatedly over the screen.

Natalie tried to gauge the distance between them, girding herself for a fight, when all of a sudden, Bella swung around and pointed her gun at Natalie.

"Don't you move," she said in a guttural growl.

Her phone rang just then, making a jangling sound.

"Hello?" Bella answered, deeply upset. "No, it didn't. No! I don't see it. It didn't go through, Hunter. What's going on?"

Apprehension traveled in waves through Natalie's body as she got ready to charge at Bella, but before she could act, a tall figure walked out of the woods toward the opening of the ruins—a well-dressed man in a camel's hair coat. He stood silhouetted against the moonlit fog and said, *"Bella?"*

She lowered her phone and spun around with her weapon raised, aiming it at him. She fired off two shots in rapid succession, and Hunter collapsed.

What happened next happened very quickly. Natalie leapt to her feet and grabbed the hot barrel of the gun with one hand, then dug her fingers into Bella's face with the other. She squeezed with all her might, until Bella screamed and pulled the trigger again, firing into the rotten ceiling beams, which splintered above their heads.

The two of them wrestled for control of the gun, thrashing around on the gritty floor, until Natalie grabbed Bella's right leg and flipped her over, rolling her onto her back, and prying the gun from her hands.

Three bullets had been fired. There were only two bullets left.

Now Natalie was on top of Bella, holding her down with her full weight, pinning her to the ground, straddling her, and aiming the Ruger gun between Bella's frenzied eyes.

Bella smiled, her teeth smeared with blood, and said, "I'll kill you and eat your soul." There was nobody named Bella here. The Bella she had once known was gone.

Natalie could taste the bitterness inside her mouth as she said, "You're under arrest. You have the right to remain silent . . ."

A snarl ripped from Bella's throat as she picked up a rusty pipe the size of a baseball bat and whacked Natalie on the side of the head with it.

Natalie flew backward, gun flying out of her hand, and blood pooling inside her mouth. Bella threw all her fury and outrage into beating Natalie off, then she scooped the gun off the floor and ran out the back of the building.

Natalie lay in an emotionless daze before everything catapulted into disbelief. She touched her bloody lips. She breathed in tiny shards of dirt and dust. Nearby was the abandoned rusty pipe. She grabbed it and, gathering all her energies, leapt to her feet, and charged headlong toward the exit.

Through the caved-in back of the ruins, she could see Bella scrambling up the incline over a pile of cement blocks and broken two-by-fours, when Hunter suddenly reached out and grabbed her.

Natalie slipped on a pile of loose boards and caught her foot in a crevice. "Ow, shit!" She could feel her ankle twinge with pain as she pulled her foot out of the hole and kept going. When she finally caught up with them, they were standing on top of the crumbling ruins, and Bella was panting for breath, visibly rattled. She had positioned Hunter in front of her like a human shield. His face was stoic. The front of his camel's hair coat was soaked in blood.

"Don't come any closer!" Bella threatened, pressing the gun into Hunter's temple. "Drop the pipe!"

Natalie didn't move.

"I'll kill him, I swear to God!"

"Keep running, Natalie," Hunter told her. "Get the hell out of here!"

"Drop the pipe!" Bella screamed.

Natalie didn't budge.

"Save yourself, Natalie," Hunter whispered. Then he reared back, reaching over his head and clawing at Bella's face. With one swift move, he tore the gun out of Bella's hands and turned it on her.

Natalie felt a liquid reaction in her gut as she and Bella locked eyes. "Bella, put your hands up. Hunter, don't shoot her!"

Very slowly, Bella raised her arms, but then tried to grab the gun back.

A shot rang out, and the bullet clipped Bella's right shoulder. She screamed as if her life had ended. A spray of blood flew up from her shredded hoodie, and she was flung off-balance. Then she scrambled to her feet and escaped into the woods, while Hunter collapsed back on the heap of rubble.

Natalie hurried to his side and knelt down beside him. He was staring vacantly at the starry sky, fingers clutching at his bloody chest wound. He blinked in the moonlight.

Natalie said, "Let me see. Let me look." She pried Hunter's hands away and ripped open his shirt. "Can you breathe?" She probed the wound, and he screamed in pain. The entrance wound was small and high. It might have missed his lungs. "Can you breathe, Hunter?"

His unfocused eyes rolled around wildly, not seeing Natalie. He gazed at everything with fear and disbelief.

She felt for a pulse and checked his eyes. "Hunter? Are you okay? Can you breathe? The bullet might've missed your lungs. It's okay. Deep easy breaths."

He pushed Natalie's hands away and gasped for air. At last he was breathing freely on his own. "I'm okay," he insisted. "Don't let her get away."

She took off her jacket, balled it up and pressed it against the chest wound, saying, "Here, put your hands over this. Apply steady pressure. I'll call for help. An ambulance will be here soon. Okay? You're going to be all right."

"Just go!" he gasped.

She stood up and checked to make sure the weapon was loaded—one bullet left—then she bolted into the woods, determined to bring her old friend to justice.

# 78

Natalie picked up Bella's blood trail in the woods and limped along after her, dialing 911. She gave the operator specific instructions, then hung up when she saw Bella on the path ahead. "Bella?" she called out.

Her old friend was a dozen yards ahead of her on the trail, her skinny legs propelling her through the woods. Natalie took off after her, but soon was reduced to kneeling on the ground, the pain in her ankle was so great.

She drew the weapon and took careful aim. There was only one bullet left in the chamber. "Bella!" she shouted. "Stop!"

Bella staggered to a halt, then turned around and watched her old friend through a maze of moonlit tree trunks. Her hair was wild. Her eyes were round and frightened. She clasped her shoulder with her left hand, and her hoodie was soaked with blood.

"I called 911, an ambulance will be here soon. Put your hands up. This is over!"

Bella shook her head. "You'll have to shoot me first."

"I'm not shooting anyone. Come back! Let me help you. Let me at least try!" Natalie's trembling hands made the gun waver. She didn't want to pull the trigger. She absolutely refused to kill another human being. "Please, Bella!" she screamed.

A hideous grin flashed across her old friend's face. "I'm dying," Bella hollered back. "So this is good-bye." She turned and ran off.

Natalie found a sturdy branch to use as a walking stick and limped after Bella, the pain in her ankle growing sharper. The woods were full of towering pines and oaks, and she could feel the muted impact in every bone and joint in her body. Soon the ground fog thickened and the woods closed in around her. She lost sight of Bella. She could hear the sound of retreat, but it was far away.

Blinking the sweat out of her eyes, she continued in vain to search the woods, every shift of wind making her shiver. She felt so exhausted, so stupefied by the throbbing pain in her ankle, that she came close to giving up. A tear slid down her face. Her head was spinning. There was almost no fight left in her.

But Natalie refused to give up. Like Joey used to say, "It's now or never."

She called in an APB for the Chevy Cavalier, then headed in the direction of Solomon Road, where Bella had parked her car. Leaning heavily against the sturdy branch, Natalie picked up the blood trail again and followed it out of the theme park, all the way back to Bella's car, its headlights probing the foggy darkness ahead. The open-door alarm was gradually losing juice.

*Ding, ding, ding.*

The Chevy's high beams coned into the woods before fading into darkness. Natalie exercised extreme caution as she approached the vehicle. Bella could have another weapon stashed away, you never knew.

*Ding, ding, ding.*

With a deep gut check, Natalie ignored the pain and kept going. She could feel the weight of the night pressing down on her as she approached the Chevy sedan. The engine was idling. The emergency taillights were flashing, creating an eerie strobe-light effect.

"Step out of the car with your hands up," Natalie called out, cautiously rounding the vehicle and approaching the driver's side door. She aimed her weapon inside.

*Ding, ding, ding.*

The front seat was empty.

The backseat was cluttered with junk—rumpled clothes, blankets, paper bags, and fast-food wrappers. Nestled among the debris was Bella, covered in blood and curled into a fetal position, her childhood violin clutched in her arms.

Feeling the fright in her bones, Natalie checked for a pulse. She took Bella's vital signs—no breathing, no muscle tension, eyes fixed and dilated.

Gripped by nausea, Natalie called 911 to check on their progress, then performed CPR. Chest compressions, rescue breaths, repeat. After five minutes, she stopped. No pulse, no heartbeat, no breathing. Bella's eyes remained fixed and dilated.

Bella had made it through one death.

She wouldn't make it again.

There was a sound in the woods behind her. Natalie spun around. The fog shifted in the moonlight, but whatever had been there was gone like a ghost.

# EPILOGUE

TWO WEEKS LATER

By the end of April, the sky was bright blue and the air smelled of honeysuckle and wild roses. Natalie followed the others down the cemetery path, her gaze drawn to the orange lichen growing on the old stones. Winged angels hovered over chiseled names so ancient they were obscured by moss, and some of the turn-of-the-century grave markers had sunk several inches, as if the dead were trying to pull them underground with them.

Today was Grace's deathiversary. Ellie placed a single red rose at the base of her marble headstone, then plucked a bird feather from the grass as a token of this special day. Natalie thought about loved ones—how they left us unexpectedly, how we were never prepared for their loss, how we never had time to say good-bye.

Hunter Rose had left for Colorado, fully recovered from his injuries, although it would take a year or more of physical therapy to regain his former strength and flexibility. After examining the evidence, the police concluded there was nothing to charge him with and no one left to press charges, never mind the fact that the statute of limitations had run out. Natalie believed that whatever punishment the law might've once doled out, Hunter had punished himself many times over.

Bella Striver was a broken soul, and her fate was not her own. Bad luck, bad relationships, and poor choices had taken away her freedom, her youth, her dreams. She was buried somewhere in this cemetery with no fanfare. Her headstone simply read: Bella Fidelity Striver, 1991–2022. No mention of the tragedies that had accompanied her untimely death, the complicated story of her life—who she was, what she believed in, and what she had hoped to achieve. No one would ever know the real Bella—the beautiful music she once made, the dark horrible nightmare her life had become.

It was easy to forgive.

It was impossible to forget.

"I think Mom would've liked it here," Ellie said quietly. "It's so peaceful."

"It's lovely," Natalie agreed.

In truth, Grace Lockhart hated it here. She didn't want to be buried here. Last year, after the funeral, they'd scattered her ashes on the lake instead, according to Grace's wishes. *Better for the planet that way. Less creepy than being buried here for all eternity—no offense, Mom and Dad.*

All the Lockharts were gathered here. To the left of Willow's headstone was Grace's marble slab. Then came Joey's and Deborah's. The empty plot was reserved for Natalie. Like that's going to happen, she thought. Over my dead body. Grace would've gotten a kick out of that.

"Aunt Natalie?" Ellie said now. "Do you want to see a picture of Asher?"

"Sure." Natalie smiled.

Ellie took out her phone, swiped her finger across the screen and held it up for Natalie to see. "That's him."

Natalie squinted down at the video. The camera panned back and forth between Ellie doing her homework and a teenage boy with a smirk on his handsome, pimply face.

"He's cute."

Ellie laughed. "I know!" She looked so vulnerable in her peach-colored blouse, her pleated navy skirt, and her UGG boots. Her eyes were red from crying, and it nearly broke Natalie's heart.

Grace's marble headstone seemed out of place. The baby-pink slab contained no flourishes, no cherubs, or urns. The carved inscription was simple. *Gone too soon from this world.*

Natalie couldn't help feeling devoured by fate, swallowed up. Her heart began to beat irregularly. Willow would have been thirty-nine years old today. Grace would've been thirty-seven. Their parents were gone. Everything was gone. History was erased.

But she still had Ellie.

And she had Luke.

"Aunt Natalie?"

"Yes, Ellie?"

"Do you believe in heaven?" Ellie peered up at her with curious eyes.

It felt good to be standing in the butter yellow sunlight among the emerald green trees, but then a wave of sadness came rolling in. "Not exactly."

"Me neither," Ellie said softly. "But we have to believe in something, right?"

"It's saddest for the family," Burke explained. Ellie's father wore a dark blue business suit and was doing his very best to be present—to be strong for his brave, sweet daughter. "It's always the hardest for those who are left behind."

Ellie began to cry, quietly at first, and Burke put his arm around her shoulder, and the two of them stood there together, while Ellie wept.

Natalie stepped back to give them some space, and Luke caught her.

He took hold of her hand, and she smiled, grateful to have him in her life. If heaven existed, then surely this was it. The two of them had fallen into a beautiful routine. The alarm went off at five. They got up and exercised together. They took a shower together. Every day, he circled his arms around her and caressed her as though he were discovering her body all over again. They were crazy in love. They grabbed a kiss here and a squeeze there. They were two misfits who fit perfectly together. He was tall and lanky with a cynical smirk that refused to let the world hurt him. He was fiercely protective of her. She adored him in ways he'd never been admired before. Her thumb rubbed away his worry wrinkles. His voice smoothed away her rough edges. They tumbled into bed with reckless abandon, but he always caught her in his strong, capable arms. Always.

Now Ellie was singing one of Grace's favorite songs, "True Colors," and Natalie listened to her pure sweet voice swirling around them, rising like a butterfly into the cool mysterious sky. She gazed at the sun and the clouds, believing for a moment that Grace and Willow and her father and mother were up there somewhere, smiling down at them. She believed in these words, perhaps for the first time. We were light and energy and dazzling colors, we were part of the sun and the clouds and the moon and the stars . . . we had the ability to see each other in our truest light, and we had the capacity to love one another deeply despite all our flaws.

Maybe that was what life was all about? You experienced terrible hardships, but you crawled out of the rubble toward forgiveness and hope, and eventually happiness.

"Aunt Natalie?"

She smiled down at her niece. "Yes, Ellie?"

"Can we get pizza at Carmen's?"

"Absolutely."

Ellie smiled. "I'm famished."

Natalie wanted to be brave for this beautiful child. Her father once told her there was a hero in all of us. In order to be a hero, you had to be brave. You had to face the things that frightened you the most. You had to be stronger than you ever imagined possible. Maybe Natalie could be that strong.

The sun was shining. The grass was green. The sky was bright blue. A mild breeze blew Natalie's hair around. She took a deep breath. Her heart raced as she surrendered herself to the morning light.

# ACKNOWLEDGMENTS

Heartfelt thanks to my wonderful agent, Jill Marr, to my rights manager, Andrea Cavallaro, and to the supportive team at the Sandra Dijkstra Agency.

Much gratitude goes to my editor, Alex Sehulster, for helping bring Natalie to life. Thank you, St. Martin's Press, and Minotaur Books' team—Joe Brosnan, Sarah Melnyk, Kayla Janas, Paul Hochman, John Morrone, David Rotstein, Cassidy Graham, Sabrina Soares Roberts, and Mara Delgado-Sanchez.

Thanks to my brother Carter for his steadfast support. Thanks to my writer's group, my family and friends. Big appreciation and thanks to the Twitter writing community, and to my spectacular readers—thank you for following Natalie so passionately, and for your love of books.

And always, always, for Doug, my heart and soul.